Readers' Praise for
Boo and *Boo Who*

"Well done! I just finished *Boo* and highly recommend it. I woke up my family when I was reading late and snorting with laughter at one of the character's antics. Thanks for a very entertaining read!"

—KAREN C., from Oklahoma

"I just finished *Boo* and can't wait to read *Boo Who.* What a refreshing read! The character development is wonderful. My wife and I grew up in a small town in Illinois, and Skary seems so familiar to us. I'm very glad I came across this book, and I'm eager to read the next one."

—RANDY M., from Illinois

"I bought *Boo* to take on vacation. While I was reading it, my husband asked why I looked sad. I told him I was almost finished with the book and didn't want it to end. It was delightful!"

—APRIL S., from Colorado

"My wife Stella and I have really enjoyed *Boo* and *Boo Who.* The author has a clever way of getting good Christian principles and characters across to readers without preaching at them."

—RICHARD K., from North Carolina

"I am so glad to see another book coming in the Boo series.... I have really enjoyed the first two. I manage a Christian bookstore, and I have recommended *Boo* and *Boo Who* to many of the book clubs that come in."

—KAT N., from California

"*Boo* is now one of my top five all-time favorite books!"

—JEANNE T., from Ohio

"I *love* the Boo series! I just finished *Boo Who,* so please tell me the author plans on writing another and another and another in the series. The characters are just grand."

—KIM S., from Oklahoma

"Finally, a book—*Boo Who*—that's intelligent *and* Christian at the same time. The story is real and entertaining with just the right touch of suspense and wackiness! I heard there were books and authors out there like this but never read one until now. Thanks so much!"

—JEN B., from Tennessee

BOO HISS

BOO
HISS

A NOVEL

RENE GUTTERIDGE

WATERBROOK
PRESS

Boo Hiss
Published by WaterBrook Press
12265 Oracle Boulevard, Suite 200
Colorado Springs, Colorado 80921
A division of Random House Inc.

ISBN 1-4000-7143-7

Published in association with the literary agency of Janet Kobobel Grant, Books & Such, 4788 Carissa Avenue, Santa Rosa, CA 95405.

Library of Congress Cataloging-in-Publication Data
Gutteridge, Rene.
    Boo hiss : a novel / Rene Gutteridge.— 1st ed.
        p. cm.
    ISBN 1-4000-7143-7
    1. Suburban life—Fiction. 2. Social change—Fiction. 3. Housewives—Fiction.
I. Title.
    PS3557.U887B663 2005
    813'.6—dc22

                                                            2005014143

Printed in the United States of America
2005—First Edition

10 9 8 7 6 5 4 3 2 1

FOR STEPHANIE BERNHARDT BYERS
whose friendship has spanned three decades

CHAPTER 1

"ALL RIGHT FOLKS, let's calm down." Mayor Wullisworth looked like he was patting the air as he tried to get everybody to sit down in the crowded community center. Martin Blarty stood a few feet away, attempting to take a pulse on why this crowd was so agitated.

It was a soccer field, for pete's sake. Sure, it was a little mysterious, but it wasn't like it was a crop circle or anything. And they'd had their share of those, until 1984, when a farmer named Bill Dunn had confessed to the prank, though he claimed he'd been possessed by alien serum when he'd done it. Rumors flew when Bill disappeared one night, leaving an empty farmhouse and all his belongings behind.

Turned out he was in Vegas, but it did make for some good headlines for a while.

"Where did it *come from?*" The woman's desperate and dramatic voice hushed the crowd and everyone looked at the mayor.

Martin bit his lip. The mayor was known for his inability to mock concern or compassion, especially for those he called EGRs, or Extra Grace Required. Martin had dealt with the town's EGRs for years, decades, and sometimes even generations. Martin's attempt to coach the mayor on how to respond to questions that lacked sensibility had finally taught him that it was really the mayor who lacked sensibility, so Martin just let it drop.

"Well," the mayor began, "we've just learned that the government

has a top secret military plan to take over the country via soccer fields."
Grumbling ensued.

Martin slid up next to the mayor and turned the mike away from
him. "What the mayor is trying to say is that though we don't know
why this soccer field has seemingly popped up in Skary overnight, we're
sure there is a reasonable explanation for it."

"What could be a reasonable explanation?" a man asked. "We don't
even have a soccer team."

True. "Listen, we're going to find out why the soccer field is there,
folks. It may just take some time. But rest assured, it's nothing to panic
about."

Martin could remember one other occasion when the town got up
in arms like this, when they decided to change a street name. A century
ago, someone had mistakenly named two streets in Skary Maple Street.
One was on the west end, one on the east. It never confused the residents of Skary because what you were talking about determined which
Maple Street you meant. You never used West Maple if you were going
to the grocery store. You never used East Maple if you needed your car
repaired.

But back when they were a tourist town, some tourists would get
confused. One man ranted, "This is worse than Atlanta and their Peach-
tree Street fiasco!" The man was also irritated that they didn't give tours
of Wolfe Boone's home, so Martin had disregarded it as misplaced
anger. But, he decided, there was no reason why they couldn't give one
of the Maple streets a new name.

No reason at all, except for the fact that the town nearly rioted over
it, and nobody who lived near one of the Maple streets wanted it
changed. So the two Maple streets remained, and everyone was happy.

"It came overnight," Mr. Runderfeld said with a grunt, clacking his
cane against the floor. "I drove by there the day before, and that soccer

field wasn't there. The next morning, it was. You got a fancy explanation for that?"

Martin stepped on the mayor's foot, a sign he would be doing the rest of the answering. "I'm sure there is a good explanation, Mr. Runderfeld. Maybe the person who owns the land wanted a soccer field."

"Who owns the land?" someone shouted.

"I'll look that up in the records, and we'll figure this out. But folks, let's just rest assured that there is nothing strange going on, all right? It's true we've never had a soccer complex or anything close to it in our town before, but there's no reason for alarm. Now if a nuclear testing site popped up overnight, that would be cause for alarm." Nobody else was laughing, and Martin's chuckle faded. "Anyway, I'm sure there's other business to address here today." He looked into the crowd. "Anybody have any other concerns?"

Silent glaring answered. Then, at the back of the room, he saw someone raise a hand. "Yes?"

A teenaged boy with curly, greasy, unkempt hair mumbled something that nobody could understand.

"Could you speak up, please?" Martin asked.

The kid nodded, but went back to mumbling, this time adding gestures.

Martin waved him up front. "Why don't you step behind the microphone so we can all hear you?"

With a slump worthy of osteoporosis, the kid padded his way up to the front of the room. Half an eye was showing when he faced the crowd. Martin recognized him as the kid that worked at the bookstore.

"Hey," the kid said like he was waving to his surfer buddies. A couple of toastmaster sessions might do him some good. "I'm Dustin, and I've lost my pet."

"Great!" Martin enthused. This was exactly the kind of thing community meetings were meant for, and a perfect distraction for the crowd, as the citizens of Skary were always suckers for lost pets. "Why don't you tell us about your pet. Give us a description, and I'm sure somebody will be able to help."

"Well, it's sort of brown and black, I guess. A little yellow mixed in. With black eyes."

Martin glanced at the crowd. By the oohs and aahs, he could tell they were already starting to forget about the soccer field.

"What kind of breed is it, young lad?" Mr. Runderfeld asked.

Dustin's sulky face lit up with pride. He scooted his hair out of his eyes. "It's a rosy!"

"Is that a kind of Chihuahua?" someone asked.

"Boa," Dustin said.

"Boa?"

"Constrictor."

The room was so quiet, Martin could hear the water heater hissing behind the wall. "Dustin, I'm sorry. I think there's some confusion here. Are you saying you lost a…a…"

"Snake."

Someone screamed in the back of the room.

Dustin looked surprised. "Oh, please, don't be afraid. Boa constrictors are not dangerous."

Martin needed to get this situation under control quickly. He stretched a grin across his face and said, "Well, Dustin, we'd be more than happy to help you find your *pet*. What is your cute little *pet's* name?"

"Bob."

"Bob. Okay. Bob."

"Well, it's kind of confusing. You can call him Bob, and that's totally fine. But Bob is kind of special."

Martin could hardly find the words to ask what made Bob the snake special, but he managed a weak, "Why?"

"Well, Bob has two heads."

Another scream.

Martin felt himself grow pale along with the three already pasty looking old ladies sitting on the front row, but he kept the grin tight on his face. "Two heads?"

"Yeah. He's a two-headed snake. A bicephalic. Pretty rare, actually. See, Bob is the more dominant of the twins. His brother's name is Fred."

"Bob...and Fred."

"Yeah. They're like Siamese twins. They share a body, and have separate necks, and two separate heads. I've had them since they were babies."

A trickle of sweat rolling down Martin's temple beckoned a subject change back to the soccer field. He looked out at the startled crowd. A woman on the third row had fainted.

"Okay," Martin said in a shaky voice, "so what we've got here is a lost snake...snakes, I mean...well, one snake, two heads...anyway, a snake that goes by the names Bob and Fred. A harmless snake, I might add, right, Dustin?"

"Yeah. Totally harmless."

"So, Dustin, I guess we should probably be...aware...when we take out the trash or move some brush, as that is probably where it's going to turn up, right?"

"Well, you would think. But actually, Bob and Fred are really domesticated. Spoiled, if you ask me." He snickered.

"What does that mean?"

"Well, you're not going to find Bob and Fred out and about like other snakes, under a rock or something. They've gotten used to being inside, and they especially like carpet and things like comforters and pillows. I'm sure they're going to turn up soon because they can't stand to be outside much. The only tough thing is that they're probably only going to appear at night because they're nocturnal."

Martin could actually hear someone crying. Dustin was completely oblivious. He addressed the crowd, suddenly very comfortable with the mike.

"And listen, if you do find Bob and Fred, they're probably going to be very hungry. They really have very healthy appetites. So if you can't get ahold of me, I'd go ahead and feed them. Any sort of rodent is fine. They're not into gourmet mice or anything." Dustin was amusing the daylights out of himself with his jokes. "Anyway, please, please, if you feed them, follow my instructions very carefully."

The room grew still. Dustin relished the attention.

"When you feed them, you must place a piece of cardboard or something between them while they're eating. Bob is the much more dominant of the two, and if you don't put something between them when they eat, Bob ends up swallowing Fred's head, and let me tell you, that is a nightmare to fix."

Martin dismissed Dustin with a feeble thank you as he ushered him off the stage. There was no use trying to get everyone under control. Hysteria reigned.

Martin turned to find the mayor. Mayor Wullisworth would surely be able to come up with some creative idea. But when he looked at him, the mayor's eyes were wide, and his mouth was gaping open. The fact that he was pulling at strands of his own hair wasn't helping Martin's confidence. "Mayor! Are you okay?"

"I-I-I hate snakes. I hate them. I *hate* them," he whispered.

Martin pulled the mayor out the back door and into the cold outside. Under enormous stress, Martin had found out, the mayor had a tendency to want to go tropical on him.

"Sir," Martin said, grasping his arm. "Sir, get ahold of yourself."

The mayor looked around his ankles, then at Martin. "What are you going to do?"

"You're the mayor, sir. I thought you might have some ideas."

"Let's pull up the protocol for evacuating the town."

Martin directed the mayor to his car. "Why don't you let me handle this? This is no big deal. I'm sure by the end of the day, we will have found this cute and, um, unique little critter."

"Critters have fur. This is a bloodsucking, slimy reptile."

"Reptiles aren't actually slimy."

"Handle this, Martin. And quickly." The mayor ducked into his car and drove off. Martin turned to find an ambulance loading an elderly woman inside.

Katelyn Downey watched out the back window as her son Willem threw the baseball to her husband, Michael. Ever the athlete, Michael caught it and pitched it back while cradling his cell phone between his shoulder and chin. He glanced at the window and gave Katelyn a short wave.

She went to the kitchen and pulled out casserole number seven. She was going to miss all those cooking days with the neighborhood ladies. It was a day well spent making large batches of casseroles, then dividing them and taking them home to freeze. On the days that soccer games, Spanish class, T-ball practice, or gymnastics meets ran late, she could just pull out a casserole and add a packaged salad.

Out the kitchen window, she saw Annette across the street edging her yard for the fourth time this month. Once, Willem had kicked his soccer ball across the street and into her grass. After he retrieved the ball, she witnessed Annette walk out and actually comb the blades of grass back into place. She painted her window shutters yearly, hid all her garden hoses after each use, measured the height of her bushes with a yardstick, and actually parked her car in the garage.

Katelyn was going to miss this dreamy street with the white picket fences, but she had a higher calling. And Annette's web wasn't long enough to reach where she was going.

Rubbing her hands raw at the kitchen sink, she didn't flinch when Annette looked up and into the kitchen window that perfectly framed Katelyn's scowl. With her designer gardening gloves, Annette's fingers rolled a wave in the air like she was strumming a harp. Her radioactive teeth glowed against her sunless tan.

Katelyn waved back. Annette's two twin girls, Madee and Megynn, provided a thorn for each of her sides. She'd been deceived by their yellow ringlet hair and saucerlike eyes. They'd been playing soccer since they were two and could run circles around Willem and all the other boys on the team. They also had a knack for snotty one-liners that evoked visions of plotting their curls' demise with a pair of safety scissors. They only had coed teams until eight. Three more years of this kind of torture and little Willem might go into the arts.

Which would be fine with Katelyn, except she'd never hear the end of it from Michael. The back door opened, and Willem trotted in, dusty and sweaty, his cheeks flushed and red. "Hi baby!"

He hugged her and ran upstairs after a toy car. Michael came in, shut his cell phone, and said, "It's official. The loan went through, and we can break ground on our dream house!" He stretched his arms out toward her, but Katelyn whirled around and grabbed the For Sale sign that was propped against the wall by the front door. She took a hammer from the kitchen and marched outside and down the front steps.

Annette had her back turned as she rolled the edger along the sidewalk. That was fine. Katelyn was willing to wait. She stood there for five yards worth of sod. As Annette turned the edger off, Katelyn banged her hammer on the top edge of the sign, driving one leg into the patchy ground beneath it.

Out of the corner of her eye, she could see Annette crossing the street, blotting her brow with her designer garden gloves. This was going to be fun.

"Katelyn?" Annette said in her practiced anchorwoman voice.

Katelyn let the hammer fall one more time before turning and greeting Annette with her own version of a smile. "Hello there, Annette." Katelyn stepped aside just enough so she could see the sign.

But Annette's attention went elsewhere as she said, "This grass! I still don't understand why it won't grow!" She began shaking her head and staring at the dirt that showed between the measly blades that made up their front yard. "It reminds me of my mother-in-law's hair before she started Rogaine." She looked at Katelyn. "And I've seen Michael out here fertilizing it to death. It must be these sweet gum trees. The shade is nice in the summer, but no good for a vital lawn."

Katelyn turned and hammered in the other side of the sign, with enough force that one slam pounded it straight into the ground.

"Oh." Annette scowled at the sign like it was a knockoff designer handbag. "You're moving."

"Yes," Katelyn said and, after a precise and practiced pause, added, "We're building."

Annette's eyebrows shot to the top of her forehead, but Katelyn kept her smile steady. "We're building" needed no further explanation. In those two small words, it was pretty much implied that your husband was making more money, you were planning on expanding your family, and you'd outgrown the current suburban perks that your particular neighborhood had to offer.

"Well," said Annette, quickly recovering her facial expression, "how interesting. So Michael's real-estate business must be going well." Her eyebrows gently floated down to their proper position.

"Very well."

"Victorian?"

"Tudor. Three thousand square feet. With a bay window."

The superiority literally melted off Annette's face. She rubbed each cheek, stared at the sign, stiffened her back, and pulled her hat down a notch. "We will certainly be missing little Willem on our soccer team."

"Where we're going, there's soccer, a spa, a charming little coffee shop, and a great church with an up-and-coming children's ministry."

A smile sprang and retreated from Annette's berry colored lips. "And where would this perfect piece of paradise be?"

This was going to be the tricky part. And it was all in the delivery. "Skary."

Annette's eyelids lowered halfway over her eyes. "Skary? Isn't that the little town that all the hoopla was about?"

"Hoopla?" Katelyn asked innocently.

"That famous horror writer lives there, and I hear they've got the most horrendous shops and restaurants. It's like a den for the devil!"

Katelyn paused, smiled, then said, "He no longer writes horror, and the town is no longer a tourist town. It's actually quite lovely, quaint even. Like something you would see in a painting."

Annette didn't look convinced. So Katelyn added, "And as the city spreads, Skary will soon become a suburb, and the real estate will sky-rocket. Luckily for me, I'm married to a man with a great sense of vision. He can look into the future and see what's going to be hot."

This was a particularly stabbing line, since Annette's husband was a history professor.

Annette scratched her ear. "I guess it will take some time getting used to a name like Skary."

"It makes it that much more charming. Irony is in, you know."

Indeed, it had taken her time to get used to the name too. But when she saw the potential of this town, and all it would eventually offer herself and her family, Katelyn decided a weird name would soon fade into oblivion. And there was always the chance it could be changed.

Annette, never one to be obvious, stretched an eager grin across her face that smothered any hint of jealousy. "I'm happy for you, Katelyn. I know you and Michael and little Willem will do well."

"Thank you, Annette. I'll miss our neighborly talks, but we're very excited."

Annette nodded and then walked back over to her side of the street, which probably didn't seem so worthy of such outrageous landscaping efforts.

Katelyn secured the sign and went back inside. Michael was standing by the kitchen sink. "You have the most self-satisfied grin on your face," he said.

She shrugged and turned on the oven. "It was just a friendly chat."

"Right," Michael said. He leaned against the sink and crossed his arms. "Katelyn, are you sure this is what you want? Because once we break ground, there's no turning back."

"The more time I spend in Skary, the more I like it."

"Why is that?"

"Because so far, my ideas have been easily sold for a few crisp, green dollar bills."

CHAPTER 2

"I'LL BE RIGHT BACK. Just sit there and relax. Enjoy yourselves." Jack did a little Japanese bow and backed out of the room. Women seemed to really like the bow. And when he greeted them with kisses on both cheeks, they would flap their hands and giggle. In the six months since he'd opened his spa, it had been a huge success. And his closest competition was the beauty parlor. They could offer a tight perm and four shades of burnt umber hair color, but they couldn't offer an avocado, citrus, cucumber hair mask with a scalp massage.

Neither could he, but he did have a good conditioner and was working on his phobia of dandruff. He also had a hard time touching people's feet, so he'd created a foot glove filled with warm oils that he would wrap the foot in before applying the massage. That way he didn't actually have to touch the foot. That was the only kind of massage he offered, because a back massage meant he might have to touch a mole, and that was completely out of the question.

But he'd found with some soft saxophone music and an array of scented candles, he could create quite a relaxing mood without having to touch anybody. He did learn the valuable lesson that you can't just mix any kind of scented candle and expect it to smell good. At one point his "jasmine moonlight" got crossed with his "mom's apple pie." He had so many scents going it smelled like "fresh barnyard." So now he stuck with the fruity scents, and the occasional spice.

His customers Melb Stepaphanolopolis and Ainsley Boone were chatting next door, reclining in two black leather chairs. They'd come in, Melb complaining of exhaustion, Ainsley just wanting to experience the spa. Since it had opened, he had also found that it was very useful in his pursuit of success to learn more about small-town women. City women he had down. Small-town women were more of an enigma.

He returned with a bowl of steaming black stones, with two white towels draped on either arm. He set it on the counter and then lifted the lid on a platter of chocolate-covered strawberries. Ainsley said, "Oh, Jack. How wonderful!"

"Do you have any cheese crackers?" Melb asked.

"No."

"Cheese dip?"

"No, I'm sorry."

"Cheese fries?"

"Just fresh strawberries dipped in Godiva chocolate."

"Nothing with cheese?"

"I'm afraid not. I do, however, have a wonderful hot stone package that is sure to relax you to the point you'll feel like you're going to melt!"

"Mmm, like cheese," Melb said, rubbing her hands together.

"That sounds good," Ainsley said. "But what's a hot stone?"

"It's an ancient technique," Dr. Hass said, going over to the bowl of smooth black stones he kept heated at the perfect temperature. "The amazing thing about this technique is that no one actually has to touch you."

With warm white towels draped over the side of the crystal bowl, Jack carried it toward the women. Steam swirled up from the black rocks like smoke from a community mall ashtray. He set the bowl on the table between them. "Now," he said in a low, calm voice, "I want you to kick off your shoes and place your arms on either armrest. There you go, perfect." He quickly draped the warm towels over their feet, explaining that the feet are extra sensitive and that the towel helps prepare the delicate nerves for the hot stone. It was a whole lot of nothing, but everyone bought it. He'd seen enough ingrown toenails to invest in countless white towels.

He gently placed several black stones on their arms and on their shins, then took two heavier stones and placed them on top of the towels on their feet.

"Now," he said, "what I want you to do is clear your mind of any distracting thoughts. Close your eyes, take a deep breath, and feel the warmth of the stones penetrate every distraction that comes into your mind."

"Cheeeese," Melb moaned.

"Okay, cheese, yes, let the stones' warmth wash away those thoughts. If you're worried about that snake, close your eyes and imagine you're in North Dakota." He'd been running a pretty successful package special designed to relieve snake worry–induced stress. He'd briefly thought about starting a rumor about a wild mountain lion on the loose, just to help business along, but that was something he would've done in the old days. He was a new creation, but he had to admit the old man was hard to shake.

"What's in North Dakota?" Melb asked. "The snake or good cheese?"

Jack spoke calmly, in a monotone. "Don't worry about the snake. Think about anything but the snake. Besides, I have snake traps set in all the rooms here, and I've smothered them with snake bait, which may account for that strange smell that wanders by occasionally. But don't think about the snake. No snakes."

The women looked relaxed with their eyes closed, except for the fact that both of them were gripping the ends of their armrests with a vengeance. He was going to have to take this a step further if he was going to get these two women to relax.

"Now," he said, maintaining the baritone seductiveness of Barry White, "I'm simply going to slide these stones up and down your arm in curves to relax your muscles."

He glided the stones up their arms and back down. Melb was starting to breath hard and Ainsley had opened her eyes and was staring straight forward. "Sssshhhhhhhh," Jack said quietly. "Sssshhhhhhhh."

"Is that hissing?"

"No, that's me, Melb." He smiled, realizing that a day at the spa for women didn't just mean relaxation. They also wanted to feel beautiful. As he moved the stones up and down their arms, he said, "By the way, ladies, one side benefit to stone therapy is that this sliding motion also creates friction, which causes your skin to shed."

Melb sat up as the stones crashed to the ground. "Jack, I'm going to need a different package. The stones aren't doing it for me."

Jack wrapped the white towel around her feet and her hands, then took a bowl of potpourri in the corner of the room. He sprinkled the potpourri delicately over each foot and hand. "Let the scent soothe you..."

Melb sat back and began to relax. Jack continued to drop potpourri all over her, hoping she wasn't going to ask for anything that required human contact.

"Melb, have you seen the new coffee shop that opened?" Ainsley asked, her eyes closed in relaxation. "Wolfe likes it. He goes there every morning."

"I asked for my coffee black, and the next thing I knew we were talking about syrup. So I assumed they were offering me a waffle, but what I came away with was a very small and dry piece of bread and a cup full of whipped cream and caramel. They need better directions for how to order, in my opinion. Speaking of Wolfe, has he come up with any new book ideas?"

"It's a process," Ainsley replied. "It takes time to come up with a brilliant novel. But to pass the time, he's signed up to be in Oliver's cousin's play."

"Lois?"

"Yep."

Melb looked startled.

"What?" Jack and Ainsley asked at the same time. Oops. He'd shown himself to be an eavesdropper. He continued sprinkling potpourri.

"It's just that Lois is… Don't get me wrong. She's talented and driven but tends to lose all sense of reality. I guess that can come in handy in the arts." Melb shrugged. "There must be something in the air. Yesterday I saw Reverend Peck blessing the farm animals for lack of something more interesting to do."

"I feel so badly for him," Ainsley said.

Melb burst into tears.

Jack stopped the potpourri and wondered if he should try incense. "Melb, what's the matter?"

"I'm sorry, I'm so sorry. I've just been so moody lately. I don't know what's wrong with me. I feel sick, and then tired, and then okay again. You should've seen me when I couldn't get my coffee the way I wanted it yesterday. I was a dead ringer for Meramusa."

"Who is that?" Ainsley asked.

"Don't you know? It was the horrible, scary ghost in Wolfe's book *The Last Soul.* She ruled this hotel, and when things didn't go her way, she'd start rattling things, like chandeliers and doorknobs. I didn't rattle a doorknob, but I think I may have rattled that nice young lady's nerves behind the counter." She looked at Jack. "And if you want to get paid, buddy, I'd suggest you do something that involves a massage." She threw up her hands. "See what I mean? I'm Jekyll and Hyde. I'm sorry, Jack. That was rude. But get those fingers going, mister. My feet could really use a workout."

Jack swallowed. He was feeling a little nauseated.

"And careful of the bunion."

Sheriff Parker walked into the smoke-filled room, waving his hand in front of his face. The volunteer fire department, which consisted of every bored male in Skary, totaling at last count one hundred and two, responded in less than five minutes, which he wasn't sure was good time considering they were four blocks away.

"Minimal damage," said Ronny, the most distinguished of all the volunteers. "Could've been a disaster."

Sheriff Parker looked at several burned-out trash cans circling the room. "What was she thinking?"

"I have no idea," sighed Ronny. "She's awfully lucky. She's in the kitchen. By the way she's reacting, I swear it's like her whole house burned down."

Sheriff Parker left the bedroom and found his way to the kitchen, where Lois Stepaphanolopolis was carrying on by herself at a small dining table. She glanced up, looked at the sheriff, launched into another round of tears, and wailed, "I'm going to jail, aren't I?"

"It is unlawful to burn trash, Miss Stepaphanolopolis. But it's just plain dangerous to burn it inside your home."

She sniffled. "I wasn't burning trash. I was warding off snakes."

"Are you telling me you set fire to trash cans in your bedroom in order to keep out that snake?"

"I tried a tiki torch first, but I couldn't get it to stand up. I haven't slept a wink. I'm so worried I'm going to wake up with a snake in my bed."

The sheriff sat down at the table and sighed. "Lois, the snake isn't even poisonous. You're telling me that you risked dying by fire to keep a snake out of your bedroom?"

"Snakes. This one shares a body. But there are two heads."

"Yes. I'm aware of its two heads. But this is sort of extreme, don't you think? You're lucky you didn't burn your entire house down, or kill yourself. You must realize that the odds are in your favor this snake won't come to your house."

"How do you know? I've had mice around here for years."

"Look at it in a positive way. Maybe the snake will take care of your mouse problem."

"That does not, in any way, shape, or form, make me feel better, Sheriff." Then Lois stopped and studied the sheriff in an uncanny way. He shifted in his seat, wondering what she was staring at. Suddenly she said, "You want some coffee?"

"Can you manage to make it without starting a fire?"

"Of course." She smiled. "But I can't promise I won't offer a fiery personality."

The sheriff lifted an eyebrow, but stayed silent.

"You know," Lois said, "you've got quite a presence."

"A presence?"

"Yes. When you talk, people listen. When you stand, you command attention."

"That's because I'm the sheriff."

"No," she mused. "I think it's something else. A natural talent."

"For what?"

She turned on the coffeepot and joined him at the table. "What would you say if I told you that I thought you had star quality?"

"I would inform you that if you're about to bribe me, you should think twice because that is even more illegal than burning trash inside your home."

"I mean it."

"What are you getting at, Lois?"

"Have you heard about my latest project?"

"I can't say that I have."

"I'm starting a community theater. I'm quite the playwright."

"Huh."

"And I've written this charming little piece, a two-act, called *Not Our Town*."

"*Not Our Town?*"

"Yeah. It's a story about this little town and all its little people and conflicts, but it's not my town. It's a love story."

"Interesting."

"There's something that screams 'lead actor' about you, Sheriff."

"Maybe it's my chronic stage fright."

"You? Please! You'd be a natural. Commanding an audience… How different can it be from controlling a town?"

"Well, if your incident is any indication, maybe I'm not doing all that well."

"Listen to you. So humble. What do you say? Will you at least read the script?"

"You can't be serious."

"Don't you see the need for a community theater, Sheriff?"

"Not really. As far as I can tell, we have plenty of drama as it is."

"Nah," she said, waving her hand at him and then getting up to pour the coffee. She handed him a mug and pulled a folder from underneath a kitchen cabinet. "Sugar."

"No thanks."

"That's the part you would play. Sugar." She handed him the script.

"Sugar?"

"Sugar Johnson. He's a new resident in the town. He has some great lines, some observations about life in his new town."

"Sugar?"

"It's a family name."

"Whose family?"

"That's backstory and not important. What is important is my need for a handsome, stoic-type fellow like yourself to bring him to life."

"You could start by naming him something other than Sugar."

"I'll think about it. In the meantime, would you be willing to give it a read?"

Deputy Bledsoe's voice crackled over the radio. "Sheriff, there's gunshots over on Patterson Street."

"I'll be right there," the sheriff said.

"Gunshots?"

"Another citizen overreacting, I'm sure." The sheriff sighed, standing and pulling his coat on.

She pushed the folder toward him. "Please."

"I'll read it through. But I can tell you with certainty, I'm not your man."

"That's something Sugar would say."

Ainsley hung up the phone and joined Wolfe in the living room, where he was reading. She brought him a mug of his favorite hot tea.

"Who was that?"

"Dad," she said, sitting on the couch. "He can't come over for dinner tonight."

"Why?"

"He sounded exhausted. Apparently this snake on the loose is really doing a number on everyone."

"It doesn't help that Dustin has posted Lost Pet signs all over the place with its picture on it."

Digging her toes into the crevice of the couch, she said, "So, I've been thinking about the nursery."

"Yeah?"

"I like the yellow. I really do. Very neutral. But I think it needs something else. And I found a beautiful green today. Just as an accent, I promise."

He smiled and ran his fingers through her hair. "I have a feeling I know what I'm going to be doing this weekend."

"It will really add to the room."

"What do you say we go upstairs and add to the chances there might be a baby up in that crib sometime soon?"

"Can't."

"Why?"

"I calculated all this out last night. If I get pregnant in the next six weeks, that would mean I'd be huge and pregnant in the spring when I'm trying to plant my gardens."

"Are you serious?"

"Sure. I mean, we've tried up until now, which would've been very convenient. But it just wasn't our time. So we lay off for two months, and then we can resume when gardening season has passed."

Wolfe rubbed his stubble. "Kind of takes the romance out of it, doesn't it?"

"Trust me. I've read all the books. The first three months the baby is here are overwhelming, and we want to be prepared."

"I'd say we're very prepared. We have a crib, diapers, clothes, toys, and until just a minute ago, a completely decorated room."

"A baby is going to change our lives. We have to be ready for it."

A knock caused Goose and Bunny to jump to their feet and scuttle to the door.

"Maybe your dad changed his mind," Wolfe said, going to the door. "He can hardly ever pass up your—" Wolfe swung open the door. "Alfred!"

"Wolfe! Greetings!"

"Alfred?"

"Wolfe. Greetings."

"It's been months since we've seen you."

"Well, are you going to invite me in?"

Ainsley swept up beside Wolfe and, before he could answer, grabbed Alfred by the arm and pulled him inside. "Of course you're always welcome in our home, Alfred. Care to stay for dinner?"

"It's quiche," Wolfe said. "You hate eggs."

"I do. But I love anything your wife makes, so I'm sure that will include her quiche. Besides, with the budget I'm living on these days, I've come to appreciate the value of such a simple food as the egg." He dropped his wool coat into Ainsley's arms and surveyed the room. "A woman's touch is here now, Wolfe," he said. "It's nice."

"I'm curious about why you're here, of course."

"I knew you would be," Alfred said. "But as your former editor and longtime friend, you should know that I'm always thinking about you and always have your best interests at heart."

"The last time you used that line, you nearly got me killed at a horror writers' boycott."

"That was a simple misunderstanding. When they said, 'We're going to cut your head off,' I thought it was a friendly chant from adoring horror fans who love stuff like that."

"Anyway." Wolfe sighed. "I've been wondering how you're getting along. How's New York?"

"Well, when you're not on top of the world, it seems like the worst place on earth. Noisy. Crowded. And expensive. I had to sell my apartment. I'm living with a friend until I can get on my feet again."

"Sorry to hear that. Any ideas about what you might be doing?"

"That's why I'm here."

"That's what I was afraid of."

"Wolfe," Ainsley said, "let the man talk. He may have some good ideas about getting your creativity jump-started again."

Alfred cocked an eyebrow as Wolfe gave Ainsley a startled expression, as if she had said too much. But she didn't care. Wolfe was at a dead end, and he needed something to spark an idea. Maybe Alfred was the answer.

"Interesting." Alfred looked at Wolfe, a wry smile delicately balanced on his lips. "Things have been slow for you, too, Wolfe?"

"Not slow. Just..."

"Slow," Ainsley said. "He's getting very discouraged."

"Why didn't you tell me, Wolfe? I could've called some people for you."

"I wanted to try it on my own. I submitted some things under a pen name."

"What happened?"

"He got rejected," Ainsley said, patting his shoulder. "And it was good stuff too. I read some of it."

"Wolfe, why are you using a pen name?"

"Because I want a fresh start. I want to know I can make it as a writer without depending on the brand that has been built around all my horror books. I don't write horror anymore, and so in essence I'm starting over."

"Yeah, but I've got connections. Believe it or not, there are still industry people willing to talk to me despite what happened to you."

"I'm not giving up. I'm just taking a little break, trying to get refocused."

"Well," Alfred grinned, swinging his arm in a flamboyant gesture, "that is why I'm here, my friend."

Wolfe actually groaned, and Ainsley had to hit him on the shoulder.

"I know, I know," he said. "You have your reservations. But let's not forget the successful transformation I instigated with your beautiful wife. She was three tarts short of becoming the next Martha Stewart."

"Alfred, just because you can do something doesn't necessarily mean it's a good idea. Ainsley is proof of that. In the end, she wasn't destined to be what she was very capable of being."

"True," Ainsley said. She figured she should throw one in on Wolfe's side, just to keep him from becoming overly agitated by Alfred's endless insistence.

"Well, if you'll hear me out, I've uncovered something truly amazing. It astonishes even me, and I'm well aware of the depth of my editorial and agentary talents."

"Agentary is not a word."

"It's an industry word. Anyway, do you want to know what it is?"

"I think I might need some food in my stomach," Wolfe said.

The timer buzzed from the kitchen. Alfred popped his hands up and grinned. "Timing is everything!"

CHAPTER 3

WOLFE WALKED ALONG the sidewalk, deep in thought. Alfred had been so passionate with his idea, and in a moment of honesty, Wolfe envied that. He hadn't felt that kind of passion for his writing in some time. He'd written a nice piece about Skary, and though moving and appreciated, it had bombed badly. He'd been informed by his publisher that he was welcome back as soon as he was ready to write horror again.

Well, he wasn't. Somewhere deep inside loomed a gigantic story, but he had no idea what it was or how to write it. He told himself it just needed to sit. Ferment for a while. When it was time to be poured out, he would know it.

And now here was the great Alfred Tennison at his doorstep once again, with another grand plan to resurrect his career. For a while he'd been thinking that his career wasn't to be resurrected. But he was starting to realize something very profound: he didn't do anything else well.

He'd tried to sell cars. He'd tried to sell books at the bookstore. He'd even tried to do nothing. But all he really knew how to do was write. What perplexed him now was why he couldn't seem to write anything. Was he that bad of a writer that a hop over to another genre caused everything to collapse?

During the quiche dinner, Alfred had tried to politely eat, though Wolfe could tell he wasn't enjoying it. Alfred explained there was a market for "you kind of writers." By "you kind of writers" he meant the kind who "think God has to be in everything." Once Alfred got past all the rhetoric, Wolfe understood him to be saying there was a whole market for what he called religious fiction.

"At first I thought they were talking about stories set in the Vatican, but no." Alfred seemed completely in awe of whatever he was trying to explain, and he was doing a fairly poor job of it. "I mean, it's nearly surreal," he said. "You know how a book won't sell if it doesn't have one and a half sex scenes or a lot of gratuitous violence, right?" Wolfe nodded, though Alfred was exaggerating. It wasn't quite boiled down to that kind of formula. Though close. "Well, these books don't have sex scenes in them. Or gratuitous violence. In fact, they won't even publish a book with something like that in it."

"That's interesting."

"Bizarre was what I was thinking, but anyway, it sounds like it could be your kind of deal. And from what I can see, there's quite a bit of money to be made. People actually like this stuff. I'm not kidding. I looked up the numbers. Turns out, lack of sex sells. Who knew?"

Wolfe walked into the recently renovated coffee shop. He'd been enjoying the routine of trying a new drink at each breakfast. It helped break up his mundane mornings. The decor was nice too. The long metal tables and aluminum chairs that had been in here before had been replaced by wooden chairs and matching, small, round wooden tables. There was art on the wall instead of hometown newspaper clippings.

He walked to the counter, where a huge selection of fancy pastries had replaced donuts. Was that baklava? Wasn't that a German pastry he used to eat at Ingrid's?

"Good morning, Wolfe."

Wolfe turned to find Reverend Peck, also a new and loyal coffeehouse customer, standing behind him. "Good morning, Reverend." The reverend liked to kill about half his morning in this place.

"How is your day going?"

"So far so good. Took a little walk, did some thinking, came in for a cup of coffee. That's about it."

"That sounds fun."

"How is your morning going?"

"Actually, it's been pretty interesting."

"Oh? How?"

"A woman came to visit me at the church, claimed she could turn it around, get people to start coming again. She said it's all in the children's ministry."

"Huh. Children's ministry. Did you mention we mostly just have adults?"

"I tried to tell her. But she insisted that she could multiply the parishioners. She would just need a box of Goldfish."

"Well, I guess that's a cross between a loaf of bread and a fish product."

"Yeah, guess so." He looked at the woman behind the counter. "Double vanilla mocha." He smiled at Wolfe. "I'm feeling a little crazy today."

Hardy Bishop could hardly believe his eyes. This was a dream come true. Booky's was now everything he'd ever wanted. He always knew money could buy happiness, and this was proof.

"I have a vision for your store," the woman with nice hair and expensive pants had said. "I think it has the potential to be amazing."

So they'd secretly planned the move. She had ideas down to every last detail. Huge posters hung from the ceiling. Recessed lighting added a homey glow. And there was aisle after glorious aisle of every book imaginable. Mrs. Downey was right. There was nothing on earth like it. Right here, in Skary, Indiana, was the most unique bookstore on the planet.

There was even a computer that scanned the bar codes and rang up the price.

But his favorite part of it all was the fact that this old grocery store, abandoned ever since the new Wal-Mart had arrived the next county over, was in use again. And it still looked like a grocery store, which was Mrs. Downey's vision for it all. It was pure genius.

Hardy looked at his watch. It was time for their grand opening! Outside he could see curious people milling about, trying to get a glimpse into one of the windows. "Dustin! It's time! Open the doors!"

Dustin didn't have a lot of expressions, but even he looked excited as he trailed over to the door, the bottoms of his jeans dusting the floor. He stood just right so the automatic doors sensed his presence and slid quietly open. "Come on in," Dustin said to the crowd of about forty. Some were Hardy's usual customers, including Wolfe, who gave him a hearty wave. Some were new customers, and that delighted him even more.

"Welcome, my friends," Hardy said as they gathered around him. "Welcome to the new location of Booky's, where we will now meet all your reading needs! Dustin, why don't you start passing out the maps."

While Dustin passed them out, Hardy continued to explain the layout of the store. "Folks, grab a buggy and get ready to read. Over here"—he gestured—"is the vegetable section. Here you will find all our books on nutrition, as well as some healthy cookbooks. At the dairy section, you'll see a nice assortment of books such as *How to Milk Life for All It's Worth* and other popular books like *Don't Cry Over Spilt Milk.* Over where the cheese used to be you'll find the bodice rippers. But some of the more serious romances you will find where the flowers used to be stocked.

"In the meats section, you'll find the philosophy and Christian living books. The Bibles are where the breads were. And in the old pet supply section, you'll find a great variety of books on animals. The gift books are where the condiments used to be. All thrillers, suspense, and horror are back in the butcher's corner. However, you'll find the mysteries on the foreign food aisle. And for those of you looking for the classics or literary fiction, a fine selection awaits you in gourmet foods. Pop fiction is on the soda aisle.

"And," Hardy said with a final grin, "if you'd like some coffee, we have some fresh and hot over on the coffee aisle!" Everyone looked enthusiastic, so he said, "Go shop and enjoy yourself. We have some couches and reading chairs at the back of the store too."

Everyone dispersed except Wolfe, who walked toward him and shook his hand. "Hardy, this is terrific. What an idea!"

"Thanks, Wolfe. Glad you could make it."

"I was wondering if you could help me out with something."

"Sure. Anything." Hardy tried to ignore the way Wolfe apparently felt the need to bounce on the balls of his feet at this moment. Maybe it was a writer thing.

"Have you heard of religious fiction?"

"Sure. Curiously, I've been having a hard time placing these in my store."

"Why?"

"Well, I don't know. I had them over by the breads, and then moved them over to the meats. You won't find any by the cheeses. The butcher block seemed kind of extreme. The freezer might send out the wrong signal. I don't know. Do you have any suggestions?"

"Not really. I'm just familiarizing myself with it now. So where'd you put them?"

Hardy grimaced. "Well, in the cereal aisle."

"The cereal? Why?"

"Because it's fortified with good stuff. Dustin suggested the canned foods, but he's never been to church and probably has never read a religious fiction book. I don't know. They just seem peculiar. Frankly, they don't really fit in." He smiled. "But they sell well."

"A friend thought I should try writing one."

Hardy laughed. "You?"

"I shouldn't?"

"I don't know. I don't think they have horror."

"I was thinking of writing something other than horror."

"Really. Can you do that?"

"I think so."

"Like what?"

"Maybe a good, cozy mystery."

"Did I mention my mysteries are over in the foreign food section?"

"Yes. Clever."

"Well, I think you're a capable writer, and whatever you decide to do, I'm sure you'll do fine with it."

Hardy turned and saw people streaming out the doors, each carrying a grocery sack. He walked over to Dustin. "This is great! People are in and out in a jiff, able to find exactly what they need!"

"Yeah," Dustin said, checking out a final customer. "But we're going to need to place an order."

"An order? We're fully stocked."

"We're completely out of every book on snakes."

MARTIN WATCHED MAYOR WULLISWORTH tug at the tuft of white hair protruding from his ear. If he didn't know better, he'd say the mayor was one snake sighting away from a Caribbean vacation. He'd ripped down all the Lost Pet posters the kid had put up.

"It's frightening the residents!" the mayor had snapped in a shaky voice. That may have been true, but it was certainly trickling down from the top.

He drummed all ten fingers against his desk like it was a typewriter, and his leg bounced up and down beneath him.

"Sir," Martin replied, "what this town needs is to see its mayor calm and collected, a reassuring voice in an uncertain time."

"This is horrible! It's horrible!" the mayor shrieked, then gnawed at the fingernails of one hand, while with the other he grabbed a pencil and busily doodled across a memo on his desk. Martin had never seen the mayor this nervous about anything.

It was supposed to be their weekly event meeting, so Martin decided that might get the mayor's mind off of his self-described "worst horror of my life."

"So part of the soccer field mystery is solved. The Brewer family sold the land, for quite a good profit, to another family, apparently not residents of Skary. I guess they wanted a soccer field. They have a right to do what they want with it. I did notice a nice set of metal bleachers has just been put in. Who knows? Maybe a soccer league would be nice around here."

The mayor nodded, and kept nodding. He didn't stop nodding. Martin resisted the urge to grab his head and make him stop.

"Anyway, the other exciting news is that Lois Stepaphanolopolis is starting a community theater!"

"A what?"

"A community theater. She's written a play and says she has people knocking down her door trying to get a part in it. She's planning a Thanksgiving Eve performance."

The mayor grumbled. "What else?"

"Trudy's little coffee shop is going well. New tables, a new counter, and a lot of different options. And I mean a lot. I never knew coffee could be had so many ways. She must order the beans straight from heaven, because it'll cost you the treasure at the end of the rainbow to try a cup. I just order Trudy's Special myself."

"What's so special about it?"

"It comes black with nothing in it. Anyway, it looks like the economy is picking up a little. For the first time in years, I see a little light at the end of the tunnel."

The phone rang, and the mayor waved it off. "I don't want to talk to anyone today." He grabbed his coat. "I've got some things to do."

Martin answered the phone as the mayor hurried out the front door. "Mayor's office."

"I hear there's a snake on the loose. Making everyone real nervous." The man had a distinct accent. "Who is this?"

"The answer to all your reptilian problems."

Dustin walked out the front door of his home, letting the screen door bang shut the way his mother hated. He didn't care.

"No calls," his mother had told him when he got home from work. Not a single sighting. Had his snakes run away? He'd been sure that within a few days Bob and Fred would have returned. He would even sneak downstairs after his mother went to bed and crack the back door open, though he was sure Bob was smart enough to make his way into the house by other means. Fred tended to do what Bob wanted more than Bob did what Fred wanted. But there had to be a dominant, and Bob was really better at it. He had a larger head and seemed to sense danger better.

Dustin had nursed the snake back to health as a baby and taught Bob and Fred how to live with each other. Though it was a small breed of boa, it had already grown to nearly four feet. He'd come home that fateful afternoon from the bookstore and found that the snake had somehow busted the Plexiglas off one side of its terrarium. He'd hardly gotten any sleep since it had vanished. He worried, wondering whether it was okay and where it might go during the day since it was more nocturnal and probably busy hunting food at night. But were Bob and Fred able to find food? He felt a lump form in his throat.

As he sat on the steps of his front porch, a long shadow crossed his face, and he looked up. A tall, paper-thin man approached, and he didn't look happy.

"Are you Dustin?" He spoke in a squeaky voice and smelled like hamster pellets.

"Who wants to know?"

"I'm Chuck. I'm the owner."

"Of what?"

"Chuck's."

"The pet store?"

"That's right," he said in a stuffy voice as he crossed his arms. "And I've got a big problem."

"What's that?"

"We're having a hard time finding rodents to feed our pets at the pet store."

"So?"

"So my suspicions are that your two-headed freak of a friend is eating all the rodents in town."

"Look," Dustin said, standing up and broadening his chest, "I'm doing everything I can to find Bob and Fred. As soon as they're back home, your rodent problem will be solved. I mail-order them special mice, anyway."

Chuck cocked an eyebrow. "Is that so? Dustin, let me ask you something. And I want you to answer me honestly."

"Sure. Whatever."

"How much are you feeding your snake?"

Dustin frowned. "What kind of question is that? I've taken superb care of that snake! It would have died out in the wild because it can hardly decide which way to go in a life-threatening situation. I've done nothing wrong!"

"Son, just answer the question. How often do you feed it?"

Dustin met this man's sharp glare. "Once a day. So back off!"

"You…you feed it once a day?"

"Of course I do. What kind of pet owner would I be if I let my snake go hungry?"

Chuck started tapping a nervous foot on the sidewalk. "Both of them?" he whispered.

Dustin was about to punch this freak. Why was he acting so weird? "Of course both of them. What am I going to do? Only feed one of them?"

"Don't they share a stomach?"

"Yeah, so?"

Chuck swallowed so loud Dustin could hear it.

"What's wrong?" Dustin asked.

Chuck said, "Boas normally eat once every week or ten days."

They both stood there silently. Dustin was calculating how much money he could save feeding them once a week. But Chuck looked angry. "Do you see what you've done?"

"Yeah, spent a whole lot of money on food!"

"You've created an eating machine. That snake is used to eating every day. That's why there aren't any mice around. It's eaten them all!"

"What will Bob and Fred eat next?" Dustin wondered aloud.

Chuck was rushing away.

"Hey! Where are you going?" Dustin yelled.

Chuck hopped into his car. "To quarantine my kids' pet rabbit!"

CHAPTER 5

"AND WHAT IS YOUR NAME, little fellow?" Lois threw her voice, but she sounded like a pig on steroids. Maybe more of a cow inflection with a little frog thrown in would work. "And what is your name, little fellow?" Eck. That sounded like a lifelong smoker attempting to sound sexy. She never knew puppets could be so hard. Maybe the pig puppet shouldn't be the one to greet the kids. Maybe the horse.

"Hello?"

Lois popped her head up from behind the cardboard box she'd fashioned into a castle. "Sheriff!"

The sheriff walked up to the stage hesitantly, like he was afraid a spotlight might catch him in its beam.

"Come on up here, big fella!" Lois urged, dropping the puppets on the floor and greeting him center stage.

"What are you doing?" he asked.

"Practicing my puppet skills. Never knew it was so hard. My hands get hot and sweaty, which makes it hard to grip these animals' mouths. Believe it or not, Reverend Peck wants to start a puppet ministry." She wiped her palms against the back of her pants, just in case she felt the need to touch Sheriff Parker. "So, what brings you by?" She noticed the script in his hand.

"Well, I read your play."

"Oh? What do you think?"

The sheriff stared at his boot-clad feet. "Interesting," he mumbled.

"You liked it?"

"Sure. But I don't want to play Sugar."

"Why not?"

"Because I want to play Bart."

"Bart's the town sheriff."

"I know."

"Well, that wouldn't be much of a stretch for you."

"But I like him. He's a laid-back kind of guy, doesn't fuss about much, and really has just a few lines. Plus, I like his loyal dog friend."

Lois tried to be tolerant. "Well, why not play Jefferson?"

"The town treasurer? He's a little nervous and tedious, isn't he?"

"Wouldn't it be fun to play someone like him, though?"

"No."

Lois sighed. "So are you saying the only way that you'll be in the play is if you get to be the town sheriff?"

The sheriff nodded.

Lois smiled. "But you *will* be in the play?"

He puffed out his ruddy cheeks and blew out the air, causing his mustache to do a little wave. "One question for you."

"Ask me anything."

"Did you plagiarize?"

"*Plagiarize?* Plagiarize what?"

"I don't know," the sheriff said. "This story just seems familiar. And I don't want to be a part of anything illegal."

Lois patted his broad shoulder. "You have nothing to worry about. I completely made this up, out of the deep places of my imagination and my life experience."

"Well, in that case," he said, managing a rare smile, "I think I will do this. You know, with Ainsley gone I get a little lonely in that big old house. Why not do something like this?"

"Why not? I'll send you a rehearsal schedule soon. Just make sure you're studying your lines, okay? There may be a few revisions here and there."

The sheriff nodded. As he made his way down the stage steps, he turned and said, "Lois, thank you."

"For what?"

"For giving me something to do with my time." He paused and said, "Besides hunt down that snake."

Lois felt her heart skip a beat. But it wasn't because of the snake.

Martin tried to relax in his favorite overstuffed chair, but there was so much on his mind, he was having trouble concentrating on any one thing. He sipped some orange juice.

His mother had always called him a worrywart—and with good reason. He was at his best when he was worrying. And he'd done his share of worrying about this town.

But no matter how much he worried, the town had seemed to be in a state of perpetual trouble ever since Wolfe Boone decided to stop writing his horror novels. And truthfully, Martin was somewhat relieved not to have to deal with tourists anymore. Though they brought a great deal of money, they also brought a great deal of strain. They tended to be pushy and inconsiderate. Now the town was quiet, just a town.

What Martin hadn't mentioned to anybody, though, was the strange visit he'd received five months ago, from a handsome man in his late thirties. He'd made an appointment with Martin, showing up right on time carrying an enviable leather briefcase and wearing a starched button-down shirt in a shade of pink that Martin thought impossible for a man to pull off. But he did.

His face was dotted with stubble, but strangely, it seemed more an accessory to his look than an oversight. His hair was short, his sideburns longer than those Martin had worn in the sixties, and he talked in an easy, conversational manner.

But the conversation was anything but ordinary. The man, whose name he couldn't remember now, asked about property, economy, income level. Martin had answered all his questions—there was no reason not to. But Martin felt like he was discussing the private hopes and passions of his wife, had he been married.

Now he was starting to see the things he'd discussed with this man come to life. He'd wondered about sports leagues. He'd pressed Martin for the coffee-drinking habits of the citizens. And he asked if the people liked to treat themselves to some luxury.

Well, at the time, no. But Jack Hass had turned that around by opening his spa. The women loved it, and according to Jack, business was endless...and legit. Now, seemingly overnight, the small coffee shop that had been home to newspaper reading and gossip swapping, offered menu items peppered with the word *gourmet*.

Yesterday, Martin had driven out to the soccer field and stood by the roadside, trying to imagine it filled with children. Skary didn't even have a school. The children were bused to the next county over. What if they did have a school? What if the town was alive with children, like it had been long ago?

Martin finished off his orange juice and fingered the pages of a script that Lois Stepaphanolopolis had dropped by earlier in the day. She told him she would like to consider him for the role of Gibb, a mayor of a small town, and one of the love interests of the story. Martin had laughed, but later on, the thought didn't seem that bad. After all, a community theater could bring some life to the town, and the best way to support it would be involvement. He picked up the phone.

And why not play the love interest? Sure, it was going to take some effort on his part to create a believable character, and he might have to start lifting weights, but there was not much in his life beyond this town that got him motivated.

"Hello?"

"Lois, it's Martin Blarty."

"Martin! Hi there. You just caught me walking in the door. I've been working on the set of the play."

"You sound tired."

"No, not at all. I'm thrilled. I've already gotten most of the play cast, and even some people to work as stagehands and run the lights. I think the show is actually going to go on!"

"Have you filled the part of Gibb, the mayor?"

He could hear her chuckle. "I only see one person playing that role, mister, and that is you!"

Martin couldn't stop a grin from stretching across his face. "Sold!"

"Oh, Martin! That is wonderful news."

"Lois, will you go out with me?" Martin was still grinning and laughing and feeling good about himself. But then there was silence on the phone, and Martin realized that he'd actually just said these words out loud. It was strange enough that he thought it, but then to say it? He groaned.

"Martin? Are you okay?"

"Fine," he whispered. "Lois, I'm sorry, I didn't mean to—"

"Did you just ask me out?"

Martin clawed his face. "Did I?"

"I'm asking you."

"Out?"

Her tone got stern. "No...I'm asking you if you asked me out."

Acid reflux was indicating that he indeed had asked her out. As it burned its way back down his esophagus, Martin was trying to remember the last time he'd had a date. He'd married his high school sweetheart, who turned out not to be sweet at all and incapable of graduating high school. He'd been single for twenty-five years and, that he could recall, hadn't had a date. So what in the world would compel him to ask Lois, of all people, to go out? She was loud and obnoxious and smacked her gum...in the most charming way.

"Ich spreche kein Englisch."

"Martin? Are you choking?"

Now that was stupid. Since she didn't speak German, she wouldn't even understand he was trying to say he didn't speak English.

"I'm fine," Martin managed.

"Are you asking me out or not?"

"Yes?" Martin squeaked.

"Was that a question?"

Martin looked around for some antacids. "Yes."

"Yes, you asked me out?"

Did he have to say it twice?

"Look," Lois said, after he couldn't answer, "if you're wanting a different part, just say so. Sugar and possibly Plum are up for grabs. Personally, I think you'd make a great mayor, but what do I know? I'm just the writer, director, and producer."

Martin combed the dead skin off his bottom lip with his two front teeth.

"But Martin, this isn't Hollywood. You don't have to go to such extreme measures to get the part you want. You can just ask."

Martin believed that in every man's life, there would be a moment of truth, that one moment in time that would never return if you let it slip away, and you would never know what your life might have been like. His fingers wrapped around the leather of his armrest. So far, Lois had sighed three times.

"Lois," Martin said, "I meant it. I wanted to ask you on a date."

He leaped out of his chair, squeezed his eyes shut, and was pumping his arm. But on the other end of the phone was complete silence. He stood in the middle of his knockoff oriental carpet, his arms flopped to his side, listening for any signs of life.

Was he on hold?

"Lois?"

"I'm here," she whispered.

"You are?" he whispered back. He wasn't sure why they were whispering, but it had been a while since he was in the dating scene, so maybe this was the new thing.

"I'm sorry," she whispered.

Martin paused. Was she sorry she was whispering? Sorry she couldn't go on a date with him? Sorry he'd asked? He didn't have much time to continue on with scenarios, because then she said, "I'm just so shocked. I can't remember the last time I've been asked on a date."

Martin smiled. This was a good sign. She was lonely and pathetic too.

"I mean, sure, I've had a few men look my way. But I wasn't ever sure they were looking at me, you know? Maybe I looked like a favorite relative. And most people just see me as overbearing, which I can be, I'll admit it. I have a mouth like a faucet and a tongue straight out of the flapper era, but I have a good heart, and most pushy people can't say that. I'm a bulldozer, I won't deny it. But there is this laid-back, mellow side of me that most people don't see. It's there, and it really is quite enchanting when I allow it to come out and play. Listen to me! I sound like I have a split personality! But seriously, in Greek mythology, I'm what they call one of those sirens, except much more placid and not so noisy. Although I can make a racket if I feel passionate about something. I won't stand down. You can't tell me to sit and stay. My bite is like my bark." Martin listened carefully for barking sounds.

"So," she continued, "I'm looking forward to you getting to know me, Martin."

"Me too," Martin stumbled. "I mean, me getting to know you. Or you getting to know me. Us getting to know ourselves."

"Pick me up at eight, tomorrow? Let's dine at that new bistro."

"What new bistro?"

"Haven't you heard? It used to be called Pete's Steakhouse."

"What's it called now?"

"Peter's House of Steak."

"Huh."

"I'm looking forward to an evening filled with surprises," Lois purred.

Martin cleared his throat of any suggestions he'd had about where to eat. Thankfully, Lois was on the ball, because five minutes ago he didn't even know he was going to ask her out.

CHAPTER 6

"DAD? YOU OKAY?" Ainsley said, glancing at her brother, who was examining his steak knife and making it glint in the dim light.

Her father was looking around, his disapproving eyes pinched like he'd stepped into the bright sun. "What have they done?"

Ainsley thought it was charming. There was an actual tablecloth on the table, centered with a votive, which replaced what used to be a napkin holder that conveniently held the salt and pepper on either side. The ketchup bottle had also been removed, and in its place stood bottles of olive oil and balsamic vinegar. The waitress, wearing all black, brought a fresh loaf of bread to the table. As she left, Butch said, "Is that Tammi?"

"Tammi?"

"From high school. Don't you remember? Stringy hair, skinny, with glasses."

Ainsley glanced behind her. Well, in this setting, that look was working to her advantage. The place was beginning to remind her of that fancy restaurant Alfred took her to in Indianapolis when he was trying to transform her into the next Martha Stewart. She looked at her dad again, and he was trying to figure out what to do with the vinegar.

"See," Ainsley said, "you take one of these small plates, and pour oil first, then vinegar. Then you dip your bread in it." The bread had melted cheese in the middle and smelled like garlic.

"I'm going to have to talk to Pete about this," her father grumbled. "I've been a patron of this restaurant since it opened, and now all of a sudden he goes and changes on me? It's like what happens to your daughter from the age of twelve to thirteen. At twelve, she's this innocent, beautiful child that adores you. At thirteen, she turns into a sophisticated ninny who is all dolled up. Everyone swears it's just part of the progression. But suddenly there's fancy clothes, an awful haircut, and makeup, all of which are supposed to improve her. But you know what? You just want the plain twelve-year-old back. She's a lot less trouble, and perfectly dependable."

Ainsley found it slightly humorous that her father was saying this as if his daughter wasn't on the other side of the table. "Dad, open your menu up. You'll see all your favorites are there."

With a skeptical sigh, he flipped it open. Butch said, "Have I told you about the things I had to eat on some of my missions?"

Ainsley nodded. "You've mentioned it a time or ten."

"Snippy, aren't we?"

"Tired. I spent half a day trying to convince Melb to go to the doctor. She absolutely hates doctors."

"Is she sick?" her father asked.

"Kind of. She's nauseated but seems to have quite a good appetite, all at the same time. But I can't get her to rest. All she wants to do is scrub floors. The closest she's come to seeing a doctor about it is calling Garth, who came over and gave her a horse pill."

"I hate swallowing big pills," Butch said.

"It was an actual horse pill. Garth claims it was all natural."

"All natural what?" Butch asked.

"All I know is that my usual homemade chicken soup isn't helping her. I don't know what to do."

"She's a big girl. She can figure it out," her dad said.

Butch was still eyeing Tammi over at the bar.

"I'll tell you one thing. This snake fiasco is about ready to make me retire." Her father threw up his hands. "See? I can't even find my favorite!"

"The twelve-ounce steak?"

"There is no steak on this menu."

"Here it is. *Steak au Poivre.*"

"What?"

"It's the New York strip you like, with the peppercorn."

"Yeah. But there's no sauce with it."

"Yeah, they're calling it a wild mushroom demiglaze. Sounds tasty!"

Her father rolled his eyes. "What's wrong with saying steak with sauce?"

Butch said, "Where's Wolfe again?"

"With Alfred, his former editor."

"Doing what?"

"Alfred thinks Wolfe might want to try religious fiction."

Butch slapped his hand on the table, startling everybody. "How dare he!"

"Dare he what?" Ainsley asked.

"That offends me."

"Why?"

"The Bible is not fiction!"

"No, no. Religious fiction is a kind of novel, like a genre. Alfred says there's a whole market for it, and now that Wolfe's a Christian, he might want to look into it. Wolfe's skeptical, but Alfred is really on top of things like this."

"Wolfe's a smart man," her father said. "He knows what he's doing."

Ainsley's heart warmed. Though her father hardly had an understanding of Wolfe's life or world, he had taken Wolfe in like a son. For the first time in years, Wolfe had a family. And this Thanksgiving was sure to be his most memorable, aside from last Thanksgiving when he almost died in a snowstorm.

Her father was suddenly distracted, watching something across the room. When she turned, she saw Martin Blarty and Lois Stepaphanolopolis weaving their way between tables, Lois guiding Martin by the hand. They were both more dressed up than she'd ever seen them. Lois had a shade of red lipstick on that could be seen half the room away.

"Isn't that cute!" Ainsley gasped. "They're on a date!"

Her father stuck his nose back in the menu.

"I would've never thought those two for a couple," Butch said. "She's a foot taller than he is."

"So what. I think it's cute. What do you think, Dad?"

"I think I'm tired of all the love in the air. I come home, and all I see are Thief and Blot cuddling on the sofa, their tails entwined, meowing some sort of lovey cat language. Not to mention the dozen or so calls a day I get for Butch from women asking about him. Do you think you might want to call at least one of them back?" He gave Butch a harsh look. Butch didn't notice because he was watching Tammi again.

He looked at Ainsley. "You're gone now, happy with the love of your life. The last thing I want to see is Martin and Lois—" He gestured toward them. "Look at those two! They're acting like high schoolers. Get a room!" he said, but not loud enough for anyone but his table to hear.

Ainsley glanced over in their direction. They were just sitting and talking at the table like anybody else. Tammi approached for their order. Ainsley hadn't even had a chance to decide, but Butch was giving her plenty of time by trying to impress Tammi with his knowledge of Middle Eastern delicacies. Tammi looked completely grossed out.

Peeking over her menu, she watched her dad observe Martin and Lois. She knew immediately. Her father had a crush.

She ordered for herself and her dad, and while Tammi was still waiting for Butch to say something she could write down on her pad, Ainsley casually said, "Lois asked me to cater the opening night of her new
play, *Not Our Town*."

"I'm having second thoughts."

"About what?"

"This play. I agreed to play a part, but it's probably going to be a
waste of my time. I'm no good at this sort of thing."

Ainsley couldn't believe it! Her father? Agreeing to be in a play? She
knew this was serious, and she had to keep her father in the play, if
nothing else, for his pride.

"You know, Dad," she began carefully, "sometimes a little competition doesn't hurt."

He glanced sideways at her. "I don't know what you're talking about."

"The play, of course," she said. "If you're worried about someone else
doing the part better than you, it might motivate you to turn on your
best...acting charm...and take a few Tony-worthy risks." She was hoping this wasn't going to take a "wink." Her dad was a very literal man,
and it was hard to *infer* with him.

Her father stared forward, seeming to get her point. "I miss your
mother," he said suddenly.

That even got Butch's attention back to the table. They looked at
each other and then at their dad.

Ainsley said, "Mom would want you to be happy."

He contemplated something silently for several seconds, then
grumped, "What's it take to get a cold glass of nonsparkling refreshment
from a mountain spring?"

Ainsley looked down. It was actually on the menu, and served bottled
for three bucks.

Wolfe stared at the ceiling of his house, while listening to Alfred's expensive loafers cross the tile with a pace short in stride and long in annoyance. "So," Wolfe said, "what you're saying now is that I shouldn't do this? You've been talking to me for days. 'Wolfe, consider it. Seriously.' Did you not say that?"

Alfred finally arrived back at the couch, but instead of sitting, he leaned against the fireplace and cleaned his fingernails.

"What is it with you? You're acting like a nervous Nelly."

Alfred paused to look at Wolfe. "You're insulting me with clichés now? You really are out of practice. We have to get you writing again."

"I thought that was the whole point of exploring this new genre."

Something was up, and Wolfe knew it. Alfred was picking at hangnails that didn't exist. Even without his manicure budget, Alfred Tennison always believed in flawless hands.

Wolfe stood, visibly startling Alfred. "All right. Cough it up. What's going on?"

"It's just that, well…there's no easy way to say this…" He sounded like he was about to announce the death of a relative.

"Just say it."

"Wolfe, you know you are a close friend, and because of that, I would never put you in harm's way."

"Okay…"

"And that's why I think this whole thing is a bad idea."

"Why?"

"You're not going to fit in."

"Fit into what?"

"Okay, let me put it this way. Do you remember Belinda Besworth?"

"The sci-fi writer? Yeah, I met her a couple of times."

"And meeting her was sort of like an event, right? I mean, she'd come to these New York literary parties dressed in silver lamé from head to toe. And who could forget her white hair molded into a single, Washington Monument spike?"

"She was different."

"Different? Anne Rice is 'different.' Belinda was from another world. And as much as she tried, she just never fit in."

"I'm not following, Al."

"I just don't think you're going to fit in." Alfred's eyes pleaded, and his back hunched as if under a hundred pound shawl. "See?"

Wolfe shook his head. "You don't think I'd fit in?"

"It's a whole scene," Alfred said with expansive big gestures. "Just like in New York, except not in New York. There are certain expectations in certain scenes. You're well aware of that. That's half the reason you always hated New York." Alfred smiled. "And why I always loved it."

Wolfe crossed his arms. "What kinds of expectations?"

"Just trust me. I have my sources."

"Who?"

"As much as you'd like to think of yourself as religious, I'm just afraid you might be perceived as a…"

"A what, Alfred?"

"A freak."

Wolfe laughed. "A freak?"

"It's a harsh and subintelligent word, but I'm afraid it's the right one."

"For a week you've been talking to me about going to this conference, and now you're afraid I might be perceived as a freak?"

"I'll admit, I was overly ambitious about jumping into this thing without doing the proper research. I take full responsibility for that."

"I was more afraid of being recognized and mobbed."

"Trust me. Nobody's going to recognize you, Wolfe. Christians don't read your stuff. They read the Bible and pamphlets. Lots of pamphlets. And self-help books with seven steps."

"When is this conference?"

"Tomorrow. In Chicago."

"Pack your bags. We're going."

"What?"

"You heard me. I'm not afraid of being called a freak, Alfred."

"I am."

"Then don't go." Wolfe eyed Alfred. "Is that what this is all about? You're afraid of being around a huge group of religious people?"

"A huge group of creative religious people in seasonal sweaters. You're quite enough as it is."

"You're coming with me."

Alfred sulked. "Do I have to?"

"It was originally your idea."

"Yes, but I'm trying to back us both out now." Alfred stepped forward and looked Wolfe in the eye. "I don't think you know what you're getting yourself into."

"We're about to find out. We leave at five thirty tomorrow morning."

Alfred stooped and pulled a folder out of his briefcase. "You might want to study this. It's all the research I've been doing about what exactly a religious novel is." Alfred smirked. "It might help you fit in."

"Thanks." Wolfe took the folder, then went to his bookshelf and pulled down a book. He carried it to Alfred. "And you might want to take a look at this."

Alfred took it. "The Bible?"

"It might help you fit in."

CHAPTER 7

"ALL RIGHT, FOLKS, let's form the line this way. That's right. Queue up right over there. Thank you, yes, thank you." Alfred smiled at an elderly lady who looked like she should be knitting, not standing in line for a horror writer's autograph. Wolfe hadn't been at the conference for an hour when he was recognized, and chaos ensued. Alfred had expected to be stoned, but instead, a mob had rushed Wolfe, and now five dozen people stood in line for his autograph. Thankfully, Alfred had thought to throw a box of Wolfe's books in the trunk. He'd really done it so that on the way back from what he was sure was going to be a disaster, he could show Wolfe this dusty old box of books as a motivation to return to the genre that had made them both famous.

So far, everything was backfiring.

"I can't believe it's him!" the little old lady said to Alfred. "What a treat!"

Alfred stepped closer to her and whispered, "You really read his books?"

"Every one of them!"

"You wouldn't know it by looking at you. Glad to see there's a heathen or two here." He grinned and winked at her.

She was frowning. "Did you just call me a heathen?"

"I'm sorry. Do you prefer to be called a liberal?"

"What are you talking about? I've been going to a conservative church my whole life! My husband's been a pastor for fifty years!"

"Step on up, don't lose your place in line," he said, nudging her forward and out of his hair. What was going on here? He looked down the line of faces. Innocent enough. Maybe there wasn't a religious authority around to control their reading habits.

Beside him suddenly was a pleasant-looking, plump woman with scholarly glasses perched on her rotund cheeks. "You're his editor, right?" the woman asked. "I'm Ellie Sherman. I'm an agent." She wore an outfit that suggested a stay-at-home mom rather than an agent, but then again he was on foreign soil. He was used to a lot of black turtlenecks, tortoiseshell glasses, and at least one useless accessory, like a silk handkerchief too expensive to use.

"Ex-editor. Alfred Tennison. I'm an agent now."

"You are?" She smiled. "You're really well known in the publishing world."

The humble shrug Alfred offered couldn't hide the humongous grin that was escaping across his face.

"Until last year," she added.

"It's part of the business."

"Of course. But I can't imagine what you're doing here."

"Just being an agent."

"You're Mr. Boone's agent?"

"More or less."

"Looking to pick up a few new clients at the conference?"

"Of course." Not.

Alfred glanced at Wolfe, who was doing just fine signing autographs and talking to all these oddly adoring fans. He took Ellie by the elbow and moved her away from the crowd.

"I could use a few tips," Alfred whispered.

"You?" she asked. "Tips on what?"

"On this." He gestured around the room, but what he really wanted to do was point at her. In any case, he was definitely the one not fitting in. "I'm fairly new to all this."

"Ohhhh," Ellie said, her eyes twinkling. "I see. You're nervous about being an agent."

Alfred closed his eyes. *An agent to these people.* But he would take what he could get, since he was never one to be too obvious.

"You've been an editor so long, this is probably completely new territory to you."

"Well, in a place other than a cocktail party, yes." Alfred added, "Where I would always drink ginger ale."

"What kind of client would you want?" Ellie asked.

"Well," Alfred began, "obviously I'd want a nonsinner." He pitched a thumb in the direction of the crowded line and chuckled, "Like none of those people."

She wasn't following. Ellie could have used a good pair of tortoiseshell glasses and at least a business suit to help Alfred feel a little more confident with any suggestion she was about to make.

"Someone who has the Bible memorized," Alfred continued, after she didn't offer any advice. "And certainly no women in short skirts. That's a definite no-no." Ellie still looked confused, so he added, "Or at least if they do wear short skirts, they should also be wearing tights. Don't you agree?"

Ellie paused and then said, "What kind of writing, I mean."

"Oh. Writing. Right."

"Is there a particular genre that you're keen to?"

Keen to. Huh. "Well," Alfred said slowly, carefully pondering his answer, "I'm keen to any kind of writer who has the promise of a two-hundred-fifty-thousand first print run."

Ellie laughed. "Good one."

Alfred smiled, but he wasn't sure what was so funny. He leaned over to Ellie and said, "Listen, as you can probably guess, I'm a little new to this kind of…setting. Is there anything that I absolutely, under any circumstance, should not do?"

Ellie looked completely amused by his question. She said, quite wryly, Alfred thought, "Just follow the Ten Commandments and you should be fine."

Alfred nodded. "Are those, by chance, posted anywhere?"

As Wolfe approached the editor, he tried to rub the slick sweat off his hands against the fabric of his plaid shirt. He was realizing just how much he'd taken the familiarity of his relationship with Alfred for granted. This was like starting from scratch, and it had been quite a long time since he'd actually had to pitch a book idea face to face with an editor. He'd attempted to sell a coming-of-age book under a pen name over the summer, but it resulted in a harsh rejection letter that suggested he might try to add something interesting, like a plot, to the book.

In his experience, there were two kinds of editors: social climbers and bookworms. Social climbers attended all the literary events they could get their prestigious name on and were regulars at any parties that served up caviar and intellect on silver platters of self-absorbing conversation. That had been Alfred Tennison, who thankfully had done a good job of representing Wolfe at places he should've been but never wanted to go.

Bookworms, on the other hand, were socially inferior and seldom left their offices. They had no desire to be known or acknowledged. They had a pure, uninhibited love for literature. They were typically not known for their bathing habits, either. They would spend hours fighting for the exact right word in a sentence, while the Alfred Tennisons of the world were calculating for the fifth time an escalating royalty rate. But often-times the bookworms would find themselves far below their entitled place on the corporate ladder, simply because they weren't social enough for the business.

"How do you do?" the man said, extending his hand toward Wolfe. He wore a sweater vest that didn't contain a single color from the striped shirt beneath it, and walked with a slight limp that drew attention to the arthritis in his hands. "I'm Harry Rector."

"Wolfe Boone," Wolfe said, shaking his hand. "Thanks for meeting with me." They sat in two leather chairs next to a fireplace.

"My pleasure," he said, his blue, grandfatherly eyes sparkling with wisdom. "I can't help but tell you how surprised I am to see you at one of our conferences. I guess it's old news about your departure from the horror world, but still..."

"According to the *Star* I've had three nervous breakdowns after being abducted by aliens."

Harry chuckled. "I suspect," he said softly, "that you were kidnapped by a different kind of adversary altogether."

"Former adversary," Wolfe smiled.

"Indeed," said Harry. "And now you're here."

"Yes sir. My agent assured me I would never fit in."

"Your agent?"

"Yes."

"Is he the fellow in the fancy trench coat who earlier insisted on praying over everyone's coffee?"

Wolfe laughed. "It makes him feel good about himself."

"Hmm," Harry said. "Sounds like he's having a harder time of it. Fitting in, I mean."

"I give him credit. He's the one that believed this might be the place for me."

"What do you think?"

"I know that I still have a lot of stories in my heart to tell."

Harry leaned forward. "What kinds of stories, Wolfe?"

Before Wolfe could answer, all of Alfred's suggestions and pages of notes flooded his mind, blocking a single, coherent word from escaping. Impressively, Alfred had been very detailed about what constituted a religious novel. And he'd also lectured him all the way to Chicago about the required and effective formula for these kinds of books, including an actual spreadsheet.

"I've studied the three top-selling religious novels of all time," Alfred had said. "Trust me. I have the pulse of the industry."

Harry was patiently waiting, and Wolfe was trying to remember the exact story line Alfred had suggested for him, being a newbie and all.

"Listen, Wolfe," Alfred had said, "you're not going to get to go in there and just publish any kind of book you want. You're going to have to present them with an idea that shows them you're on board with this kind of thing."

But right now Wolfe was drawing a blank as to what kind of thing he was supposed to be pitching. Harry looked concerned.

"Well," Wolfe began, "it's set on a prairie."

"Really."

"Yes. And in fact, there is a prairie woman in the book."

"The protagonist?"

"Exactly." Things were starting to click. "Life is hard. She is widowed and raising two children. The land is desolate, and they're trying to make their way west before the harsh winter."

"Uh-huh."

"And without warning, catastrophe strikes."

"A snowstorm?"

"The Rapture."

Harry looked stunned. That was a good sign. Maybe Alfred had come up with a pretty original idea, which was shocking, since Alfred was hardly ever original.

Wolfe tried not to skip a beat. "So half the earth's population is gone. There are a slew of covered wagons completely empty, the attached horses running wild without anybody to guide them."

"Sounds dangerous."

"But not violent," Wolfe said with a wink. Alfred had warned him that violence was strictly forbidden. "So there's this prairie woman trying to deal with the fact that most everyone she knows is gone, when she suddenly encounters something so scary it brings her to her knees."

"A false prophet?"

"A love interest."

"Oh. A cowboy?"

"A eunuch."

Harry looked completely lost. Wolfe was afraid he wasn't explaining himself very well. But Alfred had thought the eunuch would work well, since the book had to be heavy on romance but light on love scenes. At least this way there would be plenty of room for clever conversation without any temptation.

Harry asked, "Is there an antagonist?"

This was the tricky part. In many previous books that Wolfe had written, the antagonist was a heavy smoker or drinker, fond of cussing and more times than not already dead. But again, Wolfe was willing to make a few adjustments to try his hand at this.

"Remember," Alfred had said cautiously, "the bad guy is always one prayer away from total conversion."

"Yes, there is definitely an antagonist. He's sort of a well-dressed, mild-mannered kind of guy, who is often seen giving to the poor and has a soft spot for injured animals."

Harry's head had tilted to the side, like he was trying to examine something from another angle.

Wolfe quickly added, "He has a terrible temper."

Harry scratched his nose and said, "Let me see if I've got this right. You've got a story about a woman who is left behind on the prairie after the Rapture takes place, who then falls in love with a humble eunuch, who is little help against the frightful temper of the good Samaritan?"

Wolfe frowned. Oddly, it didn't sound that good when summed up in a single sentence.

Harry asked, "She wouldn't happen to be hiding dark family secrets, would she?" He chuckled and glanced at his watch. "Wolfe, what are you doing right now?"

"Bombing?"

Harry laughed. "Maybe it's time I familiarize you with this strange new world you've entered."

"Okay. And how will you do that?"

"Let's go find your agent and see what happens when I suggest we 'meditate' over some new ideas."

Wolfe laughed. "Sounds like fun."

CHAPTER 8

ALFRED HAD THE BODY LANGUAGE DOWN. There was a lot of arm patting, which was taking some getting used to, and apparently nobody did the Euro-kiss here, but other than that, he was feeling a little more relaxed.

With dinner over, thirty minutes of free time took the evening to some sort of special night session that Alfred was scared to even ask about. It was titled *Cutting Out the Bad Parts: Exercising Your Redactor Arm,* and though there were hints that the topic might be self-editing, Alfred wasn't entirely sure they weren't talking about exorcism.

The room was still swollen with eager and talkative conferees, but Alfred stood on his tiptoes, trying to get a glimpse of Wolfe. Ordinarily, he was easy to spot in a crowd due to his height. But Alfred hadn't seen him since early evening, and though he'd never felt very imaginative, he had dreamed up all sorts of scenarios, including the idea that a group might have hauled him off to another building to "pray over him."

"Alfred?"

Alfred turned to find Ellie. "Oh, hello."

"You look a little stressed. Are you okay?"

"I can't find Wolfe. Have you seen him?"

"I saw him earlier. He was speaking to Harry Rector."

Alfred smiled. That was a good sign. Mr. Rector was one of the most highly regarded editors in this business. Through his research, Alfred had actually uncovered the fact that Mr. Rector's father was responsible for some translation of the Bible. Now if that doesn't get you in the door, what will?

"How is the conference going for you?" Ellie asked.

"I'm making all kinds of contacts," Alfred lied. "Of the nonphysical kind."

"It's all about the business card." And with that, she slid one into his hand. Alfred looked down, and there was Ellie's pleasantly round face frozen in time next to her name in nearly unreadable calligraphy.

"If you push the back, it actually sings you a tune," Ellie said. Then she laughed. "I'm just kidding. But I have seen those. Who would spend that kind of money, though?"

"Exactly how long have you been an agent?"

"I'm in my fifth year."

"Good for you." Alfred grinned.

"Are you finding your way around okay?"

"Sure."

"This must be a lot different than New York, huh?"

"Let's just say I've never once prayed over my caviar."

"Well, Wolfe has just been a complete delight. He doesn't look at all like the picture on the back of his book."

"Yeah, that's been digitally enhanced."

"To make him look younger?"

"Scarier." Alfred tilted sideways, trying to get a glimpse of Wolfe, but he just saw more people. He looked at Ellie. "Let me ask you something. I've been doing my share of observing today, and I have to say, I'm nothing short of impressed. You have quite a strategy."

"Strategy?"

"Yeah. It's a little laid-back for my taste, but I'm willing to bet you score on charm alone."

"What are you talking about?"

He stepped closer to her. "Which author are you trying to steal here? I won't tell a soul, I promise."

"Steal?"

"Yeah. Surely you've got your eye on someone."

Ellie turned to him. "I'm not trying to steal anybody."

He snorted. "Right. You're trying to tell me there's not a big name here you'd love to draw your twenty percent from?" He scanned the room. "I once heard a guy promise an author he didn't even represent yet to the editor of a competing house!"

"I'm not trying to steal anyone," Ellie said. "I'm happy with my clients. I'm actually here to find fresh, new talent."

"Really?"

"Sure. You never know when you're going to discover the next Wolfe Boone!"

Suddenly a small woman was standing in front of Alfred, looking up at him like a needy child. Her thick glasses magnified dark circles and deep creases on either side of her eyes. She was trying to smile.

"She's nervous," Ellie whispered.

That was strange, because Alfred was also growing nervous at an alarming rate, especially when he noticed the thick stack of papers in her hand.

Ellie said to the woman, "Go ahead. Introduce yourself."

"I'm Rosalinda Barrington-Glauchmeier." She shrugged with a lop-sided grin. "Actually, that's a pen name. My real name is Doris Buford." She held out a hand. Alfred slid his forward, and she grabbed it with the strength of a man twice her size. "Such a pleasure to meet you!"

"Likewise," Alfred said.

Ellie smiled. "Likewise. That's cute." She looked at Doris. "He's from New York. They say things like that."

"I was wondering if you had some time to talk with me," Doris said. "I've got a manuscript."

Alfred's hand found his face as he tried to look pleasantly agreeable. "Oh, um…"

"He'd love to," Ellie interjected. "For the sake of new talent, right, Alfred?"

He glanced sideways at Ellie. "Sure."

Doris's small frame wiggled with excitement. Before Ellie could add any more suggestions, he said, "Doris, why don't we sit over here, out of the way? You can tell me about your novel."

As they sat, he couldn't deny the strange feeling that was creeping around his entrails. Was that charity tickling his fancy? A sense of goodwill toward men and short mousy women?

Was he actually being a good person? He glanced back at Ellie. She had a tight-lipped grin on her face that seemed to show a certain pride in his willingness to pay attention to Doris.

Alfred gave Doris a reassuring smile, which seemed to do wonders for her fidgeting. She took a deep breath and tried to settle into her chair.

He spread his arms wide and, with a delighted grin, said, "Doris, what can I do for you, my dear?"

Alfred took a third tissue from Doris, and blew his nose with reckless abandon. "There, there," Doris said.

Alfred couldn't stop the waterworks. And in a matter of minutes, he'd become touchy-feely. This had drawn more than a few stares, but he really didn't care. He hadn't felt this much emotion since he'd received that forty-thousand-dollar bonus nearly a decade ago.

"So?" Doris asked, ready with a fourth tissue. "What do you think?"

"What do I think?" Alfred exclaimed. "Look at me! I'm dribble!"

"I'll admit, I'm not as familiar with the New York scene as I should be, but usually when someone likes a manuscript, they just say so. However," she added quickly, "I'm all for men expressing their emotion. It really is quite a sight. What do they call you? Metrosexuals? The last time I saw my husband cry was twenty-two years ago when he got his arm cut off."

Alfred sighed, slumped, and wiped away his tears. "Doris, you don't understand. Your story…did something to me. I can't really explain it. But it…it…"

"Touched you?"

Alfred hesitated, the sexual harassment seminars he'd attended causing him to choose his words carefully. "I guess so."

"This has taken me four years to write."

"It's a powerful story, Doris. And those first chapters are amazing. I'm not one for love stories, but you've managed to win me over, and without a sex scene by page twenty-eight." Alfred sniffled. "Truthfully, it's a little hard to believe a man would go to such great lengths to save his bride, and then end up dying anyway, but you sold me on it, Doris. You sold me on it. You've raised the bar. I recently read a manuscript where I thought the protagonist was heroic because he was willing to give up his mistress, so this is quite a leap for me, as you can see."

"So does this mean you'll take me as your client?"

Alfred stared across at the woman, who was nearly swallowed by the leather chair on which she sat. He looked around the room for his only other client, who'd seemed to vanish into thin air. There he was, across the room, getting chummy with an old woman who looked like she was half a day away from her coffin.

He threw up his hands. "Why the dickens not?"

Ainsley pulled a sweater over her pajamas, buttoned up her coat, and got in her car. It was way too late to be out, but she wasn't going to sleep much anyway.

She'd spent the evening fretting. Wolfe had told her he might be home late, and though she let him leave without an argument, it was difficult. After all, she'd changed her mind about being pregnant in the spring. She realized that if she waited much later to get pregnant, it might interfere with holiday plans next fall. Who would want to try to plan Thanksgiving with pending labor? And then there was the idea of being huge and pregnant in the hot summer months, when she normally would be out fertilizing her grass.

So according to her calculations, calendar, and temperature charts, her whole plan could be blown if Wolfe didn't get home soon. And it didn't look like he was going to make it. With a huge huff, she backed out of the driveway and headed toward Melb and Oliver's.

Oliver had phoned, sounding frantic. "I've called the doctor!" he shouted.

Ainsley mustered up her calm voice. "Oliver, that's good. I'm sure he's on his way."

"No! I've called the doctor, and now Melb is about to come unglued. She hates doctors!" Ainsley realized he was shouting because of all the wailing Melb was doing. "Can you please hurry over and talk some sense into her?"

Ainsley was at their house in less than five minutes. As she got out of the car, she could see Melb's figure silhouetted against the curtains, her arm gesturing angrily at Oliver's silhouette.

She hurried to the door and knocked. It swung open, and Oliver said, "She's lost her mind!"

"Haven't you read the statistics?" Melb shouted from her vertical position on the couch.

"The ones about how many wives drive their husbands crazy?" Oliver shouted back.

Ainsley stepped into the living room and between the two lovebirds. "What's the matter?"

"She's been sick for four weeks now, and she refuses to go to the doctor. But she's getting worse, Ainsley. Today she could barely get out of bed."

"*Yet,*" Melb retorted, with a finger flying toward the ceiling, "I managed to scrub every floor in this house with vinegar!"

Oliver shrugged. "It's true. In under two hours. But despite how ill she is, she is refusing to eat anything healthy."

"He's lying!" Melb shrieked. "Oliver! What did I have for breakfast this morning?"

He rolled his gaze toward Ainsley, and in an exasperated voice said, "Cantaloupe."

"That's right. Cantaloupe." Melb crossed her arms.

"With chocolate slivers on top."

The doorbell rang, and Oliver rushed to the door as Melb burst into tears.

"Dr. Hoover," Oliver said, pulling him in by the arm.

Dr. Hoover had been retired for twenty years, but still made house calls to anyone nearby, usually at any time of the day or night. He lived twenty minutes away in the next county. He was a pretty good doctor by all accounts, except he had shaky hands, which, in some doctorly situations, could put terror into even the bravest soul.

"Please don't hurt me," Melb whimpered. She was carefully eyeing the doctor's bag.

"Melb, Dr. Hoover is here to help you. Don't you want to get better?" Oliver asked.

"What are her symptoms?" Dr. Hoover asked him.

"She's completely irrational, crying all the time, blaming me for everything yet wanting me at her beck and call. Her fuse is the length of my thumbnail, and if I mention anything that can be construed in any way other than its original meaning, she lets me have it!" Oliver slapped a harried hand against his forehead.

"Her symptoms, not her behavior," the doctor suggested quietly.

"Oh." Oliver shifted his eyes and body away from Melb. In a more controlled manner he said, "And then there's the nausea and the fatigue. She's not running a fever, but she does have frequent headaches. And"—Oliver swallowed and looked hesitant—"and she seems to have developed a healthy appetite. And by healthy I mean humongous."

Dr. Hoover cautiously approached Melb. "Not one more step," she said.

"Melb, don't you want to know what's wrong with you? Don't you want to feel better?" Dr. Hoover asked.

"No," she said, shuddering. "I just want to be left alone."

Ainsley stepped forward and sat on the couch with her, taking her hand. "We just all hate to see you this miserable. Dr. Hoover is a great doctor."

"And I promise, no shots," he said.

Melb looked suspicious, but it got her attention. She perused him with sharp eyes. "I'm deathly afraid of tongue depressors, and no, drawing a smiley face and making it do a little dance won't help."

Dr. Hoover didn't looked deterred. "What if I told you all I'm going to use is this small plastic cup?" It appeared in his hand like a magic trick.

"Are you going to fill it with chocolate milk?" Melb asked.

"No. But I do have a sucker for you if you'll be a good girl."

"Cherry?"

"Sure."

Melb glanced at Oliver, then Ainsley, who nodded enthusiastically.

Dr. Hoover opened his hand up and slowly reached toward Melb. She scowled at Oliver, looked worriedly at Ainsley, then slowly took the doctor's hand. He helped her off the couch. "Let's go into your bedroom, and I assure you this won't take longer than five minutes."

Melb nodded and followed the doctor down the hallway, glancing back once with wounded eyes at Oliver. When she was out of sight, Oliver let out a forceful sigh and turned to gather himself. He was mumbling and rubbing his feet against the floor.

Ainsley stood, approached him, and patted his shoulder. "Oliver? Are you okay?"

He gestured toward the hallway.

"I know, I know. But she'll be fine. She'll see that Dr. Hoover is here to help her, and maybe he can figure out what's wrong."

Oliver swiveled on his heel, and to Ainsley his face looked disproportionately terrified. "Are you okay?" she gasped.

"You don't understand," he whispered.

"Understand what?"

"Melb's fear of doctors is the least of my problems right now!"

"What's the matter?"

He grew stiff as he gazed at the dark hallway that Melb and Dr. Hoover had just disappeared into. Then, in barely a whisper, he said, "See that door in the hallway?"

"Sure. Where you keep the towels and the vacuum. Do you need me to get something?"

He shook his head. "I found Bob." He tore his gaze away from the door and looked at Ainsley. "And Fred."

"The snake?"

He hushed her with his hands. "It was curled up in there when I went to get Melb a cool washcloth. I shut the door." Oliver looked like he was having a heart attack. He wiped the sweat off his forehead. "I swear it was all I could do not to scream, but Melb was acting so crazy as it was, I knew I had to stay in control."

Her fingers found her mouth. "Is it still in there?"

He nodded somberly. "I've got to figure out a way to get the snake out without Melb knowing about it, or she'll really flip. But I can't get her to go anywhere or do anything. The only two places she'll go is to the kitchen and then back to the couch."

Ainsley couldn't stop looking at the hallway. She could already feel her skin crawling. But by the looks of it, she was the most level-headed person of the two of them, so she tried her best to remain calm.

Oliver, on the other hand, was clawing at his neck and profusely sweating. "But I don't know if I can take spending the night here knowing that snake is in the closet! It was so horrible, I can't even describe it. Its two heads…"

Ainsley felt her knees grow weak. "Its two heads did what?" she whispered.

"Nothing, really. But it was still horrible." Oliver shuddered. He was grabbing his chest. "I don't know if I can take another moment of this kind of drama!"

"Good news!" Dr. Hoover called as his white hair appeared from the shadowy hallway, followed by the rest of him.

"She's faking it?" Oliver asked.

"Faking it? No, no. It's quite real."

"What's wrong with her?"

Dr. Hoover had a strange twinkle in his eye. "Well, Oliver, I haven't told Melb yet. I thought you'd like to have that honor."

Oliver looked completely exhausted. "Are you serious? I thought it was always the doctor that broke the bad news."

"But this is good news. Oliver, you're going to be a father."

Ainsley's jaw dropped, and, at the same time as Dr. Hoover, she noticed Oliver was swaying and looking pale. They each grabbed an arm and led him to the couch.

"Melb's pregnant?" Oliver said, his voice as high as a little girl's.

Dr. Hoover gave a hefty nod. "There's no doubt about it. I did two tests."

Oliver's bloodshot eyes stared at the carpet, both hands shaking as they lay in his lap. Ainsley touched his shoulder. "Oliver, are you okay?"

"Give me a minute," he mumbled.

Dr. Hoover stood and offered Oliver a congratulatory handshake, which he barely managed to return. "I must be off now. I told Melb to rest for a few minutes on the bed. She was right. The tongue depressor dance didn't go over well. But she should be ready for your exciting news very soon." Dr. Hoover plopped his hat on his head and walked out the door, humming a nursery rhyme.

Ainsley turned to Oliver, not sure if she should offer comfort or congratulations. And at this point, she wasn't sure what had brought the terror to his eyes. Was he still thinking about the snake? Or was he processing the idea that he was going to be a parent?

Before she had time to offer any consolation or advice, they heard the flip-flopping of house shoes against the wood floors—Melb was coming toward them from the hallway.

"Well?" she flared. "Where's the doctor? What'd he say?" She still had a washcloth atop her head.

Oliver popped up from the couch, quite unsteadily. His cheeks were flushed to a bright pink, and he was smiling so tightly Ainsley could actually hear his teeth grinding.

"Darling," he managed.

Melb eyed him but continued her plodding toward the couch. She sat down and covered herself with an afghan. "Well? What is it?" she snapped. "All he would tell me was that it was my fault, and I should be more careful. If that doctor knew how many antibacterial soaps I go through in a month, he wouldn't be so snide with his remarks." She was studying Oliver with each angry word, and suddenly her face turned concerned. "Ollie? What's wrong?" Tears gathered in her eyes. "Am I dying?"

Oliver swallowed, and with enough gusto to sell a German-made to a Midwesterner, he threw his arms wide and beamed. "Congratulations!" he shouted. "There's a snake in our closet!"

CHAPTER 9

IT WAS A STRANGE THING to come home after midnight and find his house alive with activity, but Ainsley was busy serving drinks and there were people crowded into his living room. Alone in the kitchen, Wolfe said, "Say that again?"

"Melb's pregnant."

"No, after that."

"Oliver found the snake."

"After that."

"In his linen closet."

"No, after that."

"And they're spending the night here until they catch the snake."

"No, there was something after that."

Ainsley thought for a second. Then she sighed and checked her watch. "Oh. Yeah, forget that. You're too late. Besides, we have company."

Wolfe sulked away and joined the crowd in the living room. Oliver was sitting next to Melb, whose ashen complexion did not reveal which piece of news had brought it on. Oliver was stroking her hair, her shoulder, her elbow, visibly unsure whether he was even being helpful. Sheriff Parker, obviously awakened out of a dead sleep judging by the sheet marks that crisscrossed his cheek, was taking notes, but Butch, with his hands on his hips, looked to be the only one excited about the ordeal. He was interviewing Oliver and Melb.

"How long was the snake in your closet?" Butch asked.

Oliver shrugged, looking as if he was not sure his timid wife beside him could handle the answer. "I'm not exactly sure. Maybe one or two hours...or five."

"Five!" Melb gasped.

"I didn't want to upset you, but you wouldn't let me leave the house, and I knew if I made a phone call, you'd complain I wasn't spending enough time with you. Especially if I tried to be secretive about it. You know how your emotions have been...because of your pregnancy."

Melb patted a tissue against her cheeks. "I don't understand how this could've happened. I can't believe it. I could have sworn I went through menopause. And now I have to try to come to grips with the fact that all those mood swings are just part of my"—she could hardly finish her sentence—"personality!"

Butch said, "Okay, back to the snake. It just sat there all evening?"

"That I could tell. I mean, I only peeked in twice. That was enough for me."

Ainsley arrived in the living room with hot tea.

"I'll take one!" Melb said.

"You can't have caffeine or certain herbs," Ainsley said. "I'll make you a cup of hot water with honey and lemon."

Melb started crying again.

Butch said to his father, "Let's get over there, see what we can find out." He looked at Oliver and said, "We'll get it. Dead or alive."

"Surprised you wanted to tag along, Wolfe," Butch said from the front seat of Sheriff Parker's truck. "You may see blood."

Wolfe nodded and smiled tolerantly at Butch, who luckily liked to disappear for months at a time, only to reappear at the holidays with fantastic covert-operation stories. Though supposedly "retired" from the spy business, he hadn't specified how long he would be hanging around Skary this time. Wolfe was pretty sure only human blood made him pass out, but he was getting a little nervous…not so much about the blood but about the fire in Butch's crazed eyes.

Sheriff Parker shook his head. "I don't know what's scarier. This snake or Melb Stepaphanolopolis birthing a child."

"Be nice," Butch said. "Snakes in general are harmless creatures. When they come with two heads, though, that's a whole different scenario. It's all about knowing the enemy. And anything with two heads is the enemy." He glanced back at Wolfe. "You gonna be able to handle this?"

Wolfe rolled his eyes and decided a change of subject was in order. "How are you coming with your lines, Irwin?"

"What lines?" Butch asked.

"Your dad is taking a part in a town play that we're doing the night before Thanksgiving."

Butch turned to his dad. "Are you kidding me?"

The sheriff shrugged. "It's a small role." He paused, then added, "It's good for the community."

"What's the play about?"

"I've read through it twice, and I can't really tell you, but I do have some great lines," the sheriff said as he pulled into the Stepaphanolopolis driveway. The mood in the car immediately changed. "Butch, you got the key?"

"Yeah."

"All right. Let's go in there and get this nightmare over with."

As they got out of the car, Butch stopped them both on the sidewalk. "If I yell *Code Orange*, run as fast you can."

"Why?" Wolfe asked.

"It means we're in extreme, unpredictable danger."

"Why not just say *run?*"

Butch sighed with a long-suffering expression and said, "Just be aware of my knife. It'll fillet bone."

"You brought your knife?" the sheriff asked. "I thought I'd just use my gun."

"You haven't used your gun in years, Dad. Secondly, do you really think that they want a bullet ricocheting through their house? Now come on. Quietly. We have no more time to waste."

Butch unlocked the door, and Wolfe was about to flip the light on, but Butch grabbed his arm. "I prefer to work in the dark." He looked toward the hallway and gestured to ask whether that was the way to the linen closet. Wolfe nodded. "All right. Give me an idea about this closet. What are we looking at?"

"Linen," Wolfe answered.

"How many shelves?"

Wolfe tried to remember. He'd once opened the closet, thinking it was the bathroom. "Five, maybe."

"Maybe." Butch shook his head. "Okay, anything else?"

"Melb mentioned that's where she keeps her vacuum cleaner."

"Left or right side?"

"I don't know," the sheriff answered.

"Is Melb left- or right-handed?"

"Right, I think," the sheriff said.

"Then the vacuum will probably be on the right side." Butch drew a deep breath and pulled a large, glistening knife out of its sheath. "Stay here."

"You like working alone?" Wolfe asked.

"Most animals can sense fear, so you're better off at a distance."

He moved forward, his knife securely in his hand, raised at just shoulder level. Wolfe chuckled and glanced at the sheriff, but he seemed oblivious to the absurdity. His hand was perched on his gun. There was no way of knowing whether it held an actual bullet.

Butch disappeared into the hallway shadows. In the silence they heard him turn a doorknob. After that, several more seconds of silence went by, then the sheriff called out, "Butch? What's going on?"

Suddenly noises interrupted the still night, including grunts and a lot of "hi-YAH's," which sounded more like a Canadian neighborly greeting than kung fu, but it was over in a matter of seconds.

Butch emerged from the hallway, gently sliding his knife back into its sheath. His hair was disheveled, and he looked exhausted. "The good news is, the danger is over."

"Thank goodness," the sheriff said.

"The bad news is that Melb's going to need a new vacuum cleaner hose."

"Where's the snake?"

Butch shrugged. "I'm not sure. I'm wondering if Oliver mistook the hose for the snake. It certainly fooled me."

"So the snake's gone?" Wolfe asked.

"If it was ever there. There's a hole in the baseboard, where it could've possibly gotten in or out of the closet. It's hard to say."

"Oh, brother," the sheriff groaned. "Let's draw straws to see who gets to tell Melb and Oliver."

Melb looked worse than she did when she thought she had a communicable disease. Ainsley was gently breaking the news to her about all the foods she should avoid and how many medicines could harm the fetus.

Melb was clueless, and this was a lot to take in at one in the morning. Oliver had gone upstairs to take a shower.

"Honey and water," she sobbed, staring into her cup. "For nine months? No coffee?"

"But don't you want a healthy baby?" Ainsley asked.

Melb blinked and set her cup down. "I never wanted a baby. I've never thought I'd be a good mother. I'm too much to take care of myself. And I'm happy that I'm the only person in Oliver's life, that I have his undivided attention." She stared down at her belly, tears brimming. "I'm not ready for this. I don't know how to change a diaper. I think baby food smells like puke. How am I going to handle this? Especially with no coffee?"

Ainsley slid beside her on the couch and wrapped an arm around her shoulder. "Melb, you'll be a great mother. As this baby grows inside of you, you'll become more and more excited. And when you finally get to hold him or her, you will melt with love."

Melb folded her arms. "How do you know? You've never had a baby. I once held a puppy. Everyone else was oohing and aahing. You know what I was thinking? How many times it was going to pee on the carpet." She must've noticed Ainsley's mortified expression, because she added, "It's a hidden practical side I have."

"You're just scared," Ainsley said, returning to her kitchen, where she tried to gather up more unnatural compassion for what she was hardly able to understand. She could appreciate the practical worries, but she just assumed love would trump that. She fixed herself a cup of tea and was hoping the men would be home soon when the phone rang.

"Hello?"

"It's Dad."

"Hey…" Ainsley turned away from Melb. "How'd it go?" she whispered.

"Not good. We're not sure if Oliver mistook a vacuum cleaner hose for a snake, or if there actually was a snake in the closet and it has now escaped…possibly into some other part of their house. What I need you to do is make sure Melb is very calm and composed. I'm going to have to break the news to her, and although I have my tranquilizer gun in the truck, I don't want to have to use it."

Ainsley glanced at Melb, who looked ready for a tranquilizer as it was. "I'll do my best."

"We've got to lock up, and we're going to take a look around the outside of the house. We'll be back in about ten minutes."

Ainsley took in a deep breath as she hung up the phone. She decided against the tea. As she returned to the living room, Melb was mumbling something about dieting. "—which means I'm back on a diet again. I thought you were supposed to eat anything you wanted when you were pregnant."

Ainsley took a seat across from her, trying to think quickly. "The guys will be back in ten minutes."

Melb nodded. "I hope they found that snake. Did they say?"

"You know," Ainsley said, "while we're waiting, I could show you some relaxation techniques you'll want to use during the birth."

Melb's eyes grew wide. "The birth. I can't handle a paper cut. How am I going to handle giving birth?" Tears streamed down her face. "I'm not going to be able to do this."

"Try some big, deep breaths. Go ahead, this will do you some good."

Melb looked skeptical and complied only halfheartedly.

"Focus on something ahead of you. Think good, happy thoughts. Think about a tropical island somewhere, with warm water and cool breezes."

"Once you have kids, tropical island vacations are a thing of the past."

Ainsley rubbed her mouth, holding in the frustrated words that wanted to topple out. "Just give it a try, please."

Melb rolled her eyes, puffed her cheeks in disapproval, then stared out the back window. "Okay, fine. I'm breathing, breathing, breathing. Seeing palm trees. And sand. Oh, how beautiful is the water." Her words were nothing more than placating. "Look at that bird. How cute. And those little crabs. And the—" Suddenly, Melb jumped off the couch, gasping for air.

"Melb! It's just a fantasy!"

Melb was pointing and gesturing at the window. "Sha...sha..."

"Shark?" Ainsley frowned. "You're pretending to see a shark? Melb! This is supposed to be a fantasy where nothing bad happens! You're supposed to be relaxing!" Ainsley had reached her boiling point. "You are going to have to get ahold of yourself! Find a way to deal with this! Babies are a blessing!"

Melb, however, was furiously shaking her head, and still pointing. "Sha—" Melb was trembling all over. Ainsley didn't realize she had such a vivid imagination. "Shadow!"

"Shadow?"

Melb hurried toward her. "It just passed across the window. I swear it. It looked like a man." She turned to Ainsley. "Somebody's out there!"

CHAPTER 10

WOLFE WALKED HIS USUAL ROUTE to the coffee shop, which was now called a coffeehouse. The townspeople didn't seem to mind the name change either—what with all the frills attached. The store was seeing more business than it had in a long time. And though most people still stayed with the black coffee, a few ventured out and tried the riskier versions, such as coffee with foam.

Wolfe had gone to get coffee this morning for multiple reasons. First of all, he was completely exhausted and had finished the entire pot at home. Last night, he'd driven all the way back from Chicago, only to be greeted by a houseful of people worried about a snake, which probably was only a vacuum cleaner hose. But Oliver wasn't convinced, and so now they had houseguests who would surely stay until the snake was caught.

He was supposed to meet Alfred here in thirty minutes. They had hardly discussed anything after the conference. On their drive home Alfred had fallen asleep in the passenger's seat five minutes after they left Chicago.

He yawned his way in, and was immediately flagged down by his father-in-law and Butch. "You look wiped out," the sheriff said, rubbing his own bloodshot eyes.

"Luckily," Butch said, "I'm trained for this sort of thing, or I'd probably need a nap. But I won't sleep until I find out what happened last night."

To Wolfe's horror, the uproar continued long into the night after

Melb claimed she'd seen someone outside the back window of his house. Ainsley said the dogs had never barked, so Wolfe was immediately skeptical. Butch found footprints, but it hadn't rained in a week, so they could've been anybody's.

At least it was giving Butch something to do.

Just as Butch was getting ready to explain a tactical plan for catching the elusive shadow, the door to the coffee shop opened, and a man who looked like he'd jumped out of an adventure novel breezed in. He nodded at a few customers, apparently aware he would be pegged immediately as the stranger in town. He wore a light tan Panama shirt, with a leather vest too small for his broad chest and an overly accessorized belt that drew attention to the belly that hung over it.

He looked to be a mix between a ranch hand and fashion disaster. As he passed by their table, he smiled and said, "G'day."

"He sounds Australian," the sheriff whispered as the man approached the counter.

"It's a fake accent," Butch said. "And those aren't real snake boots, either."

They watched as the man ordered his coffee, then left without another bother.

"Come on," Butch said. "Let's go do a little investigating. Something smells fishy about this guy."

"Or at the very least a little bit horsy," Wolfe smiled. No one caught his joke.

"You coming, Wolfe?" the sheriff asked, plopping his hat on his head.

"I'm meeting Alfred." He looked at both of their serious faces. "But keep me updated."

"Will do," the sheriff said, and out they went. Wolfe went to order some coffee. He had been unable to sleep in this morning, and he had a horrible headache. Melb had confined herself to the bathroom, shouting repeatedly at Oliver to bring her crackers and Sprite.

Ainsley wasn't much better to be around. She was still reeling about an episode from last night she could only describe as "hormonal insanity." She didn't fix breakfast, and hardly left the bedroom. Wolfe could only wonder if Melb was any indication about what his life might be like when Ainsley got pregnant. But with all her crazy charts and schedules, would he ever get a chance to try? Marriage had been great, but he was certainly not prepared for the emergence of idiosyncrasies that had more than once prompted a little doubt. He loved Ainsley, and that's what kept him focused. But marriage was certainly challenging. He said a short prayer for Oliver, who he imagined was pulling out the last of what little hair he had.

Wolfe slowly drank his coffee and gnawed on a scone, relishing the serenity of the moment. But it didn't last long. The door opened, the cool air hit his face, and Alfred bore down on him.

"Coffee," he mumbled, dropping his coat on the chair and wandering off to the counter. He returned shortly, his face a little perkier. "This place has done a turnaround. They actually have a macchiato!" He gestured with his thumb and said, "And I just noticed a cell phone store across the street."

"Really?" Wolfe tried to look out the front window.

"That's exciting news. Maybe that means I can get service now. No offense, but it's like the Death Valley of the cell phone connection around here. My phone doesn't even roam. It just drops dead."

Wolfe shook his head. It was hard to imagine a cell phone store opening up. Why would a town so small that a person only had to dial the last four digits of a local phone number need cell phones?

Alfred took his seat and crossed his legs more flamboyantly than most men. His dark, shiny shoe swung as he carefully folded his hands on top of the table. "So," he said. "You have a lot of explaining to do."

Wolfe grinned. By the time he'd found Alfred at the conference, he looked ready to jump into Wolfe's arms. Apparently Alfred had become quite a quick celebrity among the writers. A few had encircled him when Wolfe found him in the main conference lounge. "We haven't even had a chance to really talk. You slept like a baby all the way home. I thought I was going to have to carry you to your hotel room."

"Funny. It was our first writers' conference, but you somehow managed to disappear for over two hours."

"I was pitching my book, like you told me to. It was time well spent. Harry Rector is a nice man."

"Well, while you were frolicking with the industry executives, I was busy watching my back. I had three ladies offer to pray over me. And 'over me' wasn't well enough defined for me to give permission. I tell you, that's a whole other world, isn't it?"

"I loved it."

"You would."

"Well, what did you do while I was gone?"

Alfred traced his hairline, and a wicked grin emerged. "I can't help but brag. I think I may have found the new It girl."

Wolfe laughed. "The It girl?"

"Doris Buford." He flicked his hand. "Her name doesn't exactly have a bestseller ring to it, but she uses a pen name and is a fantastic writer. I would even call her literary."

Wolfe frowned. "You never called me literary."

Alfred engaged him, now tracing his coffee lid. "Wolfe, you are a fine writer. No doubt about that. But Doris…now this woman has command of the language. She had me weeping." He raised an eyebrow. "I screamed once when reading a book of yours, but never cried. Except that time you played that practical joke and sent me that stupid fake ending where everyone, including the protagonist *and* narrator, gets murdered."

Wolfe smiled. "That was a good one."

"Anyway, all was not lost. I'm getting more comfortable with this religious fiction industry. And I'm pretty sure I can groom Doris to take all." He studied Wolfe. "You look terrible. You're not jealous, are you?"

"Please. I'm happy for you. I'm glad you're taking this all seriously."

"So what's wrong with you?"

"Long night," Wolfe growled. "I can't even begin to explain it."

"Trouble on the home front?"

"Well, if by 'home front' you mean that my house has now turned into Hotel California, then yes."

"I won't ask," Alfred said, waving his hand. "Let's talk about me. You know, I'm a pretty open-minded person, but I have to be honest, there were some things I saw last night that totally shocked me."

"Was it the class on levitating?"

"You're on a roll. I thought Harry said levitate, not meditate, and had he said levitate, then of course it would've been cause for alarm. I'll admit, I overreacted, but it was sort of a tense day." He paused. "I met this other agent. Nice woman."

Wolfe waited. "And?"

"That's what I mean. Nice woman."

"That's shocking?"

"In an agent, yes. Oh sure, we have our charming smiles and winsome handshakes, which fool a great deal of the literary general public. But agents can never fool other agents. Beneath all the niceties, we know the eye of a snake when we see it."

"Interesting."

"When I was an editor, we just pretended it wasn't there. After all, the agent is the lifeline, so if you want the big author, you better make nice with the big agent. But you put a group of agents together in a room, and it's death by radiant smile."

"So this woman obviously impressed you."

"She was genuinely nice. I had my claws into Doris Buford, but at the end of the night, this agent was happy that I had her, even though she knew her first. She seemed excited that I had a new client."

"I'm happy for you, Al."

"What about you? Any new ideas for a book? Did the conference finally light that long-diffused fire?"

"It was informative. Met a lot of good people."

"What about a story idea, Wolfe? I'm glad you enjoyed the socializing, but do I have to remind you that as likable as you are, you still have to have a story?"

"I know. I'm working on it. There's no hurry."

Alfred glanced at his watch. "Ooooh! Gotta go." He jumped up and pulled his coat on, swinging his expensive scarf around his neck.

"Where are you going?"

Alfred smiled gently. "Wolfe, I know this is going to be hard on you. I really do. But you're going to have to understand that you're not the center of my universe anymore. There was a time, yes indeed, where my world rotated around your star. But I've got to make a living. And as truly happy as I am that you've found your inner child, or you've aligned yourself with the planets, or—"

"Found God," Wolfe sighed.

"Right. As happy as I am about that, I can't wait around for the Almighty to inspire you."

Wolfe felt himself growing angry, but he managed to smile. "Sure. I understand. So where are you going?"

"Believe it or not, Doris Buford lives fifty miles north of here. We've got an appointment in an hour."

"Great. Good for you."

Alfred toasted the air with his coffee. "Here's to promising new talent!"

Katelyn thought she might cry with delight. Tears were actually forming in her eyes. The young man behind the counter, who looked like he was barely out of junior high but assured her he was eighteen, had a face full of expectation.

"I have bars," Katelyn said. She turned the face of the phone toward him. "I have bars!"

"Whoa," Billy breathed. "I can't believe it. Try to call me!"

She quickly dialed the number, which was displayed on a huge sign hanging in the window of the cell phone store. Within seconds, the phone rang.

"Hello?" Billy said.

"Wait," Katelyn said, holding up a finger. "I can't hear you. It sounds like it's still ringing."

"Yes, that's right! We have service, up and running!" he grinned.

Katelyn shook her head. "Hold up. It's just ringing. I can't hear your voice."

"Well of course you can! Just walk through that door and you're on your way!"

Katelyn frowned. Okay, maybe he was right. Moving toward the door might help. But when she did, nothing changed. "Let me dial again," she said.

"Not necessary. All you have to do is step fearlessly into the twenty-first century, my friend."

"What?"

"No sir, cell phones don't cause brain cancer. All right, see you soon." The kid winked at Katelyn and then hit the Flash button. "Hello?" His voice boomed through the phone.

"Hello?"

"Sorry about that. I think we might have our first customer coming in!"

Katelyn hung up the phone and walked back toward the kid. "I could hear you loud and clear."

"That's awesome."

"Who was on the phone?"

"That was Mr. Horton. He doesn't even own a microwave."

"I can't believe nobody noticed the tower going up on the highway."

"Oh, they noticed. There were all kinds of theories about what it was."

"No one knew it was a cell phone tower?"

"That was a guess. Among other things…like an alien space station."

"Don't people understand the freedom a cell phone can bring?"

"I know. It would be cool to stand out on my front lawn and call Jeff at his house."

"Who is Jeff?"

"My friend. He lives across the street."

"Right. And you could check in with your mom when you're out late."

"Oh, my mom won't let me get one. She says they cause brain cancer."

She hoped she hadn't become too optimistic about how quickly this town was going to conform. "Well, just remember, greet everyone with a friendly smile and keep it simple. We don't need people to know how to access the satellite code, just how to dial their buddy to meet for coffee."

"Right. And I'm going to have to come up with some good reasons why calling them at home wouldn't work. But I'm on top of it. I have a goal of signing up five people today."

"Very good," Katelyn said. "You sound ambitious. What did you say your last job was?"

"I sold bulletins for a dollar at the church." He shrugged at her shocked expression. "Hey, let me tell you, when you have to start selling something people expect for free, you've got to recognize the fact that you have an exceptional salesman's ability."

"Right," she said. "Well, we've gone over everything. My husband, Michael, will be in soon to check on you."

"Michael the Manager. Has a nice ring to it."

"Call me on my cell if you have any questions, okay?"

"Gotcha."

Katelyn walked outside and stood on the sidewalk. The air was so fresh and clean here. Tall pines framed the picturesque town and its blue sky. She decided a large mocha was in order. She walked across the street to the other sidewalk and headed toward the coffeehouse.

As she did, she passed a strange-looking fellow. He looked like the crocodile hunter, except for his pale skin, orange hair, and freckled face. He was curiously out of place here with his leather pants and jungle shirt. She stepped aside as he walked past. He gave her a wink and a half smile. There was a determined twinkle in his eye as he marched forward.

"That's strange," she heard someone say. She glanced to her right, and two men, totally bald, sat in front of the barber shop with their newspapers held erect in their laps. One chewed a smokeless cigar.

"That man?" the other said.

"Yeah. He's not from these parts."

"You got that right. First of all, look how he walks."

"No kidding. There's bowlegged, but then there's that."

"Suppose he's from Texas? They got some big bulls down that way."

"Naw. That's no Texan. His belt buckle's too small." The man with the cigar folded his newspaper. "No sirree. I can tell you where that fellow is from."

"Where?"

"The suburbs."

"The suburbs?"

"Strange breed of people."

"They dress like that?"

"They're as senseless with their fashion as they are with their cars and houses. The last time I checked, there wasn't a need for more bathrooms than you have people in your house."

"So that's a suburbanite."

"Things are changing, Rich. You can smell it in the air. If I'm lucky, I'll die in this decade before I see the robots take over our town." He sighed heavily. "Margaret loves all this. She can't stay out of that stupid bookstore. She claims she's drawn to the sofa. I say, 'Margaret, we got a big honkin' sofa in our own home!' It doesn't seem to matter. A sofa surrounded by books apparently is a better sofa." He stared across the street. "And now we got that!" He pointed to the cell phone store, where a few people mingled outside, looking into the windows. "Lord have mercy is all I have to say."

Suddenly the two men noticed Katelyn listening in on their conversation.

"That's another one," cigar-man whispered. "That kind of blond doesn't come naturally on God's green earth."

"It won't be long now," the other one said. "Pretty soon, all the suburbanites will take over our town."

Katelyn folded her arms and huffed away. For their information, Skary, Indiana, was not destined to be a suburb. It was far too remote to be a suburb. It was, in fact, destined to be an X-burb. But of course, these two men were too closeminded to care what that was. Or the potential this wonderful town had to offer.

She swung her shearling handbag over her shoulder and walked past the men with a dismissive flounce.

Now, where had she parked her Suburban?

It wasn't the cast of *Shakespeare in Love,* but she was pretty sure she could manage this group of people into some sort of interesting dramatics. The closest any one of them had come to actually being in a play was Martin, who had understudied in *The Lion in Winter* in college. But his prayers for the lead to grow ill or break a leg were not granted, and therefore he'd never actually performed in front of an audience.

"But," he assured her on their date, "I knew my lines perfectly. I feel confident about my abilities."

Lois had never seen this side of Martin before. She knew him only to be the fumbling sidekick and trailing shadow of Mayor Wullisworth. At dinner, he was quite charming, and though he wasn't really her type, she'd managed to say yes at his insistence they go out together again.

However, Lois also couldn't deny her attraction to the sheriff, who, to her surprise, had shown up on time to rehearsal, and even sounded enthusiastic about the fact that his role had grown larger.

She'd passed out pictures of the set design and copies of the rehearsal schedule and the newly revised play.

"Does anyone have any questions before we begin our read-through?" Lois asked.

Marlee raised her hand. "What kind of wardrobe am I going to have?"

"Yes, thank you for asking that question, Marlee. It's an important one. For most of the play, you will be wearing jeans that are too tight around the waist, several different logo sweatshirts, and your hair will always need to be tied back in a bun because you decided to do layers and it backfired."

Marlee looked disappointed. "Won't I have a gown?"

"A gown?"

"I am the love interest. Surely I get to dress up at some point, right?"

"Oh. Right. Well, we'll discuss that at a later date, but I'm probably going to go with a black pantsuit that was fashionable back in the sixties but is all I—she—can afford."

"I've actually got a great dress from my prom night a few years—"

"Who's the director here?"

"Sorry."

"Listen, folks. This isn't about you. You're going to have to enter into these roles, play these characters. It's going to take some stretching; you're going to leave your comfort zone a bit. And if that means you're wearing sequins and polyester, then that's what it means. You gotta sell your character to the audience. If you don't believe it, they're not going to. Does everyone understand?"

They all nodded.

"Okay. Now. Let's get started. Quiet, everyone. This is our first read-through. As we do this, I want you to think through your character, find your characters' motivation. Why does he say certain things? Why does she act a certain way? I want everybody to concentrate."

Everybody opened their scripts. But all Lois could think about was how good the sheriff smelled.

CHAPTER 11

"I JUST LOVE THE WAY you say that line," Lois said, scooting a bit closer to the sheriff.

"Which line?"

"You there. Stop and put your hands up."

The sheriff smiled. "I guess it's because I've said that a time or two."

"It comes across so naturally."

"What did you want to work on? I'm sure I'm the worst actor here. The list could be endless."

"Oh, you're not as bad as you think." Lois slapped his arm. Goodness, there was a lot of solid arm there. She slapped it again, just to make sure she wasn't dreaming. No, there was indeed an actual muscle bulging. She stood, walked to center stage, and beckoned the sheriff to follow. "Now," she said, "the thing that I wasn't quite buying was your affection for Lotus." *Suck in your gut.*

The sheriff stuck a finger in his ear and wiggled it around nervously. "Yeah. I know this is acting, but I can't say I'm going to be pulling it off very well. My wife passed on years ago, and I guess I'm out of practice at being a romantic. Plus, Marlee is like a daughter to me. She's been friends with Ainsley since childhood. I kind of feel weird hitting on her."

"Understood," Lois said. "Just remember, it's pretend. You're playing a role, so you have to completely enter into the head of Bart, and

Marlee is no longer Ainsley's childhood friend. She is a beautiful middle-aged woman named Lotus with an extra twenty pounds to shed."

"Right."

"It'll help when she's in costume."

"Okay."

"Have you ever heard of method acting?"

"No."

"It's the way certain actors prepare for certain roles. For instance, if an actor is playing a soldier, he might go to boot camp to see what it's like."

The sheriff took his finger out of his ear, checked it for wax, and then stuffed his hand in his jeans pocket.

"So," Lois continued, "let's do some method acting. I'm Lotus, you're Bart. Let's say we're standing in the street. We've run into each other after the annual fair."

"That's not in the script, is it?"

"No, no. See, that's method acting. You take your character out of the script, put him into a real life situation, and see how he does."

"Huh."

"So, let's say we meet on the street. You're not expecting to see Lotus. So, what do you say?"

"Hi Lois."

"Lotus."

"Hi Lotus."

"Hi there, Bart. What are you doing out here so late?"

"Lois asked me to stay."

"You must stay in character. Think of a reason why you're out here so late."

The sheriff sighed, looking a little defeated.

Lois whispered, "Like maybe you're hunting down a bad guy."

"I'm hunting down a bad guy."

"Oh, my. That sounds dangerous."

"Not really. Nothing dangerous happens around here."

"That's because we have such a strong and stable sheriff."

Red circles glowed on the sheriff's cheeks. "I do the best I can, ma'am."

She touched his arm. "Oh, don't call me ma'am. Call me Lotus."

"Okay. Lotus."

"So," she said, her finger tracing down his arm, "what are you doing now? I don't see any bad guys around."

The sheriff pulled at his mustache but seemed to try to stay in character. "I guess nothing."

"Maybe you could join me for a cup of coffee."

"Oh. Sure. Yes. Love to."

Lois smiled. "Good! You're doing terrific. Just remember, Bart is in love with Lotus, so he is probably going to initiate this little date."

The sheriff swallowed, scratched his neck, and then said, "Why stop at coffee? Why don't we go get something to eat?"

"Oh, Bart. That sounds wonderful."

The sheriff looked proud of himself. "Well, c'mon! I'm hungry!"

Lois smiled tolerantly. "Remember your manners, Bart."

"Oh." He held out his arm. "Would you be so kind to accompany me? Lotus?"

"It would be my pleasure, Bart." She took his arm, and a tingling sensation drifted from her head all the way down to her feet. They walked off the stage together.

When they stepped onto the carpet, the sheriff slapped his hands together. "How was that?"

Lois raised a seductive eyebrow. "Well," she said. "As far as I can tell, we haven't made it to the restaurant yet. Bart."

"I don't think I dressed for the occasion," the woman said.

The man gave her the signal to be quiet. She wasn't getting it, so he finally had to put his finger on her lips. He took her hand and guided her through the thick grouping of trees. Leonard Tarffeski watched these two from a distance, particularly the man, who had decided to follow Tarffeski yesterday after he got coffee. This guy was acting like Han Solo! All that was missing were two gigantic buns on either side of this chick's ears.

Jabba the Hutt is waiting for you.

"I think I heard something slither through the leaves."

Tarffeski chuckled. This guy was actually looking for the snake? This was great! What a moron!

"Before I picked you up, I found snake tracks near the junkyard."

"Butch," she moaned, "I'm freaking out."

He turned to her and gently held her shoulders. "Tammi, you have nothing to fear. I'm with you."

Tarffeski doubled over with silent laughter. This guy was something else.

"I hate snakes."

"I thought you told me your horoscope called you adventurous and fearless."

Sounds like this date's a bust. What kind of guy would take a chick snake hunting? If you want to impress her, take her to a restaurant that serves snake, you idiot.

He pulled out his knife. The girl jumped backward. It was a long knife. "Don't be afraid. I am highly qualified to use this knife. And a boa is no match for how quickly I can strike."

Tammi didn't look convinced. Tarffeski figured this guy would have another corny one-liner waiting.

"Sweetheart," Butch said, "you have no worries. With one swift flick of my wrist, I can cut this snake's head off instantly."

She folded her arms. "And exactly which head would that be? The left or right?"

"Look, if you're going to date me, then you're going to have to accept the fact that I live for danger. It's part of who I am. I can't change that about me." He swept her hair out of her eyes. "You have nothing to fear. I will protect you."

The girl actually looked convinced. And now madly in love. He was going to have to stop this nonsense. It was too painful to watch.

"But who will protect *you?*" Tarffeski stepped out of the shadows. He grinned at the two of them. Frankly, the knife was making *him* a little nervous, especially now that it was pointed toward him.

"Good evening," Tarffeski said. "What are you two lovebirds doing out so late?"

"I could ask the same thing about you."

"Impressive knife."

"It came from overseas."

"So did I."

"You're going to try to convince me that's a real Australian accent?"

"It's New Zealand."

"New Zealand. What are you doing in Indiana?"

"I'm a snake hunter."

"A snake hunter."

"A *professional* snake hunter." Tarffeski looked at Butch's knife. "But unlike you, I respect the animal kingdom." He patted the cloth sack hanging from his belt. "I have no plans to kill this strange and rare creature."

Butch narrowed his eyes. "There's something that's not right here."

"I would say it's not right to bring such a lovely woman out here in the woods just to try to impress her." He addressed Tammi. "A woman like you should be wined and dined, not taken out on a snake hunt."

"Hey," Butch said. "We have reservations at eight. So back off, snake man."

"The name is Leonard."

"He does have a cool accent," Tammi said. "I've never known anyone from New Zealand."

Leonard stepped forward. "Why don't you two kids go on, and leave the snake handling to the experts?"

"Good idea. I'm freezing. And I'm tired," Tammi said.

Butch stared him down, but then turned to Tammi. "Sure, Tammi. Whatever you want." He offered a smile. "I want you to be happy."

"Wise choice," Tarffeski said.

"I'm going to be watching you."

"Watch and learn."

"This guy is something else, isn't he? Who do you think you're fooling?"

"Be on your way, lad. I've got a snake to catch. And you have a girl yet to impress."

Butch put his arm around Tammi and walked her back through the trees toward his car.

Tarffeski laughed to himself as he listened to them drive off. Then he hurried over to the junkyard.

CHAPTER 12

IT SEEMED IRREVERENT in a way, to squeeze icing onto the strudel from a small, plastic casing. She put the strudel into the toaster just as Melb inquired about it for the fourth time from the comfort of the living room couch. Not once in her life, *ever,* had she eaten a frozen toaster strudel. The fact that it had *gourmet* written across the box did not help motivate her. And though she was a fan of strawberries and cream cheese, the very idea of making strudel in a toaster seemed so improper. She turned the box over, but the ingredients looked more like a chemical experiment than a delicate pastry dish. But this was what Melb wanted.

Ainsley walked into the living room. Melb was stretched out on the couch, sipping her decaf coffee. She glanced tiredly at Ainsley. "This stuff tastes awful. Can't you tell the difference? I think it's making me more tired."

"Your body is working overtime. Remember that. That little baby, probably the size of the nail on your pinky, is sucking all your energy. You'll feel tired for a couple more months, but then you'll start feeling really—"

Melb held up her hands.

"What?" Ainsley asked.

"Just heard the toaster pop up."

Ainsley turned back to the kitchen, but heard a knock at the front door. Fairly certain Melb wouldn't get up, she wiped her hands and went to answer it.

Upon opening the door, she saw the most beautifully dressed, pulled-together woman she'd ever laid eyes on. She was dressed in a light pink pantsuit, from head to toe, with a casual tee underneath. Her hair was pulled away from her face with a thick brown headband that matched her shoes. Delicate earrings glimmered in the morning light, along with a tiny diamond that hung around her neck. Her eyes, wide and blue and mesmerizing, held shimmery hints of color on the lids, framed with neat and tidy eyebrows. She grinned.

"Are you Ainsley Boone?"

Ainsley couldn't remember the last time she hadn't been dressed by 9:00 a.m. Her hair, she realized, was sure to look a mess. She pulled her robe closed and tried to smooth the top of her hair.

"Yes. I'm Ainsley."

The woman offered her hand. "Hi there. I'm Katelyn Downey."

"Hi," Ainsley said, shaking her hand.

"I'm sorry to drop by without calling, but Reverend Peck said…" She paused.

"Said what?"

"He said that it would be no problem. You're always up and about."

"I usually am. I have a…a houseguest… Anyway, yes, I usually am."

"I'm so sorry to bother you. Should I come back another time? I wanted to discuss the possibility of you catering an event."

"Oh. Um, no. Come in, please. Forgive the bathrobe." She let the woman in but thought it might be better to direct her to the den. "Have a seat. Can I get you some coffee? Or a…a strudel?"

"Oh, a strudel sounds fabulous! Reverend Peck has been bragging about what a wonderful cook you are."

"Well, these are…fr-fr—"

"Yes?"

"Frozen. Toaster. Encased in plastic."

"Oh." The woman smiled. "Coffee is fine."

Ainsley excused herself to the kitchen. She retrieved a cup and saucer from her china, and poured the coffee. She quickly took some sugar cubes, put them in a crystal bowl, poured half-and-half into the cream pitcher, and returned to the den with it all atop a silver platter …though her house shoes flopping against the wood floors were doing a good job of reminding her that even silver couldn't hide the fact she hadn't made it out of her bathrobe yet.

"Oh, thank you. I tell you, I don't know what I would do without my coffee in the morning. Have you seen the new coffeehouse on Main?"

Ainsley nodded.

Katelyn plopped two sugar cubes into her cup, "I'll be moving to Skary soon."

"Oh?"

"My husband and I are building. Just off Maple, near the outskirts."

"Building what?"

The woman blinked. "A house."

"So you're not actually a resident of Skary? I didn't think you looked familiar."

"Not yet. But I'm excited to be one soon. I have a son. Willem. He's five and can speak Spanish. My husband's name is Michael. He's a developer and former baseball player."

"What made you want to move to Skary? We're not exactly on the map anymore."

"Oh, you mean since Boo stopped writing. He's your husband, right?"

"Yes. And nobody really calls him Boo anymore. He goes by Wolfe."

"This is such a charming little town. It has such character. Take your house, for example," she said. "It's beautifully decorated. Sits right atop a hill. Has that wonderful porch I'm sure you two must enjoy thoroughly. Is it about three thousand square feet?"

"I have no idea how big it is."

"We wanted our son to grow up in a place where he could enjoy clean air, nice people, and convenient living. It's the best of both worlds, wouldn't you say?"

Ainsley couldn't agree, but she smiled pleasantly. She'd seen the big world, earlier this year when she was introduced to a life of fame and fortune. She didn't much like it.

"What kind of event do you need catering for?"

"In a couple of weeks, the reverend and I are going to be unveiling a brand new children's ministry at the church!"

"A children's ministry?"

"Yes! We're redoing the basement. We'll have puppets and music and all kinds of wonderful activities for the kids while the parents go to church. And it will be for all ages. We'll even paint a mural across the wall."

"I haven't heard a thing about this."

She winked. "We've kept it top secret. We wanted to surprise everyone."

"Do you even go to the church? I don't know that I've ever seen you."

"Not yet. But soon. When our house is finished."

"We don't have many children."

"You offer parents activities for children, and they'll bring their kids, their nephews, their neighbors. The power of free baby-sitting cannot be overestimated. Believe me, I pay our baby-sitter eight dollars an hour, and still have to order her a pizza." She sighed and brushed her shiny hair off her shoulders. "So anyway, what we were thinking of was having a big party after church in two weeks. We'll set up in the basement, have games for the kids, serve up some brownies and cookies and hot drinks. What do you think?"

"I can do brownies and cookies with no problem."

She clapped her manicured hands together. "Perfect! The reverend will be pleased. He says you're the best of the best."

"That's nice of him to say." Ainsley smiled. "I do try to offer a pleasant atmosphere and delicious food, no matter what the—"

"Ainsley!"

Katelyn jumped in her chair, spilling her coffee onto her pink pants.

"Oh dear!" Ainsley grabbed the linen napkin on the tray and rushed to Katelyn's side. "Blot, don't rub," she instructed her. "I'll go get a stain stick."

"Ainsley!"

"Who is that?" Katelyn asked, blotting rapidly and looking toward the living room area.

Ainsley cleared her throat. "That's um, that's…Melb. I'm taking care of her while her…her house is being…purged of excess company."

"Oh."

"Nice lady," Ainsley said quickly. "She's just pregnant and—"

"Ainsley!"

"I'll be there in a minute!" Ainsley shouted, then gasped at her own loss of temper. She looked down at Katelyn, who was still blotting, now with disapproving eyebrows. "I'm sorry," Ainsley said. "I didn't mean to shout."

"Listen," Katelyn said, dropping the napkin onto the silver platter and standing, "I better get going." She pulled a card out of her designer handbag. "This is my number. Call me when it's a better time for you, and we'll talk about the details."

Ainsley looked at it. Her lipstick color matched the pink lettering. Katelyn carried her bag over her shoulder, sliding on a pair of gloves before she allowed Ainsley to open the front door for her. "It was a pleasure," she said, and trotted down the front steps. Ainsley watched the petite woman pull herself into an oversized SUV and disappear behind the tinted glass as she shut the door.

"Ainsley! Where are you?"

Ainsley sighed, slammed the door shut, and stalked toward the living room, where Melb hadn't moved an inch. A line of crumbs from the strudels sat upon her chest.

"I've been calling your name for five minutes," Melb complained.

"I was in the middle of something."

Melb sat up, the crumbs falling onto the couch. She dusted them onto the carpet. "You're not going to believe this!" she said.

That was the truth. She couldn't believe it. What one person could do to an entire, perfectly organized household! At least Melb had actually gone to get her own strudel from the kitchen.

"I felt the baby kick!"

Ainsley couldn't even muster up any kind of expression except the irritated one that had seized all her features.

"Did you hear me?" Melb asked.

"The baby is the size of half a peanut," Ainsley said firmly, holding up her pinky finger. "You can't feel it yet."

"You just know it all, don't you? You have this idea of how you think the whole world should run, and if it doesn't run according to your highly developed schedule, then somebody somewhere is doing something wrong."

Ainsley wanted to kick something. So instead she ran upstairs, slammed the door, and fell onto her bed in a heap of tears. It wasn't yet eleven, and she already felt exhausted enough to sleep! And she *still* wasn't dressed. She tore off her robe and lay in her pajamas, wiping her eyes.

Melb Cornforth Stepaphanolopolis was testing Ainsley's longstanding idea that she was, indeed, the perfect hostess.

Wolfe walked along Main, to the corner of Pine, where there was a wonderful view of the countryside. He used to do this when he was brainstorming a book. It was hard convincing people that staring at nothing in particular was the majority of how a writer worked, but back then, he didn't have too many people to convince. His life had changed drastically over the last several months. He'd gone from isolation to having a wife and hopefully children soon. He'd inherited a stable father-in-law and an imaginative brother-in-law, but nevertheless, it was a family. He'd learned how to be a friend and in return had gained friends. What he'd lost was his ability to write. And standing at the corner where so many ideas had often come to him, it was strange being able to think only about what he was unable to do anymore.

With the Spirit of God filling him now, was there no room left for a good story? He was certainly glad to have joined the faith. It had brought him the peace he'd searched for his whole life, but what he seemed to lack was direction. Why wasn't God showing him what he was supposed to write? Every word he attempted seemed a worthless effort. It was as if an entire chapter of his life was over.

He heard a car behind him. Turning, he saw Martin pull up to the curb and get out.

"Morning, Wolfe," he called as he approached.

Wolfe met him halfway. "Hi Martin. How are you?"

"Fine. What are you doing all the way out here on Pine Street?"

"Working."

"Okay." Martin stuck his keys in his pocket. "Well, since you're not doing anything, can we talk?"

"Sure."

Martin directed Wolfe toward a park bench nestled against a grassy knoll. That was one of the most delightful things about Skary—how many benches one could find. It had been Martin's idea. He'd proposed that when a loved one died, instead of sending flowers, you could contribute to the Memory Bench program. A new bench would be put in, and your loved one's name would be put on a plaque in the middle of the back of the bench. It was a huge success, and Martin said there were now more than a hundred benches all around the town. Even on his long walks, Wolfe never had trouble finding a place to sit.

They sat down on the memory of Mr. Elijah Samuel Smith.

"What's going on?" Wolfe inquired, noticing Martin's dreadful expression.

"It's kind of hard to talk about." Martin's wringing of the hands was proof of that.

"Well, whatever it is, you can certainly confide in me."

Martin gazed at the sky. "I'm in love."

"Really?"

"I don't talk much about my love life. Mostly because I haven't had one in the past twenty-five years. I just believe it's a private matter. I don't think it's right to go around talking about it."

Wolfe nodded, realizing they were getting ready to talk about his love life.

"But," he continued, "the problem is that I'm so out of touch with dating that I'm afraid I'm going to need some advice. What kind of advice can you give me?"

"Me?"

"Sure. You managed to snag the hopelessly romantic Ainsley Parker, so surely you've got some sort of charming secret you can spread around."

Wolfe shrugged. "It was by the grace of God, Martin. I did everything wrong. The only thing I had going for me was the fact that Ainsley's other option was the overly ambitious vet, Garth Twyne, who managed to keep pushing her away by his underhanded tactics."

"Oh, now, don't be so humble. I know you had to have done something to keep Ainsley's heart."

Wolfe tried to think. "Well, I guess I was just myself. I tried to let her get to know the real me, even though I was pretty sure that would make her turn and run."

"But you had the advantage of being a famous horror writer. I mean, as much as she despised what you did to the town, it had to at least be intriguing. I, on the other hand, am an accountant. I'm much more comfortable around a multiplication table than a dinner table, especially with a beautiful woman sitting across from me."

"Don't sell yourself short, Martin. You have a lot to offer. If it weren't for you, this town would have been gone a long time ago."

"Managing a town is one thing. Managing a woman's heart is quite another."

"Well, you seem sensitive to the fact that women take a special touch. That's at least a step in the right direction."

"I just wish that there was something dazzling about me, you know? That movie star quality, I guess."

Wolfe thought for a moment. "Martin, let's talk about a person you admire. Maybe there're a few things you can borrow from that person. You shouldn't change who you are, but you could certainly take notes and perhaps find some of those qualities hidden deep within yourself."

"That's awfully philosophical, but I guess I could give it a try. Why not?"

"Okay, good. Name someone you truly admire. Someone that embodies what it means to be a great man."

Martin thought for a long time, staring at the sidewalk in front of them, his arms crossed over the top of his chest. He looked to be thinking so hard, Wolfe didn't want to interrupt him with a suggestion or two, like perhaps Churchill, or one of his new favorites, C. S. Lewis.

"Got it," Martin finally said.

"Great. Who?"

"Butch."

"Butch?"

"Butch."

"Butch Parker?"

"Yeah."

"Ainsley's brother?"

"Yes, Wolfe. How many Butch Parkers do we know?"

"Right. Butch. Okay, fine. So what is it about Butch that you find so admirable?" Wolfe couldn't wait for his answer, because as far as he was concerned, Butch was one of the wackiest guys he'd ever known.

"Well, for starters, he's a complete stud."

"How's that?"

"It's no secret what a dangerous job Butch has. I mean, he can't give a lot of details, but we know enough to know that man has got nerves of steel and guts made of iron."

Wolfe closed his eyes. People really believed this stuff? Couldn't anyone see through Butch's Clint Eastwood facade?

"So...you want to have a dangerous job."

"Not per se. I'm Walter Mitty's timid brother." Martin slumped. "But I would love to have some of those stories, you know? Just for some dinner conversation. Have you seen the way a room crowds around Butch, even when he's simply talking about the weather? Plus, I wouldn't mind having his hair. I have no idea how it spikes like that, but I've tried gel, and that's not the magic formula."

"Listen, this woman that you're in love with wants to know you. And besides, you have some stories to tell. They may not be filled with covert operations that may or may not be embellished, but Martin, you're an admirable man. Do you believe this woman is interested in you?"

"We've been on one date. I really enjoyed myself, and she seemed to as well." Martin turned to him. "And believe it or not, I did it on a whim. I just asked her out. No warning or anything. Just said it. Fell out of my mouth like a bread crumb."

"See? And she said yes, and you two had fun, right?"

"Right." He slumped again. "But I haven't had the nerve to call her again. Every time I think about doing it, my stomach cramps up, and I have to lie under a heating pad for twenty minutes and then go do bath salts."

"First of all, you'll probably want to keep the bath salts thing out of general conversation…just until you get to know her better."

"Yeah?"

"But most of all, just be yourself and let her know that you really like being around her. Women are drawn to men whose whole focus revolves around them."

"So should I call, ask her out again?"

"Definitely. And there's no reason not to bring her a small bouquet of roses. Don't go overboard, because there's a fine line between enthusiastic date and aspiring stalker, but just let her know in small ways that you think she's special. As you grow closer, you'll learn what she loves, and you can cater a few special things to her liking."

A small smile spread across Martin's lips, and Wolfe could see a thousand ideas springing inside his head. "She does seem to like to go to nice restaurants."

"If she likes German, there's a great place called Ingrid's. I'll get you directions."

They stood, and Martin pumped his hand like they'd just closed a multimillion-dollar deal. "Thank you, Wolfe! I knew I could count on you."

"You're welcome."

"Not a word to anybody. Promise?"

"Sure," Wolfe grinned. "But can't you tell me who this dream woman is?"

"Not yet. One step at a time. But I can assure you of one thing. As soon as I know she's mine, I'll tell you her name and shout it from the rooftops!" He started toward his car and then turned back and said, "Say, if you're still having trouble coming up with a book idea, maybe you could write one about how to get a woman. That's gotta be a hot seller, right?"

Martin hurried off to his car, waving as he drove away. Wolfe sat back down on the bench, wondering if he'd just been demoted to the status of self-help guru.

CHAPTER 13

IT WAS FIVE O'CLOCK in the afternoon when Ainsley finally got herself dressed. By that time, it was useless to put on any makeup. She was just going to have to wash it off in five hours. As she pulled her hair into a ponytail, she couldn't help but think of how together that woman was this morning. Katelyn. That was even a pulled-together kind of name. Ainsley was always a name that wasn't easy to explain. And hardly anyone ever pronounced it right on the first try. "Paisley with an *n* and minus the *p*" was the only way she could describe it.

She dusted off her jealousy and went downstairs. Wolfe was somewhere in town trying to find himself, and then would be at the bookstore most likely. She made a list of dinners for the week and then wrote out her grocery list.

At the store, she tried to keep focused, but it was hard. On one hand, she hated what all this was doing to her relationship with Melb. Yet she was so exhausted trying to manage all that was required in that relationship, could she imagine another day with Melb in her house?

She was picking through an assortment of bell peppers when someone cleared her throat behind her. When she turned, there was Melb.

"Hi," Ainsley said quietly.

"Hello." Melb threw her nose in the air.

Ainsley tried to keep her composure. "Look, I'm sorry about this morning, okay?"

"You sound real sorry."

"What do you want from me, Melb? I'm doing my best to accommodate you. But you're pushing your limits."

"I'm sorry. I didn't realize there was a limit to friendship."

Ainsley bit her tongue and took a deep breath. "You're welcome to stay at my house as long as you need to."

"No need. I'm going to call Ollie's cousin, Lois. She'll take us in."

Ainsley clutched the plastic bag in her hand. "Melb! Stop being such a martyr. If you could just understand that…that…"

"That what, Ainsley?"

There was going to be a way to explain this, and it had to be done with great care. "It's like this. I have my world. You have your world. My world is very…structured. You are more…carefree. I'm just having a hard time adjusting to some of your personality traits, traits that are often confined to one's home."

"You're saying I'm a slob."

"I did not even use a word close to that!"

"Well, from now on, we can keep our personality traits to ourselves. I'll have Oliver come by to get our things later tonight."

Ainsley watched her sweep past, feeling both relieved and guilty. She closed her eyes, trying to remember exactly what Jesus had said about dying to yourself, your needs, your comforts. Yes, that's right. He said die to yourself, your needs, your comforts. She turned, watching Melb walk toward the meat counter.

Without any more hesitation, she chased after her.

"Melb! I'm sorry. Please, come stay with me again. I won't be such a grump. I promise I'll do better. Please, I want you to stay."

Melb stood with her back turned. Ainsley hoped it wasn't too late. Had she offended her friend forever?

"Melb?"

Melb slowly turned around, but when Ainsley saw her face, she gasped. She was as pale as the white floor on which they stood. "Melb!" Ainsley grabbed her shoulder.

Melb collapsed into her arms.

"Come in," Lois said. Martin tried not to stare, but she looked stunning tonight. Her lips looked amazing painted in red, and not everyone could pull off pink eye shadow at the same time. Martin hadn't come into her home on the last date. He didn't think it was appropriate for a first date. Of course, he wasn't sure what was appropriate for a date anymore. With women's lib and all that, it could easily confuse a man like Martin. He'd browsed Hardy's new bookstore for some tips, but even that lost him. There was a lot of talk about different planets, but nothing of practical use.

"I'll just be a moment," Lois said. "I need to get my shawl."

Martin's insides tickled. A shawl. This was one classy lady. Martin walked around the living room, admiring her knickknack collection. On top of an upright piano, a collection of old pictures were gathered together like they were going to sing bar tunes. Martin looked carefully at each one, recognizing Lois in most of them. He studied a black-and-white picture of a baby, smiling broadly considering the lack of teeth.

"That's my ex-husband," Lois said from behind him.

Martin glanced back at the picture. "The baby?"

"It was the only picture of him I could stand to look at. It reminds me he was once an innocent human being instead of the bloodsucking monster he became. It also reminds me of the level of maturity I was forced to deal with for so many years."

"I was married once too."

"So you understand how painful it can be when a marriage falls apart."

"Sure." Martin stared at a clock across the room. "It hurts when someone just stops loving you."

"It hurts even more when they decide to love someone else."

Martin tilted his head to the side and took Lois's hands. Trying to get past the fact that he was actually touching her, he said, "I'm so sorry, Lois. Did he leave you for a younger woman? Some men are bad about that."

"He left me for an older woman." She dropped her hands from his.

"You got left for an older woman?"

A wash of bitterness hardened her features. "I hear these women complain about losing their husbands to younger women, and I just want to scream. I say, 'Look, deal with it. Try being left for an older woman, and see what that does to your sense of self.'" She looked at Martin and smiled. "But I'm long past it."

"Oh. Good." Martin took a step back and said, "You look so lovely this evening. And you should know, I'm taking us to a new restaurant tonight. We're going to the next county."

"Really?"

"Yes, indeed, my fair lady. To a fine German restaurant called Ingrid's." Martin was thoroughly amusing himself with how dashing he'd suddenly become. He was inclined to throw in a British accent.

"Sounds romantic, Martin. You've put a lot of thought into this."

He took her arm and guided her to the door. "If I thought any more about this, I'd need another head."

Ainsley watched from the kitchen as Dr. Hoover hovered over Melb in the living room. She couldn't see Melb. The back of the couch was in the way. All she could see was her dark curly hair sticking off one end of the couch, and her tennis shoes on the other side. If Dr. Hoover's facial expression was any indication, this was serious.

He finally stood upright and packed his doctor's bag. He turned off the lamp and joined Ainsley in the kitchen.

"Is she going to be all right?" Ainsley could hardly hold back tears.

"All her vitals are good. But she absolutely must rest. For at least two weeks. I don't want—"

The front door flew open, and Oliver rushed in. "Where is she?"

Dr. Hoover put his finger to his mouth and beckoned Oliver into the kitchen. Oliver's eyes grew wider with each step. "Is she okay?" Oliver almost whispered.

Dr. Hoover put a steady hand on Oliver's shoulder. "She's fine. She's sleeping, which is exactly what she should be doing. I was just explaining to Ainsley that Melb really needs to take it easy for the next couple of weeks. She's probably been exerting herself. Maybe trying to get the nursery ready or shopping for the baby's clothes."

Oliver shook his head. "No. She's been too tired to do anything."

"Dr. Hoover, could stress have contributed to this?"

"Sure. She shouldn't be under any stressful situations right now. She needs to relax. Completely relax." Dr. Hoover walked toward the front door. "I will call and check on her tomorrow. In the meantime, make sure she eats right and gets plenty of rest."

Oliver and Ainsley stood in the kitchen, staring at each other. Then they both looked at the couch on which Melb was dozing. Oliver ran a hand down his face. Ainsley touched his arm. "Oliver, don't worry. I will take care of Melb. She can stay here, I will keep an eye on her and make sure she is resting and eating right."

"It's just that this is our big sales week at the store. I have to be there."

"I completely understand. I promise, she's in good hands."

Oliver nodded, hugged Ainsley, and said, "I'll keep my cell phone on. Call me if you need me."

"You have a cell phone?"

"Yeah. Haven't you seen the new store? Call me," Oliver said. He gave her the number, then headed back out the door. "I'll be home late tonight. Tell Melb I love her."

He shut the door quietly. Ainsley leaned against the counter, burying her face in her hands and trying to take some deep breaths. She had two catering events to plan for, and now Melb to look after. But she knew she had to. After all, she'd caused at least some of the stress in Melb's life.

She looked toward the couch, where the once peacefully slumbering Melb was now sawing logs.

"Lord, help me," she whispered.

"I want to tell you, Martin," Lois said as they ate their dinner, "that you're doing a fantastic job playing Gibb." She'd had her doubts. Martin, after all, wasn't exactly heroic-type material. But there was something about the way he'd confidently stepped into the role, like he was born to play it—and the way he was eating that cabbage like he had the intestinal tract of a robot.

She'd decided to forgo the cabbage but was enjoying the sausage. Most of all, she was enjoying Martin. She'd never considered him an interesting man, but now he was. She'd not realized how much effort he'd put into keeping the town alive, and all the trials he'd faced along the way.

He set the impaled cabbage back on his plate and looked at her. "Really?"

"I'm serious. I'm so impressed. You have quite a lot of talent."

"Talent. Now that's not something I hear every day."

"Apparently it reaches far beyond the town hall."

"I have to admit, I was skeptical. But I'm glad I'm involved now, if only to know you better."

"I'm glad we're getting to know each other better," Lois said. "But I want to take it slow too."

"So I should take the ring back?" A grin emerged. "Kidding."

"I knew you were," Lois smiled back. "You have a good sense of humor."

"Thanks. I don't get to use it a lot. Mayor Wullisworth, well, let's just say he doesn't do humor. Or irony. Or sarcasm."

"You've worked for him a long time."

"Yes."

"So what's his take on this snake problem? Anything happening?"

"He's afraid of snakes, so I'm handling it. But there's not much to handle. We sort of just have to keep everyone calm until the snake shows back up."

Suddenly, there was a strange noise coming from his breast pocket. He looked as shocked as Lois felt. "Oh!" he said suddenly. He reached in and pulled out a cell phone. He looked at it and said, "Excuse me. It's the mayor." He rose from the table and walked to the corner of the restaurant. He was gone for about a minute, then returned. "Sorry," he said, sliding the phone back into his blazer. "I'm pretty new to this cell-phone thing. I don't know exactly what I'm doing, when I should answer it, et cetera." He cleared his throat. "The mayor thought I should have one, so he could track me down anytime he wanted, as if he doesn't already do that."

"Is everything okay?"

Martin looked a little worried. "Everything's fine. Nothing that can't wait until later tonight when we're finished."

"Martin, if you need to go, I understand."

He looked up at her. "No. I want to stay. I'm really enjoying the evening."

"Me too."

And then his cell phone rang again.

"You should answer it."

Martin pulled it out of his pocket, hesitated, then answered it. "Yes? Uh-huh…uh-huh…but can't this wait?… But sir…uh-huh…okay. Good-bye." He shut his phone and stared at his plate.

"Are you okay?" Lois asked.

"Yeah. But we'd better eat fast. The mayor needs me."

The foot massage that Ainsley had ordered from Jack Hass had worked. But unfortunately Jack seemed to get sick right there in front of them, so Ainsley sent him home. Melb was practically drooling when Ainsley walked in with the plate of cooked peas and carrots. Melb turned, looked at the plate, and sat up a little. "Who is that for?"

"Dr. Hoover said you have to eat well."

Melb stared at the steaming vegetables. "What is that?"

"Peas and carrots."

"I'm going to gag."

"Melb, if you're ever going to feel better, you're going to have to rest and eat right."

"But peas and carrots? Why can't we start off with something a little less intimidating, like a cheese steak?"

"I promise, it won't kill you."

"At least tell me you put butter on them."

"No butter."

Melb sighed and laid back down. "I think I'd rather be dead."

Ainsley pulled up a chair next to the couch. "Look, I'll make you a deal. If you eat this plate of carrots and peas, I'll let you have a cookie."

"A cookie? What kind?"

"I've got chocolate chip and oatmeal."

Melb's face lit up. But as soon as she looked at the plate, her enthusiasm wilted. She was shaking her head vigorously.

"C'mon," Ainsley moaned. "It's just one plateful. You can do it."

"I can't."

"Then no cookie."

Melb sighed loudly. Ainsley heard Wolfe walk in the front door.

"You think about it, and I'll be right back," Ainsley said. Taking the plate back to the kitchen, she met Wolfe as he was putting his coat up. "Hi."

"Hi," he said, embracing her. "How was your day?"

"Dramatic. How was yours?"

"Dull."

"We make a good couple."

"Do I hear moaning?"

"Long story," she said, bringing him into the kitchen. "I'm trying to feed Melb carrots and peas."

Wolfe raised an eyebrow. "Melb can't feed herself?"

She whispered, "Not if it's a vegetable, apparently. She passed out today at the grocery store, and Dr. Hoover has ordered her on no stress. I told Oliver I would look after her because he's got some big thing going at the car lot."

"Why are you whispering?"

"She has to maintain a stress-free environment. Can you go turn up the heat?"

"Why?"

"She might get cold."

"It's a perfectly normal temperature in here."

"But she's been lying down all day. That can make a person cold."

"Ainsley, Melb is fine. Fuss over her a little bit, make her comfortable, but then let her be."

Ainsley felt tears rush to her eyes. "You don't understand."

"Understand what?"

"I feel responsible." Ainsley wiped at her face.

"You didn't cause this." Wolfe turned her toward him. "You understand that, right?"

"I've got to go feed her these vegetables."

Wolfe stopped her. "Why don't you let me?"

She couldn't hold in a laugh. "You?"

"What? I'm just going to take the plate in to her."

"It's a little more complicated than that."

"Why?"

"You think you're just going to march in there and give her the peas and carrots, and she's going to eat them?"

"I don't know."

"Well, I can tell you that she's not."

"So what? I'll just leave the plate there. If she gets hungry, she'll eat it."

"You're just going to let her starve to death?"

Wolfe was chuckling, the kind of chuckle that comes out when you think you're talking to someone who might have gone insane.

Ainsley grabbed the plate off the counter. "You just don't understand. I'll do it. And please, go turn up the heat!"

Alfred gave Doris a short wave as she looked up from her kitchen table and observed Alfred on the phone. *Just another minute,* he mouthed to her. Doris was currently working on a fourth draft of her manuscript. Alfred had done his research, and he knew the top religious publishers to send it to. He'd strike gold with all three of them, and then it was going to be a matter of dollars and cents.

But his ambitions didn't stop there. He'd learned a lot in that one-day conference. More than he would've liked to, at least a few months ago. However, he was beginning to see that this religious thing Wolfe had gotten himself involved in was quite profitable—the only problem being that his most profitable religiously turned writer wasn't writing. And he didn't want to put all his eggs in one Doris Buford basket.

Alfred Tennison had not risen to the top of the industry by watching the literary world pass him by. No, indeed.

"Alfred?"

"I'm here, Geoffery."

"Sorry to keep you waiting. You know how it is."

"Of course."

"Back to your question. No, none of these guys are on my client list. I've never heard of any of them."

Alfred smiled, expecting the superior tone in his voice. "I know.

They're a well-kept secret. But they continue to make the bestsellers list week after week."

"What bestsellers list?"

"Let's just say that I've found the pot at the end of the rainbow."

"I wasn't aware you'd turned to drugs."

"Pot of gold, Geoffery."

A moment of silence passed. He figured Geoffery was snickering into his shoulder. Geoffery was a snickerer. Everyone knew it. At parties, he spent half his time with his mouth buried in his shoulder.

But Alfred took the high road. That's what people on his side of the aisle did. Took the high road. Just like Ellie Sherman. So he waited.

"A pot of gold, eh, Alfred? Last I heard you were bunked with an old college roommate in Queens."

"I'm doing a lot of traveling."

"Huh. I haven't seen you at any parties lately."

"I don't party anymore." Alfred squeezed his eyes shut. Goodness, he was becoming Wolfe's "mini me."

More snickering. Alfred felt his chest constrict, holding back the words that wanted to climb out of the bile in his stomach. This was harder than it looked.

"I'll have you know," Alfred inserted into the snickering, "that before the month is over, I'm going to acquire a client list worth over fifty million dollars."

"Interesting."

"But thank you for your time, Geoffery. Always nice to talk with you."

"Keep in touch, Alfred."

The line went dead. Alfred turned to Doris. "How's that scene coming along?"

Doris shrugged. "I don't know. I've severed his arm, there's blood all over the floor, and I'm trying to think of something clever for him to say."

Alfred nodded. "Excellent. But I don't think we're going to get away with blood on the floor. Keep working on it."

CHAPTER 14

MARTIN TOOK THE MAYOR by the arm and led him into the back hallway. "We need to talk." Martin closed the door to the room where it seemed the entire town had gathered. It was one of their largest town meetings ever, at the noon hour at least.

"What is it?" the mayor asked. Martin noticed the mayor's hands were shaking, and he was having trouble concentrating.

"I just don't think it's a good idea."

"What's not?"

"What that man suggested. Leonard? Tarffeski? With the weird accent?"

"He's from New Zealand."

"First of all, if you put a snake hunter up in front of everyone, you're going to invite hysteria. People are going to think this is a bigger problem than it really is."

"This man assured me he's an expert. He has a good game plan. And you're the one that agreed to bring him here in the first place. The fact of the matter is that until this stupid snake is caught, our town is not going to sleep well. The sheriff's office has reported more traffic accidents in the recent days than in our entire town's history! Plus, if you haven't noticed, everyone seems to be in a really bad mood."

"But sir—"

"Martin, trust me. People feel empowered when they have knowledge and a way to help themselves. This Leonard assures me they will have both."

Martin rubbed his tired eyes. He wasn't losing sleep over a snake, but he had enough on his mind as it was. "Sure," he said with a faint smile. "You know best."

The mayor slammed his hand into Martin's back. "Now, let's get this meeting going. We have a long agenda today."

The murmuring hushed as the mayor bounded up to the podium. Martin stood a few feet away, eyeing Leonard. *Please don't start a panic*, Martin prayed.

"Good afternoon, fellow Skary citizens!" Where was the mayor getting all this energy? "I'm thankful for the great turnout today. I know you all have a lot on your mind, so we're going to get this meeting started. First of all, you may remember that the last time we gathered, there was some concern over the mysterious soccer field that seemed to emerge overnight. Well, the good news is that we've solved the mystery. I'd like to invite to the podium Mrs. Katelyn Downey. She and her husband are developers, and as you may have noticed, our little town does seem to be evolving."

Martin watched a petite blonde make her way up next to the mayor. A tight baby blue silk suit hugged her small frame. Her purse and shoes matched.

"Katelyn," the mayor said, "why don't you address the citizens of Skary? Tell them a little bit about the vision that you shared with me."

"I'd love to, Mayor Wullisworth." She patted her hands together as she slid behind the podium. "Let's hear it for our wonderful mayor!"

The crowd looked confused. Nobody had ever clapped for the mayor before, or been beckoned to do so. Martin led the way hastily, slapping his hands together like a trained seal. The rest of the crowd slowly followed, and then it all died down.

"Well," Katelyn began, "thank you for that warm welcome. First of all, I'd like to tell you how absolutely in love we are with this beautiful town called Skary. We see so much potential." She grinned at the entire crowd like everyone there was a personal friend. Martin spotted Lois near the back. He wanted to wave, but her concentration was on the woman up front. "You may have noticed a few wonderful changes around here. I've noticed you've taken to the cell-phone store. And just let me say, we had to pull a lot of strings to get the company to consider putting a tower up. But luckily for you, you're near a major highway, so it was in their best interest.

"To answer the mayor's question, yes, we built the soccer field. Our son, Willem, is a huge soccer fan, and one of the best male players in his preschool league. Sports, as you may know, is an important development tool for young children. It not only helps their motor skills, but what we're finding is that it also helps their social skills as well."

Martin studied the crowd. They looked like they were trying to decipher a foreign language.

"We're just as delighted as we can be about how that coffeehouse has turned out. And we've noticed its patrons enjoying a few additional menu items." She winked, her thick black eyelashes sticking together momentarily. "As you may have noticed, we've broken ground on our new home, and it will hopefully be ready in just a few short months. In the meantime, we'll continue to invest in Skary, and bring about change in a way that will make this little town the It place of all X-burbs!"

She spread her arms, as if expecting applause. None came. But Martin could sense that something was about to. He hadn't made it to the podium when the shouting began.

"Who do you think you are?"

"I love the new bookstore!"

"Coffee comes two ways, lady! Black and not black!"

"Cell phones cause brain cancer!"

"We can't be bought with all the money in the world!"

"Oh yes we can!"

Chaos erupted. Martin flew up beside Mrs. Downey, but she didn't look like she needed the help. Though a bit flustered, she tried to calm the crowd by inserting a few calming words.

"We're not here to take over your town, just improve it," she tried. The crowd never heard her.

"You shouldn't be afraid of change. We're changing you for the better."

Again, no one heard her.

"We're taking a huge gamble. Shouldn't you be grateful?" she asked, this time with an annoyance in her tone. It was useless. Everyone had lost their mind.

"Excuse me," Martin said to Mrs. Downey. "Let me try."

Katelyn stepped aside, whispering, "These people are insane."

"You have no idea," Martin whispered back. He leaned toward the microphone. "People, please. Folks, really. We must calm down. We can talk about this in a civilized manner." Nobody stopped shouting. Martin sighed, then said in a loud voice into the microphone, "If you don't calm down, we can't talk about the snake!"

Silence. Everyone took their seats again. Martin smiled. "Now, before that, we're going to let Mrs. Downey finish what she had to say. She won't be taking questions today, but we'll have another meeting soon to address all your concerns." Martin stepped aside and let Katelyn move back to the microphone.

"Thank you," she said. "Listen, my friends. There is nothing to fear. Skary is going to become a dream town. It's already got so many wonderful attributes. It's warm and cozy. The people are friendly. Main Street is just a dream. And strangely, the entire town seems devoid of rodents. That's always a plus. Trust me when I say, Skary, Indiana, is going to be hot property very soon."

Before anybody could shout, Martin slid up next to Mrs. Downey and said, "All right. Thank you, Mrs. Downey. Very intriguing. I, for one, have to say that I've really enjoyed the new bookstore. A bigger selection on easy-to-find aisles. And who doesn't want their town to be known as 'hot,' right?" Martin grinned. Nobody grinned back. "All right, well, let's get to the second reason we're here today. As many of you know, we have a snake loose."

Katelyn was walking off the stage and he heard her gasp. The rodent mystery was now solved for her.

"We are lucky enough today to have a snake expert with us." He watched the mayor shake Leonard's hand and point him toward the stage. "Leonard Tarffeski is a real-life snake hunter, folks. And he's here to help us find Bob and Fred." Martin forced a smile. The crowd seemed genuinely intrigued. All eyes were on Leonard as he stomped onto the stage. There was no doubt: he certainly had a presence about him.

He tipped his hat to the crowd. The ladies swooned. Martin tried not to roll his eyes but instead extended his hand to Leonard and gave him a polite nod. "Leonard, I'll turn this over to you."

"Thank you, Martin," Leonard said in his distinct accent. Martin stepped aside, but not far enough away that he couldn't jump behind the mike again if need be. "Ladies and gentlemen, it has come to my attention that you have a very rare and special kind of snake on the loose. I'd like to help you find it, so you all can sleep at night."

Martin glanced at the crowd. They looked eager.

"So," Leonard continued, "first of all, Bob and Fred is a rosy boa. Rosy boas are a small breed of boas. They only grow to about three to four feet long, so I can assure you nobody is going to be squeezed to death, though you might want to keep a close eye on your Chihuahuas and Yorkies. Poodles are probably okay, but just to be safe, go ahead and cage all those smaller breeds for now."

The crowd started to murmur, but Leonard held up steady and sure hands. "Let me finish, everyone." The crowd quieted. "Dustin, the snake's owner, tells me that Bob and Fred have become accustomed to living indoors, and that they enjoy soft, comfortable things such as pillows and blankets, even couch cushions. But knowing snakes like I do, I am more inclined to say that Bob and Fred are probably still quite timid, and if they're going to appear, it will be at night, and only after they sense the house is quiet. So," he said in a booming voice that indicated he was about to say something important, "I have a sure way of finding this snake. Everyone must listen carefully, though."

The room grew completely silent. Even the heater kicked off.

"The first thing I want you to do is go and check under every appliance you have, behind every bookshelf, under every sofa. You want to find all the dark corners you can. Check your shoes, your boots, boxes, storage containers. Snakes like to feel as if they're in a cave, so think like a snake. Where would you hide?"

"Behind the toilet!" one man offered.

"It was a rhetorical question, but thank you. Now, I'm expecting that most everyone has already done this."

Most of the crowd nodded.

"All right. Then we go to phase two, which is the absolute best way to catch a snake. This is what I want you to do this evening. First of all, while it's still light outside, go around your house and plug any holes or gaps you have. Look around piping, in closets, near your air conditioner or heater, near appliances. And don't let the smallness fool you. A snake can squeeze through a hole half its own diameter."

Many people were taking notes.

"Once you've done that, then prepare your house. By that, I mean make sure that your entire house is quiet. Don't run the dishwasher. Turn off all your clocks. Don't run a dryer. And if you have pets, go ahead and take them up to bed with you. You'll want to also make sure your house is very dark. So you're going to want to turn out even your night-lights, and draw your curtains."

Martin grabbed a pen and paper so he could take notes.

"Now, once you've got your house dark and quiet, take a flashlight and a bag of flour. Carefully go through your house and place a line of flour across every doorway. Pay special attention to laundry rooms, pantries, and closets. If you've got a washer and dryer in a pantry room, you also might think about getting some plastic bags, like you would get from the grocery store, and stuffing a few behind them. Then sit very still. Wait thirty minutes. If you don't hear any bags rattling, then you can go on upstairs. Sleep normally. Then, when you wake up in the morning, you'll be able to see if the snake has come out to play during the night."

Martin looked up from his notes. The crowd was silent. Yet, they didn't look particularly scared, either. It was almost a look of…determination. Maybe the mayor was right. Maybe they felt empowered.

"So, let's do this. If you find the snake's tracks in your house through the flour, meet me tomorrow morning here, at the community center. We'll be one step closer to catching Bob and Fred and putting all your minds at ease!"

Martin started clapping, because Leonard looked so desperate for it. A few followed. Martin shook his hand. "Thank you, Leonard. How completely fascinating. I would have never thought to do the flour trick." He smiled. A few smiled back. Okay, it wasn't mass hysteria. Martin looked at the mayor. "We've got one other thing on the agenda."

The mayor stepped back onto the stage and said, "I'll handle this one, Martin. Thank you." He raised the mike and looked out at the crowd. "Now folks, this won't take long, but I need you to pay attention, because we've got a real problem. I was informed by the gas company, the electric company, and the water company this week that a vast majority of you are suddenly not paying your bills. When I looked further into this, I discovered that the problem seems to be with our cell phones. Now, I realize many of you got the shock of a lifetime when your first bill came. One resident told me her cell phone bill was nearly three hundred dollars." A grumbling followed. The mayor held up his hands. "Now, now. Settle down. The solution to all this is that you absolutely must read your contract. You're charged by the minute, and it also depends on what time of day you're using your phone, and where in the town you're actually standing. Apparently if you're on the west side near Maple, you're going to be charged a roaming fee as well. So folks, you're going to have to pay attention to all this. And use some common sense. If you're at home, and you need to call a neighbor, pick up your house phone and dial the four digits. You've saved yourself from dialing three additional numbers and about twenty bucks."

Katelyn was standing near Martin and asked, "What does he mean by four digits?"

Martin whispered, "It's a small town. We just dial the last four digits of the phone number if we're calling someone else in Skary."

"So that's it for now, everyone. I love the flour idea, don't you? Have a wonderful day!"

Katelyn took Martin's arm and headed out the back door with him. "I'm going to have to talk to people later about all these changes, Martin. I have an appointment in a few minutes. But I wondered if I could have a moment of your time."

"Sure."

"I'm interested in that vacant store on Main Street."

"Where the hardware store used to be?"

"That's right."

"We could definitely use another hardware store. We have to go to the next county just to buy some nails."

She smiled sweetly. "I have different plans for that property."

Martin blinked. As far back as he could remember, it had always contained some sort of hardware store. It had certainly had different owners, but it was always hardware.

"Not hardware?"

She shook her head. "No. It's actually going to be called Come and Play."

"Come and play what?"

"It's a miniature gym, with bright colors and plastic play stations."

"What's it for?"

"Children, silly. You join with a monthly membership, and then you come and play with your child."

Martin blinked, trying to follow. "You come and play with your child and do what?"

"Oh, it's really much more than playing. We'll have all sorts of different and creative ways to interact with your child. It looks like playing, but what you're really doing is teaching your child."

"People pay for this?"

"Oh, it's very popular. Everyone in my affluent suburb loved it. We actually had to turn people away. By the time he was three, my son Willem knew how to ask for nearly anything in Spanish."

"I'm sure that's quite handy in your crowd of people." Martin said.

"I'm telling you," Katelyn said. "This is going to be a hit."

Martin couldn't deny the fact that everything else she'd laid her hands on seemed to turn to gold. She glanced at her watch. "I have to run." She offered her hand. Martin shook it with great care. "I'll see you soon, Martin."

Martin watched her leave, then decided to go to the grocery store. He needed some flour.

Ainsley wiped her face with the Kleenex and tried to pull herself together. But with each look in the mirror, her chest would heave and she would be back to square one. She turned and walked into her bedroom. "Good grief!" she whispered harshly to herself. "Get yourself together!"

Walking quietly into the hallway, she listened carefully. She could hear Melb laughing. That was good. She'd stuck in a video for her so she could have a chance to come upstairs. She had a meeting in ten minutes and she hadn't even gotten dressed yet!

Besides that, she was plagued with guilt. When Melb had refused to eat her broccoli and bagel at lunch, Ainsley had caved and given her Gummi Bears instead.

"Death by Gummi Bears?" Wolfe had chuckled over the phone.

Ainsley had hung up on him. He didn't understand. Nobody understood. She'd never felt so alone, so out of control, and so guilty all at the same time.

Melb seemed to be sitting on the couch, enjoying the video, and staying out of the kitchen, so Ainsley tiptoed back into the bathroom. She had to do more than get dressed. She actually had to look professional. This woman…Katelyn…as pulled together as they come, expected a woman equally as pulled together. Once upon a time, this didn't seem so hard. Just a few months ago she was the next Martha Stewart. Now she was just a bad version of herself.

Katelyn had gushed about her reputation, and so far she'd only been seen in her bathrobe. If she didn't hurry, this time she'd be in her pajamas with splotchy, sticky skin.

She pulled on a T-shirt and then a brightly colored cardigan. She decided on her dark khakis and brown flats. Wolfe had bought her a nice, soft leather briefcase for her birthday, so that should finish off her look.

Now, what to do with the hair? Katelyn's was perfect. Not a strand out of place. Held back from her face with a leather headband as if to expose the flawless skin that showed every touch of color like a painter's palette. Ainsley decided to try a little colored lip gloss. She glided it over her lips, and next thing she knew, the mascara wand was in her hand.

The careful artistry of stroking her lashes was interrupted by *"Ainsley!"*

The wand fell down her cheek and onto her sweater, leaving black skid marks. Ainsley's mouth dropped open. She wanted to cry. She wanted to scream. She wanted to—

"Ainsley!"

Ainsley swallowed back her tears and walked out of her bedroom. At the top of the stairs she called, "Yes, Melb?" Her voice wobbled, but Melb wouldn't notice.

"This is so funny! I just had to tell you that. This is absolutely hysterical!"

"Oh. Good." Ainsley turned back to her room, looked at the clock, and stripped. Okay, she might have to go with a frumpier sweater. She pulled on a color-blocked number, which did not go with the khakis. She changed to black pants and black boots, which required black socks. Rushing back into the bathroom, she scrubbed her face raw, but the mascara was still barely visible.

"Foundation."

She fumbled through her drawers, trying to find the one bottle she owned. "There!" She opened it up, spilled some onto her fingers, and first started rubbing into the half of her face that had fallen victim to the mascara. It had been a long time since she'd worn foundation, but she was pretty sure it was just a matter of blending.

The doorbell rang. Ainsley turned. "The baby-sitter," she breathed. "Okay. Okay. Okay." She rinsed her hands and kept the bottle on the counter so she could finish up. She raced past the living room, where Melb seemed oblivious as she stared at the television and roared with laughter.

She opened the front door. Amber, the fifteen-year-old daughter of one of the church members, stood smacking her gum.

"Hi Amber," Ainsley said.

"Hi. How much do you pay?"

"Well, why don't you come in and we'll talk about this?" Ainsley led her to the kitchen. "What do you charge, Amber?"

"I've never baby-sat an adult."

"Well, how about I pay you twenty bucks?"

"For an hour and a half?"

"Not enough?"

Amber paused then said, "Yeah, I guess that'll be okay. What do I have to do?"

"Basically just keep her happy and comfortable. She's going to want cookies and candy, but under no circumstance should you give them to her. A couple of crackers should be fine, and she can have one glass of juice, but no more, or she'll have to get up and go to the bathroom."

Amber glanced toward the living room with a bit of fear in her eyes.

"In case of an emergency, be sure to call the sheriff, okay? But if you need to get ahold of me, I'll be at the deli."

"Which one?"

"There are two?"

"There's a new one, just opened yesterday."

"Oh. Well, I'm going to be at the one on the corner."

Amber nodded, her arms still loosely crossed in front of her belly. She was giving Ainsley some odd looks, but what more could she do? It was a last resort. She knew one thing, she couldn't possibly leave Melb here alone.

Amber said, "So it's okay that she watches television?"

"Yeah, sure. Just keep putting in videos if you have to. I need to run upstairs and get my stuff. Do you have any questions?"

Amber shook her head.

"Okay." Ainsley hurried upstairs, grabbed her briefcase, and decided she was just going to have to wear a ponytail. She quickly brushed her hair and secured it to the back of her head. Gathering up the papers and recipe books scattered across her bed, she threw them into her briefcase, then zipped it up and ran to the door. Stopping just short of the hallway, breathing hard, she felt like she was forgetting something. She closed her eyes, trying to remember. Recipe books. Grocery list. Idea list. Decorating list. Her heart pounded inside her chest. The ticking of the hallway clock brought her eyes wide open.

"Oh!"

She was already five minutes late, and she hadn't even made it out the door yet. Scrambling downstairs, she yelled a good-bye and ran out the front door. "Please don't leave, please don't leave, please don't leave," she murmured. Her goals were much less lofty now. She just wanted to get there before the very pulled-together woman left.

Katelyn drummed her fingers against the paper that was spread where a tablecloth would normally be. She'd expected a waiter to at least come by and write his name out in crayon, but there were no waiters at this deli. Just paper tablecloths and only eight sandwiches, five of which contained meat products that Katelyn refused to eat. She'd ordered a side salad and a tea.

Checking her watch again, she wondered what everyone thought was so special about this Ainsley Boone. She'd come highly recommended by all the townspeople, but so far she hadn't impressed Katelyn one tiny bit.

Maybe there was a small-town hierarchy that Katelyn was going to have to familiarize herself with. From what she could tell, it was apparently important to be related in some way to the sheriff, who didn't appear to wield any special power, but had a mighty big presence nevertheless. It probably also didn't hurt to be married to the likes of Wolfe Boone, admittedly a handsome fellow, though Katelyn hadn't seen him do much more than wander the streets and drink coffee.

Through years of painful experience, Katelyn had found how very important the hierarchy was. She'd made it her goal to study it in every situation. No matter what circumstance she found herself in, she could immediately assess who held the power, whether it was at the garden club, a church fellowship, or a book club. Always, *always,* there was someone who was honored for their importance. She sipped her tea and stared out the store front. She was having serious doubts about her decision to use Ainsley Boone.

Just then the door flew open, the chimes announcing an arrival. Ainsley rushed toward the table like a strong north wind.

"So sorry," she said, her voice trembling. She was swiping hair out of her face and at the same time trying to unbutton her coat. "I hate to be late. I'm never late. Please accept my apology. I'm so terribly horrified."

Katelyn stood, not knowing what else to do. The poor woman looked like she was about to collapse. "No, it's okay. I just grabbed some lunch. It's no problem."

"I'm sorry, I really am." Ainsley dropped her coat onto a chair, and her briefcase fell to the floor with a thud. "Oops. Hold on, let me get that." She stooped to retrieve it, then hit her head on the table as she rose. "Ouch!"

"Are you okay?" Katelyn gasped.

She rubbed her head. "I'm fine," she said with a smile, though Katelyn thought she saw tears in her eyes.

"Please, sit down here. Relax. Everything's fine."

Ainsley set her bag down, this time with an exhausted look on her face, and fell into her chair. "You'll have to excuse all this. I normally am very prompt."

Katelyn plastered a smile on her face. "Again, you come highly recommended."

Tears streamed down her face. "Thank you."

"Oh…no…don't…" Katelyn was at a loss for words. She wasn't sure she'd ever seen a woman cry before. Plenty of men, but no woman in her circle of friends, that was for sure. She handed her a napkin.

Ainsley smiled, but her nose was turning red, and her eyes were wet and shiny. Katelyn looked closer. Oddly, she appeared to have makeup on only one side of her face. If this woman was considered "pulled together," she wondered what the rest of the Skary women were like!

She was breathing deeply, gathering herself. Finally she said, "The baby sitter was late."

"The baby-sitter? Oh, I know what you mean. Baby-sitters are hopelessly unreliable. I've been through five in the last eight months. They all claim my little Willem is uncontrollable, but in reality, they're just not able to render control. The kid is five, you know? I mean, do they really expect him to do everything they say? It takes some creativity to get your kid to eat his dessert."

Ainsley smiled and nodded, but looked lost. Maybe they shouldn't talk about kids.

"Anyway, let's hear what you've got planned for this big church event."

"Right." She reached into her brown leather bag, the only fashionable thing on the woman. A high ponytail paired with a boxy sweater went out in the late eighties. But then again, so did those kinds of boots. Luckily her expertise was food, not fashion.

"Well, here is what I thought we would serve. You want something that involves as little mess as possible, since we're going to be indoors in the basement. We know it's going to be cold enough to serve hot drinks, so I've got those listed on the side. I figure everyone is going to expect a lunchtime atmosphere, so I developed some finger foods that are deceivingly rich. They'll look great on the trays, but we won't have to serve a lot because people will get full easily. For dessert, we're going to have children running around, so I stayed simple, and have three items that won't need forks or napkins."

Katelyn read through the list. Shockingly, it was perfect. Maybe this lady did know what she was doing. "What's the cost?"

"I've got it circled on the bottom right-hand corner on the fourth page."

Katelyn flipped it over. "Are you serious?"

"Too much?"

"Too much? No! I can't believe you can do all this for that amount of money!" She looked up at Ainsley, who for the first time looked delighted. "That's amazing."

"It's what I do. People don't have a lot of money around here, so I've learned to cater on a budget."

Katelyn smiled broadly. "Well! This will allow for decorations, too!"

"That includes decorations."

Katelyn set the paper down on the table and clasped her hands. "Unbelievable."

"You like it."

"I love it!" Katelyn handed back the paper. "I think this is going to be the best indoor children's picnic ever!"

"Actually it's the only one we've had. I'm so amazed at what you've done to the church basement."

"Kids love murals and puppets and music. I think it'll be a big hit." Katelyn found her wallet and made out a check. She handed it to Ainsley and said, "You're hired."

Ainsley slumped with relief. "Thank you so much. I really thought I'd blown it."

Katelyn checked her watch. "I've got to run. You have my number. Call me with any questions." She stood and shook Ainsley's hand.

"All right. Thanks."

Katelyn pulled on her coat and grabbed her handbag. She could say one thing for this town—it was full of surprises.

CHAPTER 15

MARTIN HOPPED OUT of his car and shouldered through the crowd toward Leonard, who stood on the top step at the community center, looking uncharacteristically overwhelmed. The mayor was behind him, tapping the man's back like it was a drum.

Nearly knocking an old woman over—though he didn't feel bad because she was yelling with the might of four men—Martin reached Leonard and the mayor, out of breath and hardly able to ask, "What is going on?"

Leonard took a few steps back, pulling Martin with him and then turning his back so they'd have a chance to hear each other. "It's the flour."

"The flour?"

"The flour trick. To catch a snake."

"What about it?"

Leonard glanced back at the crowd. "Well, um…well…"

"Spit it out!"

"Apparently the flour revealed that everyone, unbeknownst to them, has some sort of critter living in their house."

Martin turned toward the crowd. Their eyes were wide, their faces desperate. He looked back at Leonard.

Leonard continued. "We've had reports of snake tracks, mouse prints, lizard prints, and someone even claims they've got an alligator hiding in their house."

Martin slapped a hand to his forehead. How could he not have seen this coming? Of course everyone sleeps better when they're not aware of what lurks behind the walls. A woman screamed hysterically, causing Martin and Leonard to glance back. It was Lois Stepaphanolopolis.

Martin forced his attention back on Leonard. "So what are you going to do about this?"

"Me?"

"Yes, you! You got everybody into this!"

"My expertise is with snakes, not rodents."

Martin grabbed Leonard's shoulders and turned him toward the mayor. "See that?"

"What? The mayor doing aerobics for no reason?"

"Yeah. The mayor doesn't deal with things like this well, and he's been acting strangely lately, so you better figure out a solution and fast. We don't need mass hysteria in this town right now. For the first time in a long time, we're seeing a little hope for Skary, and I will not have it undone by the likes of you!"

Leonard's casually set eyes grew wider with each word.

"Now fix this mess!" Martin yelled over the madness.

Leonard and Martin watched the sheriff and two deputies pull up. There was so much shouting and screaming, Martin wasn't sure if either one of them could be heard. He signaled the sheriff to get his bullhorn.

"I-I-I'm not sure," Leonard stuttered, "what I should do."

Martin sighed and grabbed Leonard by the arm to bring him toward the crowd. The sheriff stepped up and handed Martin the bullhorn. "What in the world—"

"I'll explain in a moment," Martin told the sheriff. Then he said to Leonard. "Now. Follow my lead, and for crying out loud, look confident, as if you expected this all along."

Martin put the bullhorn up to his lips and said, "Folks, we need you to calm down. Please, everyone. We've got to settle down before we can address the situation."

One by one, the people in the crowd hushed. Martin drew in a breath and glanced at the mayor, wondering if he might want to take the bull by the horns, so to speak. He was standing to one side, staring into space.

"Okay. First of all, let's get some organization going, since obviously the objective of this is to find the boa constrictor. So step over to the right if you believe the tracks you saw in your flour were those of a small rodent. We're talking mice, rats, hamsters, anything like that."

About forty people stepped to the right.

"Okay, good. Now, step toward the back if you believe the tracks you saw were of a small reptile, body width no more than an inch or inch and half. This includes lizards, as you'll have the foot and body or tail tracks."

About twenty people stepped toward the back.

"All right, great. Now, step to the left over here if the tracks you found in your home were about three inches wide or more."

Four people stepped to the left.

Martin turned to Leonard, who was about to trot down the stairs toward the people on the left. He grabbed his shirt and yanked him back. "Not so fast, snake boy."

"What?" Leonard frowned. "We've got four potential candidates here."

"I realize that. And they're going to hang tight. But see these other sixty people? You're going to go down there and in some rodent-authority way make them understand that every house has rodents, and that just because they're aware of them now doesn't mean anything unusual is going on. Use statistics. People like statistics."

"I don't know any statistics about mice and lizards."

"Then make some up. I don't care. But what I better see when you're done is a whole bunch of people who love and appreciate their rodent friends. Got it?"

Martin gave him a little shove forward, until they both noticed one person still standing in the middle where the crowd had once been: Lois Stepaphanolopolis.

"Um…Lois? What are you doing?" Martin asked, now able to hand the bullhorn back to the sheriff.

Tears glistened in her eyes. "I don't know where I should go."

"You had tracks last night?"

She nodded.

Martin approached her. "Okay, well, what kind of creature do you think you have in your house?"

She sniffled. "A stranger."

"What's all the chaos in town about?" Alfred asked. He handed Wolfe his coat as he stepped inside.

"What chaos?"

"At the community center?"

"Oh, that. I think they were having a town meeting or something."

"Looked like a riot to me."

"You're going to have to keep your voice down," Wolfe instructed him as he hung his coat up.

"Why?"

"Well, it's kind of a long story, but—"

"Hi Alfred!" Ainsley appeared in the entryway.

"She's not keeping her voice down," Alfred observed.

"Nobody has to whisper."

Wolfe frowned. "I thought she was being overstimulated."

"I got her calmed down." Ainsley looked at Alfred. "Do you want to come see her?"

Wolfe was about to protest, but Alfred said, "See...what?"

"She's feeling much better," Ainsley announced proudly, bringing Alfred along by the arm.

"Who is?"

Wolfe trudged along behind, his hands stuffed in his pockets. How much more of this he could take, he wasn't sure. Last night he'd taken Ainsley out for dinner, hoping to relax her a little. She was relaxed for the whole dinner, but as soon as they got home, it all came undone. Aliens had abducted his common-sense, clearheaded wife and replaced her with—

"Isn't she just a breath of fresh air?" Ainsley asked, sweeping her arm toward Melb, who was sitting up on the couch eating raw carrots.

Alfred jabbed his thumb that direction. "Her?"

"Melb. Yes."

Alfred glanced at Wolfe, who could only shrug and encourage him with an expectant look.

Ainsley added, "She's got the rosiest cheeks, wouldn't you say? And look at that smile."

On cue, Melb turned and gave them a big smile, her cheeks full of crunched-up carrots.

"Uh...yes. She's so..."

"Healthy," Ainsley declared. "That's her third vegetable today."

Alfred, being the gentleman he always tried to be, smiled and graciously looked interested. But it was too painful a sight, so Wolfe said, "Alfred, why don't we step into my office? We can talk there."

With the door closed, Alfred's gentlemanly disposition slid off him like a silk gown. "What kind of freak show did I just witness?"

"Don't ask. I'm waiting for E.T. to return my wife." Wolfe sat down at his desk and offered Alfred a seat. "So you seemed excited on the phone."

"Yeah. For one, I can get cell phone service. But besides that, I have a new direction in my life."

"Being an agent again."

"Not just any agent," Alfred said with a dramatic gesture pointing toward the ceiling, "but the top agent in this industry."

"What industry?"

"You know…the 'religious' industry." Alfred fanned himself with his hand. "Is it hot in here, or is it just me?"

"It's hot. Ainsley has the heat turned up to seventy-five."

"Good. Because for a second there I thought I might be feeling guilt."

"Why is that?"

"Well, I have to say, I find it hard to mix the two. Business and religion. I mean, they don't seem to coexist all that well. But Wolfe, I'm telling you, there is money to made in this industry. And you'll be proud to know that I've actually resigned myself not to steal anyone's client."

"You've come a long way."

"I know. But the thing is, I don't actually have to steal anybody. Tons of people don't even have representation."

"Really?"

"And not just people, but megastar people. Some of them have been on the religious bestsellers list for years. Decades!"

"They don't have agents?"

"Nope. I've called everyone I know and a lot of people I don't. So I'm going after them."

"Seems like they've done okay without an agent."

"Yes. But one can always do better, my friend. They're probably not making near what they're worth. I've looked up some sales figures. Astonishing."

"Well," Wolfe said, leaning back into his chair and entwining his fingers, "I'm glad you've found a new direction."

"How's your writing coming along?"

Wolfe mindfully kept his expression unchanged. "Fine. I've got some good ideas going."

"What ideas?"

"Top secret for now," he said, taking a cue from his brother-in-law. He actually said that with a straight face.

Alfred's eyebrows shot up. "Interesting. You of course know I'm open to seeing whatever you've developed."

Wolfe nodded.

"But you'll have to understand that I won't be at your beck and call like before." Alfred crossed his legs. "My client list has grown, and will continue to grow."

"You've got one other person."

"True. But she does require a lot of my attention. She's new to this. I left her last night writing in a descriptive violent scene. It was half a page and it took her three hours. I finally had to say to her, 'Doris, it's a severed limb. Make the guy convulse and writhe and get on with it.'"

"I thought it was a love story and they don't like violence."

"It is, and I know. I had a hard time finding a good place to add the gore, but we finally decided on a bizarre mattress accident. The two characters were headed into forbidden territory anyway, so it worked out perfectly. The more I study it, violence is acceptable, but it has to be written in an accidentally-happened-and-nobody's-responsible way."

The office door opened, and Ainsley poked her head in. "Honey,

I'm running to the store. Melb's taking her morning nap, so you two keep it quiet. She should sleep the whole time I'm gone, but if she wakes up, there's a glass of milk in the fridge for her."

"Okay," Wolfe smiled.

The door shut, and Alfred said, "Don't look now, but your life has done a one-eighty."

Sheriff Parker drove toward Lois's house, handing her one tissue after another as she sobbed uncontrollably in the passenger's seat. At the only stoplight in town, he glanced back at Thief, whose ears were laid flat in annoyance. He'd never ridden in the backseat before. And until lately, all he'd wanted to do was stay at home with Blot. But like with all men, that got old after a while. For the last couple of days he'd followed the sheriff out the door and hopped into the cruiser. The sheriff didn't ask questions. He didn't have to. He was a man.

"I'm just so scared," Lois cried, grabbing the sheriff's arm as if he weren't trying to drive a car. He patted her hand gently, then laid it back on her lap.

"We'll figure out what's going on, Lois. I promise. You don't have to worry."

She dabbed her face. "I trust you. I know you're not going to let anything bad happen to me."

"What I mean is that we haven't had a violent crime here in four decades, so the odds are in your favor."

Lois shook her head. "You don't understand. Whoever it was walked all through my house! You can see the footprints everywhere." Her voice climbed in pitch. "They went through my refrigerator!! They were in my bathroom!" She covered her mouth with her tissue and added, "Even my bedroom closet. I feel so violated. Who would do this to me?"

"Lois, I'm going to need you to calm down and tell me everything you remember."

"That's the problem. I don't remember anything. I've been so tired with this play that I passed out as soon as my head hit the pillow."

"Were any windows broken? Doors open or unlocked?"

"The back door was unlocked, but I always keep it that way. It's Skary, Indiana. Why would I lock it?"

The sheriff pulled onto Lois's street and then into her driveway. Deputies Bledsoe and Kinard followed. The sheriff got out of his car and opened the door for Lois, helping her to her feet. "I don't know if I can ever go in there again."

"Is your front door unlocked?"

"Yes, I ran out of the house screaming this morning." She pulled her coat around herself. "I'm still in my pajamas."

The sheriff looked down. She wiggled her house shoes. "Kinard, stay with Ms. Stepaphanolopolis. Bledsoe, come with me."

The sheriff reached the front door and turned the knob.

"Sheriff!" Lois called.

He turned. "Yeah?"

"Be careful."

The sheriff nodded, and at the tip of his tongue were the words, *If I don't come back, know that I always loved you.* He stood there stunned. What in the world would compel him to think that way? He looked in the darkened house, wondering if his life was indeed in danger. He placed a hand on his gun, causing Bledsoe to take a step back.

"Sir, what's going on?" Bledsoe whispered. "You okay? You zoned out there for a second."

The sheriff swallowed, trying to regain his composure, and then to his everlasting relief, he realized why those words floated through his mind. It was from the play. Lotus says, *"Be careful,"* and Bart's reply is, *"If I don't come back, know that I always loved you."*

"I'm fine," the sheriff replied. "Let's get in there and see what we can find. Be careful not to step on any of the flour tracks. Apparently they're everywhere."

The two men moved inside, tiptoeing over the chalky white footprints scattered about the small living room. It looked like Lois had put flour through every doorway, and tracks showed that whoever it was, they'd been all over the house.

The curtains were drawn, so Bledsoe turned on his flashlight. The flour was tracked all over the place. The sheriff indicated that Bledsoe should join him in the kitchen. Once there, the two men followed the trail to the refrigerator, then to the counter, and then to the dishwasher.

The sheriff shone his flashlight onto the counter. "Look at this."

Bledsoe came by his side. "Crumbs."

"Looks like whoever did this decided to help themselves to a snack."

Bledsoe raised an eyebrow. "And cleaned up after themselves."

The sheriff said, "Go check out the garage and backyard. I'm going to the bedroom."

The sheriff lit his path down the hallway, where two sets of tracks were clearly cast into the carpet. He looked into the bathroom, but nothing seemed out of order. Across the hallway was Lois's bedroom. He walked in, straddling the footprints in the doorway. The last time he'd been here, there was a smoky smell. He could still detect the scent, mingled with a host of floral Plug-Ins he noticed all over the place. The footprints tracked over to the closet, so with careful steps, the sheriff made his way over. The door was already open, so he peeked in.

Clothes on hangers were cram-packed together, and he wondered if the woman had ever cleaned out her closet. A large rack of shoes hung on one wall, and sweaters were folded neatly along three open shelves.

Bledsoe had walked into the bedroom. "There's nothing out of place in the garage, and the backyard looks fine."

The sheriff walked out of the closet and said, "I know who's been here."

CHAPTER 16

REVEREND PECK WAS BEGINNING to feel like a prisoner. He'd missed the town meeting yesterday and had every intention of showing up this morning to find out if anyone had found the snake. But instead, he held a paintbrush in one hand and a paint bucket in the other.

The ever-energetic Katelyn Downey stood by his side. "It looks great, doesn't it? I love the rainbow. And that's one of the kids' favorite Bible stories. They're going to walk down here, take one look at this mural, and squeal with delight."

It was hard to complain. After all, no one had ever taken as much interest in his church as this young lady. And he'd never heard the word "squeal" ever mentioned outside the farm. But he was starting to feel like he might not be the boss anymore. When he'd suggested he might like to take a break and go to the town meeting, Katelyn replied, "Reverend, with all due respect, one of us has to stay here and paint. We have a lot more to do and only a few short days."

So he was stuck painting in the dark, lonely basement, when what he really needed to do was prepare his sermon. He'd had to stay up late last night, and now he was tired.

The door to the basement swung open, and a long shadow stretched across the floor, followed by a shorter one.

"Willem!" Katelyn exclaimed, and a little boy bounded into his mother's arms. Katelyn turned to Reverend Peck. "This is my son, Willem. Willem, this is Reverend Peck."

"Hi William."

"Willem."

"Oh. Will…em. Hi."

The boy shyly hunkered into his mother's arms. A tall man walked toward them.

"And this is my husband, Michael."

They shook hands, and Michael grinned warmly. "Looking forward to becoming members of your church, Reverend," Michael said.

"Well, your wife sure has brought some excitement to the place."

Michael looked at the walls. "She can really turn things around, can't she? Sweetheart, I have the extra paint, stencils, and games in the car."

"I'll help you unload." She dropped Willem to the floor and said, "Why don't you stay here, honey, and look around? Tell Mommy what you think when I get back." The boy watched his mother leave up the basement stairs. Then he turned and stared at the reverend.

"How old are you?" the reverend asked with a smile.

"Five."

"Five. That's a nice age."

Willem looked at the wall. "Did you paint this?"

"I sure did, with your mommy's help."

"Noah's ark."

"That's right."

"You're missing a color in your rainbow."

The reverend looked. Indeed, he was. Purple. "Thanks for catching that. I'll add it as soon as your mom returns with the paints."

"So this is going to be the kids' area?"

"Yes it is."

"I hate it."

"You hate it? Why?"

"You don't even have a coffee bar."

"Sure we do. We serve coffee upstairs every day."

"For *kids*. I like a double mocha hot chocolate. I can't go to church unless I have it."

"Well, sorry. The best you can hope for, young man, is some juice and cookies. After story time."

"Story time?" he whined. "We're not having interactive videos?"

The reverend stifled a laugh. "What?"

"Never mind," the boy huffed. "I hate this place. I don't know why my mother and father want to move here. It's stupid."

"You know," the reverend tried, almost forgetting the little pipsqueak was a kid, "your parents feel like this is the best place to raise you. There're a lot of good things about a small town."

"Like what? Stupid rainbows and boring stories?"

"Didn't your mother teach you any manners?"

He crossed his arms. "I'm just being realistic. Kids are going to hate this. I've heard the story of Noah a thousand times, and you know what? It doesn't get any more interesting when you tell it in Spanish."

"I don't speak Spanish."

"I do. And I'm learning German."

Katelyn returned with two more buckets of paint. "Mommy!" the kid sang, running into her arms.

"What do you think of the room?"

"I want to help paint!" he declared, jumping up and down.

Katelyn ruffled his hair. "Isn't he just a delight?" She squeezed his cheeks. "Why don't you help your dad carry some stuff downstairs from the car?"

"Okay!" He bounced up the stairs.

As Katelyn set the paint down, the reverend recovered from the shock of his previous conversation. "Katelyn, your son doesn't like this."

"Like what?"

"This room. This place. He called the Noah's ark mural stupid."

She batted the air with her hand. "Oh, Reverend Peck. That's silly. My son doesn't use words like that."

"He called it all stupid."

She stopped what she was doing and stood up. "Well, what you have to understand about five-year-old boys is that they don't really have command of their language. So Willem might say the word *stupid* but really mean something else altogether." She put her hand on his shoulder and handed him a picture book. "Now, why don't you thumb through this?"

"What is it?"

"It's the story of Noah. I thought you'd like to read this for our first story time on opening Sunday."

"Story time?"

"We're going to have a ten-minute part of the service where you read to the kids before they go downstairs for children's church. It makes them feel important and loved, plus the Noah theme will help tie in the mural."

All the reverend could see was Willem's scrunched-up, scowling face.

The sheriff dismissed the deputies and approached Lois, who was sitting near the curb. He helped her to her feet. "Why don't you come inside?"

"It's safe?"

"Yes, it's safe." He took her hand and led her inside. "Sit down on the couch here."

She slowly sat down, keeping her eyes fixed on the sheriff. "What's wrong?" she urged.

He smiled. "Nothing, Lois. You're perfectly safe."

"How do you know?"

"What size shoe do you wear?"

"Seven."

Sheriff Parker gestured toward the floor. "Recognize those footprints?"

Lois's gaze slid downward, and she frowned. "Are you saying those are my footprints? Impossible! I never got up once last night."

"Do you think that you might sleepwalk?"

At first, Lois shook her head vigorously. "Impossible. I wear a sleep mask."

"But study the footprints carefully. It looks exactly like a morning routine." The sheriff guided her focus toward the bedroom. "First to the bathroom. Then the closet. Then the kitchen." He looked at the tracks on the living room carpet. "Do you come in and turn on the morning news while you eat breakfast?"

She slowly nodded.

The sheriff smiled. "Mystery solved."

"I do this all with a mask on my face?"

"Sure. It's routine. Habit. You don't need to see to do it."

Lois slumped, throwing her tissue to the side. "No wonder I'm so tired in the mornings."

"If you'll get me a dustpan and a broom, I'll help you clean up."

"I think I'd rather go get some breakfast. Care to join me?"

The sheriff took the hint immediately. He was getting good at this. "Breakfast? Sounds tantalizing."

"Could be. We could order an omelet and share it."

"That means we would have to sit next to each other."

"I can't think of a better way to spend my morning. Let me just go change into something tight and uncomfortable, and I'll be right out." The sheriff watched her avoid the flour footprints as she walked toward her bedroom. This was fun.

"Don't be too long…Lotus."

She turned around. "Lotus?"

He laughed. "I'm sorry. I'm breaking character, aren't I? But you have to admit, I'm getting good at this."

Lois looked a little annoyed. She was one heck of a serious director. He wiped the smile off his face and returned to his character. "Sorry."

"I think breakfast is off."

"Off? Why? Because I laughed?"

A terrible frown had crossed her face. "You obviously need to work harder on your character."

"Hey, that was pretty good back there. Bart would've been up for an omelet."

Now Lois looked depressed. "Right. Bart."

"What? Should he have played a little harder to get?"

"No. It was fine."

"You look upset. Lois, you're going to have to tell me what to do here. This is the first time I've ever been in a play. And this method acting stuff is new to me."

She tried to smile. "I know, Irwin. Don't mind me. I'm just being grumpy. Work on your lines today, and I'll see you tonight at play practice, okay?" Lois disappeared into her bedroom.

He sighed and threw up his hands. No matter what role they played in his life, Sheriff Parker could never understand women.

Leonard Tarffeski walked out of the fourth and final house, sweat pouring off his face. Dustin waited for him by a tree in the front yard. "Any luck?" the kid asked.

Leonard blotted his forehead with his sleeve. "Sorry, kid. Nothing. If there was a snake in there, I would've found it."

"But what about the tracks? Snake tracks, right?"

"Possibly. But probably too small for a boa that's been fed every day. Judging by the pictures you have of your snake, he's one fat dude."

Dustin sulked. "Great. I'm never going to find my pet."

"I'm going to find that snake if it's the last thing I do. You can bank on that."

"Thanks, dude. So what now?"

"You let me handle this. Aren't you supposed to be at work?"

"Yeah. Ten minutes ago."

"You'd better get going. But I should warn you, Dustin, there are people who are going to want to capture your snake for their own personal gain. You can't trust anyone else, or you may find your snake traded to the black market." Leonard patted him on the shoulder. "Don't fear. I'll get your snake back."

Dustin nodded and walked to his car. After Leonard smiled and gave him a short wave, he turned and balled up his fists. This task was becoming more and more frustrating. Not only was this rare and priceless snake on the lam, but Leonard had unforeseen competition now. He'd done a good job of convincing Dustin of his noble deeds, despite the fact that Dustin seemed as inept in real life as he did in cyberspace. He would never forget the day that SNAKE_DUD68 arrived on the sloop. It took everyone a while to realize that he'd misspelled his screen name and left off the *E*. But "dud" was as good a description as any. He'd always pipe into the conversation with his supposed knowledge of snakes, and more than half the time he'd get his facts wrong. Plus, the guy was like an open book, which was part of the reason Leonard's plan was working so well. By the third week Dustin had joined, he'd given out all his personal information (most likely trying to impress the chicks on the sloop), including his social security number. Lucky for him, he couldn't type, so he'd left off two digits and added an *S* for some other number. But all that information had come in handy for Leonard when one day Dustin announced that his rare and enviable snake had gotten loose.

Now he just needed to find that snake.

Butch had watched Leonard stand on the steps of the community center and shamelessly wave his ego flag. A small group had gone with Leonard. The larger group had been directed to the pet store where apparently they were going to get a lesson on rodent control. His father had taken charge of some hysterical woman. And the mayor, on tenterhooks, was being led away by Martin. So the only one left standing was a small man in overalls named Gordon.

Butch had approached him after the dust had settled. "What are you still doing here?"

He shrugged. "Waiting for someone to tell me what in the world I have in my house."

"You have tracks?"

"Yep."

"Snake tracks?"

"It was about yea wide," he said, opening up his hands to measure six inches across. "Looks to me like I've either got an anaconda or a potbelly pig."

It took ten minutes to get to Gordon's house, which was near the edge of town. It was an old farmhouse, the paint peeling off the wood like a cheese slicer had gone down the side of it.

Butch followed Gordon in the front door. "This is my wife, Alda."

Alda sat on the sofa in the living room holding a shotgun, her hair wound back into a bun at the nape of her neck. Alda looked like she knew exactly how to handle a shotgun, so Butch just smiled, said a hello, and tried not to make any sudden moves. "Why don't you show me those tracks, Gordon?"

Gordon brought him to the back of the house, near the kitchen. He pointed to the flour. Butch stooped down to take a closer look. Sure enough, there were large tracks, nearly six inches wide, going through the flour. And they continued on toward the basement in an *s*-like sequence.

"What's down there?" Butch asked.

"Aw, not a whole lot. Some cattle feed. I do a lot of wood cutting down there. It's just a bunch of junk."

"I need a flashlight."

Alda rummaged through some drawers in her kitchen and returned with one. The light was dim, but it would do. He shone it down the stairs, where the flour faded with each step. So whatever it was had gone down the stairs, not up them. Which meant whatever it was had a high probability of still being down there.

"Is there another way out the basement?"

Gordon shook his head. "We had the door cemented over. There's a window, but it's high, and an animal couldn't get to it."

"You have a light down there?"

"Naw. Burned out in '69," Alda said.

Butch squatted at the edge of the stairs, trying to figure out what would make such a large track. Suddenly an idea popped into his head. He stood, Gordon and Alda hovering right behind him. "I need a phone."

"Alda, go get the phone," Gordon said.

She handed him the shotgun and left.

"What for?" Gordon asked.

If Butch's theory was right, there was a lot at stake here, and the last thing he needed was a trigger-happy farmer's wife blowing a hole through him and the basement wall at the first sign of trouble.

Alda returned. "Here you go." She plopped a cell phone into his hand.

"Gordon, I'm going to need a rope. And Alda, can I get a cup of coffee?" Both went to fulfill their separate tasks, allowing Butch the room he needed to maneuver. He didn't need a rope or coffee, but he needed them out of his hair for a moment. When they were out of earshot, Butch made a phone call.

"Bookstore, Dustin speaking."

"Dustin, this is Butch. Let me ask you something. You say that Bob is the more dominant of the two heads."

"Yeah, that's right."

"So what happens to Fred when they're slithering along?"

"Oh, he just sort of gets dragged. Sometimes he'll put up a fight, but that just puts them at a standstill. So mostly he just gets dragged."

"Okay, thanks." Butch hung up the phone and looked at the tracks. That could account for the wideness. Fred's head being dragged alongside the body.

"Cream and sugar, son?" he heard Alda call from the kitchen.

"One and a half tablespoons of sugar and three ounces of cream." Butch clutched the flashlight and headed down the cold cement steps as he heard Alda opening kitchen drawers, trying to find a measuring spoon. He fingered his knife with the other hand. His footsteps echoed as he descended into the dark box. Standing on the last step, he listened carefully for any sound.

After a few moments, he started hearing a noise from the far corner, over by where the cattle feed was stacked.

"Got a rope!" he heard Gordon call from the top step.

"I forgot to mention I'm also going to need some pliers. Needle-nose if you have them."

The wood above him creaked as Gordon went back out to the shed. Butch aimed his light over to the corner. He blocked out everything else around him and controlled his fear.

With careful steps, he made his way around a pile of junk and to the corner. The sound became clearer as he approached with deft footsteps. He knew one thing for sure. He was going to have to move those feed sacks if he was going to see anything. And you don't move a feed sack with one hand.

He found a box to set his flashlight on, facing the beam toward the sacks. He pulled out his knife and put it between his teeth for easy access. Then, one by one, he slowly moved the sacks. The sound became more prominent with each movement he made.

He had three sacks to go. He moved one, and as he went for the next to last one, he stumbled backward, dropping his knife. After getting over the shock that he'd actually *yelped*, he bent forward, picked up his knife, and peered between the remaining sacks and the corner wall. There, coiled tightly, was a two-headed snake.

One head was obviously bigger than the other. But nevertheless, four soulless eyes were staring back at him. He'd been in a lot of dangerous situations, but he'd not once felt his knees shake. The snake was fat and thick but not exceptionally long. It looked like it didn't want to be disturbed, so with great care, Butch stacked three of the sacks back and stepped away. He climbed the stairs as he heard Alda call, "I've got your carefully seasoned coffee up here."

Butch emerged and shut the basement door behind him. Alda didn't look pleased. She shoved the coffee into his hands. Butch smiled and took a sip. "Delicious," he managed, despite Alda's growing scowl. Gordon returned with needle-nose pliers.

"Maybe we should call that snake hunter. He's the expert, after all, and probably more qualified to handle this situation," Gordon said.

"No need. The snake isn't down there," Butch said confidently. "I shut the door to make sure whatever it is you do have doesn't go down there. That is now a secure location, so whatever you do, don't open that door, or it immediately becomes unsecured."

"What do you need the rope and pliers for?" Gordon asked.

Butch handed the potently stale coffee back to Alda. He took the rope and pliers from Gordon like he knew what he was doing. He didn't have a clue. But he was trained to think fast, and that didn't stop in a farmer's house.

He carefully coiled the rope against the bottom of the door and then set the pliers in the middle, with the sharp end sticking up.

"What'd you do that for?" asked Alda.

"If it is a snake you have, then it will be scared off if it thinks another snake has a territorial claim over the house. Snakes don't see well, so to him, it will appear to be a snake." It was a bunch of bull, but bull can be sold with the right kind of cockiness.

Gordon and Alda looked down at the rope and pliers. Both shrugged. "Okay. Well, how long do we keep the basement door shut?" asked Gordon.

"Three days," Butch said. "If you don't see any more activity surrounding the flour, then I'd say you're in the clear, and the snake has been scared off. If you see tracks in the flour, go ahead and call the snake hunter."

That seemed to bring some relief to both their concerned faces. Gordon shook his hand. "Thank you, son. Thank you."

Butch smiled, decided not to thank Alda for the coffee again, and walked outside. As far as he was concerned, he'd come face to face with the Loch Ness monster.

CHAPTER 17

"STOP, STOP!" LOIS YELLED from four rows back. The actors onstage turned, defeat heavy in their shoulders. "What was that?" She rose from her chair and floated down the center aisle. "Marlee, do you expect me to believe you're the kind of woman these two men want?"

Marlee was about to answer. But in the theater, Lois never asked a question that she intended someone to answer.

"The fact of the matter is that you're going to have to push yourself in this role, Marlee. Lotus is a complex woman, with a lot of complex emotional components. Yes, on the surface she may appear to be handling the love of two men with grace and dignity, but underneath, what is happening to her?"

"She's—"

"Losing her mind, that's what! She's envious!"

"Envious of what?"

"Women who only have to deal with the affections of one man, that's what! How she longs for a quiet, simple life. But yet how can she deny love?"

"So you want her to be moody?" Marlee asked. "I can do moody."

"Not *moody*, Marlee. Misunderstood."

"So in this scene, when she slaps both men at the same time, she's misunderstood?"

"No. She's just mad. But that's Lotus for you. She's not intimidated by anger." Lois sighed as she looked at their perplexed faces. "Okay, it's late and you all look tired. Go home, get some good rest, and we'll come back here tomorrow night with some fresh blood in us. In the meantime, be thinking about your character, okay? What makes him or her tick? What motivates your character to do the things he or she does?"

"Mental illness," she heard someone whisper. She ignored that.

Everyone dispersed except Sheriff Parker, who came toward Lois as she gathered her things. A sloppy grin looked like it was about to fall off his face.

"I don't suppose Lotus would be up for a late night piece of cheesecake?"

Lois stood upright and swung her bag over her shoulder. "In case you haven't noticed, Lotus is a little irritated."

"But Bart always brings a smile to her face."

Lois rolled her eyes. "Not tonight, Irwin. I mean, Bart. Whoever you are." She brushed past him. Glancing back like any self-respecting woman shouldn't, she noticed how wounded the sheriff looked as he walked the opposite way out the front doors of the auditorium. With a grunt, she turned and called, "Bart?"

It took him a moment, but he finally figured out she was calling him. "Yeah?"

"Maybe you could stop by Saturday, help me paint some of the set."

His face lit temporarily. "Okay. I'll bring the coffee and donuts."

Lois nodded and continued toward the back exit where her car was parked. This play was going to be a disaster. Nobody understood anything about their character, least of all Marlee, who couldn't seem to get out of her late-twenties mind-set. And despite Lois's best directing attempts, Marlee didn't look a day over thirty-six.

Outside, the night had turned frigid. Lois tucked her chin into the collar of her coat as she walked to her car. Pulling her keys from her pocket, she reached for her door and heard, "Hello, Lois."

Wolfe tiptoed down the stairs, each creak of the wood announcing his presence. He'd just finished talking Ainsley off a cliff, and then she'd fallen asleep mumbling something about vegetable crackers. Melb had become quite the late-nighter, and it was only a few minutes before that she'd finally gone up to bed. Ainsley said that Oliver had been asleep since eight.

The rehearsal had let out late, and Lois was in a particularly grumpy mood, so the fun and games of it all had vanished, and now for everyone there was real fear of dropping a line. He'd been diligent in his memorization. Why not? He didn't have anything else to do. And though he'd wanted to offer Lois some tips on basic story structure, he wasn't sure that would be well received, so he just kept his mouth shut and tried his best not to be bothered by the fact that the story didn't have a climax and that the conflict and resolution both shared the same page of the play.

Now all he wanted was a big, fat sandwich and a tall glass of milk. It was nearly eleven o'clock. In the kitchen, Goose and Bunny huddled in the kitchen and whined. This had all been hard on the dogs. Accepting Ainsley into their family wasn't the problem, but the recent activity inside their home was wreaking havoc on their predictable dog lives.

Wolfe went to the garage and got their dog food. He poured it into their bowls, but they didn't move to their dishes. "Come on, kids. Dinner's waiting. I know it's late." They stayed put, and actually hung their heads and whined. Wolfe stooped down to their level. "What's wrong with you two?" He scratched their heads. "Listen, I know things are weird around here. We've got houseguests who aren't exactly conventional. And I've noticed that Ainsley doesn't pay as much attention to you as she usually does. I'm sort of in the same boat. But life will return to normal. I promise. You're both probably feeling ignored, and that's understandable. After all, most nights I don't get home until late with all these play practices." He gave them both a good rubdown. "All right, go eat."

Both slid closer to the floor and lowered their heads. Wolfe's growing concern was interrupted by a tapping at the back door. He could see someone standing outside. As he approached, he recognized his father-in-law's badge.

"Hi," Wolfe said, opening the door. "What's going on?"

The sheriff came in and glanced around. "Everyone asleep?"

"Yeah, except me. I was just about to make myself a sandwich. You want one?"

"Sure. Thanks." He followed Wolfe into the kitchen. "I'm glad you're up, Wolfe. I need to talk."

Wolfe had his back to the sheriff as he poked his head into the refrigerator. So luckily he didn't see Wolfe squeeze his eyes shut. That was the last thing Ainsley had said tonight before she went into a thirty-minute tirade that somehow included Wolfe's unwillingness to help fold Melb's laundry. Except Ainsley had never asked him to, and there was a part of him that wasn't sure he could fold other people's underwear.

Wolfe took out all the ingredients and laid them across the counter. "Talk?"

"Yeah," the sheriff said, plopping down on a barstool. He glanced at the dogs. "What'd these two do, dump on the carpet?"

"What? No. They're fully trained."

"Really. That's the exact same look Thief gives me when he doesn't make it to the box. I'm the sheriff. I know guilt when I see it."

Wolfe rubbed his temples and tried to breathe deeply. He was *not* having this conversation, was he? "They're just tired."

"Anyway, I thought you could give me some advice."

"Advice?" Wolfe slapped mayo onto the bread and whisked it from side to side.

"Yeah. I'm going crazy, Wolfe."

"Why?"

"I think I'm in love. But it's so complicated, and I just don't trust myself right now."

"What's complicated about it?"

"I'm not sure what part of myself is really in love."

Wolfe tried to hand the sheriff his sandwich without looking like that statement was at all odd. "Right, I see."

"It's Lois," the sheriff sighed. "I think I'm in love with Lois."

"Lois, Oliver's cousin?"

"Yeah. I know. The Queen of Menopause."

"No, no. Not at all. Lois is a fine lady. Eccentricity can be attractive, especially when it comes with hot flashes."

The sheriff didn't show a hint of a smile, but he was biting into his sandwich at the time. Wolfe decided he'd better can the humor and listen to his father-in-law. The man was obviously distressed.

"So you're not sure about your feelings for her?"

"To tell you the truth, I'm not sure if it's a fantasy or not. One night Lois and I went out together as Bart and Lotus, just for some help with my character. She called it method acting. You should try it with your character."

"I might. My character's dead, so I could just lie around all day."

"The problem is that I don't really know if my feelings for Lois are because I'm pretending to be Bart, or if they're for real."

"Well, how do you feel about Lois when you're not Bart?"

"That's the problem. I can't seem to leave Bart behind. He's a smooth guy, you know? He always knows what to say and when to say it. He's got these great little lines in the play that make all the women crazy. And so whenever I'm around Lois, I can't seem to be myself. I always go into Bart, because Bart always knows what to say. I, on the other hand, just fumble my words and act like a complete idiot."

Wolfe lost his appetite. He set down his sandwich. "So what you're saying is that whenever you're around Lois, you pretend to be Bart?"

"It's a little game we play. She becomes Lotus, and we do our thing. But that just makes me more confused. Do I really have feelings for Lois, or am I in love with Lotus? And who am I, anyway? Me, or Bart?"

Wolfe felt a tickle in his belly, that tickle you feel right before you giggle at the most inappropriate time and at something you absolutely shouldn't. Wolfe squeezed his stomach muscles and stuck his tongue to the roof of his mouth just to make sure nothing escaped.

The sheriff continued. "The other thing complicating matters is that I think I have some competition."

"Really?"

"Gibb." The sheriff cleared his throat. "Martin, I mean."

Wolfe shook his head. Of course! That was who Martin was talking about. "You think Martin is dating Lois?"

"I know he is. I've seen them out."

"So what are you going to do?"

"I don't know. That's why I'm here. What should I do?"

Wolfe went ahead and took a bite of his sandwich, just to give him some time to try to think up a rational answer in this very irrational circumstance. After forty thorough chews, he swallowed and said, "Obviously, you've got to find out who, exactly, is in love with Lotus. Lois."

"Right. And whoever it is, which woman is he in love with?"

"Good point."

"So step one is going to have to be this: I'm going to have to talk to her as myself. No word-savvy Bart. Just me."

"That's a good idea."

"And we'll see if there's chemistry. I should talk about work and family and see what happens, right?"

"Right."

"Maybe just talk about work. I don't want to scare her off."

"Okay."

"But you get my point. I'm going to have to come through as myself."

"Yes."

The sheriff finished off his sandwich and gulped his milk. He wiped his mustache and handed Wolfe his plate. "You make a good sandwich. Ainsley's been so out of the loop lately, maybe you should start cooking, eh? It's not like you work or anything."

"Yeah…"

"I guess I better head out." He pulled his jacket on. "Don't breathe a word about this to anybody. Especially not my family. They see me as a rock, Wolfe. The stable part of this family. If they sensed that I was in any way coming unglued, it could really do some damage."

"My lips are sealed."

The sheriff slapped his arm. "Good. Thanks. I'll see you tomorrow." Wolfe let him out the back door and locked it. He plodded into the kitchen to put the sandwich stuff away. Goose and Bunny were still acting strangely.

"What is up with you two?" Wolfe asked. "Do you need to go outside?" They both remained motionless.

Wolfe sighed and put all the sandwich stuff into the refrigerator. All he wanted to do was go to bed and forget all the conversations he'd had in the last two hours. His mind was mush, and his emotions were teetering. He was about to flick off the kitchen light when he noticed Oliver's coat on the back of the couch. Soon enough he would be properly trained by Ainsley as to where his coat should go, but for now Wolfe decided he'd better divert any potential conflict-causers.

He grabbed the coat and went to the coat closet. He noticed the dogs slipping to the other side of the room and decided he was going to have to call Garth, the vet, in the morning. Just as he was reaching for the door to the coat closet, he heard someone whisper, "Don't scream."

"No…no, not at all," Lois replied the third time Martin asked her whether he'd freaked her out. "Seriously, it's Skary. Someone sneaking up on you in the dark is usually no reason for concern or alarm." She said this while clenching one hand over her wildly beating heart.

Martin smiled. "I just wanted a little bit of time alone with you. I didn't want to say this in front of the entire cast."

"Say what?"

He stared at the gravel. "I'm just quite fond of you, Lois. And it's not like me to look at a woman. I haven't looked at a woman in years. Didn't even know I was still capable of it. But then you came into my life…"

Lois's heart melted. Martin Blarty was not a man that she would've looked twice at a decade ago, but this was not a decade ago. This was midlife. At midlife, there are certain things that don't bother you anymore, like the fact that a man is three inches shorter than you are. As a mature woman, your standards haven't slipped, they've just deepened to include Volvos instead of Corvettes. There is nothing at all wrong with quiet dependability and a surplus of air bags.

Lois touched his hand. He almost flinched, but recovered nicely.

"Martin," Lois said, "you are one of the kindest, sweetest men I know."

Martin's expression sagged. "But?"

"But what?"

"There's always a 'but' after that statement."

Lois laughed. "We're not in high school anymore."

"Oh. Right." He smiled. "The thing is, Lois, that I don't have a lot to offer. I'm not a powerful man, and I don't have a lot of talents beyond my small world of numbers."

"You have more talent than you know, Martin. You don't give yourself enough credit."

"Credit can be dangerous in the wrong hands," he joked, then shook his head. "See? Even my humor revolves around numbers."

Lois laughed at his joke, but inside she was feeling somewhat conflicted. Though she was strongly attracted to the sheriff, his stupid antics weren't giving their relationship much hope. He seemed to like her only if she pretended to be the fictional character of Lotus, whose dreamy eyes, silky hair, and knockout body were nothing Lois could compete with at this stage in her life. Was that all that man wanted? A hot young Jaguar?

Martin stood before her looking as awkward as a pocket protector on a tuxedo. Yet there was something about Martin…a strange, quiet confidence that rested in his gentle eyes.

"I've said something wrong," Martin sighed.

"I'll say," Lois replied.

Martin glanced at her with a startle. "What did I say?"

"It's what you didn't say."

The poor guy looked ready to pass out.

Lois continued. "I'm still waiting for you to ask me out again." She folded her arms just for effect.

"Oh! Uh, yes, of course!" Martin slapped a hand to his cheek. "Lois, how can you think I wouldn't want to go out with you? I'm waiting around in the dark for a chance to talk to you."

"As I'm sure you're well aware, Martin, women don't always make a lot of sense. We're not neat and tidy like a column of numbers. We're more complicated...like the English language. How did you do in English, Martin?"

"I can't say I did all that good."

"Just remember. Like so many words in our delightfully eccentric language, women oftentimes have more than one meaning, if you catch my drift."

Martin appeared not to.

Butch walked out of the coat closet like it was the men's bathroom. "Hi Wolfe," he said casually. "Have you put the sandwich stuff up yet?"

Oliver's coat dropped to the floor, and Wolfe watched Butch walk toward the kitchen. He managed to get his feet working in order to follow him.

"What are you doing in my coat closet?" Wolfe demanded.

"Hi kids," Butch said to the dogs, who gathered at his feet with expectant looks on their faces.

"Butch! Answer me!"

"Wolfe, calm down. You're going to wake the dead."

"Have you been in there the whole time?"

"For about an hour. I slipped in while you were upstairs talking to my sister. Then I heard a car pull up, so I stepped inside the closet. I didn't want my presence to be compromised. Turns out I made the right decision, since the car ended up being my dad's."

"Why would that matter?" Wolfe asked, eyeing the peculiar sway that Butch seemed to have over his dogs. "And why are Goose and Bunny being so friendly to you?"

Butch pulled out three strips of bacon from his pocket. "I never leave home without these. They've worked wonders in all parts of the world, taming animals and bribing people for information." He fed the dogs the remaining pieces. "That's why they didn't alert you to my presence. They felt guilty for taking food from someone they obviously should have alerted you about. Bacon is one of the most powerful weapons in the world."

Wolfe couldn't begin to find words to dispel the stunned feeling that had paralyzed his body. Butch was slicing the bread. "I thought Dad would never leave. Someone's going to have to talk some sense into that man. He has one love in his life, and that's Mom. It's understandable to lose one's mind every now and then. Dad isn't perfect, and the older he gets, the more he lets things slip. But I'm going to have to talk some sense into him."

"You can't do that. Nobody is supposed to know."

"I was standing in the closet, Wolfe. I heard everything."

"How are you going to explain that?"

"I'll tell him you told me."

Wolfe felt himself growing angry. He looked up at the clock. It was after midnight. He was exhausted. And now he had to deal with his brother-in-law hiding in his closet and acting as if that was perfectly natural.

"Besides being creepy, you've really violated my privacy. I mean, what if I'd been...you know...with my wife?"

"First of all," Butch said with a chuckle, "I knew that wasn't going to happen. You have houseguests, and I happen to know Ainsley's well-planned schedule wouldn't allow for that on the same night you have play practice. Second, I make it my business to know people's schedules and habits. It's what makes me as dangerous as I am clever. For example, I happen to know that every night before you go to bed, you come down and make yourself a sandwich."

Wolfe fumbled a few words before finally blurting out, "Why in the world are you hiding anyway? Why not just stop by or call on the phone?"

"It's classified."

Wolfe suppressed a scream.

"I'm just kidding," Butch laughed. "But that sounded good, didn't it?"

"I want an explanation."

"Look, I've uncovered some highly sensitive information, and the fact of the matter is that I don't know what to do with it or how to handle it."

Wolfe wanted to reach out and strangle the man.

"I'm serious," Butch added.

"Highly sensitive information," Wolfe growled. "In Skary, Indiana."

"It has to do with the snake."

"I'm listening." Anything that could get Melb and Oliver out of his house was worth listening to.

"Well, while Mr. Snake Expert had his ideas about how to capture that snake, I had some of my own. And I found it."

"The snake? You found the snake?"

"For the next couple of days, it's safe and hidden. But after that, I'm not sure."

"Where is it? Let's go get it!"

"Not so fast," Butch said. "It's not going to be that easy. First of all, if Leonard Tarffeski catches wind of this, we're going to have ourselves a real fight. That man is an imposter, but more than that, he's out for money. All he cares about is capturing that snake and most likely selling it on the black market."

"So? Let's give it to him and move on."

"Wolfe, that snake is a boy's pet."

"He's nineteen."

"So what. He's raised that snake since birth. Unfortunately, Tarffeski has convinced Dustin that he's on his side. Dustin isn't going to trust anyone but that snake charmer."

"So we get the snake, return it to Dustin, and be on with it."

"I know this seems simple to you, Wolfe, but you're going to have to slow down and think things through."

"Like what?"

"For starters, the snake looks to weigh about twenty pounds."

"Twenty?"

"He's huge. He must have been feasting on raccoons or beavers or something. And I've seen a lot of wacky things in my line of work, but I've never gotten chills like I did when those two heads were staring at me."

Wolfe couldn't resist. "You were scared?"

"My line of work doesn't require the removal of fear. It requires the control of it."

Wolfe sighed and leaned forward on the counter. "So why are you telling me all this? What does this have to do with me?"

"It's a two-man operation. And more than anyone else in this town, you've got the experience."

"I don't have any experience with this."

"Sure you do. You wrote a book about it."

"A book about what?"

"Snakes. Don't you remember?"

"I wrote a book that had a snake in it. And contrary to popular belief, just because I put it in a book doesn't mean I'm an expert."

"Well, the snake is a complete monster. Surely that's in your arena."

"I write horror but try my best not to live it."

"Look, either you help me get this snake and get it back to Dustin without Tarffeski cluing in, or you resign yourself to living with Jekyll and Hyde."

Wolfe's head pounded, and his eyes were burning with fatigue. After a few moments watching Butch eat three slices of bread, Wolfe finally said, "Fine. I'll help you. But I need some rest."

"We'll start our operation tomorrow at o-nine-hundred."

"Shall I open the back door for you, or would you like to leave out a window or something?"

"Cute. There are a lot of myths about what I do, Wolfe. But we do use doors from time to time."

Wolfe walked him to the back. As Butch stepped outside he said, "And remember. Not a word about this to anyone."

Wolfe's eyes rolled back, but he wasn't sure if it was from exhaustion or exasperation. He quietly closed the door and turned off all the lights in the house. Climbing the stairs with intentional quietness, he finally made it to the top and to his bedroom. Lifting the covers with a gentle hand, he slid under the sheets and for the first time since he'd decided to make a sandwich, he inhaled a deep breath. *Finally. Bed.*

He rolled over to take Ainsley into his arms, but to his surprise grabbed an empty pillow instead. Sitting up, he clicked on his bedroom lamp. Her side of the bed was completely empty! The bathroom light was off, and the door was open. He looked on the other side of the bed, just to make sure she hadn't fallen out. Carpet stared back.

He hopped out of bed, checked the bathroom, then checked the closet. "Ainsley?" he whispered. "Ainsley!"

As he rounded the corner into the hallway, he ran right into her.

They both screamed, then covered each other's mouths. Wolfe whisked her into the bedroom and closed the door.

"What are you doing?"

"What are *you* doing?" she whispered back.

"Coming to bed."

"At this late hour?"

"I...I needed some time to wind down. Why aren't you asleep?" She moved past him and into bed.

"Ainsley? You didn't answer my question," he said, crawling in beside her. "Why aren't you in bed?"

"I was checking on Melb."

"Why? She's sleeping."

"I know. I just wanted to make sure she was okay."

"Isn't Oliver sleeping right beside her?"

"Yes, but he snores so loud, I don't think he could hear if she needed help. I watched her breathe for a few minutes, though, and everything seems fine."

"What kind of help would Melb need in the middle of the night? She's sleeping!"

Ainsley rolled over in a huff and dragged all the covers with her. Wolfe sighed and turned out his light. He hadn't read a lot of books on marriage and had pretty much been winging it with Ainsley since they first met, but common sense told him there was a rule that allowed a woman to discuss her own mental breakdown ad nauseam, but the man was not to mention it under any circumstance.

So Wolfe stared at the ceiling and listened to Oliver's tuneful snoring.

CHAPTER 18

As if God was shining down on Ainsley this morning, Oliver had announced to her that he was going to take the morning off to spend some time with Melb. Ainsley was dressed by eight, and spent ten minutes gawking in the mirror at herself. It had been a while since she'd worn this much makeup, but she felt beautiful. Her hair was put neatly into place, and her cheeks shimmered with a soft pink.

Downstairs, even Wolfe commented. "You look radiant!" he declared, pulling her into an embrace.

"I've got to go to the church regarding one of my catering jobs." She stepped back and noticed he was fully dressed. "Where are you going this morning?"

He shrugged. "I'm spending some time with your brother."

"Why?"

"Well, it looks like he's going to be around here more, so I should get to know him better."

"That's so sweet!" she said. They didn't mention the fight last night, and sometimes it was better to just ignore things that happen in the early morning hour when one person is not right in the head.

Wolfe was obviously exhausted and had lost all common sense. He craved sleep more than Melb's health, but Ainsley couldn't blame him. She was exhausted too. However, Melb came before her needs, and that's just the way it was. Wolfe would learn.

In the meantime, she had the important task of measuring the church basement to see how many tables could fit down there. And she arrived right on time!

"Good morning, Reverend!" Ainsley said as she flung open the sanctuary doors.

The reverend looked startled until he saw her. "My girl! How are you? You look as beautiful as ever." He hugged her with warm arms.

"Thank you. I'm here to take some measurements of the basement."

"You too?"

"What do you mean?"

"Katelyn is downstairs doing that exact same thing."

Ainsley started toward the basement door.

"Wait," the reverend said, gently grabbing her arm.

"What's the matter?"

He guided her to a pew where he offered her a seat, took the pew ahead and turned around to face her. "I need your opinion."

"Sure. What about?"

"Things are changing mighty fast around here, Ainsley. And I know I'm old and probably out of touch with a lot of things, but I can't help feeling a little overwhelmed."

"What kinds of things are changing?"

"The basement, of course. And I'm not saying that's a bad thing. It's just a new thing. We've never really catered to children, you know? When I was growing up, I sat right next to my parents through a two-hour sermon, and I remember listening to the whole thing from the age of six. Now we've got murals and drink bars and televisions. It seems like the whole religious world is passing me by."

"Reverend, this is your church. If Katelyn is suggesting something you don't like—"

"No, not at all. She's been very gracious, and frankly, she has brought a lot of life and activity to this old church. I'm not complaining. I just hope I can keep up."

"You'll do fine," Ainsley said, patting him on the arm.

"I've been praying for a long time for this church. And I know God well enough to know that it's a rarity to have a prayer answered the way you think it should be. I always imagined my powerful, charismatic sermons might be a big draw someday, but it looks as if it may be the new cappuccino machine."

"Reverend, your sermons are always powerful."

He batted his hand in the air. "No matter. God will use me how He wants. I can serve coffee just as well as I can serve up a good speech. And if it means people will start attending church, who am I to stand in the way of that? So the whole world passes me by. So I'm left standing in the dust of the technology age. So I still prefer a cup of black coffee from an old pot. God is still God and I'm still on this earth at His beck and call." The reverend's shirt pocket vibrated. "Excuse me," he said, and he answered his cell phone.

"Corner booth by the kitchen," Butch told the waitress at The Mansion Restaurant. Wolfe followed them both and took his menu as he sat down.

When the waitress left, Wolfe said, "Most people like to be away from the kitchen."

"Wolfe, this booth was chosen with our utmost privacy in mind. If we're by the kitchen, it's too noisy for other people to hear what we're saying, and like you said, this is usually the most isolated part of the restaurant."

"Why couldn't we meet at the new coffeehouse?"

"Because that's the exact wrong place to meet. Most people are there alone, pretending to read newspapers while they eavesdrop on conversations." He looked up as the waitress approached. "Two poached eggs, two pieces of toast, a glass of orange juice, and ten slices of bacon. For you, Wolfe?"

"Just some coffee."

The waitress returned to the kitchen, and Butch said, "All right. There're some things you're going to need to know."

"Like where the snake is."

"Not so fast. One thing at a time. First of all, you're going to need to be trained in the handling of boas."

"Why would I need that?"

"Because you're going to be handling a boa."

"I'm not touching any such thing."

"Just listen, will you? If we're going to do this, we're both going to have to approach this snake like the pet that it is. So the first thing you should know is that although a boa's bite can cause a lot of bleeding, it isn't fatal and doesn't hurt more than a cat scratch. And in fact, it won't even bleed if you can manage to keep your hand or arm completely still when the snake strikes."

"Sure. No problem."

"Don't be sarcastic, Wolfe. I'm just giving you the facts."

"A plan would be nice."

"The first part of the plan is to make the snake familiar with us. We're not sure how much Dustin handled the snake, but we know it was probably handled at least a little. However, it's been gone from that environment for so long, it may not be used to human touch."

"You're not serious. We have to touch it?"

"Wolfe, how on earth do you think we're going to capture it? With pleasant conversation and an invitation for cheesecake?"

"I'm not touching it."

"Hear me out. The first thing we have to do is find a large, cloth bag a little larger than a pillowcase because it's definitely not going to fit in a pillowcase. We place the bag near the snake. It will be drawn into it because it's dark. Once it is in there, we close the bag, and then we begin to start touching the bag. We sort of stroke the body of the snake until it gets used to being touched. After that, you will remove the snake and hold it against your warm body—"

"Or your dead body."

"It sounds extreme. But once we get it in the sack, we can probably transport it. It's going to take both of us though."

Wolfe massaged his temples. "I can't imagine holding a snake, much less a two-headed snake."

"I won't lie. It was freaky. The sack will help. We won't have to look at its heads."

"How in the world do we get to the snake in the first place? Won't it hear us coming?"

"Snakes don't have ears, Wolfe. But they do feel vibrations. That's where my training will come in handy. I can teach you to walk without making a sound."

Wolfe downed his coffee. This was not the solution he had in mind for the mother of all maternal crises, but it was the only one that seemed somewhat plausible. *If the snake's caught, Melb will have to return home and Ainsley will have to return to normal.*

Butch was slicing his eggs. "You know what I've found in life, Wolfe? There's not much to fear. I've been in some of the most danger-ous situations imaginable, but God delivered me. And even if death had come, my life would've continued on in a better place. Is a two-headed snake going to get your heart pounding? You better believe it. But just think of all the great stories you can tell about how you handled a two-headed snake. Surely that's fodder for a book."

"I'm not looking for fodder," Wolfe lied.

"Well then you must be looking for a way to get your life back to normal."

He couldn't even pretend to lie about that.

"So will you help me?" Butch asked, finishing up his breakfast and stuffing bacon into his jacket pocket.

Wolfe leaned back in his chair and took a deep breath. A lot was riding on this, mostly at a personal level, but the town was still reeling from it too. It would sure make the sheriff's job easier. Plus, he couldn't deny, there was a certain amount of manliness at stake.

"Okay," Wolfe sighed. "I'll help you. But I am not holding the snake against my 'warm body.' "

Butch nodded and pushed his plate back. "We'll just have to get creative."

"That's what scares me. So where is the snake?"

"At Gordon and Alba's farmhouse, in the basement." Butch stood and threw down a few dollars. "I'll be in touch."

"Where are you going?"

"I've got to go see my dad, talk some sense into him about this fling he thinks he needs."

"You'll do no such thing!"

"He's my dad, Wolfe. I don't think you have a lot to say."

"Your father came to me and confided in me about a personal matter. He expects me to keep it private."

Butch laughed. "Private. That's funny."

"What's so funny about it?"

"Nothing is private, Wolfe. And by nothing, I mean nothing. I can access anything from anybody anytime I want."

"Good for you. But you are not going to talk to your father about this. Unless he spills the beans to you, you're not going to talk to him about it."

"You're going to physically stop me?" Butch said, puffing out his chest.

"If I have to."

"I'd like to see that. I have four black belts."

"Well, I have knowledge of a certain snake. And its whereabouts."

Butch's chest deflated. "You got me. Information is one of the most deadly weapons around. All right. I'll back off Dad. For now. But all bets are off after we find that snake." Butch moved past him.

"Butch, what's the deal? Don't you want your father to find companionship?"

"Why? He's got me."

"Hi," Ainsley said. She stepped down the basement stairs as timidly as a mouse-hunting kitten. She didn't want to admit it, but this Katelyn Downey made her unsure of herself.

"Oh, hi," Katelyn said. She was covered in paint and had ratty old overalls on, but the look did nothing to ruffle her perpetual air of perfection. Setting down her paintbrush and wiping her hands on her rag, she met Ainsley halfway. "Good to see you."

"Thanks. You too," Ainsley said. How did she get her hair to do that? So perky. Before now, Ainsley's seemed admirable because of its lack of split ends.

"You sound tired. Are you feeling okay?"

"Oh, yeah, fine. Just up with the…the…"

"Kids? I know how it feels. It can wreak havoc on your eyes." She smiled and avoided Ainsley's gaze. Ainsley touched the puffy patch of skin below each eye. She didn't think they were that noticeable. "So? What do you think of the mural?" Katelyn asked.

"It's nice. Makes this room look so colorful."

"We're going to be adding purple carpet. We'll have a TV in that corner, a puppet castle over there, and then of course a little beverage bar. All proceeds go to God, which will teach the kids to give."

Ainsley wanted to point out that it would only teach them to expect something in return, but then she spotted the tape measure. Her curiosity disrupted any further thought. "The reverend said you were down here measuring."

"Yes. I'll be honest. I've been worried about space. I wanted to get an exact idea of how many tables we can fit down here."

Ainsley pulled a tape measure out of her purse. "I can tell you that."

"Here," Katelyn said, taking a piece of paper out of her pocket. "The measurements are written down there."

Ainsley took the paper and studied it. Measurements down to every detail, including the small window that of course would need to be centered with the table.

"Eight-foot tables?" Katelyn asked.

"Yes," Ainsley said. "So that means two tables on the east wall,"

"And one on the west," Katelyn added.

"But we can add a four-foot table for drinks over on the south wall."

"Exactly. Right by the beverage bar." She clapped her hands. "That will be perfect."

"And will keep the traffic flowing in one direction."

"Which is always important." Katelyn said this while studying Ainsley's shoes.

Ainsley couldn't decide if she loved or hated this woman. Here was a lady who embodied everything dear to Ainsley. She understood that the way a room is laid out is of utmost importance. She understood décor and fine food and table settings. She was energized by things being exactly right, evident in her attention to detail on the mural and Ainsley's shoes. So why did this woman aggravate her so?

Not knowing what else to do, she decided to stare at Katelyn's shoes. They were multicolored canvas. Which of course would go perfectly with paint-stained overalls. Ainsley glanced down at her own shoes and—

She gasped. Katelyn turned back to the wall, and Ainsley stared down at her feet. Mismatched shoes?! How could it have happened? They were close, one a dark brown, one a soft black, but still. She wanted to sink into the floor and cry.

Instead, she decided to try to hold her head high. She noticed a photo album lying on the table. It gave her something to do other than continue to horrify herself, so she decided to go take a peek. "What's the photo album for?"

Katelyn followed her to the table. "It's one of my Creative Memories albums."

Ainsley flipped open the first page. Each picture was framed perfectly with dainty pink and green mats, plus festive stickers and typed labels. She looked closer. It was a picture of Main Street. She turned the page, and the next page. They were all pictures of Skary. And as she got to the middle of the book, she began seeing pictures of the new coffeehouse, the bookstore, the new deli, and then the cell phone store. At the back of the book were pictures of the church. Ainsley bent over the book, hardly believing her eyes. There on one page was a drawing of their church, with two other buildings surrounding it, plus a deluxe playground.

Katelyn said, "Those are just some drawings I did. Just playing around with some ideas."

"That's our church."

"Behind the church is the multiplex, which will house a gym, a theater, and classrooms. On the other side are the offices and children's area."

Ainsley couldn't believe what she was seeing. After getting over the shock and pure, undeniable envy of how perfectly organized these pictures were, along with color-coordinated stickers and mats and page numbers, she then had to deal with the idea that Katelyn Downey had a much bigger plan for Skary, Indiana, than just adding coffee flavors. She flipped back through the pages, trying to grasp it all. She did notice, with more than a bit of pleasure, that Katelyn didn't seem to know colors all that well. Throughout the pastel-colored album, touches of red in the form of arrows clashed conspicuously.

Ainsley closed the book and turned to Katelyn, who was busy fixing her ponytail. As she was standing there observing how masterfully Katelyn could use her fingers (and not a brush) to accomplish such a task, something extraordinary happened to Ainsley, something she was not sure she'd ever felt before.

"That's an interesting choice of red you've put in your album." Ainsley stood with one foot behind the other, feeling equally empowered and ashamed by her snide remark. What had this woman done to her? It was jealousy in its worst form, and she knew it. But that didn't wipe the self-satisfied smile off her face.

Katelyn smiled back. "That's actually not red. It's called Crimson Blood."

"Among pastels?"

"To stand out. It represents all the territory that I haven't fully con-
quered yet."

Lois Stepaphanolopolis divided her clothes. On one side of the closet
were "Martin outfits" which consisted of polished cotton shirts, jackets,
and pants in more modest cuts, such as black pantsuits. On the other
side were Sheriff Parker–appropriate clothes—more polished cotton
with plunging necklines and bright colors, paired with a few floral wrap
skirts. And of course everything had shoulder pads. Lois didn't mind
that she hadn't updated her wardrobe since her twenty-pound weight
gain of '87. She knew how to make an outfit look good. It was all about
the walk and the shade of lipstick.

It had been years since she'd dated, and even then, weeks went by
between dates, so having two men interested in her at one time was
extraordinary and nothing short of miraculous. She could admit it—she
loved the attention.

She was still unsure which man was right for her. Martin Blarty was
not her type, not by a long shot. She had few rules about men she dated,
but one of them was that he had to have a larger shoulder span than she.
Though a smaller man, Martin did carry himself well, and something
about him made Lois feel that no matter what the crisis, he would come
through. There was this sense that he had a solution for every problem.
He was the kind of man that might have entered every relational challenge he could think of into a spreadsheet of some sort, and calculated
out their chances of coming through successfully. He wouldn't be pur-
suing her so hard if he didn't think it could work. And though her heart

didn't pitter-patter at the sound of his voice, she couldn't deny that the way he treated her made her feel special.

Then there was Sheriff Parker, a.k.a. Irwin, a.k.a. Bart. He was much more of an enigma. The man's intense stare could buckle her knees, and she loved the way she had to stare *up* into his eyes. A certain power exuded from him. He walked with a purposeful stride. Strutted, actually. But he carried it off well, especially for his age. She couldn't shake the feeling that he was a little confused about who he should be in love with. It was a common hazard among actors. They start to believe the role they play, and therefore project their playacting emotions into real life.

Lois backed out of her closet, after organizing her shoes according to heel height, and closed the door. One thing she knew for certain. She was going to have to keep these two men as separate as possible. The less they knew about each other, the better. She was not in an exclusive dating relationship, so there was no reason she couldn't or shouldn't test-drive both varieties. But she knew for certain that she couldn't play one against the other. Both men had fragile egos, and with that came the risk of losing it all. A couple more weeks dating them both would help her figure out which she was more attracted to. It was simply a matter of keeping a distinct record of heart palpitations.

Lois went to the kitchen to fix herself a healthy salad with a side of loaded potato. But before she could even get the pound of cheese out of the fridge, she heard a knock at the front door. She smiled as she fluttered across the living room. She just knew it was one of her favorite men, possibly with roses or chocolates. Smelling, she was sure, like the cologne she loved.

She swung open the door. Well, she was right about the roses. And the chocolates. And the cologne. Martin and Irwin stood shoulder to head under the porch light.

CHAPTER 19

"GENTLEMEN," LOIS SQUEAKED. "What...what are you both, um, doing here?"

The two men glanced at each other and then at Lois. "Well," Martin began, "we came to woo you."

The sheriff said, "But apparently we both had the woo idea."

"I like to woo with roses."

"I woo with dark chocolates."

"I would have rung before I wooed except I really wanted to surpwise—er, surprise—you."

Two woos. Huh. "Who wooed first?" Lois asked.

"We arrived to woo at the same time," the sheriff said.

"The chances of that are actually astronomical," Martin added.

"Well," Lois said, not knowing what else to do, "why don't you both come in?"

The men looked at each other, both obviously concerned. But neither looked like they wanted to turn down the invitation either.

"Sure, why not?" the sheriff said, and both men squeezed through the doorway at the same time. Lois shut the front door and offered them each a seat.

"Martin, let me put the roses in some water." She smelled them and said, "They're beautiful, thank you."

"Chocolate?" the sheriff asked, opening the box.

The array of chocolates beckoned her attention. "May I see the map?"

"What map?"

"It's on the inside of the lid." She took it from him. He looked confused. Possibly because he'd never known there was a map. The map was the only thing one needed to stay away from the possibility of biting into one with orange filling. "Yum. This one looks good." She took a truffle.

The sheriff glanced at Martin and grudgingly offered him one too. Martin took the middle one. "Thanks," Martin said, popping it into his mouth. Then he made a face. He didn't look at the map.

The sheriff closed the box.

Lois put the roses in a vase and offered the men drinks. Both declined. She sat across from her two suitors, crossed her legs, and folded her hands together.

"Well," she said after several seconds of awkward silence except for the orange chocolate smacking inside Martin's mouth, "I guess it's obvious that I've been dating both of you. I didn't want to hurt either of you, but the fact of the matter is that I'm attracted to you both."

Martin and the sheriff smiled at each other. In a woman's world, that would've jump-started a cat fight.

"You each have certain unique qualities that I'm attracted to. I was hoping you wouldn't find out about each other, but now that you have, I think that's probably healthy. Keeping secrets is never a good way to start a relationship."

"All right. Fine!" Martin blurted. "I wear heel lifts!"

Lois hastily added, "I meant concerning me. Dating both of you."

The sheriff was staring at Martin's shoes, and Martin was staring at the box of chocolates. She was losing control of this situation. If she was going to have the two men she adored in her house at the same time, the attention was going to have to be on her.

So she did what any self-respecting drama queen would do: she fainted.

"Good-bye, Doctor. Thank you for coming." Wolfe said and shut the door quietly, though a jolt of satisfaction caused him to smile. But it had worked! He'd called Dr. Hoover earlier that day and asked him to come over and assess Melb. It was just as he'd expected. Dr. Hoover had given Melb a clean bill of health and told her she should start exercising. *By packing your bags,* Wolfe had thought, but he didn't quite have the snake issues resolved. Very soon, though.

Nevertheless, he knew this would bring a great deal of relief to Ainsley, who had been feeling guilty for everything that had happened to Melb. Now they could get on with their—

What was that noise? He followed it into the kitchen. Ainsley was pouring some berry-colored drink from the blender into a glass. Wolfe followed her into the living room, where she gave it to Melb and then adjusted her blanket.

Wolfe followed her back into the kitchen. "What do you think you're doing?"

She opened the refrigerator and pulled out a sack of carrots. "Juicing carrots. Why?"

"Didn't you just hear what the doctor said? Melb is fine. She should go about life normally."

"People drink carrot juice, Wolfe."

"You're acting as if you didn't hear a thing Dr. Hoover said."

"I'm juicing carrots. Is it a federal crime?"

"Don't be sarcastic with me. I saw you pull the covers over Melb's feet."

Ainsley finally turned to him, a determined fire in her eyes. "What is with you? Why do you care so much?"

"Why do I care so much? First of all, you're my wife. I hate seeing you like this. You're utterly exhausted, and you never stop. You just keep going and going. And now you've been given the green light to stop, and you can't."

"You're overreacting."

"Take a good look around you! I don't know how to say this, but you've totally lost your mind!" He paused, waiting for a possible slap to the cheek. There was no slap, but plenty of tears had begun running down her cheeks. "Oh no. Please. Please don't cry. It's just a temporary insanity. Easily remedied."

"You don't understand. This isn't about Melb. It's about coordinated handbags and shoes."

"Sure it is." he said softly, but he didn't have a clue what she was talking about.

"I just feel incompetent, Wolfe. I feel like…like…"

"Like…what?"

"I feel like I've been outdone."

"Outdone?"

"There's this woman named Katelyn, and I swear she is the perfect woman. She looks like she stepped right out of a magazine, and I'm not talking about the co-op magazines. A real fashion magazine. She's so pulled together. And even when she's *not* pulled together, she's pulled together. I feel so useless when I'm around her. She makes me want to crawl in a hole." Ainsley glanced toward the living room. "I guess this has made me feel useful, important. I'm helping save a little life, and what better thing can a person do?"

Wolfe held her shoulders. "Ainsley, you are not useless. And there is no such thing as perfect. This Katelyn woman may seem pulled together on the outside, but let me assure you, everyone has weaknesses. And what I've found true in life is that the more perfect someone seems on the outside, the more imperfect they are on the inside. They're putting up a front, making everyone think they've got it together. You are one of those rare people in life that has it all together on the outside *and* the inside."

She wept harder, and fell into his arms. "Wolfe, that is the nicest thing anyone has ever said to me."

"It's true." He blotted her face and swept her hair out of her eyes. "You don't need to prove anything to anybody. You're a capable, smart woman, who is compassionate and caring to a fault." He lowered his voice. "Ainsley, the longer you continue to treat Melb this way, the longer you're enabling her."

"Enabling her?"

"You're not making her face the fact that she has a baby on the way, and she's going to have to accept this and prepare for it."

"So what you're saying is that I'm not doing her any favors."

He sighed with relief. "Yes. That's what I'm saying."

She nodded. She suddenly looked exhausted. "I'm going to bed."

"Are you okay?" he asked.

"I just need some rest. Listen, don't say anything to Melb, okay? There's going to be a right time to do this, and it's not now. But I've got to rest. Can you handle it this evening?"

"Sure." He hugged and kissed her with a smile. "I love you."

"I love you too," she said, with the first genuine smile he'd seen on her face in days. "Thanks for speaking the truth." He watched her walk toward the stairs.

Then, from the living room, Melb screeched, "Where's my tea? I could die of thirst with how hot you keep this house!!"

Wolfe geared himself up for a long night.

Martin poked along the five-block stretch of street between Lois's house and his. It was dark and cold, just like his soul. How in the world was he supposed to compete with Sheriff Parker? The man was practically a legend! Was Lois just being nice when she said she was attracted to both of them? Sure, the flowers seemed to be a hit, but Martin had sampled the chocolate, and it was nothing to snub your nose at. Two caramels and a cherry later, he himself was almost ready to marry the sheriff. Next time he would definitely have to go with the sweet stuff.

Dragging his feet along the pavement, he contemplated giving up. But he couldn't shake the feeling that Lois really was attracted to him. After all, she'd gone on more than one date with him. She just as easily could've said she was seeing someone else. That, at least, lit a little flame of hope in his heart.

He gazed at the night sky as he walked up the sidewalk toward his house. Maybe there was something he could do to make himself more attractive. He'd read that hair implants were becoming less and less expensive. Rumor was that old Farmer Gordon had had it done, when seemingly overnight he'd stopped wearing his John Deere cap and Alba had taken to lipstick again. He scratched his cold head and then felt in his jacket for his keys.

And of course he had to ask the all-important question, was Lois

Stepaphanolopolis the right woman for him? A woman wasn't like a spreadsheet. There were plenty of unpredictable factors that didn't fit into the nice, tidy boxes on the screen. Like, for instance, her blood sugar issues, which they'd found out about tonight when she suddenly passed out on the couch.

Martin had not a clue what to do. The sheriff took the role of hero. He laid her on the couch and felt for pulses and other throbbing things. Martin just stood back and watched, then fetched a washrag when ordered to.

"Martin?"

"Ah!" Martin stumbled backward. Someone stood in the shadows of his porch. "Who's there?" he wheezed.

He heard a chuckle. "Good grief, Martin. It's just me." The mayor stepped into the moonlight. "The boogeyman hasn't been to Skary in at least a decade."

Martin punched his key into the doorknob. "What are you doing here this late anyway?"

"I can't sleep," the mayor said, following him inside. "You didn't answer your cell phone."

Martin flipped on the lights and noticed it sitting on the dining room table. "What can I do for you, sir?"

The mayor sat down in Martin's favorite chair and dropped a bag he was carrying to the floor. "Well, we've got a crisis."

Of the heart, Martin lamented, but tried to concentrate on the mayor. Of course, there was always a crisis, so what was new? "What kind of crisis?"

The mayor pulled out a stack of mail. "These. I've been getting letters and phone calls like crazy!" He set the mail on the coffee table, then he hopped up from his chair and rubbed his hands together like he was trying to start a fire.

"About what?"

"People's opinions, mostly. Everyone feels strongly one way or the other. Some people think we should be open to the idea of becoming a suburb…or an X-burb, whatever in the world that is. Others think it's going to be Armageddon. They swear it will be the end of life as we know it."

Martin took the mail and sifted through it. "What do you think?"

He paced the floor. "As you and I both know, this town is always on the brink of bankruptcy. We could use some financial incentive, and there seems to be a couple ready and willing to make it happen. On the other hand, we will most likely lose all our small-town values. I mean, you can't be modern and still exist in a shell, as we've done. We've managed to keep our town away from all the madness of the world. But it was only a matter of time before they found us."

"So either cease to exist or lose who we are."

"I'm afraid those are our only two choices," the mayor said. "But we've got to do something. Make some sort of decision. And soon." Martin started to hand the mail back to the mayor, but he said, "No. You keep those."

"Why?"

"Maybe you'll get a sense of what we should do, after you read them all."

"But sir, this is your town. You're the one who should make the decision."

"You're as capable as anyone of knowing the pulse of the town."

The pulse of the town, perhaps. The pulse of a woman, not so much.

Martin rose and stood in front of the mayor. "Sir, I know this snake thing has everyone's nerves stirred, but I'm worried about you. You seem pretty anxious, and you're not sleeping. You can't sit down for more than five minutes. There is the stress of all the new things happening in town.

Maybe you should see a doctor." It was the most diplomatic way of say-ing, *Last time there was a crisis, you lost your mind and thought you were in the Caribbean, so you can see why I might be concerned.*

"Martin, you worry too much. Now, I have to go. I need to get in my five-mile run."

CHAPTER 20

WOLFE WIPED THE SWEAT OFF his brow and drove carefully so as not to draw attention to himself. As Butch had explained, if you drive too fast, you're going to get pulled over. But drive too slow and you look suspicious. Three over the speed limit, he'd instructed. Wolfe had rolled his eyes, but now he found his attention glued to the speedometer.

Butch had contacted him last night, about thirty minutes after Ainsley had gone to bed, using the phone rather than the closet. Wolfe didn't ask, but he steeled himself for a conversation he knew he needed to have with Butch. It would be one of those conversations that starts off with the awkward line, "Don't you think it's time to stop fooling yourself and others with this charade?" He realized this was not going to be a popular view. Many Skary residents regarded Butch as a local war hero, but it was a shame they couldn't see Butch for who he really was. And at Wolfe's age, he just didn't have the patience for it.

However, he could take care of that after they figured out what to do with the snake. Life was all about priorities, and right now, his number one priority was getting Melb back home. He had noticed that Ainsley didn't cater to her as much this morning, but she also hadn't had "the talk" with her by the time Wolfe left. Maybe she didn't want Wolfe breathing down her neck about it.

Ainsley also looked more refreshed this morning. She had that youthful glow in her cheeks, and her eyes sparkled. It was a gigantic relief.

Wolfe checked his watch. Right on time.

"Whatever you do," Butch had said, "don't be late. Timing is critical for our operation. Gordon and Alda go out for one hour every morning to tend to their cattle. I've calculated the time it will take, including fear and apprehension, and one hour should be sufficient. But don't be late! And for goodness sake, don't be early, either."

The perspiration had beaded and clustered on his forehead. He was running exactly on time. The farmhouse was ten minutes up the road, and he had eleven minutes to spare. He slowed down by two miles an hour, just to compensate. But not too slow. He didn't want to appear "suspicious."

"Don't tell a soul," Butch had warned. "Nobody can know about this. If they do, our cover will be blown, and you may risk having Melb and Oliver as permanent houseguests. Don't tell Ainsley or my father or anyone you know. This has to stay between us. If Tarffeski gets wind of this, the snake's gone and he's pocketed a lot of money. This snake belongs to Dustin, and we're getting it back to him and him alone."

Wolfe had to admire Butch's sense of justice. Wolfe would've just handed the snake over to the snake hunter and been on his way. Now he was on his way to breaking and entering, but at least it was for the sake of a heartbroken pet owner.

Butch's final words had been, "And don't bail on me, Wolfe. I need you there. I can't do it alone. I'll never forgive you if you don't come help me. Plus, you'll be driving the getaway car. I'll find my way there by foot, but we'll need something to haul this snake away in."

Suddenly Wolfe's Jeep lurched forward, made a horrible noise, lurched forward again, then lost acceleration. He pulled to the side of the country road, white steam spewing from underneath the hood. "No! No!" Wolfe scrambled out the door. He opened his hood, and a hissing sound filled the peaceful country side. "No!" He clawed at his hair and took a few steps back. "Now what?" He could attempt to run, but he would be way too late. His shirt dampened with sweat. His first instinct was to pray, but he wasn't entirely sure what he was on his way to do was going to be blessed by the Almighty in the first place.

Nevertheless, he was going to need a miracle.

Ainsley waited for Melb to return downstairs from her bath. Her anxiety over the impending conversation had caused her to juice eight glasses of carrots, but it gave her something to do with her hands. This was not going to be an easy conversation, yet as she'd fallen asleep last night, she knew Wolfe was right. She was enabling Melb. She'd done it unintentionally, but regardless, the damage had been done. In the deepest place in her heart, she'd wanted Melb to appreciate and love this baby. She couldn't fathom how anybody wouldn't want a baby. Sure, Melb was a little older, but this was a gift from God!

Behind her, Melb galloped down the stairs. She had a cornflower blue towel wrapped around her head and smelled like she'd bathed in lotion. "Oh, that felt good!" she said, joining Ainsley in the kitchen. She stopped and stared at the carrot glasses.

"Those aren't all for you."

She patted her heart. "Thank goodness. I was hoping for a Pop-Tart."

"I have your favorite pastry dish in the oven."

"That's what I smelled!" She grabbed Ainsley and hugged her. "You're the best! Is it the one with cream cheese?"

"Yes. And blueberries." It was a devious tactic, but Ainsley hoped it would help ease the pain of what she was about to say.

Melb sat down on a barstool. "I've been secretly wishing for it."

Ainsley smiled and handed her a cup of decaf. "Melb, we need to talk."

Melb looked up as she was about to sip. "Talk?"

"Yeah. I've got to confess some things."

"Isn't the reverend available?"

"Not sins. Well, not really sins. I've just been…been a little misguided, I guess you could say."

"That sounds sad. Can I have more cream?" She handed the coffee back to Ainsley.

Ainsley added more cream and handed it back to her.

"And an ice cube. I don't want to scorch my mouth."

Ainsley took the cup and plopped an ice cube in it.

"You were saying?" Melb asked, blowing on the coffee.

"It kind of concerns how I've been treating you."

"Oh, let's not hash over that, Ainsley," Melb said. "Sure you've been a little moody lately, and have said some things that coming out of your mouth have been nothing less than shocking, but we're friends. And friends forgive one another. I mean, did I complain once when you forgot to feed me dessert after dinner? No. I simply dropped a few subtle hints, and that was it. If you ask me, I think you've been under too much stress lately. Maybe it's because Wolfe doesn't seem to know what work is anymore. I mean, if he's not going to write, shouldn't he be doing chores around the house or something? I'll leave that between you two, but it's just been a simple observation I've made while recovering from the unfortunate incident at the grocery store." She sipped her coffee. "Okay, a little too sweet, but thanks for trying."

Ainsley crossed her arms and lowered her tone. "I meant how I've been coddling you."

"Coddling me?"

"I've been catering to your every need."

"Well, if I'm not mistaken, that's what you do for a living. Cater."

"What I'm saying is that I haven't helped you deal with any of this. I've been trying to protect you, I guess, from anything going wrong, or you feeling any more badly than you do about this baby. I guess I thought if I made your life comfortable and easy, you might decide that having a baby wasn't so bad after all."

Melb didn't look happy. "What are you saying?"

"I'm saying that it's time you took back your life, Melb. Get off the couch, start living again! You have a lot to do in the coming months. And I'll help you along the way. We can think of a color and theme for your baby's room. Go shopping for clothes. It can be fun!"

"Fun. Ainsley, by definition, middle-aged means that you're incapable of bending down to pick up anything that is drooling. Especially twenty times a day."

"You're a strong woman. I know you can do this. You have a tiny baby depending on you. You have a husband who needs assurance that you're going to be there for him, too."

Melb's eyes teared up. "I don't even know where to begin."

Ainsley tried not to let it distract her. "Begin by getting dressed every day, by planning for this baby. Pick out a boy name and a girl name. Make appointments at the hospital once a month, or at least have Dr. Hoover come over. Start deciding what you want to do with the baby's room. You will have plenty to keep you busy."

Melb was staring at the tile floor, but her eyes were sparkling with that determination Ainsley had seen when she was trying to lose all that weight before her wedding. Ainsley even noticed her hands had moved over her belly. "It's real, isn't it?" Melb whispered.

"Yeah! It's real!"

Melb smiled a little. "It's real. I'm going to have a baby. Oliver and I are going to have a baby!"

Ainsley embraced her. "What more joy could there be?"

"That pastry."

Ainsley laughed with Melb and went to get the pastry out of the oven.

"You know what else, Ainsley?"

"What?"

"I'm going to move back home."

"But what about the snake?"

"I'm a pregnant, middle-aged woman. Bring it on."

Wolfe's heart had never pounded so wildly in his chest. He was walking in circles, now wishing he'd signed up for that cell phone plan. What was he supposed to do?

Down the dusty road a large smoky cloud rose from the horizon. In its center was a vehicle, racing along the center of the road is if it didn't expect to see another soul for miles. As it neared Wolfe, the dust settled, and Wolfe could tell it was a station wagon.

It pulled to the side of the road. The sun glared off the windshield, and he couldn't tell who was in there. But soon the passenger door opened, and Oliver Stepaphanolopolis stepped out.

"Wolfe! What in the world are you doing out here?" Oliver sauntered up, looking at the raised hood on Wolfe's Jeep. "Car trouble, huh?"

Wolfe nodded. Maybe he could catch a ride back into town with Oliver. But he knew there wasn't enough time to get back to Gordon's farm.

"I was just taking this fine station wagon out for a test drive. Where you headed?" Oliver asked. "You want a lift?"

Wolfe nodded but said, "No."

"What are you going to do? Just sit out here and hope it starts?"

Wolfe dug his toe into the gravel.

"Are you okay?"

Glancing at the station wagon, he turned to Oliver. "Who's driving?"

"That's Sam Bavitt."

"Doesn't sound familiar."

"He's a lawyer from the next county over."

Not from Skary? That was good. And a lawyer. Could come in handy.

"Ollie, you up for a little adventure?"

Oliver didn't look like it. Both men checked their watches. Wolfe realized they could make it if they left now and sped all the way there.

"It's top secret. What you hear stays between us and our lawyer."

Oliver glanced back to the car. "I've got a bad feeling about this."

"Let's just say, if this operation is successful, your life may get a lot easier."

Alfred Tennison straightened his tie, his slacks, and his hair while sitting in the small though luxurious waiting room at the religious publishing house. Tapping his fingers against his briefcase, he tried his best to remain calm and in control. After all, none of these people knew that he'd become a religious agent out of desperation. As far as they were concerned, he was the well-known editor of Wolfe Boone, and might be able to swing the once-prolific novelist toward publishing with them.

Truthfully, the power rested with Alfred. And nobody needed to know that Wolfe Boone had pretty much lost all ability to write. He could use Wolfe as leverage to publish Doris Buford. And then he could torture Wolfe until he put something down on paper.

Admittedly, he was more nervous about being among religious people. He might say the wrong thing. Offend someone. It was hard to tell what was acceptable among this crowd. But he'd been practicing. From the unsullied Ellie Sherman, he'd learned that a gentle smile and a quiet, confident demeanor seemed to be one of their favorite traits. So he'd taught himself to kill the ear-to-ear grin. And he thought the hands-folded-in-front-of-the-belly look offered a lot of promise. Of course the Catholic jokes he always liked to crack were out. But he was hoping he could still use a little humor to warm things up. And just for kicks he'd actually parted his hair. He'd seen that on television once, and though it wasn't going to win him any fashion awards, he hoped it offered a subtle hint of his regard for the "straight and narrow."

"Alfred Tennison?"

Alfred looked up at a fine, tall, stately looking gentleman in a cotton short-sleeve polo shirt standing over him. As Alfred rose, he couldn't help but notice the casual slacks. Dang. He was overdressed and six inches shorter. This was not good.

"Yes," Alfred said, shaking his hand.

"Mike Jefferson. I'm the publisher. Why don't you come into the conference room."

"Thank you."

Alfred followed him around the corner. Another man was sitting at the table going over some papers. He rose and shook Alfred's hand. "Neil Bryant. Executive editor. Pleased to meet you, Mr. Tennison."

"Please, call me Alfred."

They shook hands with Alfred, and he sat down across from them.

Neil was tieless, and his hair was hanging below his ears. He wasn't sure what kind of establishment he'd found here, but they certainly weren't up to par in their dress code. Especially considering the stack of Bibles in the corner. However, in his research he'd found that this publishing house had earned the most revenue in the past three years.

"We're glad to have you here," Mike said. "And certainly curious about why. We know you were Wolfe Boone's longtime editor and that you left the industry when he did."

"That's right," Alfred lied. *Banished* was a more accurate word for what happened, but there was no reason to go there. "I'm an agent now."

"No kidding?" Mike said. "That's terrific."

"A religious agent," Alfred added.

Mike and Neil glanced at each other. "Interesting."

"I'm building up my client list, and we can talk about that in a moment, but I wanted a chance to pitch to you a book by a woman named Dori Ford." Doris had agreed to go with the Dori Ford pen name since it was her name minus an S, B, and U. "I've done a lot of research in this market, and I have to say I'm impressed, and as you know, it takes a lot to impress a New Yorker."

"We'd love to see what you have. Has, um, Mr. Boone shown any interest for writing this kind of fiction?" Mike asked.

"Oh my, yes. The man is practically a walking religious tract. But like any brilliant artist, he requires time to mold and cultivate his ideas."

"Is he going to be writing…horror?"

"He hasn't decided yet. Wolfe is capable of writing just about anything, so we'll see what direction he decides to take his brand. But whatever that may be, you know it's going to be an instant success."

Mike folded his hands together. "Well, why don't you tell us what Ms. Ford has to offer?"

Alfred smiled. "It's a nonviolent, sexless adventure-suspense-romance with absolutely no controversy in it whatsoever. And let me just add that all conflict is resolved in a loving, timely manner."

"What?" Oliver shouted angrily as he drove them toward Gordon's farmhouse. "Are you kidding me?" Oliver's face was turning red.

"I know this sounds weird," Wolfe said from the back of the station wagon, "but it's the best way."

"Weird is an understatement," Oliver grumbled. Sam, the lawyer, was strangely silent in the front passenger seat and looked as though he was contemplating whether he'd been abducted by aliens.

"Look, all you have to do is stay in the car. As soon as we have the snake, we'll get out of here, and that will be the end of it."

"Do you know how much trouble you could get in? Besides, farmers are notoriously fond of shotguns."

"Look, Butch has an entire plan worked out. If you could just go a little faster, we'll get there in time, get the snake, and be gone before anyone knows it. By the way, you can't mention this to anybody."

"That will cost you a retainer of two hundred and fifty dollars," Sam interrupted. "Then I'll be your attorney, and I can't say a word to anybody. The law says so."

"I can't believe this," Oliver sighed. "I take the station wagon for a test drive, and the next thing I know I'm involved in grand larceny!"

"It's technically breaking and entering, since the farmer doesn't know he possesses the snake," Sam said.

"Whatever!" Oliver fumed. "I'm involved now, and there's no turning back."

"But just think about how Melb will feel knowing the snake is back where it belongs."

Oliver settled down a bit and glanced in the rearview mirror at Wolfe. "That's the *only* reason I'm doing this. For Melb."

"There it is," Wolfe said, pointing to the farmhouse at the bottom of the hill. "Pull over there, by the big tree."

Oliver groaned and pulled the station wagon to the side of the road.

All three men opened their doors. Wolfe looked at his watch. He was three minutes late already. Butch was probably having a heart attack. "Okay, you two stay here, I'm going to meet Butch on the other side of the farmhouse. When we have the snake, we'll bring it here, and then we'll take off."

"Oh no. I'm going with you. You've already gotten yourself into enough trouble, Wolfe. Somebody needs to be thinking clearly."

Sam said, "Technically, if I'm going to be your lawyer, it's better for me not to actually witness your crime. I'll stay here."

"Sam, just get in the driver's seat, and be prepared to race away when we get here, okay?" Wolfe looked at Oliver. "Are you going to be okay? You look distressed."

Oliver wiped the sweat off his top lip. "I'm fine. Let's just get this over with."

"Follow me," Wolfe said, and he started running toward the house. But he had to slow down because Oliver couldn't keep up. When they made it to the north side of the house, Oliver was wheezing.

"Just give me a sec," he said, trying to catch his breath.

Wolfe looked at his watch. "Come on. Butch is waiting." Wolfe and Oliver slid along the wall and then around the corner. There, waiting by the basement window, was Butch. His eyes widened as he noticed Oliver.

"What is going on?" Butch demanded. "You're four minutes and five seconds late, *and* you bring someone with you?"

"It's a long story," Wolfe said. "We can trust Oliver. And he might come in handy." There was no need to mention Sam at the moment.

Butch shook his head. "You're a disaster, Wolfe. Come on, time's wasting. We've got to get in there." He held up a laundry sack. "This is what we're going to put the snake in. I'm hoping the snake is hungry, or else we may not get it to go in by itself, in which case we're going to have to pick it up and put it in. There's a small mouse at the bottom."

Wolfe felt lightheaded.

"You," Butch said, pointing to Oliver, "stay out here. We'll lift the snake up to you and through the window, and you pull it through. When we're all out, we'll go. I'm assuming you brought a car, Wolfe?"

"Yes. It's Oliver's."

"Fine. Whatever." Butch slowly pried the window open. Looking around one more time, he then turned on his belly, slid backward, and disappeared inside the window. "Come on, Wolfe!"

Wolfe tried to get control of his nerves. And he wasn't sure what he was more nervous about: being caught by the farmer or the snake. Either way, it was going to be hard to explain it all to Ainsley. After all, he'd given her the indication that he trusted her to handle the situation with Melb, and now he was taking it into his own hands.

"Wolfe! Come on!" Butch called from the basement.

"You'd better go," Oliver said.

Wolfe knelt, then flopped over to his belly and slid backward. He was much taller than Butch, but he still managed, unfortunately, to fit through the window easily. The ground was only inches from his feet when he slid through, and he dropped down. Butch was over near the corner.

"He's still there!" Butch said. He turned to Wolfe. "Walk with your feet flat. That will cause much less vibration."

Wolfe approached, feeling awkward about his attempt at the non-tiptoe approach. It didn't matter, because he was sure his pounding heart vibrated everything else. Butch was removing the feed sacks. Then he beckoned Wolfe closer. "You got to come look at this. The two heads! Amazing!"

Wolfe put on his "how interesting" expression, which he'd used often at literary parties. He peered over the remaining sacks, willing himself not to gasp. It was hard. Bob and Fred, with their innocently average names, were nothing of the sort. "Weird," Wolfe whispered. Then he drew back.

"Okay, I'm going to set up the sack over here," he said, pointing four feet to the right. "I've got to rig it so it stays open a bit. When he smells that mouse, he's going to go right for it."

Wolfe checked his watch. They seemed to be doing okay on time, if Butch was right about their schedule. Butch set his stopwatch. "We'll give him ten minutes, and then we're going to have to force him in there."

Alfred was not quite as smooth as he would've liked to be, but he thought he did a fairly good job communicating Doris's story in a way that shouted *bestseller* while keeping it firmly planted in its literary roots. Alfred was a master at reading body language, and he watched both men carefully as he touched on different points.

For example, they seemed to lean forward as he was describing the premise of the book. But when he attempted to show the conservative writing style, by pointing out such things as death by bizarre mattress incident, they looked down in a more uncomfortable state. By the end of it all, though, they did seem genuinely interested.

Neil said, "Alfred, you may have the wrong impression about what kind of publishing we do. We're out to tell a good story. Sure we have boundaries, but they're boundaries that can easily be worked around with a bit of creativity. I think Ms. Ford could certainly come up with some better ways to kill off a character."

"That being said," Mike added, "it's a very promising story. And looking over these sample chapters, her writing style is absolutely magnificent."

"Real talent," Neil said. "I think we should take this to committee, see what happens."

Alfred smiled broadly. "That is great news. I think you'll be delighted with her. She is really a nice person, too."

"Good," said Mike. "Alfred, I must say, I'm curious about your other clients. Most agents work with many writers. You're new to the business, but do you only have two clients?"

Alfred folded his fingers together calmly. This was going to take finesse. "It is true that I only have two at the moment, but I am selective about my clientele. I can tell you that in a couple of weeks, I feel sure that I am going to be representing some of the biggest names in religious publishing. Some of these people have been on the bestsellers list numerous times, for weeks at a time. I'm in the process of acquiring them even as we speak." Alfred hesitated, knowing the next move could be considered a bit tacky, but he was feeling a good rapport with these fellows. This could be the thing that definitively tipped the scales in his favor. He did not want them to think of him as a two-hit wonder. He took a piece of paper out of his briefcase and slid it toward them. "These are just a few of the writers I intend to eventually represent."

Mike took the paper and looked it over. By the surprised look on his face, Alfred could only guess he was thoroughly impressed. Mike handed the paper to Neil. Neil, however, didn't look surprised. He was frowning, and then looked to be suppressing a smile.

"A. W. Tozer. Oswald Chambers. Francis Schaeffer. Charles Spurgeon." Neil glanced up, and his cheeks were turning a little red.

Alfred remained steady. They doubted him, but then again, they didn't know how capable he was of doing the impossible.

"Alfred," Neil said. "These men are dead."

CHAPTER 21

"THE SNAKE'S NOT MOVING," Butch reported for the fifth time. Wolfe was standing nearby, silently praying that God would look past his criminal activity and intervene by pushing that snake into the sack. But his prayers seemed to be bouncing off the thick concrete walls of the basement. "We're going to have to go in."

"Go in where?"

"Go in, as in take control," Butch said. He checked his watch. "We don't have a lot of time to spare. You ready?"

"No I'm not ready!"

"Wolfe, we've already lost four minutes. We don't have the time. Now come over here and help me pick it up."

This guy was unbelievable! But Wolfe watched in awe as Butch moved the rest of the bags to fully expose the snake. "I'll grab up here, you grab toward the back. You'll have to try to anchor it, keep it steady. We'll see how much Bob and Fred like to be picked up." Butch stepped forward, clearly expecting Wolfe to follow.

Wolfe's feet felt as heavy as feed sacks. He glanced back, and Oliver was on his stomach, his face peering through the window. He looked like he was about to be sick.

Of all the horror scenes he'd written, this topped everything. He hadn't touched a snake since his middle school biology class. Bob and Fred, seeming to sense his fear, raised both heads and looked right at him. Behind him, Oliver gasped.

"Come on, Wolfe," Butch said. "Let's go! Get a grip. They're sensing you're scared."

Wolfe clenched his jaw and shuffled forward, because he couldn't lift his feet.

"Move slowly, very slow movements," Butch instructed. "I'll grab the upper part of the body first, and when that is secured, then you take the back part."

Wolfe moved into position. Nausea swirled in his stomach. Bob's tongue was flicking. Fred just looked observant. Wolfe wiped the sweat off his upper lip, grimaced, and reached for the thick snake. Behind him, Oliver was making noises Wolfe wished he could, including girlish whimpers.

"Good," Butch said. "Now, hold this position. I want to see what they do."

Surprisingly, Bob and Fred just looked around, as if wondering why they were suddenly two feet off the ground. But neither looked to be an imminent threat. Butch looked back at Wolfe and smiled. Wolfe managed to smile back. He was conquering a fear. It felt good.

"Okay," Butch said, after a moment, "let's see if we can get them into the sack."

"You think they'll go willingly?"

"There's a mouse in there, plus it's dark and cool, so they'll be drawn in."

"Tell me what to do."

"Just control the tail end. Keep it steady." Butch stepped forward a bit, and said, "I'm trying not to look into those four eyes. That's really freaking me out."

Wolfe chuckled. Perhaps there was an element of normalcy in Butch after all.

"Holding the sack open," Butch said, as if Wolfe couldn't see for himself what was going on. But he kept silent. "Sliding the heads in. There we go. Good boys. See, they like it."

Wolfe couldn't help but notice that it was that kind of innocently optimistic line that would always get one of his characters killed off. *See? There's nothing to be afraid of.* And that would seal their doom.

But surprisingly, Bob and Fred went into the bag easily. Wolfe held the tail, then helped the snake on in. Once it was inside, Butch drew up the strings that closed the bag. Both men let out a huge sigh of relief. Butch stuck out his hand for Wolfe to shake and said, "Well done." Pride swelled in Wolfe's chest.

"Okay, let's hoist this through the window and get out of here. Gordon and Alda could be back any minute. Help me put the feed sacks back."

They stacked them, then Butch carried the sack with Bob and Fred over to the window. "You're taller, so you're going to have to hand this up to Oliver."

"Me?" Oliver gasped. "I don't think so."

"It's in the laundry sack, Oliver. He can't bite you. And boa bites aren't fatal anyway," Butch said.

"However, Melb's can be." Wolfe smiled a little.

"Oh, all right. Hand it up." Wolfe hoisted the bag up, and Oliver grabbed it and pulled it through the window.

"Wolfe, you're going to have to help me up, and then move a box over, and we'll pull you through."

Wolfe lifted Butch by the foot, and he crawled through. Then Wolfe went to get a small box to give him the extra inches he needed. As he was pulling himself through the window, Butch said, "Hurry! I hear a car coming."

Wolfe looked toward the gravel road but didn't see anything. He scrambled through the window and got to his feet.

"Come on!" Butch said, and the three men raced toward the group of trees where Oliver had parked the station wagon. "Hurry, boys!"

As they were running, the snake juggling by Butch's side, Wolfe was trying to decide how best to break the news to Butch about Sam. But then Butch stopped in his tracks, and Wolfe and Oliver did, too.

"What's wrong?" Wolfe asked.

Butch turned back to the house. In the distance, a cloud of dust encircled a truck as it headed for the farmhouse. "The window. We forgot to close it."

"Come on, we gotta go," Wolfe urged.

"No. I have to go close it. I don't want them to suspect anything." Butch took a deep breath and handed the sack to Wolfe. "You go. Get the snake out of here. I'm going to go shut the window. I'll meet you back at Oliver's house."

"How are you going to get back?"

"The same way I came, Wolfe. Now go."

Wolfe and Oliver took off. Wolfe glanced back once to find Butch edging carefully toward the farmhouse. They finally reached the car, where Sam stood leaning against the door.

"Sam!" Oliver huffed. "Open the hatch! It's the button conveniently located by the driver's seat."

The back door of the station wagon flipped open, and Wolfe put the snake in the back.

The three men, including Sam, stood catching their breath.

"I hope Butch will be okay," Oliver said.

"He will be." Wolfe looked at the car. "Who's going to sit in the backseat…in front of the snake?"

Each man was shaking his head vigorously.

"I'm in front," said Sam.

"Me too," said Oliver.

"I'm not sitting anywhere near that snake," said Wolfe.

Oliver smiled. "Well, luckily for us, this particular model of station wagon will fit three adult men comfortably up front. Plus everyone gets a cup holder."

Melb folded the last of her clothes and closed her suitcase. It was going to be hard leaving this comfortable though warm house. If she didn't know better, she might think she was living with a couple of reptiles, the way they had the heat cranked. But Ainsley was right. It was time for her to face reality.

And she was up for it. For the first time in weeks she felt energized, including a tingle of excitement for the baby. She was also starting to crave healthier foods, like chicken-fried steak instead of chocolate cake. So maybe there was something to Ainsley's obsession with health food. Ainsley told her that if she listened carefully, her body would tell her exactly what it was needing. Right now it was french fries.

But she didn't have the time. She had to get packed and get back to the house. She wanted to surprise Oliver. She knew he was missing home and that work had been hard on him lately. She intended to go home and prepare a big dinner. Carrying her suitcase, she walked downstairs.

But she was surprised to find Ainsley crying in the kitchen.

"Ainsley?" Melb touched her shoulder.

Ainsley jumped and then buried her face in her hands.

"Oh, honey, don't cry. We're still going to see each other. Seriously. There's going to be plenty of time for us."

Ainsley rolled her face sideways to look at Melb. "That's not why I'm crying."

"Oh."

Ainsley sat up and wiped the tears off her cheeks. "Melb, I'm feeling so inadequate. I've never had a self-esteem problem my whole life. Even when my mother died, Dad gave me so much attention and love that I've never doubted myself one day in my life. But now I wonder if I've just been fooling myself all these years."

"How so?"

"I just always thought I was really good at what I do, you know? But now I'm seeing that maybe I'm not quite as good as I thought."

"Honey, you're the best cook I know."

"But I'm talking about the complete package. Sure, I can cook. But can I cook with the proper makeup on?"

Melb was lost. And somewhat distracted by the pastry left on the table. She tried to focus back on Ainsley.

"Honey, I'm sorry, I'm not following."

"There's a new woman in town."

Melb perked up. "A new woman?"

"You've been on bed rest, so you probably haven't seen her. But she's…she's…"

"What?"

"Perfect."

"How so?"

"In every way, Melb. Her hair, her makeup, her clothes, her son, her husband, her car. You should see how she carries herself. It's confident but not snobby." Ainsley sniffled. "Melb, have you ever met someone that you consider a better version of yourself?"

Melb thought for a moment. "I guess had I had a chance to meet her, Princess Di."

"Right," Ainsley sighed. She blotted her face and then offered a smile. It was the same smile she plastered on her face right before she was about to offer a diced vegetable. "Listen, Melb, I'm really proud of you. I think that every day this baby is inside you, you're going to grow to love him or her more and more."

"I feel good," Melb said. "I'm going to go home, clean up the house, and enter back into my world. It's going to be hard, but if I hurry, I can make it back in time to see my soap!"

Ainsley laughed.

"Ainsley, listen, whoever this woman is, whatever she's like, I can't imagine her being more warm or kind than you are." Melb reached out and squeezed her into a hug. "Keep your head high. I know one thing is for sure. She can't make a pastry like you can. You're the absolute best! Can I take the rest of this home?"

"Sure," Ainsley smiled, and pulled out the tinfoil.

"I'll load the car. Back home I go!"

Comfortably seat three grown men was a bit of an overstatement. They sat shoulder to shoulder as Oliver drove back toward town. Sam sat in the middle, and Wolfe was on the outside.

"I'm sorry to take you away from work like this," Wolfe said. "I know you've got that big car thing going on down there, and it's probably a nightmare to leave."

"I made it up. There is no big thing going on at the lot. I just couldn't be around Melb anymore. She was driving me crazy. I thought I was literally going to go insane. I knew Melb was in good hands with Ainsley, so I gave myself a little break."

"Are you and Melb okay?"

"You know how when you open the refrigerator, and you see a plastic bowl of leftover spaghetti and meatballs, you get all excited because it's exactly what you were craving? You open it up, and to your surprise, it's not spaghetti and meatballs, it's chicken marinara. You love chicken marinara. It's one of your favorites. But you thought you were getting spaghetti and meatballs, so you're trying to adjust your taste buds for the new dish."

Wolfe wasn't sure he was following.

"Melb is the love of my life. She always will be. But I guess after the wedding, you start realizing you may not have married the meatballs. You may have married the marinara."

"Gotcha…" Wolfe cleared his throat. He was getting hungry.

Sam said, "Where are you two going to keep the snake?"

"At Oliver's house, just for now," Wolfe said. "Their house is empty since they're staying with us. And I'm thinking by tonight we'll be able to connect with Dustin and get the snake back to him."

"Why not just take the snake over now?"

"Butch wants to avoid that Leonard Tarffeski fellow. Says he's bad news and that he wants to capture Bob and Fred just for the black market. Butch has a weird soft spot for lost pets. He doesn't want Tarffeski around."

"I think the guy's kind of cool, with his accent and all," said Oliver.

"I don't know. All I know is that this town is going to rest easier when that snake is back where it should be."

"I'll sayyyyy!! *Ahhhhhh! Ahhhhhhhhhhhh!*" The car started weaving violently from one side of the road to the other. Wolfe hit the right side of his head on the window, and then banged the left side of his head with Sam's. *"Ahhhh! Ahhh!"*

"Oliver!" Wolfe screamed over the madness. "Oliver, slow down!!"

But Oliver kept weaving and speeding and shrieking. Wolfe managed to notice that he was staring into the rearview mirror more than at the road. Were the farmers after them? When Oliver stopped weaving for a moment, Wolfe turned around but saw nothing out the back window except a dust cloud.

Oliver was stuttering, trying to say something. Sam was pale. Wolfe was about to ask what in the world he thought was following them when he saw it. Bob and Fred's heads, slithering over the top of the backseat.

"They've escaped the bag!" Wolfe shouted.

"I know!" Oliver shouted back.

"Pull over, pull over!" Wolfe urged. But on gravel, going high speed, it was nearly impossible to slow down quickly, and the car fishtailed, causing Bob and Fred to tumble forward into the backseat. As soon as the car stopped, the men fell out.

"Close the door!" Wolfe hollered at Oliver, and Oliver slammed his door shut.

Oliver was trembling from head to toe. "Now what?"

Wolfe peered through the station wagon window to see what Bob and Fred were doing. They didn't look happy, especially Bob.

Wolfe closed his eyes and, with confidence worthy of Butch Parker, said, "We're going in."

CHAPTER 22

SAM HAD TO DRIVE BACK to Oliver's, Wolfe was banished to the backseat to make sure the snake didn't escape again, and Oliver was busy checking his own heart rate.

"I can tell you one thing," Oliver finally said after much silence and heavy breathing, "that snake is not going inside my house. Not even for a minute."

"Look," Wolfe said, "we'll get to your house, leave the snake in the car, and wait for Butch. When he arrives, we can come up with a new game plan."

Sam said, "Well, I'll tell you one thing, this station wagon handles beautifully! I feel like I'm driving a luxury sports car."

Oliver managed a smile. "I knew you'd like it, Sam. And as you saw, it handles erratic driving pretty well too."

Once they arrived at Oliver's house, Oliver said he needed a drink. Wolfe looked in the back of the station wagon. He'd double-knotted the laundry sack, and Bob and Fred hadn't moved much since. Maybe they were enjoying the mouse. He prayed they wouldn't swallow each other's heads. The men already had enough on their hands as it was.

Oliver was stumbling toward his front door, large sweat circles under his arms. Sam followed. Wolfe shut the door and prayed Butch would arrive quickly…and safely. That's all he needed—Butch held at gunpoint by Farmer Gordon. Plus, he wanted to brag a little about how he got the snake back in the sack by himself, despite Oliver's screaming unhelpful suggestions behind him.

Inside, Oliver was barely able to hold the cup still, but he managed a few swigs. "That was by far the scariest thing I've ever done."

Wolfe smiled. "But you have to admit, it was quite an adventure."

"The reason I stay in Skary, Indiana, is because nothing exciting ever happens. I'm about ready to move to the big city. I thought I'd seen it all last February. I guess not." He took another swig, then raised his glass to Sam and Wolfe. "You two want some orange juice?"

Sam said, "No, I'm good, Oliver. But I tell you, I'm seriously considering the wagon. Great handling."

Oliver smiled. "I know. And leather seats; just in case you accidentally wet yourself, it cleans up great. Not that I did, but if you did, it would." Oliver poured himself more orange juice.

Wolfe stepped to the back door and opened it. He needed some fresh air. He was worried about Butch. How long should they wait before they went after him? Butch had impressed him. The way he handled that snake without any hint of fear. No...despite his fear. Something in him said that Butch was going to be just fine.

Nevertheless, he prayed this day would be over soon.

Oliver and Sam joined him on the back porch as Oliver was explaining air bag features.

Melb saw the station wagon as Ainsley pulled into their driveway. Her heart swam with love. "Would you look at that?"

"What?" Ainsley asked.

"The station wagon! Oliver must've turned in his BMW for a more family-friendly car. Isn't he just a treat?"

"It looks like a nice one."

"Oliver is a dream. I'm going to fix him his favorite TV dinner tonight. He's going to be so glad to be home, to have life back to normal." She patted her belly. "Well, almost normal." She squeezed Ainsley's hand. "Thanks for the ride."

"You're welcome."

"Are you going to be okay?"

"I'll be fine. How about you?"

"More than fine. Thanks for being such a good friend." Melb stepped out of the car and pulled her bag from the backseat. She felt a bit like clicking her heels and singing a Julie Andrews song. Ainsley drove off, and Melb stood in the driveway of their home, taking in the smell of grass and trees. Life was good. God Himself had to have put this baby inside her. He believed she could be a good mother, so why shouldn't she? She was capable of maternal instincts, especially if she would stop watching those stupid soaps, where not a maternal instinct could be found. Yes, today was the first day of the rest of her life. She was going to conquer it without fear. She would be determined! Capable! And joyful!

Melb marched up her driveway toward the station wagon. It was a light blue... Perhaps Oliver was hoping for a boy? She giggled and peeked inside. Automatic, that was good. Looked to have "the package" as Oliver always liked to call it. Even leather seats! Wow!

She looked in the back and saw a bag of laundry. Poor Oliver. He had taken to doing his own laundry now. She didn't blame him. Ainsley starched like they needed medieval armor. Melb dropped her suitcase and opened the back hatch. She pulled the bag out and almost dropped it! How many days had the man gone without his laundry done? She slammed the door shut and marched into the front door and straight into the laundry room. She put the sack on the floor.

Her Oliver was going to have his laundry done just the way he liked it!

But it would have to wait. Her soap was on.

Wolfe was rocking back and forth in one of Oliver's patio chairs when he thought he saw movement inside the house. He jumped up, causing Sam and Oliver to stand, too.

"Butch is back!" Wolfe said, running inside. Sam and Oliver followed. But they were all surprised that it wasn't Butch standing in the living room. It was Melb.

"Oliver!" she said, her hand slamming against her chest. "What are you doing here?"

Oliver tried to contain his shock. "Oh, uh…you know…just… uh…"

Sam stepped up. "I'm Sam Bavitt. You husband here is quite a salesman. He's about to sell me a car on the first test drive."

"You must be an awfully special customer," Melb smiled. "Oliver normally doesn't invite his customers over!"

The men all smiled and nodded. Melb didn't seem to think it was odd Wolfe was there, but since he was unemployed, people saw him mostly as a drifter these days.

Melb suddenly frowned. "It's not the blue station wagon out there, is it?"

"Yes! It's a fabulous car. I'm looking forward to driving it home at a safe speed on a paved, two-lane, divided highway for my wife to see."

Melb looked disappointed. Oliver stepped forward. "Honey, what's the matter?"

"Oh, nothing. I just thought that it might be a surprise for me…and the baby."

"Sweetheart, listen. I would never pick out a car for you without you testing it first. And besides, if I'm not mistaken, you're more of the minivan type, are you not? Especially with a sun roof, automatic doors, and hidden storage?"

Melb grinned. "You know me well, Oliver." She took his arm and leaned her head against his shoulder. "I'm back, my dear. We're back. We're going to be staying here."

"At the house?"

"Yes! Ainsley and I had a long talk this morning, and I'm seeing things differently now."

Oliver glanced sideways at Wolfe. He didn't look happy.

"What kinds of things…differently?"

"Well, for starters, we need to be in our home. I need to be getting on with my life. We need to be setting up the nursery and planning. Now I know the snake is a concern, but the chances of the snake actually still being in our house or anywhere near our house are so slim that I don't think it should dictate our whole lives!"

This provoked a chorus of nervous chuckles.

"You're going to see a new me, Oliver. I'm inspired to be a better woman. A better mother. A better wife. You will never have to worry about your laundry again!"

"Honey…um, I haven't been worried. I mean, Ainsley's been doing my laundry, and—"

"Oh, Oliver. Always the gentleman. But the fact of the matter is that I saw the big bag of laundry in the car, and I happen to know you like a lighter starch. So fear not! Your laundry will be done by this evening!"

Oliver stared at Wolfe, who tried to keep a steady, normal look on his face. Sam's eyes were widening by the second. A lot of communication needed to take place with only a few subtle facial gestures to do it. Wolfe was nodding and grinning, trying not to mouth the words, *We have to get her out of here!*

Oliver turned to Melb and said, "That's um…so nice of you. The laundry, I mean. Where, exactly, did you put the laundry?"

"In the laundry room, silly," Melb said, slapping his arm. "Listen, you want me to fix you a sandwich? Sam? Wolfe?"

"No," they all said in unison.

Wolfe said, "Oliver, you know, last time I drove by your lot, I saw that amazing green minivan. That hasn't sold yet, has it?"

"Oh…um…no, not yet," Oliver said, his mock-joyful voice a little too forced, especially with the unusually large grin on his face. It looked like invisible fingers were pulling his lips back.

"Maybe Melb would like to go and look at the minivan. Now."

"Oh, that can wait," Melb said. "I'm over the station wagon. We've got plenty of time to decide on cars. I just want to stay in my house and enjoy it. I've missed this house! Your house is fine and everything, Wolfe, but it's a little big and kind of on the warm side. You should consider a heat pump."

"I think we need to celebrate!" Oliver said, throwing up his hands, startling everyone in the room. "I want to take you out, Melb. Right now! I don't want a second more to go by without us celebrating this new child! We haven't even celebrated yet!"

Melb looked amused. "That's true. And I am looking pretty fabulous right now."

"Baby, I'm taking you to the new deli and buying you a double-decker!"

Sam put his hands on his hips. "What about my car?"

"Oh...uh..." Oliver looked to Wolfe for help.

"Maybe I can finish up the paperwork for you, Oliver. I was, after all, trained by your very hand." And fired, too, but why mention it?

Wolfe could tell Oliver didn't like the idea, but nobody had come up with anything better.

"Sure. Why not?" Oliver squeezed Melb tightly. "Come on, honey. We'll take your car, and they can drive the station wagon back." Thankfully, Melb's car was parked in the driveway and not the garage. They all walked out the front door. Oliver was about to lock it, and Wolfe had to think quickly. He had to have access to the house. He wasn't about to leave the snake there. Besides, Butch was going to arrive any minute.

Wolfe doubled over, holding his stomach. "Oh..."

"Wolfe! Are you okay?" Melb asked.

"Yeah...I think I just need to go to the bathroom. I'm feeling a little..." Wolfe peered up at Oliver, who looked like he wasn't sure if Wolfe was faking it or not. Oliver looked a little nauseated too. "You guys go on," Wolfe said, grimacing. "Oliver, Sam and I will lock up. I don't want to spoil your day."

Oliver looked like he'd had enough, but he nodded. "Sure. Just lock up."

"I'll call you," Wolfe said, "as soon as the deal is closed."

Wolfe continued to hold his stomach as he watched Melb and Oliver pull out of the driveway. He then turned to rush into the house. Sam said, "I'm waiting here. I don't want to see you get sick."

"I'm not really sick, Sam. I had to do that so I could go back inside."

"Whatever. I'm staying here."

"I'm going to get the snake."

"And then what?"

"Then we'll figure out what to do with it."

"What about my car?"

Wolfe sighed. "Yeah, okay. We'll go, finish up your car, and you can be on your way." He hurried inside and strode down the hallway. He opened the door to the small laundry room that led out to the kitchen.

"No!" Wolfe grabbed his head as he stared at the laundry sack, flat against the floor. The tie was in a loose knot. Wolfe moaned as he looked around the laundry room. He tried to get a look behind the washer and dryer, but the space was so tight he didn't have a good angle. There was certainly room for a snake to crawl back there.

Then he noticed the small dog door that led out to the garage. Opening the garage door, he scanned the floor but saw nothing. Boxes and lawn equipment lined the walls, but it would take an hour or more for him look through everything. This snake seemed to be able to escape through anything, so who knew where it was now!

Wolfe closed the door to the laundry room and joined Sam outside. Sam was looking at his watch. Wolfe had already blown it with Oliver once. He didn't want to blow it a second time, and he could tell how important this sale was to him.

"Sam, let's get you to the sales lot so you can drive this baby home!" Wolfe tried his most enthusiastic expression. But all he could think about was that the snake was now loose in Oliver and Melb's house, and Butch had yet to turn up. Plus, his car was on the side of a country road. He couldn't have made up better conflict in a book if he'd tried.

Lois stepped back, framed the stage with her fingers, and extended her hand with a gesture that indicated Marlee should begin.

Marlee cleared her throat.

"Stop, stop!" Lois said, waving her hands. "Marlee, you can't clear your throat. First of all, you sound like a man when you do that. The second I indicate you should begin, you must be in total and complete character. You're not just saying lines here. You must *become* Lotus. You must think like her. Do you understand?"

Marlee nodded. "I think so. But I've got ten more minutes, and then I've got to go color my hair."

"No, no, no, no. *No!*" Lois shook her head. "Don't you understand her?"

Marlee stood in the middle of the stage, blinking. They'd been at this for two hours. It was past lunchtime, and Lois was growing hungry and irritated. Even with the extra work, Marlee didn't seem to be catching on. She could certainly stand up there and look poised, but Lotus was more than just a striking pose. She had a certain depth and majesty to her. There was the outward Lotus, but then there was the inward Lotus. Marlee so far had managed to capture the way she would wear her eye shadow, but that was just about it.

Lois walked up onstage and straight to where Marlee stood. "Lotus," she said, "would never, *ever* tell anyone that she colors her hair."

Marlee's mouth was hanging open, which of course Lotus would never be caught dead doing. Lois gently took her finger to the bottom of her chin and pushed her mouth closed.

"Marlee, it is more than just talking. It is more than just making sure that you say all your lines while standing to the left, so your good side will show. Oh yes, I've noticed. And there's nothing wrong with that *if* you are able to pull off the character. Lotus is a complex woman, with a deep heart and a heart-wrenching decision to make. Two men love her." Lois felt herself getting choked up. "Both men are worthy of her love. Don't you see the tragedy in all this?"

Marlee sort of shrugged. "I think it's cool. I've never had two men in love with me before."

Lois sighed. "Go on. I'll see you tonight at the rehearsal. I appreciate that you took the time to come by and work on it." Lois watched Marlee bound down the stage stairs, grab her bag, and disappear.

Lois walked off the stage and gathered her things. Just a few short nights until the play. Things were not coming together like she'd planned. Most everyone was doing okay, and she had to admire the cast for working hard on their lines, but beyond that, it was just a bunch of people onstage making their way through.

Behind her, she heard clapping. She whirled and saw someone walking up the aisle, emerging from the shadows. "Hello?" Lois said.

"Hi." It was Butch Parker, Sheriff Parker's son.

"Yes?" Lois said. She wasn't sure she'd ever really talked to his son before.

"I'm Butch Parker, but then again you already know that, don't you?"

"I suppose I do. What can I do for you, Butch?"

"Do you have a moment?"

"Sure, I guess."

"Good. I'm here to talk about my dad."

Leaving Sam in Oliver's office to fill out some additional paperwork on the car he was trading in, Wolfe rushed to a vacant office to call the sheriff's house. Again. It rang and rang, with no answer. Wolfe couldn't remember feeling this fretful since he was courting Ainsley. His imagination was running wild about where Butch might be. Still at the farmhouse? Exhausted from a long walk home? Waiting at Oliver's house, wondering where everyone was?

Wolfe slammed down the phone and went back to see about Sam. He had a lot to do, the least of which was to somehow communicate to Oliver that the snake was most likely loose in his house somewhere. But the first order of business was to get Sam off and running with his new car. Then he could concentrate on other things. He brushed his sweaty hair back and tried to look at least somewhat urbane.

"Sam!" he said boisterously as he rounded the corner into Oliver's office. But Sam was holding his head in his hands. The pencil was sitting on the desk. "Sam?"

Sam looked up at Wolfe and flopped back in his chair, like he'd just been told he had six months to live.

"Sam?" Wolfe scooted around Oliver's desk and sat in his chair. "What's wrong? Some hard questions there on the paperwork? Just skip over them. No big deal, okay?"

Sam was shaking his head. "I don't know. I just don't know."

"Know…"

"I'm having buyer's remorse, I think."

"What? No! No. No buyer's remorse. It's probably just indigestion."

"I'm sitting here thinking, what kind of guy buys the first car he finds on the first test drive he takes?"

"The kind of guy who knows what he wants in life, that's who!"

"It's a station wagon. Diverse, yes. Practical, of course. Perfect for hauling the dogs around. But is it sexy?"

Were they still talking about cars? He'd not once thought of a car in that way, but then again, he wasn't in the car business. He tried to think as Oliver would.

"Well," he began carefully, "it depends on what you're looking for in a wo—car. If you're looking for one that's going to land on the cover of a…magazine…then the station wagon is probably the wrong car for you. But you're a deeper man than that, Sam. You know that life isn't all about flashy…paint, and um, high-priced tires. When you add it all up, don't you want someone…thing…that you can depend on?"

Sam rose and walked out of the office. Wolfe followed right behind him, joining him at the front as he gazed out the window at his Mustang parked just outside. For a long moment, he just stood there and stared at it. Wolfe bit his lip, willing himself not to say anything. Oliver had taught him that the first person who speaks loses. And no matter what, Wolfe was not going to speak first. So in the meantime, he found himself admiring the Mustang. It was a nice car.

Finally, Sam spoke. "I think I'm more of a bikini guy." He shrugged and looked sheepishly at Wolfe. "What can I say? I'm a lawyer. So I have to compensate in other ways."

A sharp pain sliced up Wolfe's neck and over the top of his head, to right between his eyes. "Sam, please. I know it's been kind of a crazy day." He placed a hand on the man's shoulder. "But you love this car. You were so eager to buy it back at Oliver's house. You couldn't wait to get here. Remember? What was it about the car that made you want to buy it? Right then and there?"

"I don't think it was the car, to tell you the truth. I think it was the adventure. I mean, it was dangerous, you know?" Sam said, clenching his fists. "I was driving the getaway car! That was hot! We could've been shot at! Or arrested!"

"Life is full of adventure, right?"

"I'm a small-town lawyer. Not really." Sam patted him on the arm. "Sorry. But thanks for your time. Tell Oliver I'll be back when I have more of an idea of what I want. Tell him I've got my eye on the gorgeous red number up front."

CHAPTER 23

LOIS LAUGHED WITH DELIGHT. They'd been chatting for fifteen minutes or so. "Oh, Butch. You are so funny! You're just like your dad. He's always had such a great sense of humor."

"He's a fine man," Butch said.

She glanced at her watch. "Well, it's been completely wonderful getting to know you, Butch. I'm so glad you came by to introduce yourself. I've got to run and get ready for rehearsal tonight. We're doing our first run-through."

"One more thing," he said. "Before you go."

"What is it?" She loved the way Butch's eyes twinkled, just like his father's.

"Lois, I think you're a fine woman. I really do. And that's why I'm here. I just don't want you to get hurt."

"Hurt?"

"As you might have guessed, I figured out that you are seeing my dad."

"Sure. We're not keeping it a secret."

Butch lowered his voice. "It's just that...there's another woman."

Lois grabbed her chest. It felt like she'd just been stabbed. "Another woman?" Lois whispered. "No, there can't be. Your father is so fond of me. And while I realize...well, there's another man involved...your father is completely aware of the situation." Lois narrowed her eyes. "Who is she?"

"The love of his life," Butch said, a strange tenderness in his voice.

"The love of his life? But he's been forthright about his feelings for me."

"I know. He does that. He goes astray every once in a while. Sort of loses his mind. It's not his fault, really. He gets confused."

Lois folded her arms. "Confused? He's a grown man. Surely he knows what he wants."

"You would think. But my father just can't seem to let her go."

"Who is she?"

"I can't say. It's a very private matter for him."

"It's Karla Lee Tucker, isn't it?"

"Who?"

"The flirt. Hello? From the barber shop?"

"Lois, it doesn't matter who it is. I just thought it would be the right thing to do to come and tell you. My dad will always love this woman. He can't help it. You're such a lovely woman, you deserve someone who can give you their full attention."

Tears stung the corners of her eyes. She looked away, toward the stage. If only life could mimic art. If only endings could turn out just right.

"Are you going to be okay?" Butch asked.

Lois nodded, wiping her nose. "I'm not sure how I should handle this. I mean, it's going to be a little awkward considering the play and all."

"Women always get the last laugh, don't they, Lois? I'm sure you'll figure out a way to bow out gracefully. Like calling it off first." Butch was still smiling in that gentle manner...the same as his father. It gave a reassurance...a feeling of safety that went far beyond a deadbolt.

Lois stood and hitched her chin up a notch. Oh yes. She would get the last laugh. She would find a way to preserve her dignity. And the whole world would learn that Lois Stepaphanolopolis was a woman not to be reckoned with!

Sam had been kind enough to drop him off at Oliver's house. Inside, Wolfe had looked under every sofa cushion, every blanket, in every dark corner, under every box, inside every cabinet. But the snake was nowhere to be found. He figured he should direct his attention to the house, first, as that would seem the more ominous place for Melb to discover the snake. Then he would move to the garage.

Thankfully, in the confusion and chaos, he had forgotten to actually lock Oliver's house up. Because of it, he'd gained access easily, and was now hoping for some sort of miracle. Either the snake or Butch showing up would be nice. Or even Sam returning with a change of mind.

Just as he was making his way through a stack of towels in the bathroom, he heard the garage door go up. He froze, trying to decide what to do. He could sneak out the back door and run for it. Or he could do what Butch would do. With swift strides, he raced down the hallway toward the front door. And just as the back door to the garage opened, he slid into the coat closet.

He kept his breathing shallow and tried not to sneeze. He could hear their voices as they came in through the garage and down the hallway. And he was realizing what an absolutely stupid idea this was. He'd lost his everlasting mind! Except that he thought there was a chance he could find the snake first. Being around Butch had somehow induced him to adopt this strange behavior. All he knew was he was in the Stepaphanolopolises' coat closet, and hearing every word they spoke.

"I like the name Susanna," Melb said. "Or Shelly."

"I like Stephanie."

Stephanie Stepaphanolopolis? Hope she's born a genius.

They giggled, and he could hear them clanging around in the kitchen. He had a choice to make, and he needed to make it quickly. The way these two lovebirds were acting, he might be here all day. And even if Oliver left, Melb would still be here. Why hadn't he thought this through? The only thing that would work was if Melb left and Oliver stayed home. Of course that wouldn't happen! Oliver would surely be itching to get back to the car lot to see how everything was going.

He tried to listen to see if he could gauge what was going on. There was silence and then, "Oh, honey! Kiss me again!"

Wolfe squeezed his eyes shut. He was going to have to come out of the closet and now. This was by far the worst thing that could happen. Besides being morally wrong, it quite possibly could cause his death by sheer embarrassment. He could slide out, hopefully unnoticed, and pretend he was in another room and had been there all along. This could work. But he had to act fast.

His hand wrapped around the doorknob, but then he heard, "I wish I could stay all day, sweetheart, but I have to get back to work. I'll be home this evening, though." He could just see Oliver's eyebrows popping up and down. His hand froze on the doorknob. Now what? Should he go? Stay? Pray that Melb would leave too, for some shopping time?

"When you come back home, this house will be sparkling like it was brand new."

"Now don't exert yourself. You're carrying a mighty precious package in there."

Guilt swept Wolfe like a swarm of locusts. What if Melb came upon the snake? While with child? He was just going to have to go out there and come clean. It was the right thing to do.

He was about to turn the doorknob when the door flew open, and he was staring right at Oliver's pale, shocked face, mouth opening wide in preparation for what could only be a man-scream. Wolfe did the only thing he could think of. He slapped his hand over Oliver's mouth and whispered, "Don't scream!"

Oliver's breathing quickened to a rapid pace. Wolfe bent forward and looked to see if Melb was anywhere nearby. Apparently she was still in the kitchen. He could hear her humming.

"Wh-wh-wh…"

"Sshhhh," Wolfe said. "I'll explain everything later. Right now you have to get me out of here, without Melb seeing me."

"Why?"

"Trust me. She doesn't need to know the information I have."

Oliver looked over his shoulder and stuffed Wolfe back into the closet.

"What are you doing?"

"I'll get you out. But she's coming." Oliver slammed the door in his face and said, "I don't think I'm going to take a jacket today. It's starting to warm up."

"But it'll get cool when the sun goes down, honey. You better take one."

"No, I don't think so. I've got a long-sleeved shirt on."

"It's supposed to drop into the forties tonight."

"Then I guess I'll just have to come home early."

There was a pause, and then a giggle. "I can see what kind of grief a little Oliver is going to give me, can't I? No jacket, Mommy!"

Wolfe smiled a little. That was cute. Then he waited. And waited. And waited. Then the door flew open and Oliver grabbed his arm, whisking him out into the light. "Hurry," he urged. "To the garage door and into the garage. Climb into the backseat and *get down!*"

Wolfe rushed through the hallway, praying that wherever Melb was, she wasn't going to jump out and see him. When he safely reached the garage, he ducked into the car and quietly closed the door. Oliver was making gestures and whispering, none of which Wolfe could understand. But he figured Oliver was telling him to stay down and keep quiet.

As he lay on the floorboard of Oliver's immaculate car, Wolfe wondered if he'd hit an all-time low. Is this what his life had come to? Sneaking around in his friends' houses, hiding in dark cars, lying to his wife? Of course his intentions were good, but wasn't this entire thing about control? Trying to control his life, to set it back to some kind of normalcy? Maybe he was fighting against something that was supposed to be. Maybe God wanted Melb and Oliver to stay with them, if only for Wolfe and Ainsley to learn to be selfless. Why couldn't he have just let things go? Let Ainsley find her own course, instead of lecturing her about how insane *she'd* become? Why couldn't he just be happy he had a home to offer two people in need?

Cramped and on his side, staring at the back of the driver's side leather seat, Wolfe couldn't help but feel a little sorry for himself. He'd turned his life over to God, decided to stop writing in a controversial genre, and in general had become a better person. He'd of course won the woman of his dreams, and that was nothing to snub his nose at. But could he really accept the fact that his life was to change so drastically that writing would be gone forever? He couldn't imagine it, yet for months he'd found little to no inspiration to write anything that mattered. His attempt to immortalize Skary, Indiana, had been a hit with the sparsely populated town but nowhere else. His agent had all but abandoned him for fresh, hot Christian talent, if you could use the terms *fresh* and *hot* with the word *Christian*. His days were long and boring, watching his wife skip around town with complete direction and motivation that he envied.

Perhaps the only person he could really relate to was Butch Parker. Weren't they really pretty much one and the same? Whatever Butch used to be, which was still in question, he wasn't any longer, so he relied on embellished operative stories to feed his sense of self-worth. Maybe that's why it grated on Wolfe's nerves so much…because he was in exactly the same boat.

Resting his head against the back door, Wolfe stared out the dark window of the car, waiting for Oliver to come back. He'd created a real mess. He was going to have to clean it up. The idea that they'd come so far and risked so much to get that snake, only to lose it again in the very place that could cause him the most grief, baffled his grasp of irony.

He closed his eyes and realized it had been a while since he'd prayed for help. He could spend quite a lot of time praying, but he was beginning to realize that it wasn't often he prayed for help. Maybe he'd been used to going alone for so long, it was hard to remember Someone was there to go along with him.

Wolfe closed his eyes and took a deep breath. *Father, forgive me for not relying on Your strength and trying to accomplish everything on my own. Also, forgive me for breaking into Gordon's farmhouse. I feel so weak. I feel like my life is one chaotic, out of control—*

The driver's side car door flew open, and Oliver fell in. "Keep your head down. Melb is starting to suspect something. Stay down!"

Wolfe tried to lower his knees as best he could. He could feel the car roll backward and hear the sound of the garage door lifting up. Bright afternoon light flooded the car, and Wolfe felt vulnerable and exposed. But he kept down.

"Bye, honey!" Oliver said, waving at Melb, who'd stepped out the front door for some reason. Oliver accelerated backward like he had dreams of NASCAR. And before long, they were out of sight of the house. Wolfe sat up.

"That was close," Wolfe said.

Oliver was frowning at him in the rearview mirror.

"What in the world would cause you to do such a stupid, idiotic, ridiculous thing as to hide in a closet at my house?" Oliver's eyes bulged at him in the mirror and hardly regarded the road in front of him.

Wolfe was about to offer an apology when Oliver said with a sigh, "Look, I shouldn't be mad. I guess I should even be grateful. After all, you captured that stupid snake *and* sold me a car today."

Wolfe woke up from where Melb had been a permanent fixture in his home. It was a nice, comfortable couch, perfect for a midday nap. Wolfe wasn't really a napper. And in fact, he couldn't remember the last time he'd actually taken a nap. But there was no better way to deal with one's problems than going unconscious. He awoke to what sounded like bags rattling in the entryway. He sat up and rubbed his eyes. Goose and Bunny, full of worry about why their owner had suddenly taken to their pastime, had sat on the floor beside him and watched him slumber.

Blinking twice, he realized it wasn't a nightmare. His life had gotten complicated, beginning with the fact that Oliver was now not speaking to him.

Oliver had driven Wolfe to his house, ranting about how in the world he was going to tell the new and improved Melb that there was indeed a snake in their house. Wolfe didn't have any good ideas. Telling her now would only bring on hysterics. But the risk of not telling her and letting her "stumble upon it" might create a circumstance beyond hysteria, and as Oliver continued to remind Wolfe, *She's with child*.

Which Wolfe took to mean, *She's in a fragile emotional state, let's not wreck this.*

No matter how Wolfe tried to explain the situation or apologize, his effort seemed incomplete and insincere. The friendship was in jeopardy. From the kitchen, he heard voices. He rose from the couch and stumbled into the kitchen.

"Alfred?"

"Good morning. Oh, wait. It's not morning. I was suddenly confused by the bathrobe, slippers, and unshaven face." Alfred's way of implying he was on the verge of a nervous breakdown.

Wolfe looked at the packages on the table, then at Ainsley. "You've been shopping? Don't you have that big thing at the church tomorrow? Normally wouldn't you be spending your afternoon baking up a storm?"

Wolfe's head pounded, and then the realization hit him that he was also going to have to find a clever way to tell Ainsley he'd misplaced her brother. Maybe he should go back to sleep.

"Every career woman needs an outfit to accent her talents," Ainsley smiled. "To inspire her."

"Speaking of inspiration," said Alfred, "have you—"

"I don't have anything. Not even a small piece of a story. Not even an idea. I may get to do some research in jail, which might spark a few ideas, but I have nothing. Okay? Off you go."

"Wait," Alfred said, yanking his arm away from Wolfe. "First of all, you look terrible."

" 'Wait,' Alfred, usually indicates that what you're about to say has enough worth to keep the door from slamming in your face."

"I'm worried about you. Seriously."

"I'm fine. But in no mood to talk."

"Good. Then I'll do all the talking."

Ainsley pulled a pink suit from the bag.

"Darling! Fabulous!" Alfred exclaimed.

Ainsley twirled around, holding one of the outfits in front of her. "What do you think? What does it say, Alfred?"

Alfred studied it like a fine oil painting. "It says you're a sophisticated modern woman who chooses to deliberately keep her small-town roots because she doesn't feel the need to oversell her beauty."

Wolfe cocked his head to the side. How'd he come to *that* conclusion? It looked more like a cupcake to him.

"Yes! Yes! That's it!" Ainsley gushed. She hugged Alfred. "That's exactly the look I was going for."

"With perfection," Alfred said, winking. "Now, Wolfe, shall we go into your office?"

"Why?" Wolfe asked.

"I have some important news."

"Well if it's not about me, I don't want to hear it."

Ainsley and Alfred exchanged worried glances.

Alfred tried again. "I think I've had a religious experience."

"Oh, great. That's just great. Now what am I supposed to do? If I say no, I don't want to talk, I've made myself look like a complete you-know-what!"

"Because of my religious experience, I can't fill in the blank for you, Wolfe."

"Oh, all right. Let's get this over with. Come on," Wolfe said, stomping to his office. He could hear Alfred and Ainsley whispering behind him.

Wolfe fell into his office chair.

"In all seriousness," Alfred said, his hand over his heart, "I want to know if you're okay." He quietly shut the door behind him.

"Do I look okay?" Wolfe said, throwing his hands in the air. "Look at me, Alfred. Do I look like the all-time best-selling horror novelist that you once knew? Do I look like a brilliant writer? Do I look like a man who has complete control of his life?"

Alfred looked like he might answer him.

"The answer is *no*, Alfred. Look at me! I'm a loser. I've written one meaningful thing since leaving the world of horror. And though I'm glad I wrote it, it seems to be the only thing I'm capable of. I can't find a single thing to write about. Nothing!"

"You know the best stories are in the places you least expect them to be."

"I've recently been in three of the most least-expected places you can imagine, so you can take your unexpected places theory and try it on your other client."

Alfred was looking at him the way one might observe a dying dog on the side of the road. But Wolfe didn't have anything more to say.

"Okay, just sit and listen for a moment, will you? Now, first of all, I want to confess some things. I know that I wasn't exactly the model of confidence when I introduced you to this religious publishing thing. I wasn't sure what to expect from it, and to tell you the truth, there have been a lot of surprises along the way, not the least of which was how well you fit in with those people."

"Christians, Alfred."

"Right. I was recently at one of their publishing houses, pitching a very agreeable story, which they became interested in, but they wanted to know more about you."

"Like how washed up I am?"

"*No.* They wanted to know what kind of person you are. They were curious about why you left the writing world as you did, and what has become of you now."

"What'd you tell them?"

"I told them what a wonderful man you are, Wolfe. How you've changed my life, and the lives of others around you. How you stood up for what you knew to be right, and no matter what temptations came your way, you were determined to stay the course. I told them what a good person you are, that's what I told them."

Wolfe rocked back and forth in his chair. "This morning I broke into an old farmer's house and stole something that didn't belong to me. Then I lied to my friend's wife, snuck back into my friend's house, attempted to find the stolen item that was inadvertently misplaced. After that, I botched an important deal that has probably ended the friendship, but since that wasn't enough, I broke back into his house, hid in his coat closet and listened to him and his wife kiss."

Alfred's face was frozen with shock.

"But I am a good person." Wolfe was enjoying Alfred's inability to find words. "So tell me more about the religious publishers."

"Okay…for one, they don't particularly like the term *religious*. After all, as they pointed out, every book has an agenda, so there's no reason to treat them differently. And apparently they're what're called evangelicals. Here's an interesting fact for you… They don't actually put halos around Mary's head. That's a Catholic thing."

"How'd you know that?"

"I was describing what I thought would be a lovely cover for Doris Buford's book."

"Oh."

"Listen, Wolfe, the reason I came by is simple: to tell you that I think this is your niche. You're going to fit right in, and you're going to find something that works. I really believe that. The more I talk to these people, the more I'm convinced that you're one of them."

"What about you, Al? Where are you in all of this?"

Alfred paused in a thoughtful way. "A few weeks ago I would've called myself a casual observer. But I'm being drawn in. I won't lie. And it was all because of one experience."

"What experience was that?"

"Do you realize that there are several dead men whose books remain bestsellers even to this day? You don't find that in any other market, my friend. And these people have been dead for decades, some even centuries. I was shocked. I learned this after failing to attempt to acquire them as clients. Because they're dead. Dead! Can you imagine? You just don't find a lot of dead authors on a regular bestsellers list."

"So what are you saying? You're going to kill me off so I'll hit the bestsellers list?"

"Funny. And a good idea. But actually what I'm saying is that it has given me an understanding. What these people are writing, it's timeless. Fads come and go, as you know, and some of them thankfully faster than others. But truth...now that stands firm."

For the first time in his life, Alfred Tennison looked genuinely passionate about something that didn't affect his salary. Alfred opened up his hands like a book. "You, my friend, have talent. You have a gift. And I think you're going to find that when that story comes, whatever it is, it's going to fit perfectly with everything else in your life. Including your religion. That's all I had to say." Alfred stood and offered his hand.

"Where are you going?"

"I'm not going anywhere. But it sounds like you need to go to confession."

CHAPTER 24

LOIS HAD TAKEN A BUBBLE BATH to try to relax before rehearsal. She knew she had to be focused, no matter what her love life looked like. After all, the show must go on. She'd tried not to let herself become irritated by how distracted all her actors seemed to be.

Wolfe, usually the one who seemed most able to concentrate, was running around asking about Butch Parker, of all people. She did *not* need to be reminded of Butch or their earlier conversation. Marlee had apparently gone three shades too light and was now wondering if her head was creating a glare in the spotlight. Of course, Lois didn't care what Sheriff Parker was doing at the moment, which didn't look like much, except staring into space. Then there was Martin, eagerly trying to please her while letting her know he might have to leave early because of a suburban crisis at the mayor's office. He implied that the crisis at the mayor's office might be the mayor himself, but he didn't elaborate.

She clapped her hands to get everyone's attention. "All right. I want you all to know how much I appreciate how hard you've worked on my play. Without actors, this would never come to life. The success of this play is on your shoulders. One little dropped line, and it could all come crashing down like an unsecured backdrop on a fly rail. I want everyone to just relax, enjoy the process. Before we do a complete run-through, we're going to do Act 2, Scene 8. This is such a critical scene, and nobody seems to be getting it. I want you to *feel* your characters. Get in

touch with them. Understand what it is they want, why they are motivated to do what they do. Places everyone. And remember, have fun.
Marlee, get to *stage right!*"

Marlee whizzed over to the other side. The woman still didn't know
her stage left from her stage right. It was maddening. Lois fingered her
hair for one last fluff and drew in a deep breath. "Now, let's take it from
the top. I want everyone concentrating. The focus should be on one
woman. Me and Lotus. Understand?"

Everyone nodded. The lights dimmed. Wolfe stepped forward.
*"News in a small town travels fast. And it wasn't long before everyone caught
wind of Gibb's affections for Lotus. He was able to control the whole town,
but could he control the one woman he ever loved? Could he win Lotus
back?"*

Wolfe stepped back, right on cue. Marlee walked forward, humming and skipping along next to the painted backdrop of trees. They
discovered early on that Marlee couldn't skip and whistle, so now she
was humming. If ever there was a casting mistake…

"Lotus?" Martin walked in, right on cue. She loved that intense look
he could give when he played Gibb, the mayor. His eyebrows would
scrunch together. His lips would spread tight. He dragged his left foot
in a somewhat unattractive way, but overall, he owned the character of
Gibb.

*"Why, Gibb. What are you doing here on this fine afternoon? Bird
watching?"*

*"If ever there was a more beautiful humming bird, I don't think I've
ever seen it."* Lois had to add that line to compensate for Marlee's lack of
whistling ability. Originally it had been a bluebird. *"What are you doing
here?"*

Marlee tried as best she could to look in despair. *"I shouldn't say."*

"Why not? It's me. Gibb."

"It's complicated."

"I know complicated. You're talking to the mayor who single-handedly brought this town back to life after our most famous actor, the great Plum Blazey, was so tragically killed. The town grieved, and wondered what in the world would come of it. But we've rebounded, and look at us now. We're thriving, despite the fact that we're known as the town that killed the greatest actor to ever live. I know and can handle complications."

Marlee turned to him, right on cue. "Okay. It all started the night before last."

"Wednesday?"

"Tuesday."

"Well, that would be two nights ago."

"I know. The night before last."

"But it's not evening yet."

Lois had to add those lines in attempt to compensate for Marlee's perpetual dazed and confused look. She figured Lotus could be a bit of an airhead. It wouldn't take much away from the character.

"It doesn't matter what day it was! The fact of the matter is that I've fallen in love with Bart!" A bit melodramatic, but she managed to carry it off.

"The sheriff? But how?"

"The same way it always happens with you, Gibb. You're married to your job. Hasn't it ever occurred to you that you might not be the marrying type? Oh sure, you love the romance of it all. But when it comes to commitment, you really just can't manage it."

"I've been a changed man for a long time. You just haven't noticed."

"Gibb, you haven't been changed since you were in diapers."

Lois howled. That was a good line. Everyone turned to her.

"Don't look at me!" she yelled. She clapped her hands, indicating everyone should stop for a moment. "We haven't addressed this yet, so now is probably a good time. The fact of the matter is that you're going to have to anticipate some laughs from the audience. Don't jump into your next line. Wait until the laughter settles down, give it a little pause, or the audience is not going to hear the next line, which is so vital to the play. Okay?" She gestured toward Martin.

"Change, Lotus, comes from the gut, not the diaper pail. And I know what I've lost. I know that you were the perfect woman for me, and I blew it. I was selfish and uncaring. I always thought the grass was greener on the other side, and I never realized what I—"

"Martin, I need you to be more pathetic. Slump your shoulders and look like a loser."

Martin nodded, complying.

Marlee turned again, this time toward the audience so they could see the angst in her face. The angst turned out to be an awkward grimace, but at least it was emotion. *"Gibb, you will always be special to me. But I can't take the risk anymore. I love Bart. And I always will."*

The sheriff entered on cue. *"Somebody call my name?"*

"Bart!" Marlee squealed, jumping into his arms and hugging him. She'd written in a kiss, but everyone was totally grossed out by it. Bart extended his hand toward Gibb. *"Gibb."*

Gibb didn't shake it. *"I won't shake the hand of the man that stole my woman."*

"I didn't steal her. You let her go when you refused to give this spectacular woman the love she deserved."

"I'm still the better man."

"You're a good mayor, Gibb. You've done a lot for this town. But it's time to let Lotus go into the arms of the man she truly loves."

Lois sat back in her seat as the lights faded. The lines were said perfectly. The set turned out better than she expected. The lights were right on cue. But there was something not right. Something that was holding this play back from being what she'd envisioned it to be.

In the dark, Lois knew who it was. She was standing center stage with hair color 49 glowing in the dark.

Ainsley was cooking as fast as she could, whipping up batter for cookies, cupcakes, and brownies. She'd spent her day shopping, then trying on her clothes. Now she was behind on everything she needed to do for the church celebration tomorrow. She'd never waited until this late to prepare for a catering job.

She was just about to pour the fourth batch of brownies into the pan when the doorbell rang. She smiled. Right on time.

She wiped her hands and did a quick check in the oven mirror. She'd bought this little number yesterday. It was a cotton sweat suit with silk trim and a matching T-shirt to go underneath. She'd spent an hour this evening getting her ponytail to look like she hadn't thought twice about it.

Opening the door, she said, "Hello, Katelyn!"

"Hi Ainsley!" Katelyn walked in wearing belted jeans and a long-sleeve T-shirt. Her hair was pulled back on top, with a few wisps hanging around her face. At her side was a young man, who Ainsley guessed was her son. "I brought Willem as an expert taste tester."

"Willem, welcome to our home," Ainsley said, bending down to his level. "I bet you like chocolate chip cookies, huh?"

"They're not my favorite."

"Oh. Well, I've got brownies, too. Do you like brownies?"

"Depends how moist they are."

Ainsley stood up and looked at Katelyn. "A little chef in the making, isn't he?"

"I've enrolled him in cooking classes this winter."

"How…how old is he?"

"Five," she said, walking into the kitchen. "I know, he seems a lot older, doesn't he? He's in all the gifted programs."

"What's he gifted in?"

"Life." Katelyn scrutinized a plate of cookies like they were about to do something very impressive, like get up and walk away. "So tell me how it's going. It smells wonderful. They are doing wonders with those boxed brownie numbers, aren't they?"

"They're all from scratch. Please, go ahead and try one."

Katelyn picked one up and took a nibble. "You'll have to share your diet secrets with me later. How do you stay so slim? What are you wearing? A size two?"

Ainsley frowned. "No, I'm a size…size…"

"I've got a ton of out-of-date clothes you can have. So you've got the drinks taken care of?"

"We'll have tea and lemonade."

Katelyn made herself comfortable on a barstool while Willem sat on the floor to play with the dogs. "Tea and lemonade. That's cute. This town, as quaint and tender as it is, is ready to be shaken up a little, don't you think?"

"Shaken up how?"

"Don't pretend you don't see how enthusiastic the citizens are about some of the changes that have been made. This sleepy little town was just begging for a slice of the modern life. And that is the genius of a 'burb, no matter what kind of 'burb it is." Katelyn watched Willem while she spoke. "It's having it both ways, you see. You get all the perks of modern life, while enjoying fresh air, green backyards and towering trees."

Ainsley stirred her batter, trying to keep her calm. "But what about the values that keep a small town safe? Those will be in jeopardy, won't they?"

"Oh, those can be implemented in creative ways. Believe me. I lived in a suburb for years, yet we still managed to work in that root beer float you all are so fond of."

"I'm not talking about root beer floats. I'm talking about values. I'm talking about how we all look out for one another. How we know every-one's relatives, even those that don't live here. I'm talking about the expectation that when you walk down Main Street, at least one person is going to wave at you. And if you get sick or have a baby, you're going to have meals for four weeks straight."

"Honey, listen. Meals are no problem. We have a list. It assures that all funerals and births will be covered by a choice of five different casseroles, including bread and salad. We even have pre-signed cards for any occasion. The Card Coordinator just sticks them right in the mail whenever one is needed. All she needs is a stamp, which we of course reimburse her for on a monthly basis out of our Generosity Fund, where we've raised money by selling off the extra frozen casseroles at the end of the month. It's actually so self-maintaining that we don't even have to call each other anymore. Everyone knows what they are supposed to do and they just do it."

"I've always done most of it myself. A few people help, if it's a really big family."

"See? This way you only have to work on the first Tuesday of every month, which will leave more time for you to expand your company."

"Sounds complicated."

"Oh, you'll get the hang of it. I can show you how to program your cell phone to remind you that you're on casserole call if you want."

"Maybe another time."

She took another bite of brownie. "You really should try the boxed kind, Ainsley. They taste just as good."

"Oh, but you should try my lemon tart. It can fool you. It's dusted on the top with powdered sugar so you think it's going to be nice and sweet, but as soon as you bite into it, it's really sour." Ainsley folded her arms and stared hard at Katelyn. This was a woman she was beginning to not like much at all.

"Willem, honey, we have to go."

"So quickly?" Ainsley left the smile on her face.

"Tomorrow is going to be a big hit. But right now I have to go to the town hall."

"Why?"

"I have to address the picketers who are marching up and down the front steps and making reference to the devil."

Wolfe was not sure he'd ever felt more exhausted. The anxiety over the day that had followed him from place to place since this morning seemed to build with every hour. If he could just put himself out of his misery. Or find Butch. He'd managed to make it through the rehearsal saying most of his lines correctly, and trying his best to portray the ghost of a dead actor who had now become the narrator to the love life of a small town.

Lois had lectured everybody about what time call was, then had to explain that no, she wasn't going to call them on the phone to tell them to come, that it was the name for what time the cast arrived before a play. She then set out the schedule for the final rehearsal.

He was walking out the back when he felt a hand on his shoulder. It was the sheriff.

"Hey there!" Wolfe said. "You did a great job tonight. Really. You don't have the easiest part."

The sheriff shrugged. "Thanks. It's kind of fun."

"You look upset. Are you okay?"

The sheriff pulled Wolfe into a quiet corner. "I think I've upset Lois. All week I've been trying some suggestions from Butch. I don't know how, but he knew about Lois. The guy's got a sixth sense or something."

"Um…what kind of suggestions?"

"Well, you name it, I've tried it. I wore a hot pink shirt. Butch said that it shows I'm secure with my manliness. I tried to text-message her, but I got a little confused. I tried to send *U R 2 GR8,* but I think it might've read *R U 280#.*"

Wolfe winced. That probably didn't go over well.

"She's been pretty cold to me tonight. I've tried to talk to her several times, and she just kind of blows me off. I can't imagine what I've done. My only thought is that maybe she's decided she likes Martin better."

Martin had scurried out of there ten minutes ago mumbling something about picketers and the mayor's new jogging habit.

"Maybe she's just nervous about the play."

"Maybe. I don't know. To tell you the truth, Wolfe, I'm having a hard time figuring this woman out. I'm trying really hard. I swear it. But when you get down to it, I don't know what to do with her or how to make her feel secure. Things are so much different these days. Love seems different. How do I know what she's thinking?"

"I can't say I'm an expert on women," Wolfe said, "but I can tell you that I was once a really good writer, and if I had to guess, the best way to figure out Lois is to take a close look at her play."

"What do you mean?"

"Study it, you know? Every writer puts at least a little bit of himself or herself into the work."

The sheriff looked down at the script he was holding. "The thing is...I don't get this play. Nothing about it makes sense. Except the ending. Bart gets the girl. That's all I know. It jumps around so much it nearly makes me dizzy trying to figure it all out. So I stopped trying to figure it out. I just say my lines when I'm supposed to, and everything seems to work out."

"Maybe you need to read between the lines. Why is this character of Lotus so important to the play? to the writer?"

"I'm a logical man. I see things in black and white."

"For example, my book *The Empty House*. It was about an old, abandoned house that's surrounded by ghostly legends. A lonely teenager makes it his home and becomes attached to the ghosts there, who end up killing anyone who tries to harm him. Years later, I realized that grew out of my feelings of abandonment when my parents died."

The sheriff was shaking his head.

"I wish I could be of more help," Wolfe said.

"Maybe I'll give it a try. Go home and study it, figure out what she's trying to say about the world. Right?"

"That's a good start."

"Well, thanks."

"Hey, have you seen Butch today?"

"Butch? No, I haven't. Not since early this morning. Why?"

"No reason."

"He may be at the rally."

"What rally?"

"Over at the town hall. I'm headed there now. Apparently there's an uproar over flavored coffee or something." The sheriff left, and Wolfe fell against the wall, slapping his hands against his face.

The last thing Lois had told them was to get a good night's rest so they'd be refreshed for tomorrow's dress rehearsal. Good luck with that.

"Oliver?" Melb asked. "You seem uptight. Are you okay?" She'd watched Oliver move from room to room all evening, like he was looking for a set of lost keys or something.

"Just a stressful day at work."

"Look, I know Wolfe isn't the most talented salesman who ever lived, but there will be other cars."

"You can't think that way," Oliver said, coming out of the guest bedroom for the fourth time this evening. "Every car could be your last."

"Well, sit down, will you? You're making me a nervous wreck."

He stopped and looked at her with sincere eyes. "I'm sorry. I don't mean to do that. How are you feeling otherwise?"

"Good," Melb smiled. "I'm feeling optimistic about our future, very relaxed." She glanced at the clock. "Oh my goodness! Oliver, hurry! Fluff the pillows! Pick up the newspapers on the floor! Oh! Where's my dust rag?"

"Why? What's wrong?"

"The reverend will be here any moment!"

"So?"

"He's our pastor! We can't possibly let him see how we really live! Hurry! Over there! Close the door to the movie cabinet!"

The doorbell rang.

She ran across the living room scooping up everything she could. She dumped it into the coat closet.

"How do I look?"

"Fine."

"Do I look serene?"

"You are breathing hard."

The doorbell rang again.

"Why is Reverend Peck here, anyway?"

"I asked him to come by and bless the baby and our future and our...secular sports magazine! *Ahh!*" Melb waggled her finger at the coffee table. "Oliver, get it, hurry!"

Oliver rushed over, and as he was sliding it under a couch cushion, Melb answered the door. "Reverend Peck, so nice to see you. Won't you come into our home?"

"Thank you," he said, stepping in.

He was about to take off his coat. "Oh, you better keep that on. It's chilly in here," Melb said, stepping in front of the coat closet just in case he got a crazy idea like putting his coat in there.

He shook Oliver's hand. "I hear congratulations are in order, Oliver. The secret's out."

"It was Wolfe's fault!" Oliver shouted.

The reverend's hand slipped from his, and Melb gasped.

"The baby's not yours?" the reverend whispered through the frightful expression on his face.

Oliver turned bright red. "The baby? I thought we were talking about... Yes, I mean. The baby's mine. Of course, the baby. I thought you were talking about...the dust on the floor. Wolfe left the door open today."

"Oh."

"Can I get you something to drink?" Melb said, eyeing her over-wrought husband. "We're so thankful you could come by tonight."

"I can't stay long. I still have a few things to work out in my sermon for tomorrow. You two are coming to the special celebration, aren't you?"

"We wouldn't miss it," Melb smiled. She had no idea what he was talking about, but then again, she'd been out of the loop for a while.

"Your new little one will have a children's area."

"You must be excited," Oliver said.

"I'm an old man. Change is hard. Life goes so fast these days, much faster than I'm able to keep pace with. I just hope I'm doing the right thing."

"This town is changing. We've gone from famous to obscure to a magnet for all that is suburban," Oliver said. "I can't say I mind. Business will increase for me, and that's a good thing."

"But what about our child? We have a chance to raise him or her in the small-town way that we were raised," Melb said.

"I had an outhouse," Oliver replied.

Melb smiled. "Skary, no matter what it's been through, has always been peaceful, gentle, filled with nice people. There just isn't any pretense here." She glanced over at the sofa to make sure the magazine wasn't sticking out from underneath the cushion.

Reverend Peck said, "God has always been with this town. I suppose all we can do is pray, and trust Him. We don't have a whole lot of choice." He turned to Melb. "Speaking of prayer, I believe you wanted a prayer to bless the precious child inside of you."

Oliver put his arm around Melb and said, "And if you could, pray that all reptiles within twenty miles of Skary would die."

CHAPTER 25

WOLFE COULDN'T EVEN MANAGE to speak without yawning. Ainsley hadn't noticed. She was too busy fretting about an uneven hemline she'd discovered this morning. Wolfe suggested she just change. Or at least that's what he thought he suggested. Judging by her reaction, he thought he might've suggested she swallow carpet tacks.

He was sitting alone in the pew, as she was downstairs preparing something or other. They'd come early, so most of the parishioners hadn't arrived yet. The church was quiet. Misty morning light swam through the room in straight, crisscrossing beams.

What little sleep he'd managed was fitful at best. He was more than worried about Butch. The man's fanciful imagination about being a covert operative had apparently not translated into managing his way off of Gordon's land. How was he going to explain all this if Butch didn't show up?

And then there was Oliver, who'd been into the whole thing by accident and was no longer speaking to Wolfe. Bob and Fred could be anywhere in the house. Or long gone again. But Oliver had warned him not to even try to come back over. The last thing Melb needed was to find out the snake was in their house.

So here he sat. His entire world cracking and breaking like frozen glass. One wrong move and it could shatter. He was finding out that with relationship comes great risk for conflict and anger. He hadn't been out of his solitude for but a month when he'd been accused of poisoning the sheriff's cat. It had seemed the entire town hated him.

Then he'd made a mistake that had gotten him fired while working for Oliver at the car lot. Oliver eventually forgave him, but it wasn't overnight.

And now, here he sat, Oliver mad at him *again* for another flub over a car deal, and Butch possibly in harm's way. Even his wonderful marriage was proving to be a challenge.

There was a part of him that longed for the solitude again. It was safer, wasn't it? People couldn't hate him because people didn't know him. He might fail, but nobody would know about it. Now he was vulnerable. What was good about that?

A few parishioners were arriving, but Wolfe continued to sit quietly and ponder what used to be. Surely there was a balance. Somewhere.

He studied the cross that hung behind the pulpit. What would have made Jesus walk among people? People, he'd found, were unpredictable, hard to understand, testy, especially when they don't get their way, and most of the time overly emotional. Why would He even want to be around it all?

In Wolfe's view, life among people was a lot of extra work.

"Don't turn around," someone whispered behind him. So he turned around. It was Butch. "Don't turn around!"

Wolfe faced the front again. Relief and anger exchanged places in his heart. "I've been worried sick!" he said. "Are you okay?"

"I'm fine."

"Why didn't you contact me? Tell me you were okay?"

"I couldn't. I'm being followed. By Tarffeski. Since yesterday. He's here now. Three o'clock." Wolfe shifted his eyes. Tarffeski was on the other side, reading a bulletin.

"Butch, don't you think you're a little paranoid?"

"That kind of statement is the exact reason I had to keep you out of the loop for a while, Wolfe."

"You probably should just leave me out completely. I botched it all yesterday. I lost the snake."

"I have the snake."

"What?" Wolfe turned around.

Butch glanced around and then whispered, "If you can manage to keep your mouth shut, I'm going to be able to close the deal soon. But I have to do something about Tarffeski first. It's too risky right now. I've found out that this snake is worth a lot more than I originally thought, and Tarffeski will stop at nothing to get it, including posing as a religious man. Please. With that kind of shirt? You need to keep a low profile about this. Don't say a word to anyone about it. And I mean *anyone*. Do you understand me? You already blew it the first time. You've got a chance to do it right this time. I'll be in touch. Until then, keep your mouth shut. Don't even say the word *snake*. Got it?" Butch slipped out of the pew and left the building.

Wolfe turned to face the front, just in time to see Oliver walk down the aisle and give him a dirty look.

Reverend Peck stayed in his prayer office. He could hear the congregation gathering outside, ready for worship. He was the only one who was not.

After all these years, last night Reverend Peck came to the conclusion that he was, indeed, a simple man. And maybe that was why his church had always remained small and perhaps ineffective. Sure, there had been times when he'd made a difference. He certainly couldn't deny that. But for the most part, he continued to pastor a small-town church that was more their affectionate possession than their source of victory. He knew that God often worked in small ways to accomplish His bigger picture, but he wasn't sure how small a thing He could work with.

The reverend sat in his favorite chair, his fingers tangled together, and asked God to bring a new, younger man. He was too old for this. He was starting to see that life was different now. Skary had been sheltered for so long that people didn't know what else was out there. But he knew the world would eventually come knocking. And now it had. In the form of a petite blonde and her incorrigible son.

Who didn't bother to knock as she came through his office door with cheer at her side.

"Good morning!" she sang. "It's our big day! I just checked with Ainsley, and the refreshments are set to go. She's done a terrific job decorating, too. It's going to be perfectly festive. Now, I wanted to go over the service schedule with you. I've set up a stopwatch on your podium just so you can keep track of time. Ainsley's set to start the coffee ten minutes before you're finished, so we'll want to be prompt. You'll open as usual, with praise and prayer reports. Let's keep it to three each. People tend to be long-winded, and since we have the children's story time added, we don't want to let things lag, especially since Lois has that cute little puppet show for the kids downstairs after their story time. Oh, and we have the special music—"

"What special music?"

"Didn't I mention it? Our guest singer will be doing a lovely rendition of 'When the Saints Go Marching In.'"

"Who is the guest singer?"

"Me. I'm assuming you've been practicing your children's story—Noah's ark?"

All eight pages of it.

"Now, we've got two minutes, and then you're on. Are you okay? You look a little pale."

"No, I'm fine. I'm just—"

Katelyn shoved a piece of paper in his hand. "This is the order of service, just in case you forget. Any questions?"

The reverend shook his head, and Katelyn smiled sweetly at him. "We're so blessed to have a pastor like you. You are one of those rare men who stands up for what you believe in and isn't afraid to speak the truth. Now go out there and preach the Word of God! Oh, and keep the sermon to fifteen. We'll need time to hand out the brochure on the new children's ministry afterward."

Reverend Peck stood and followed Katelyn out of the prayer office. He walked onto stage and greeted everyone with one of his favorite scriptures, Psalm 20:1–5. He looked down at the schedule. In bold letters it read **PRAYER AND PRAISE TIME (3 ONLY)**. The reverend looked out across the crowd and said, "Would anybody like to share a praise or a prayer request?" He did this every Sunday, but there was never much response. There used to be a lot of the elderly praying for health concerns, but they'd died off due to poor health, and the praise reports were popular until the reverend had to point out that the intention was to acknowledge what God did rather than human accomplishments, such as a hole-in-one.

However, to his surprise, more than a few hands popped up. The reverend pointed to Elwood in the back pew. "Yes?"

"I'd like to pray that this town would be kept safe from the evil plotting of the devil."

"Okay…"

A woman stood and said, "I'd like to praise God for the way my business has picked up! Almost twenty percent in the last two weeks!"

"I'd like to ask for prayer for our teenagers, that they would not be tempted to wear anything that reveals a belly button."

"I'd like to praise God for the fact that I can feel safe knowing my elderly grandmother can call me on my cell phone if she needs help."

And back and forth it went. The reverend was trying to keep track of numbers, but he was so astonished people were actually speaking he lost count. Finally, amidst the shouting, he raised his hands to settle everyone down.

"My friends," he said, "I know this is a difficult time for us all. We see our town changing, right before our eyes. And while we can appreciate some of the modern benefits we're encountering, it's disconcerting to see things change—"

"We can't hear you!" someone shouted from the back.

Reverend Peck looked down at the microphone that was perched, as it always was, on top of his podium. He tapped it a bit. "Is this thing on?"

Before he knew it, Katelyn was by his side. "I'm so sorry, Reverend. I forgot to give you this." She stuck a plastic headband to the back of his skull that wrapped around his ear and then had a small, narrow wire that extended from the back of his ear to a couple of inches from his mouth. She whispered, "It's a wireless microphone. That way you can move around if you want. Sorry, go ahead." She was clipping something to his belt buckle.

The reverend looked across the congregation. Everyone was staring at him like he was about to say something important. He'd done a lot of preaching in his life, but never with anything on his head, though there was the time that a bird had gotten in and managed to dump breakfast right on his crown. It had really worked well into his message of the day: Living in Humility.

"Okay…um…like I was saying…" He couldn't really remember what he was saying. Something about the old and the new. Well, he was certainly a picture of that, wasn't he? An old man standing up there with new technology strapped around his head. He couldn't decide if he looked awkward or ridiculous. Either way, the service had to go on. He looked down at the schedule Katelyn had printed out for him. Story time.

"Today," the reverend said, trying to ignore the wire hanging in front of his mouth, "we're going to start a new tradition in our church." He could've predicted the few grumblings at the word *new*. "As many of you know, we're beginning a children's ministry, and along with that, every Sunday we are going to have a story time. So, if all the children will come up front, we are going to read the story of Noah's ark!"

He spotted two kids in the congregation. One little boy was already coming up to the front. The little girl was clinging to her mom, whimpering and shaking her head vigorously. The boy, dressed in slacks, a white shirt, and a tie, looked like a miniature deacon. All he needed was a plate. As he approached, the reverend recognized him as Willem, Katelyn's son.

"Anyone else?" Reverend Peck asked hopefully. "Okay, then." Reverend Peck sat on the top step of the platform and Willem didn't look like he needed any direction. He sat down on the floor with his back to the congregation, crossed his legs, and folded his hands in his lap, slumping a little. Reverend Peck greeted him with a warm smile. "Good morning, Willem."

"Good morning."

The crowd chuckled. It was a sweet moment. Maybe Katelyn had the right idea.

"This morning, we are going to read the story of Noah. Do you know about Noah?"

Willem nodded.

"It's one of my favorite stories in the Bible." Reverend Peck opened up the picture book and began with page one. "Once upon a time, there was a man named Noah. Noah loved God and always tried to do what God told him to do. He was very obedient to God." The reverend glanced up, smiled at the crowd, then looked at Willem. But Willem was frowning at him. Pointedly. Of course, nobody else could see this, thankfully, because Willem's back was to the crowd. The reverend tried to continue. "One day, God spoke to Noah and told him to build a great big ark, which is like a boat." Willem was now rolling his eyes into the back of his head and making monster faces. The reverend looked down at the book. He'd already lost his place. "Um…a big ark, which is like a boat. God was displeased with the people of the earth, because *they were being bad.*" Willem gave him an evil grin and stuck his tongue out. The reverend was sure he couldn't hide the shock of that. He cleared his throat, and looked up at the crowd, who seemed oblivious to the distraction. They were all smiling and tilting their heads like a baby was being baptized.

The reverend tried to focus. "Everyone laughed at Noah and made fun of him because of his obedience to God. They told him he was not in his right mind." The tongue was still out, but now the eyes were squeezed shut. Apparently closing one's eyes was a more evil form of dishonor in a five-year-old's world. The reverend grew angry. He just wanted to get this over with. He flipped the page.

"But Noah did not let that distract him. Instead, he listened to God's voice and designed the boat exactly the way God wanted it." Willem had now proceeded to make a gagging motion. The reverend wanted to take the kid by the collar and drag him down the aisle to his parents. But that wouldn't exactly be a great way to start a new tradition. There was already a redhead on the fifth row who looked like she feared for her life.

The reverend flipped the page and turned the book so Willem

could look at the bright, colorful pages. He was going to have to do something to get this kid's attention.

"You see, the people of the day were incredibly evil. And by evil, I mean as close to a monster as you can get. They were violent, murdering each other without reason. In fact, rumor had it that sticking your tongue out could get you beaten with a stick." Willem's tongue slid back into his mouth. "All these people had no regard for their Maker, didn't care that God had given them warning after warning. So God got very, very, *very* angry."

The heads weren't tilting to the side anymore, and Willem's eyes were growing wide. The reverend slapped the page over, just for effect. "Little did they know that their disregard for God, and for Noah's warnings as well, would lead to a horrible and violent death for each and every one of them. Now, when Noah had finished the boat, God instructed him to bring a male and female animal of each kind onto the boat. When Noah had gathered each animal and then his family, God shut the door to the boat. And then rain began.

"Inside the boat, Noah could hear the screams of the people drowning, begging for him to open the door. But Noah would not. They had not listened to him, and now it was too late." The reverend smiled at the congregation, but too many jaws were dropping for anyone to smile back. He flipped the page. Little Willem was looking a bit pale.

"So Noah and his family passed their time while it rained by shoveling manure to try to keep the horrible stink down. You've got all those animals and no place to use a bathroom, and I'll tell you what. I think Noah might've been tempted to dive off the side of the boat and into the water, you know what I mean? Noah was six hundred years old. You can only shovel so much manure before you start losing your will to live."

The reverend flipped the page and smiled. "By this time, everybody on the entire earth was dead, including men, women, and children;

puppy dogs and little rabbits. It rained for forty days and forty nights, and the flood remained for a hundred and fifty days. Luckily the rain stopped so they could get a little fresh air. The boat came to rest on top of a mountain, and the flood waters began to recede. Noah opened a window and let out a bird called a raven to see if it could find dry land, but it only flew back and forth. Then Noah let out a dove, but it came back because it couldn't find a place to land. Can you imagine the depression he was struggling with? They didn't have Xanax back then, my friend."

Willem was wide-eyed. "Did they ever see dry land again?"

"The second time the dove was released, it returned with an olive branch."

"I hate olives, but I would eat it just to be nice to God."

"The third time, the dove did not return."

"Was it dead?"

"No. It had found dry land. By this time, Noah was six hundred and one years old. He'd been in the boat for a year. He'd gone half mad at the smell, but he was glad to be alive. Then God told him and his family to release all the animals and to leave the boat. He told them to repopulate the earth, which I'll let your mother and father explain. God promised never to flood the earth again, so He put a rainbow in the sky as a reminder of this promise."

Willem looked genuinely relieved. "God's never going to kill all the evil people again?"

"Nope. In fact, He said that even though we have evil tendencies from childhood, He will never flood the earth again. And you can always believe God's promises." The reverend looked down. Oops. He'd forgotten to flip pages. He flipped to the end and pointed to a nice, colorful drawing of Noah and all the animals standing by the boat with smiles on their faces and a rainbow over their heads. "There's some puppets waiting downstairs for you in our new children's area. Go on, now."

Willem hopped up, his eyes still wide. He started to walk off, then turned back around and said in a quiet voice, "That was really cool." Then he walked down the aisle.

The reverend cleared his throat, stood up and shut the book. "Now, how about some special music?"

Ainsley worked quietly in the corner while observing Lois's puppet show. Willem was there by himself, but then a little red-haired girl had joined him. Lois definitely had a gift for puppets, and was thoroughly entertaining the two children. Ainsley had rearranged the food table four times waiting for the crowd to arrive downstairs.

Thumping down the stairs came Katelyn. "Ainsley, I don't know what to do. Reverend Peck has gone way over his allotted time." She looked at the table. "Oh no. See? The ice is melting in the tea. And look. The sandwich bites will get soggy."

"What's the holdup?"

"He's just preaching and preaching and preaching. I mean, I'm all for letting God keep me strong while the world around me changes, but people are getting hungry and we have melting ice."

Ainsley hadn't heard any of the sermon. She'd been downstairs preparing the food and drinks.

Katelyn rushed to the table. "The fruit is getting too juicy. When fruit just sits, it turns to mush."

"Why don't you see what you can do about all this? I'll be right back." Ainsley rushed upstairs and entered the sanctuary quietly, taking a seat in the back. The reverend looked like he was still going strong.

"My friends, the world is always going to offer you a choice—several choices, in fact—of who you want to be. And the world is offering this town a choice of who we want to be. Changes may be coming all around us. It has been true throughout all of history. Things cannot stay as they are. But you are fearfully and wonderfully made, capable of embracing things you fear. After all, isn't it change that causes us to reach high for answers and at the same time fall on our knees for help? If everything around us remains as it always has, we are never forced to grow.

"When Noah came off the boat, hadn't his entire life changed? Everything he knew to be true about life was now gone, and he was literally starting over, an entire new earth at his disposal. Yet God said to him, 'As long as the earth endures, seedtime and harvest, cold and heat, summer and winter, day and night will never cease.' It can seem in life that nothing is sacred. Friendships come and go. People die, people are born. There is health, and then there is sickness. Life is prosperous one moment, destitute the next. You are favored, and then you are scorned. But one thing never changes, and that is God. And His promises stand true. As long as the earth is spinning around, the seasons will come, reminding us that life changes. Just as it is true in the seasons, change has its purpose. We may not understand it now, but if we stand with the One who does not change, we will make it through any season in our life. And that is a promise as sure as the rainbow in the sky."

Reverend Peck took in a deep breath and stepped back from the podium, pulling off the gadget attached to his head. Suddenly the crowd erupted in applause. Ainsley's throat swelled tight with emotion, and she wiped away grateful tears. She stared down at that stupid hemline she'd been obsessing about all morning and let out a laugh. Then she felt a hand on her shoulder.

"Hey, are you okay?" Wolfe stood above her. She rose and hugged him.

"Yeah. I'm good. These are tears of relief, believe me. Can you herd the crowd downstairs for the refreshments? I want to go talk to the reverend."

"Sure."

Ainsley walked up an end aisle to avoid the crowd and try to catch the reverend, who was headed to his office. She hurried her steps. "Reverend. Reverend, wait."

He turned. "Ainsley."

"Reverend, I just wanted to thank you."

Ainsley noticed his hands were trembling as they held a picture book of Noah's ark.

"Are you okay, Reverend?"

"A little shaken up. I've never done that before." He looked at her. "At the last minute, I decided to change my sermon. As I was going up there. Right at the very moment I stepped behind the podium, I set my sermon aside. I'd intended to preach a sermon on…"

"On what?"

He smiled a little. "Something comfortable. Anyway, my dear, I'm glad you enjoyed it."

"No, Reverend, you don't understand. It wasn't an enjoyable sermon."

"It wasn't?"

"What I mean is that it helped me. It was a hard thing to do to stand up there and say things that aren't popular, but you did it, and because of it, I now know it's okay to be me. I can be a part of change and still be myself, all at the same time."

The reverend smiled, and then looked behind Ainsley to find a line of people formed, waiting to talk to him. Ainsley noticed it too.

"Now that's quite a change," he laughed.

Wolfe was admiring the mural on the wall—although he had an entirely new view of the ark and all its various smells now—while enjoying one of Ainsley's famous brownies. But even her perfect brownies couldn't distract him from the burden that Butch had laid on him. Oliver had made it obvious he didn't want to be near Wolfe by moving to the opposite side of the room. But if he could tell Oliver that the snake was not in his house, he might at least defuse some of the conflict.

Butch's warning seemed completely stupid, and Wolfe was growing tired of these antics. His family still apparently wanted to buy into all these tall tales. But what good was that doing Butch? Somebody needed to tell him to be himself, that he didn't need to create these lies to make himself look better, no matter what level of elusive talents he had.

He turned to find Oliver across the room. He was standing by Melb eating a plateful of food. Sure, the last time he'd gotten Oliver involved, things had turned south, despite Butch's warning to keep it confidential. But that had really been out of his control.

He needed to tell Oliver. Just for everyone's sanity. He would ask Oliver to keep it quiet, and no harm would be done.

"Where you going?"

Wolfe turned to find Leonard Tarffeski standing behind him holding a cup of punch. He smiled like they were old buddies. Tarffeski turned his attention toward Oliver, across the room. "You've been staring at that guy like he was somebody important. Is he?"

"Just a friend."

"We haven't been formally introduced." Tarffeski said. He held out his hand. "Call me Leonard." Wolfe shook it quickly. "And you're Wolfe Boone. I'm not a big reader, but everybody knows who you are." He sipped his punch. "So I haven't caught that snake yet."

"Is that so?"

"I wouldn't still be hanging around if I had."

"Any leads?"

"A couple." He looked across the room at Oliver again. "I think some people are hiding some things."

"Why would anybody hide anything? Everyone wants this snake caught."

"Maybe a few people have found out its value. Maybe you have."

"No amount of money is going to make that snake adorable, let me assure you," Wolfe said. "This town just wants it back in the hands of its owner."

"Dustin."

"Yes."

"The true ownership of that snake may be up for dispute, but I won't go into that now. However, if you know anything at all about its whereabouts, you should tell me. This snake has been aggravated and taken out of its element. I'm sure it's unhappy, and unhappy snakes are not fun to be around. Especially when they have two heads."

"I find it hard to believe that you would come all the way from New Zealand just to hunt a snake."

"Then you don't know much about snakes." He finished off his punch. "Nice church service. My grandmother used to read me stories from the Bible. I don't remember them quite like that, but nevertheless, it was a nice service." Crunching his cup he said, "Tell your brother-in-law that he can sneak around all he wants. But he's no match for a professional snake hunter. Now I have to go."

"Where are you going?"

"To get another one of those unbelievable brownies."

CHAPTER 26

MARTIN CHECKED HIS WATCH. It was almost time to go to Monday night rehearsal. His stomach was a mess of acid and indigestion. Lois, in a strange turn of events, had started to pay more attention to him. It made his heart swirl and turned his mind to mush. He'd been going over his lines all day, just so he wouldn't drop one when she looked his way. She'd even walked him out after practice Saturday night, and said hello to him three times at the church. He'd brought her some punch in the basement as she stood at the end of the rainbow mural.

But other things required his attention as well. Like the fact that the mayor had not come in to work and was still nowhere to be found. People were calling all day, worried about the fate of Skary, Indiana. For the most part, through the years, he'd managed to keep the trials of the town fairly quiet. But people could see the change coming. Some embraced it, happy to have the luxuries of the outside world right at their fingertips. Others grew more and more fearful with every new arrival.

Martin wasn't sure where he stood on the matter. For him, the town had always revolved around numbers, so if the numbers were good, he was happy. If the numbers were bad, he wasn't happy. This, however, evoked more complicated emotions. Whether numbers were good or bad, Skary was always Skary. Now Skary was becoming something else. What that was, nobody knew yet.

Martin looked at the clock and decided to gather his stuff together. He was finding favor with Lois, so the last thing he wanted to do was be late for rehearsal. She'd stressed how important it was to act in a professional manner, and take the show seriously. He closed his briefcase and snapped it shut.

"Martin, glad you're still here."

Martin whirled around to find Mayor Wullisworth stepping into his office. He fell onto the couch and pulled out his pipe. "I've been doing some thinking."

"Sir, I have to—"

"And I came to a profound conclusion, Martin. This was nearly life altering. But I think it's a good analogy."

Martin swallowed. He hoped it wasn't a long analogy. He tried to make the glance at his watch obvious, but the mayor was tamping his pipe in double-time.

"Martin, a town is like a woman." He paused, his gaze thoughtfully cast to the ceiling. "You pamper her, give her what she needs, make her feel special. Maybe put a sign up that tells the entire world how proud you are of her."

The *Pride in Skary* sign had fallen down years ago, but Martin kept quiet.

"You buy her things. Nice things. You invite people to come look at her beauty, even when you know good and well she isn't the prettiest that ever lived. But still, you love her beauty, the beauty others don't see. And you remain loyal to her. Marry her, even. Yet you always run the risk of something, Martin."

"Getting your heart broken?"

"Becoming outclassed by her."

Martin blinked. He wasn't sure if they were still talking about the town or not. The mayor puffed on his pipe. "We've got a long night ahead of us, Martin. We're going to have to come up with a game plan to get this town back in order. Gather up some notepads. It's time to do some heavy-duty brainstorming."

With his briefcase hanging at his side, and each breath barely able to fill his lungs, Martin said, "I can't do that, sir."

"Come again? Didn't hear you."

Martin cleared his throat. "I can't do that. Not right now. I have to be somewhere."

Mayor Wullisworth's eyes narrowed behind the white stream of smoke that created a haze in front of his face. "You have something more important to do than deal with a town in crisis?"

"Yes. Sir."

The mayor leaned forward. "You're going to that play practice."

"Yes."

His nostrils flared, blowing the smoke away from his pipe. "Of all things to abandon a town for…"

Martin couldn't help but smile. "A woman is the most worth it."

Lois found herself trembling from head to toe, and with every thought of *her* came another round of shivers. It wasn't that she didn't like the girl. She was perfectly fine when unattached to clever lines and unforgettable men. But Marlee was just not pulling it off. No matter how many seductive looks she threw from one side of the stage to the other, she still had not created a character worthy of the attentions of either of these men.

They'd come to intermission, and Lois was beside herself. The entire play hinged on the character of Lotus. If she wasn't believable, nothing else would be either. She'd considered the fact that she might indeed be somewhat hormonal. The news that the sheriff was seeing someone else had been a tremendous blow to her self-esteem, though she thought she'd handled it in a pretty mature way. She'd done what any half-insane lovesick playwright would do.

"I've rewritten the script," she announced as everyone regrouped for Act 2. Why couldn't she evoke those kinds of expressions out of them during rehearsal? That wide-eyed, stunned look was just the thing she'd needed from both Bart and Lotus in two separate scenes!

"What do you mean you've rewritten the script?" asked Wolfe. Always critical of other writers.

"It's the last scene," she said, and everyone scrambled for their scripts and started flipping pages. "It's a simple change. It doesn't affect most of you. If you'll turn to page sixty-four, I'll give you the new line."

Everyone was ready.

"Okay, we have Lotus coming onstage carrying her suitcase. Everybody following?" The crowd nodded. "She runs into Bart on the street. And Bart thinks she's leaving town because she's carrying her suitcase. Now, let's read the lines. Start with Bart's line."

"Lotus, you're leaving? Why now? I thought we loved each other. I thought we were meant to be."

"We are meant to be, Bart. That's what I've been trying to tell you." Marlee pretended to hold up her suitcase like she would onstage. *"I'm coming back to you."*

"You are?"

"Okay, stop, stop right there. That's where we're changing the lines."

Wolfe said, "Good thinking, Lois. Those lines were a little canned."

"The new line will be after Bart says, *'I thought we were meant to be.'* Everyone have a pencil ready?"

Everyone nodded.

"Lotus replies, *'We aren't meant to be, Bart. That's what I've been trying to tell you. I'm going to marry Gibb.'*"

Stunned silence was broken only by pencils falling to the ground.

"What?" several asked at the same time.

"I'll repeat it one more time. *'We aren't meant to be, Bart. That's what I've been trying to tell you. I'm going to marry Gibb.'*"

"Are you saying that the entire play ends with Lotus marrying Gibb instead of Bart?" the sheriff asked.

"That's what I'm saying." She smiled.

"But Lois," Wolfe interjected, "you have built the entire play around the idea that the audience is going to want Lotus to end up with Bart. They are meant to be. If Lotus ends up with Gibb, the audience will feel let down. You can't just change it like this in the last hour."

"Why not? I'm the playwright." She folded her arms and stared down Wolfe.

"What's the motivation?" Wolfe asked. "Why would she suddenly want to be with Gibb?"

"I don't know," Lois said, swinging her foot back and forth like a schoolgirl. "Maybe Gibb's the better man for her. Maybe Gibb is more interested in her. Maybe Gibb isn't seeing other women behind her back."

Everyone glanced at one another, but Lois stared right at the sheriff. His perplexed look didn't deter her.

"So," she said, "that's how it's going to end. Bart will skulk offstage like a whipped puppy, and Gibb will come onstage. They'll run toward each other. Lotus will drop her suitcase and jump into his arms. The lights will go down."

Wolfe threw up his hands. "That makes no sense. Besides that, it's the night before the show."

"Love rarely makes sense, does it, Wolfe?" she said. "Now, places, everyone. Let's run Act 2 with the kind of zeal and zest that you showed me in Act 1." Everyone dropped their scripts and walked backstage.

Lois uncrossed her arms and sat down in the front row. Now she had the tedious task of giving Marlee such severe stage fright that come tomorrow night, she would hardly be able to stand.

There was only one woman with enough hormonal energy to play this love maven, and it wasn't going to be a bottled blonde.

"Katelyn," Ainsley said as she opened the door.

"Hi Ainsley. Can I come in?"

"Sure." Ainsley opened the door wider and let her through. "Is everything okay? Were you pleased with how the event went yesterday?"

She nodded. "You did an exceptional job. Everyone had a great time, don't you think?"

"Yeah. And I think people are excited about the children's area too."

Katelyn, however, did not look excited. In fact, she looked a little sad.

"What's the matter?"

She shrugged, and tears filled her eyes. "It's hard to explain."

"I'm here to listen. Whatever is on your mind."

She looked up and tried to smile. "That's the thing. You are so nice. People here are nice. I went to the boycott the other night, trying to explain why this town needs what I have to offer. But you know what? This town is just fine the way it is. People here are happy. Do you know that? Really, truly happy. They're not always wanting more. They're just living, with whatever they have. They don't have all the modern luxuries of suburbia, but they have each other."

She caught a tear with the back of her finger. "In my world, Ainsley, it was all about one woman being better than the next woman. It's a quiet competition. Nobody really says that's what is happening. But it is. We don't have real friendships. We have packs, like we're wild animals defending our territory." She started crying harder, and Ainsley walked over to put her arm around her shoulder.

"It's okay, don't cry."

"It's not okay. What am I doing to this town, Ainsley? It was perfectly fine before, and now I'm turning it into the exact kind of place that I'm leaving. I can't stand to be around that anymore. My life is chaotic. I drive my son from one activity to another, hoping that at some point he'll be better at *something* than the twins across the street. I'm so incredibly organized with my meals, yet we never really sit down and eat together. Michael works so much that when we get this new house built, I'm probably going to be spending most of my time alone, like I usually do. And then I'll be in a town that hates me for what I did to it."

"Katelyn, nobody hates you. Sure, there are some people scared about what they're seeing, but we knew it would happen eventually. Nobody thought Skary, Indiana, could remain the same way forever."

"I sat in that service yesterday and listened to Reverend Peck. I was worried that he was going too long, that people were starting to get hungry. But I realized something. My whole life, I've been trying to change everything around me to make myself happy. The reverend talked about change yesterday. I realized that maybe what needs to change is me. Maybe I need to stop trying so hard to be perfect." She looked at Ainsley. "Take you, for example. You seem extraordinarily happy despite the fact that you wear two different shoes sometimes."

"Katelyn, listen. Everyone has insecurities. Believe me. And as lovely as this town is, we're struggling to stay on our feet from month to month. Sometimes God works in mysterious ways. And maybe what you and your husband have to offer is just what this town needs to stay afloat."

"And maybe what this town has to offer is just what I need to find happiness again. Do you know how hard it is to find matching shoes for every single outfit?"

Ainsley laughed, and the phone rang. She didn't answer it, but Katelyn looked distracted. After four rings, she said, "Aren't you going to answer it?"

"They can call back."

"Don't you have voice mail?"

"No."

"Well you should answer it. It could be an emergency."

"If it's an emergency, they'll hang up and call back." The phone stopped ringing, and Ainsley smiled.

Katelyn said, "See? That's what I'm talking about! In my world, a ringing phone never goes unanswered. Never! But you stand next to it and calmly declare the phone has no power over you."

The phone rang again.

CHAPTER 27

AINSLEY MADE HER WAY through the small crowd that was standing outside her dad's house. She could see Wolfe standing in the doorway.

"Wolfe!"

"Ainsley," he said. He took her hand and walked her inside.

"Where's Dad? Is he okay?"

"He's in the kitchen."

Ainsley rushed in and saw her father's face. That assured, stoic expression that she'd come to depend on her whole life had been wiped away by fear. He looked up, and when he saw her, he offered a gentle, reassuring smile, but he could not hide the uncertainty in his eyes.

"Dad, are you okay?"

"I'm fine. I'm fine. I wasn't here. I was at play practice."

"What happened?"

"Looks like a back window was broken out," Wolfe said. "They came in through there and sort of ransacked the place."

Ainsley looked around. Closet doors were open, the pantry door.

"Whoever did this did a real number upstairs," her father said.

"What did they steal?" Ainsley asked. "Mom's jewelry?" Her heart sank.

"No. Far as I can tell, they didn't take anything except an old, empty suitcase."

"A suitcase? Why would they take that?"

"I don't know," her father sighed.

"Are you okay?" Ainsley asked. He looked really upset.

"I don't know when was the last time we had a burglary in this town," her father said. His two deputies shook their heads too. "It sure feels weird, I'll tell you that. Knowing somebody has been in this house, uninvited, looking for who knows what. Maybe guns, I don't know."

Ainsley couldn't believe what she was hearing. This was not a violent town. They had hardly any crime. Maybe Katelyn was right. Maybe what she was bringing to this town was only going to harm it. This had to be the work of an outsider. Nobody in their right mind would break into a house knowing it belonged to the sheriff.

Ainsley tried to hold back tears and be strong for her father. "Where's Butch?"

"Around here somewhere. I think he's out looking for clues."

Wolfe said, "I'll go find him."

Ainsley laid her head against her dad's chest and stared at the broom closet, its contents strewn onto the kitchen floor.

"I know you didn't mean to drop that line tonight, Marlee, but the fact of the matter is that you did. I was once in play where a fellow actor jumped from page thirteen in the script to page fifty-four. The rest of the cast followed and the play was over within ten minutes. Now I've worked awfully hard on this play. It took me twenty years to write. The entire town is going to show up expecting to see a full-length play, and we're going to give it to them. You simply cannot flub up any more lines."

"But all I said was *we* instead of *I*."

"You've added an entire person to the scene just by saying *we*. You say *we* and everyone is looking around for the other person, you see? It's confusing." Lois folded her hands together and looked directly at Marlee. "Now I understand that probably what caused all this mess is that you're nervous. Are you nervous?"

"I wasn't. Until now."

"Let me give you a few tips. I've done a lot of theater over the years, and one thing that helps is to make sure the night before the show to think about all the hundreds of people that are going to show up to see you perform. That way you've already faced your fear, so when you actually see their beady little eyes, you'll be prepared. Granted, it's a little different when you step out onstage and can actually hear them breathing, maybe even whispering about your hair color. But just ignore all that. Your focus should be on not screwing up." Lois paused. "Are you okay? You look a little pale."

"No, I'm, um, fine. I'm just...I can't even remember the first line of the play!"

"That's because you don't have the first line; Wolfe does. Now listen, don't panic. If you start feeling your heart race, you're already up a creek. If that happens, you might as well throw in the towel. The key to being the lead actress is being calm, cool, and collected." Lois leaned forward. "Honey, let me take your pulse."

"I'm fine. Lois, please. I'm fine." She brushed the hair out of her eyes and visibly tried to gather herself. "I'm perfectly capable of playing Lotus. I've done lots of speeches at school, and I give Mary Kay parties all the time. I'm not afraid of a crowd."

This chick wasn't going down without a fight. Lois felt a little desperate. She didn't know how or when, but Marlee Hampton was going *down.*

Marlee stood and said, "Now, I've got to go so I can be plenty ready for tomorrow night's show."

Lois said, "I'm sure it will go fine."

Marlee walked toward the door. "All I care about is that my makeup looks good."

At the back of the house, Wolfe found Butch, bent down examining some dirt with a flashlight. "It's him."

"Who?"

"Tarffeski. These are prints from those ridiculous boots he wears."

Wolfe crossed his arms. "You're telling me you think Leonard Tarffeski broke into your father's house for that snake?"

Butch stood, his hands on his hips, still studying the "crime scene" around him. "I know for certain. Tarffeski's been on me like a hound dog. He knows I have the snake, and he's going to do anything he can to get it." Butch glanced at Wolfe. "The snake is safe, by the way. It's a fascinating creature to watch. I don't know how they've done it, but it seems Bob and Fred have finally managed to learn, at least for the most part, to work together. That's the only way they could've gotten all the way to Gordon's farmhouse. When they fight, they are at a standstill and can't go anywhere."

Wolfe bit his lip. This was getting to be ridiculous. When was it going to stop? Butch continued to create this imaginary world around him. Maybe he broke into his own house to finish off the fantasy. Who knew?

"Butch, come on. Are you trying to convince me that Tarffeski would actually break into the home of a sheriff just for a stupid snake?"

"It's not just any snake, Wolfe. This is a bicephalic rosy boa constrictor. Do you know how rare it is to find one full grown? They almost always die when they're babies. Bob and Fred are extraordinary. And they're worth about thirty thousand dollars."

"Thirty thousand dollars."

"There're a couple of things not adding up, though. And you better believe I'm going to get to the bottom of it."

"Like what?"

"First of all, Bob and Fred are a rosy boa. Rosy boas are native to California." Butch turned off his flashlight. "And Leonard Tarffeski claims he's a snake hunter from New Zealand."

"So?"

"New Zealand doesn't have any snakes."

Dustin had been dreading this day for a while. He'd kept Bob and Fred's terrarium up since they left, but it was beginning to become clear that Bob and Fred weren't returning. He'd refused dinner tonight, worrying his mom half to death. But he didn't feel like eating. It was time to say good-bye to Bob and Fred forever.

He touched the photograph that was stuck to the mirror in his room. And the snakeskin that was nailed to his wall. It was the first skin they'd shed for him. All around were reminders of Bob and Fred, but he couldn't look at them anymore. It just made him sad.

Two knocks and his bedroom door flew open.

"Mom, I said I wanted to be alone," Dustin said, his voice strained as he held back his emotion. He didn't want his mother to see him cry.

"There are two people to see you, Dustin. Butch Parker and Wolfe Boone."

Dustin's eyes grew wide. "Are you serious? He's here, in my house?"

His mother nodded, turned to the side, and said, "Come on in."

Dustin couldn't believe it as the two men walked into his bedroom. They both looked around and then greeted him with a handshake.

"Hi Dustin," Wolfe said. "Good to see you again."

"Yeah, dude...me too."

"Dustin, hello. I'm Butch Parker."

Words would not form in his mouth.

"Thanks for seeing us."

"Yeah...dude...I can't believe you're standing in my room."

Wolfe said, "Who? Butch?"

"Butch Parker, dude! Who else! You're so cool, dude. You're like a legend!"

Butch slapped him on the back. "It's always nice to meet a fan."

"I'm more than a fan. Are...are all the stories true?"

"As you know, Dustin, I can't discuss the details, but I can't deny them either."

"Whoa. That is awesome. Have you ever killed anyone?"

"That's classified."

"Of course, yeah, of course." Dustin found himself needing to straighten up his room as he invited the men in. He didn't really have anyplace for them to sit except for his two stereo speakers. He dusted them off with his shirt and offered them. "Well, I can't even imagine why you are here."

"I'm here to talk to you about your snake," Butch said.

"Bob and Fred! Have you found them?"

"I need to ask you some questions."

Dustin looked skeptical. "Why?"

"Leonard Tarffeski has been around here, talking to you about the snake, hasn't he?"

"What if he has?"

"What has he said to you, Dustin?"

"He told me not to discuss the snake with anyone. He was the only person I could trust. He's a professional snake hunter."

"What did he say to do if you were reunited with the snake?"

"He was mostly concerned about my snake's well-being. He said I should contact him if someone brought me the snake, because it might require medical attention." Dustin shifted his eyes back and forth between the two attentive men. "I'm not sure I should talk about this anymore."

"Dustin, I'm not sure this man has your best interest at heart. How do you know he isn't in this for himself?"

"I dunno." Dustin stared at the carpet beneath his sneakers. "He said that I had to be careful, because people see Bob and Fred as freaks. They don't understand them, so they might hurt them or even try to kill them. He said I shouldn't trust anyone but him." Dustin shrugged. "Makes sense. He's a snake lover too."

Butch leaned over, his full attention on Dustin. "Dustin, I need to ask you something, and I need you to be honest with me."

Dustin felt anxious. He'd always admired Butch Parker, and since he was a little kid had heard the stories about him. But Leonard's words kept ringing in his ears. *Trust nobody. They're out to hurt your snake.*

"What's the question?"

"You claimed you found Bob and Fred as a baby in the wild near your home. But I know for a fact that's impossible, that you couldn't have found them in the wild."

Dustin stood up, sticking his hands in his pockets. "Why do you know that?"

"I'm right, aren't I?"

Dustin didn't answer.

"I know this, Dustin, because rosy boas are native to California, not Indiana."

Dustin looked at Butch, then at Wolfe, then back at Butch. "It's none of your business."

"Did you steal it?"

"No! I would never steal anything!"

"Then how did you get it?"

"Leonard was right! You all are out to hurt the snake."

"No, Dustin, we're out to find the truth. Things are not adding up here, and until we find the truth, this situation is not going to be resolved."

"It doesn't matter anyway. They're gone for good. They haven't been seen for weeks now." He shook his head. "They don't know how to survive in the wild. They'll never make it."

"Where'd you get the snake, Dustin?"

Dustin stayed silent.

"Tonight, my dad's house was broken into. They're looking for suspects right now. If I were you, I would tell us right now where you got that snake, because if you don't, you're going to be added to the list of suspects who have a history of stealing in this town."

Dustin looked into their eyes. They doubted him. Both of them. He had a reputation to uphold, and it wasn't as a thief.

"I bought it off eBay."

"EBay?"

"A version of eBay, for pet lovers." Dustin looked away. "I can show you the receipt if you want."

"How did you get it?"

"Just like on eBay. You bid for it. This guy had found it, his son had wanted to keep it, but he thought it was too freaky, so he put it up for auction. I outbid everyone and bought it for a thousand bucks." He shrugged at their open-mouthed looks. "What? I live with my mom. What else am I going to do with my money around here?"

Butch looked at Wolfe, then at Dustin. "Okay. Interesting. Dustin, have you told anyone outside this town about your lost snake?"

He shook his head, but then said, "Besides the sloop."

"The sloop?'

"It's what we call it. It stands for snake loop. It's an Internet chat room for snake lovers."

CHAPTER 28

WOLFE SLEPT IN, though it didn't do much for his fatigue. He'd tossed and turned all night, worried about his father-in-law, worried about Ainsley worrying, worried about the fact that the play was going to be a total disaster, and just to top it all off, worried about his lifeless career.

When he wasn't busy worrying, he was going over the lecture he was preparing in his head for Butch to get real and stop deceiving people with this charade he'd created. He couldn't believe the way Dustin had practically fallen down and worshiped the guy. Sure, Butch got the information he needed from Dustin, but wasn't he exploiting the kid's idealism just a bit?

Then he'd go back to worrying, and Oliver's anger toward him consumed the rest of the night.

Downstairs, he found Ainsley busily working at making food for the play. "Good morning...or should I say afternoon?"

He laughed and hugged her. "It's not quite that bad, is it?"

"Well, I'm getting ready to offer you a sandwich instead of scrambled eggs..." She looked up at him. "You still seem tired. Are you okay?"

"I'm fine. Just hoping I don't make this play more of a disaster than it already is by forgetting all my lines."

"The play's not good?"

"It's...different."

"Hey, change is good. I'm not even making brownies for tonight. I decided to try a few new recipes, just for something different. And tomorrow, for Thanksgiving, I'm cooking a ham."

"You are?"

"I am. A ham. Me. Can you imagine? So you want a sandwich?"

"No. I'm going to go see Oliver this morning."

"I saw Melb at the store yesterday, and she looked great."

"Was Oliver with her?"

"No. But she did say that Oliver has been worrying her lately, that he's been acting strangely, pacing all around the house like a nervous cat. Maybe he's growing a little anxious about the baby. I'm sure it will pass."

"I'll see you after a while." Wolfe pecked her cheek and got in his Jeep, complete with a new carburetor, to drive to Oliver's house. Butch's warning to tell no one about the snake seemed a distant memory. What harm could it do, really? Especially if he could get Oliver away from Melb, he knew Oliver would keep the secret, no matter how mad he was at him.

He knocked twice on Oliver's door before he answered. Oliver's expression was nothing short of surprised. "Wolfe…what are you doing here?"

"Can I come in?"

"Um…now's not a good time."

"Oliver, I know you're mad at me, and I can understand that. I promise I won't keep you long. Do you have to get to work?"

"We always close the week of Thanksgiving. Listen, why don't we—"

"Is Melb here?"

"No. She's out getting some last minute items for the Thanksgiving dinner."

"Great. Oliver, there's something I have to tell you."

"Wolfe—"

"I know you're mad at me. Just hear me out. Please." Wolfe edged around Oliver into the entryway. "We're friends, and that's the least you can do."

"I'm not mad. Really. I'm over it. I know you didn't mean any harm. Seriously. We're fine."

"Oliver, I came over to tell you that you don't have to worry about the snake."

"Why?"

"I can't give you the details, but the snake is definitely not here in your house, and is in a very safe spot."

"Really?"

"I wouldn't lie to you. You're my friend, and I feel horrible about what happened. You, after all, were just an innocent bystander. Can you forgive me?"

Oliver was nodding, but Wolfe noticed a trickle of sweat. It glistened at his temple, then rolled down his cheek and under his chin. He slapped at it like it was a mosquito.

"What's wrong?" Wolfe asked.

"Nothing. Off you go. I've got a ton of things to do. Thanks for stopping by, though. Glad about the news."

Oliver had turned Wolfe and was pushing him back toward the door when someone behind them said, "Well, well."

"Oh no," Oliver groaned.

Wolfe turned to find Leonard Tarffeski standing a few feet behind them, a slap-happy grin crinkling up his menacing eyes.

"Tarffeski." The very word sent a shiver down his spine. He looked at Oliver. "What is he doing here?"

Oliver threw up innocent hands. "What? I thought I had a snake in my house. I knew if my pregnant wife found out, she'd have my head and then move me to another state. What was I supposed to do? It only made sense to call the snake hunter, no matter what you and Butch thought about him."

Tarffeski was still grinning. "Hmm. I can only imagine. So you say the snake is safe and sound, is it?"

"Look, Tarffeski, you're not getting to the snake. It will be returned to the owner. You have no business in Skary anymore. You should leave."

"It's a free country, the last time I checked. I've grown rather attached to this little town. Maybe I'll stick around for a while. Love the coffee."

Wolfe looked at Oliver. "I can't believe you called him!"

"Hey, I'm the innocent bystander in all this. Remember?"

Wolfe looked at Tarffeski, then at Oliver. This was just great. Now he'd really made a huge blunder. A scorching heat strangled his neck; he thought he might be having an anxiety attack. He quickly turned and went out the door, rushing to his Jeep.

It wasn't yet 10:00 a.m., but his nightmare was in full force.

Martin gulped down another cup of decaf while he sat in his car outside Lois's house. He'd been there for two hours, but then realized maybe not everyone in the world rose as early as he did. He'd not checked in at the office yet, but right now, he didn't care much about work. His loyalties were divided, and he knew it. He couldn't concentrate on saving the town and loving Lois. One or the other had to give.

So he'd decided to come over and talk to Lois. To wear his emotions on his sleeve. He was going to declare his love for her and make her decide. He couldn't go on competing with the sheriff, no matter how much he respected the man. Maybe it was because he did respect him that he was forcing a decision. Whatever the case, he wanted Lois to know how he felt, just in case he hadn't made it clear before.

But since he'd arrived so early, he'd been having second thoughts. He'd fetched coffee twice just to kill time and try to get a clear head. He'd chosen decaf so he wouldn't be jittery, but that hadn't helped. His skin was crawling like a mountain of ants.

And now he had to go to the bathroom. Great.

He opened his door and stepped out carefully. For two hours he'd been trying to gauge whether Lois was awake, but he'd seen no signs of life. However, the curtains were drawn, so there was really no way to tell.

It was ten. Everyone was up by ten. His stride was long and confident as he made his way to her front door. He knocked with a pleasant, gentlemanly tap and jutted his chin up just a notch for a show of subtle, manly confidence.

But she didn't come. Maybe she wasn't home. Maybe she was already at the theater, getting ready for tonight's performance. He was nervous about tonight. He wanted to do his best, but Lois was so much on his mind that he couldn't think straight.

Suddenly the door swung open. Lois was standing there in her pajamas, with her sleep mask perched on top of her head like a pair of sunglasses. She gave him a lazy smile.

"Hi Lois. I didn't wake you, did I?"

"Well, sunshine, what brings you by? You haven't been here in a while."

Martin hedged. Sunshine? She'd never called him *that* before. Maybe things were going a lot better than he thought. He tried to act cool. "Well, we've had a lot going on, you know, with the play and all."

"It's a nice night. Maybe we should go for a walk."

"After the play, you mean?"

"There you go again." She blinked awkwardly against the morning's sun. "What do you want from me?"

Martin swallowed. Was he supposed to tell her now? Like this? Well, she was asking.

"I want your love, Lois. I want to love you for the rest of your life."

"New Mexico."

"What?"

"You heard me."

"You want to move to New Mexico?" Martin frowned. "Don't you like Skary?"

"I'd do anything for you, sunshine. You know that."

Martin covered his mouth, because he wasn't sure what was getting ready to come out next. He thought it might be a marriage proposal. He'd always wanted to be the kind of guy that seized the moment.

"So you love me too?" Martin asked.

"New Mexico."

"Uh…?"

"It's the Land of Enchantment."

"Oh…right. Enchantment." Martin was trying as hard as he could to be enchanting. But was it enough? He didn't even have a ring. It was as if gravity were pulling his knee down. He kept looking into her eyes. And even in their strangely fixed, groggy state, they mesmerized him. As if in slow motion, his knee bent ever so slightly, and he lowered himself toward the welcome mat on which he stood, his kneecap landing right on the *C.* His heart pounded like the hooves of racehorses.

"Lois?"

"This is what I've always wanted. I promise I'll make you proud."

"It is?" Martin took her hand, and she looked down like she'd just noticed he was below her. "Lois, you're the most terrific woman I've ever met. I think we would make a great couple. And I want to take care of you for the rest of our lives, no matter where in this crazy world we end up." He wheezed out the next string of words. "Lois, will you marry me?"

There was a long pause. Lois was staring at a nearby tree now, her eyes thoughtful and reflective. Martin's chest was constricting. Maybe he should stand. His back felt like it was going to go out.

But then, as graceful as a gazelle, she looked down at him, a loving softness in her eyes. And she said, as tenderly as he'd ever heard her speak, "I just want the very best for you. And if this is what you want, then we'll make it happen."

Martin couldn't blink. He couldn't speak. He couldn't breathe. Had she just said yes? Was that a yes?

"I don't have a ring," Martin said, choking back emotion. "But I will get you one. I promise!"

"You can just put it in the mail."

Martin stood up. "In the mail?"

"Now I have to go. But you know how much I love you, right?"

Martin nodded. Kind of. "I'll see you tonight?" he asked, and kissed her on the cheek.

"Good-bye."

"Good-bye."

Martin doubled his stride as he nearly skipped to his car. Lois was standing in the doorway, watching him. He gave her a toot on his horn as he drove off.

This was by far the best, if not the strangest, day of his life! He was engaged!

Lois stepped back from the front door and didn't bother to close it. She scratched her scalp and walked toward the kitchen. Why was there light all over the house? She looked down. Was she in her pajamas?

She turned. Why was the front door open? She gasped and hurried to close it, peeking outside. Nobody was out there, and the street was quiet. The morning sun made her squint. She closed the door, then stood with her back against it for a moment. After a few minutes, the fog lifted.

Lois slogged toward the kitchen, shaking her head. She must've been sleepwalking. She laughed as she stuck two pieces of bread in the toaster. She'd been in the middle of the strangest dream! How odd. She'd been dreaming of the time she'd gone to her father, whom she hadn't seen in months, and asked if he would pay for her to attend college in New Mexico.

She'd almost gone too. She'd been following a boy there. They'd broken up a few weeks before she was to enroll. And thank goodness, too. She'd realized after they broke up that college was not for her.

There was no way she would've been able to engage in that kind of commitment.

She glanced at the clock. She'd overslept! She had to hurry and get to the theater. Tonight was the big night!

Wolfe wondered why confessing everything to the reverend was not making him feel any better.

"Wolfe," the reverend said, "I know you're anxious about all this, but I'm going to have to ask you to stop clawing the arm of the pew. We just refinished the wood."

Wolfe balled up his hand. "Sorry."

"You're sure you're not trying out a new novel idea on me? That's quite a story."

"I wish." Wolfe shook his head and then lowered it into his empty hands. "I feel horrible. I've made a huge mess, and I don't know how to help the situation."

He felt the reverend's hand on his back. "Listen, my friend. I've learned a few things recently. I was about ready to throw in the towel. Really, I was. I thought all these years I've been swimming upstream, making no progress, not helping anyone in any real way. But Sunday all that changed for me."

"Why?"

"I realized there are certain things in my control, and certain things that aren't. I can only control a very small part of the universe. It's so minute nobody would even take a second look at it. But it's what I can control, and nothing else. I thought this town was passing me by, you know? But I realized that the only thing that's passing me by is life, if I don't get up every day and expect God to do something big. He doesn't always work in the way we think He should. I've been praying for this town for years. I didn't expect an answer to arrive in a big coffee cup with a cell phone by its side. But here it is. And you know what? All I need to worry about is what God put me in charge of. God put me in charge of delivering His Word to His people every Sunday, and being here for the community in any way I can. I do that faithfully, and everything else will fall into place."

Wolfe was nodding, but he wasn't sure how to apply it to his situation.

"Wolfe, you can only control so much. Everything else will take its course."

"Everything you're saying is true. But I have to tell you, I don't feel much better." He kept his hands folded in his lap to avoid any more damage to the furniture.

"You know what I always do when I can't seem to shake it off?"

"What?"

"Remind myself that no matter what is happening, there are others who have it worse off than I do."

The sanctuary doors flew open, and Martin Blarty rushed toward the reverend like he'd just witnessed a natural disaster. He was breathing hard, pumping his arms to increase his speed, when he finally reached them on the second pew from the front. "Reverend," he said, leaning over to catch his breath.

"Martin? What's the matter? Is someone hurt?"

Martin shook his head and finally stood straight up. He was grinning. "I've got the most unbelievable news!"

"What?"

"I'm getting married!"

CHAPTER 29

LOIS CHECKED THE PROPS and the costume changes for the third and final time. Everything was ready to go, and all the actors had arrived right on schedule. It was here. Finally! Her big night. The only distraction had been Wolfe, who had tried to talk her into changing the ending back to the way it had been originally written. But Lois wouldn't budge. She knew how to draw emotion from an audience, and it wasn't by writing a predictable ending. Wolfe might be the expert in writing horror, but he wouldn't know a romance if it took him to dinner.

She went backstage and encouraged everyone with a confident nod, except Sheriff Parker, to whom she gave a deliberate cold shoulder. He didn't deserve the time of day, much less any encouragement. She found Marlee at the makeup mirror getting ready to apply the Ben Nye. "Oh, honey, you can't apply your own makeup."

"Why? I'm a Mary Kay expert."

"But the diva never does her own makeup. It's a longstanding theatrical tradition. It can bring bad luck if you do." Lois pulled up a stool. "Honey, I'm going to make you into a woman you will never forget."

Wolfe stood backstage, going over his lines one final time. The sheriff came up beside him. "Have you seen the crowd out there?"

"No. People are actually here?"

"Tons of people. Take a peek." He parted the curtains slightly, and Wolfe looked out. People were streaming in. Ainsley was taking a seat on the front row with Melb and Oliver. The sheriff let the curtain fall back into place.

"This theater is going to be packed," Wolfe said.

"I'm nervous," the sheriff said. "I've never done anything like this before."

"You'll do fine. Do you have the new ending down?"

"Yeah. I still can't figure out what I did to make Lois so mad. Do you think the new ending has anything to do with it?"

"I don't know. It's pretty weird. I mean, she builds the entire play around the idea that Lotus should be with Bart, not Gibb, then changes it at the last minute. Everyone is going to hate this play. I swear we may hear a boo-hiss at the end. And maybe get a few tomatoes thrown in our faces."

"Well, at least I'll be offstage for it all."

"Yeah. I end it all with some crazy explanation about her change of mind."

The sheriff chuckled. "Good thing you're supposed to already be dead." His laugh faded. "I don't know how I'm going to get her back, but I'm going to do it. I think I love that woman. I'm not kidding. It's a weird thing, because I never thought I would love another woman besides my wife. But Lois brings a lot of different things to my life. Makes it exciting again."

Wolfe wasn't sure how he should break the news that Martin and Lois had gotten engaged. Lois didn't seem nearly as excited as Martin was. When they'd first arrived at the theater, Wolfe was walking in with Lois and said, "Congratulations. I heard the good news."

Lois had responded, "I know. She's about to fall to pieces."

Wolfe didn't know what that meant, and Lois had continued on into the theater without another word.

He stood there wondering if he could manage to get himself into any more awkward situations. He'd avoided the house all day long just in case Butch wanted to come by and question him about something. He figured if he could just get through this play, and possibly Thanksgiving dinner, without discussing it, then he could find a good time to tell Butch that he'd alerted Tarffeski to the fact that someone had the snake, and since Tarffeski was already suspecting Butch, he was pretty sure this was a bad thing.

The sheriff fidgeted, looking over his script, glancing up to see if Lois was walking by. How painful this was going to be for the sheriff. Love was always full of surprises, a prime example being his marriage to Ainsley. But frankly, there was no reasonable explanation for this. And maybe Wolfe shouldn't try to come up with one.

Then, from around the corner backstage, came a horrific scream. The sheriff took off running, and Wolfe followed. As they came around the corner, they saw Marlee in a heap of tears and Lois standing there with a makeup brush.

"What's wrong?" asked the sheriff.

Marlee was crying so hard she couldn't even speak. Lois was just shrugging and trying to find a few words of explanation.

"Lois, what is going on?" Wolfe asked as the rest of the actors crowded around.

"I don't know," Lois finally said. "One minute I'm doing her makeup, the next minute she's crying."

Marlee looked up, and black ribbons of mascara were falling down her cheeks. "This is awful!" she declared.

"What is awful?"

"Look at me! Look at my makeup! I can't go on like this!"

"I'm sure Lois can fix the mascara," Wolfe said, though he did notice, strangely, she looked more like a clown than a woman.

"I can't be seen like this. Look at all this blush. And my eyes look like blue cupcakes." She looked at Lois. "Where did you learn to do makeup?"

"It looks fine to me. Lotus is a woman who wears a lot of makeup. She's not afraid of a little color."

Marlee's hands were shaking. Wolfe said, "Marlee, you're going to have to calm down. Get ahold of yourself. The show starts in five minutes."

Marlee, in barely a whisper, said, "Every woman knows a blonde with my complexion can't carry off blue eye shadow and red lipstick."

"Can't we wash it? Start over?" Wolfe asked.

Lois looked at Marlee. "I don't know if she can pull this off. She's shaking like a leaf."

"Marlee, look at me. Concentrate. Let's do Scene 5, when the sheriff asks you if you would like to dance. Remember that scene?" Wolfe looked at the sheriff. "Say your line."

"Lotus, it would be an honor if you'd dance with me."

"Double espresso, periwinkle, onyx," Marlee said, her stunned expression frozen to her face.

"Sounds like she's trying to order coffee," the sheriff whispered.

"Strike-a-pose rose," Marlee said.

Wolfe bent down to her level. "Marlee, you're going to have to snap out of it."

"Mocha blush duet," she said as she looked at Wolfe.

The sheriff said, "Somebody go get this woman some coffee! She wants some coffee!"

"She's reciting makeup colors," Lois said.

The room grew still.

"Marlee," Wolfe said, "can you tell me where you are?"

"Whipped cocoa," she murmured.

"I'm telling you, she needs coffee."

"Let me try," Lois said, stepping closer. "Marlee, honey, I want you to listen to me very carefully." Marlee focused on Lois, and for the first time blinked her eyes. "Good. Now, can you tell me what Lotus says to Gibb at the end of Scene 6?"

Marlee blinked again, and her mouth fell open an inch. Everyone leaned forward, willing an answer out of her. But after a few moments, her mouth closed and nothing was said.

"Marlee," Lois said, "can you tell me what color of lipstick a woman with medium skin tone, green eyes, and blonde hair should wear?"

"Warm tones in the brown family."

Lois turned to the crowd. "I think her nerves finally got to her." Lois lowered her voice. "I've been afraid this might happen."

"What are we supposed to do?" the sheriff asked.

"The show must go on."

"How?"

Lois drew in a deep breath. "I will be playing the role of Lotus."

Well into the second act, Wolfe was pleased. The crowd seemed engaged, and he was actually having a lot of fun. During one part of his narrative, he'd made eye contact with Ainsley and nearly started laughing, but for the most part, the play was holding up well. But then again, they hadn't come to the ending. He hoped the crowd was familiar with the literary term *tragedy*.

Wolfe stood offstage, waiting for his cue. He was pretty impressed with all the actors. Everyone had really turned it on for the performance, and was giving a hundred and ten percent. Even the sheriff had looked like he was really weeping in the scene when Lotus tells Bart about Gibb.

Wolfe closed his eyes and mentally rehearsed his upcoming scene, but was interrupted by a tap on his shoulder.

"Butch! What are you doing here?" Wolfe whispered.

"I need to talk to you."

"We're right in the middle of the play! I'm getting ready to go on!"

"It's important. Tarffeski's on to me. He confronted me today, told me he knew I had the snake, and said he would get it, no matter what."

"Can we discuss this afterward?" Wolfe glanced toward the stage. It was almost time for him to walk on. He looked back at Butch and noticed he was holding a suitcase. "What's that for?"

"The snake's in here."

"What?!"

"I had no choice. Tarffeski's in the audience, waiting to pounce on me. I had to do something. I figured he wouldn't come backstage while the play was going on."

"You took your father's suitcase?"

"It's the only way I could transport Bob and Fred from one place to the other safely. See, it's got a buckle instead of a zipper, so they can't weasel their way out unless you undo these two buckles."

"Why are you telling me this?"

"Because, like it or not, you're involved. You're going to have to keep an eye on the snake until after the play. If I'm back here too long, Tarffeski will get suspicious. I've got a plan to expose him for who he is and convince Dustin he's not to be trusted. But for now, we just have to keep the snake safe."

"But…wait…" Wolfe reached for him as he walked away but came up empty-handed. He realized his cue was ten seconds away. "Butch!

Wait! I can't watch the snake! I'm in the…" He stepped onstage and into the spotlight. He was so out of breath he could hardly get his next line out. *"As you can imagine, Lotus was torn between the two men she loved. What was she to do? How would she ever know for sure who was the right man for her? Who could she trust to watch out for her?"* Wolfe couldn't help but glance sideways to make sure the suitcase was still there. He looked back toward the audience, keeping his composure. He saw Butch slide into a seat at the back. *"Lotus was going to have to search her heart. After everything she'd been through with Bart and Gibb, she knew there was only one right man for her. And she was about to find out who that was."*

Wolfe slid offstage and stood by the suitcase. Thank goodness the show was almost over. But something told him that was when the drama would really begin.

Lois stood in the wings, waiting for her cue. She felt like she was flying. It had been years since she'd been onstage, and she was still owning the audience. They hung on her every word, noticed every time she touched Bart or Gibb, and cried when she cried. At least a few did. There was a certain energy in the room that made the impending climax that much more spectacular. The crowd was holding its breath, waiting to see which man Lotus would choose.

This was what she'd been waiting for, what every actress strives for. That one scene that would define her for the rest of her acting career. The lights were slowly coming on, and a tingling sensation rushed through her. Thankfully, it sounded like Marlee had been shut up again. Lois had to send Wolfe back there a third time to get her to stop wailing. It was breaking everyone's concentration. She drew in a deep breath and reached down to grab her prop, the suitcase. But strangely, there were two suitcases. One was right next to her, and the other off to the left, hidden a little. Why two? Had the first one broken, and someone brought in a replacement at the last minute?

The lights were almost completely up. She rushed to get the second one. It was fancier anyway, with adorable buckles instead of a zipper. Wolfe was coming around the corner just as she walked on, and he thought she heard him yelp, but she had to ignore it. She was already onstage. Maybe he'd stubbed his toe. This suitcase was awfully heavy for a prop. Had someone put a brick in there?

She watched Sheriff Parker stroll across the stage toward her. There was a certain pain in his eyes. It looked a little too real. But that was the price he paid for double-crossing this woman. Humiliation in the form of a good theatrical slap.

"Lotus, you're leaving? Why now? I thought we loved each other. I thought we were meant to be."

"We aren't meant to be, Bart. That's what I've been trying to tell you. I'm going to marry Gibb." The gasp from the audience nearly caused a breeze. She stared hard at Bart, and at this point Bart was supposed to skulk offstage like a whipped puppy. But there was no skulking. Bart wasn't moving. Why wasn't Bart moving?

She looked across to stage left, and Martin was preparing to enter as Gibb. He looked a little confused, since Bart wasn't going anywhere. The crowd was quiet.

"Did you hear me, Bart? We aren't meant for each other. I'm going to marry Gibb." She went ahead and dropped the suitcase since it was so heavy anyway and she always made good use of her props. It fell to the ground with a dramatic thud, then tipped over. Bart still didn't budge.

Apparently not knowing what else to do, Martin decided to walk on. Lois ran into his arms, and Martin swung her around just like they'd practiced. *"I love you!"* he added. That wasn't in the script, but she went for it.

"I love you too, Gibb." She glanced behind her and Bart wasn't off-stage yet. The lights were about to fade on them and come up on Wolfe, who was moving into place.

But suddenly the sheriff said, "No, you don't."

Lois dropped from Martin and turned. "Yes, I do."

"No you don't. You don't love him and you know it. You're just getting back at me. But your true love is Bart. Me. You love me."

Lois didn't have to act. She was so stunned she did the unthinkable and looked out at the audience. They looked to be anticipating the next line as eagerly as she was. What was she supposed to say?

Bart…the sheriff…whoever…walked toward her and took her hands. "I love you. And you know how I know that? Because I haven't felt like this in years. You make me feel alive again. My whole life used to revolve around my job and my cat and my family. My cat got hitched, my daughter got hitched, and my job is my job. But you are the one thing that can make my heart feel young again. Let me take care of you. Let me love you for the rest of our lives."

The crowd came alive with satisfactory murmurs. Lois didn't know what to say. Was he talking to Lotus? Or her? Or both? She looked into his eyes, and something told her that they weren't onstage anymore. This was real life.

"Not so fast!" From behind her, Martin shoved his way between them. "You can't just come in here and expect her to fall for you just like that. I'm the one who has won her heart, not you. You heard her. She's going to marry me!"

"Not without a fight," Sheriff Parker said.

"I'm not scared of you. Bring it on."

Before Lois could even motion for the lights to go down, the two men were brawling right there onstage. The audience was cheering and clapping and thoroughly enjoying themselves. She looked back at the men who were wrestling and stumbling all over the stage. With one hefty push, the sheriff shoved Martin backward, and he fell over the suitcase in the middle of the stage, causing both buckles to pop open.

Lois stepped a few feet to the side, realizing at some point she was going to have to come up with a clever line, because Wolfe looked like he'd been zapped with a stun gun. With the men still wrestling, Lois decided to address the audience. She wasn't exactly sure what she was going to say, but maybe some witty remark about middle-aged men and their wrestling abilities would get everything back into focus.

She opened her mouth, but what came out was a scream. She shut her mouth quickly, but the scream kept going. And then another scream. It was the audience. People were screaming. She turned and realized why. She started screaming too.

"Snake! It's the snake! *Snake!*" Panicked voices were announcing the obvious fact that the two-headed snake was slowly emerging from the suitcase. Lois could only think of one thing. A two-headed snake was stealing her show.

The adage was right: never act with animals or kids. They'll always upstage you. Well, she wasn't going to be upstaged without a fight.

But before she could do anything about it, a man from the fourth row bounded up onto the stage and, with one swift motion, snatched the gun out of the sheriff's holster, then grabbed Lois and turned her to the audience. Lois wanted to shriek, but the man said, "Shut up and you'll be fine."

He then addressed the audience. "Listen up. I just want one thing, and if I get it, nobody gets hurt. See that snake? I leave with that snake safely in my possession, and nobody gets hurt. But one wrong move, and this lady isn't going to make it to see Bart or Gibb. Got it?"

Lois watched the crowd cling to one another, their eyes wide with fright. She could hardly breathe.

"Now, I'm going to take this snake and move slowly out of the theater, and as soon as I feel safe, I'll let the lady go. But if anybody makes one wrong move, you're going to regret it."

The man started to bend down, but out of the corner of her eye, Lois saw something move and tackle him, causing Lois to fly forward and land on her stomach. She rolled over to find the sheriff flipping the man over and cuffing his arms behind his back. And then, just as quickly, he turned to the snake, which was hissing from each mouth, grabbed it just behind its necks, and stuffed it back into the suitcase. He quickly buckled it closed.

Then the sheriff rushed over to her and scooped her off the ground, which was no easy task. "Are you okay?"

She nodded and touched his face. He was bleeding just above the brow. "You saved me."

"I would do anything for you. Just give me a chance."

She leaned forward and kissed him on the lips. "I'll give you a chance."

Suddenly the crowd erupted in applause. People were on their feet, clapping as loudly as they could, wiping tears from their eyes. Lois looked over to Wolfe, who had the end line for the entire play. But to her surprise, he was lying unconscious on the floor.

"Oh no! Is he okay?" Lois gasped.

"He passes out at the sight of blood." The sheriff set her down and took a step back. "Take a bow. You deserve it."

And so Lois stepped to the front of the stage. She stretched out her arms like an eagle about to soar. Below her she could hear people saying to one another, "What an ending!"

"I never saw that coming!"

"How clever to use the snake!"

Lois bent forward, swept her arms in front of her until they dangled to the floor, then lifted herself up and smiled broadly at her new fans.

Throwing kisses to them, she said, "Good night! And God bless!"

CHAPTER 30

"SMELLS GOOD. Is there anything I can do to help?" Wolfe asked, joining Ainsley in the kitchen at her dad's house.

"It's almost ready. But I do have a favor to ask of you."

"What's that?"

"Can you go up in the attic? There's a box in the corner, and it has something special I want to use for the Thanksgiving dinner."

"Sure. Where is it again?"

"Just go up in the attic, and it's in the corner by the window. You can't miss it."

"Okay." Wolfe went out to the garage and pulled down the ladder. He climbed up. The attic was stacked with boxes and memorabilia all over the place. He wasn't even sure he could get to the corner. Luckily, due to the window, the room was well lit.

Trying to make his way through it all, he accidentally stumbled and knocked over a box. Papers and photographs spilled everywhere.

Wolfe groaned as he knelt to try to pick it all up. But as he did, he noticed something peculiar. These didn't look like normal photographs. And in fact, as he looked closer, he realized they were combat photos. And the papers looked like official government documents. He flipped through them and saw Butch's name, as well as his picture among other soldiers.

"What are you doing?"

Wolfe looked up to find Butch coming up through the attic door.

"I-I'm sorry, Butch. I thought you were at the station. I accidentally knocked over this box. It belongs to you. I was just gathering it all up to put it away."

Butch walked over to him and looked down at the box. "I don't keep super classified stuff here. Just some good memories." Butch knelt beside him and picked up one of the pictures. "What a story this was."

Wolfe stared down at the obvious evidence of Butch's past, shame sweeping through his heart. "Butch...I want to say I'm sorry. It's hard for me to admit, but I doubted you. I doubted this. I thought you were making it all up."

Butch smiled. "It's pretty unbelievable. Some of the things I've gone through are downright scary. They'd make some great stories if I could tell someone."

Wolfe stood up, holding two photos in his hand. "What if the stories happened to be fiction?"

"What do you mean?"

"I mean, they're changed up a bit. It's a real story, real people, disguised in a fictitious setting."

Butch knelt down and stared into the box. "Cleverly disguised."

"I could bring these stories alive, Butch. Everything you've been through."

"Some of them may sound far-fetched, but it's all really just about being human and surviving what seems impossible through the grace of God."

"And maybe half the battle is at home, where you can't tell anyone what your life is really like." Wolfe paused. "I'd be honored to be your storyteller."

The two men embraced and patted each other on the back.

"Why don't we talk after Thanksgiving dinner?" Butch asked.

"Good idea. Besides, I was supposed to be fetching some box for Ainsley. She said it's in the corner."

"I can help."

They walked through the crowded attic and found the corner by the window, but Wolfe didn't see a box.

"All that's here is a baby cradle," Wolfe said. "What box is she talking about?"

"This was Ainsley's cradle. I can't believe Dad has kept it all these years. Hey, there's a note in here. Has your name on it."

Butch handed it to him, and Wolfe opened it up.

It read, *Congratulations. You're going to be a dad.*

Martin waited by his front window, gazing out at the fall leaves, waiting for the mayor. He'd intended to spend Thanksgiving alone. After last night, he didn't want to be around anybody. It was an embarrassing moment when Lois and Martin figured out that apparently Lois had been sleepwalking when she agreed to marry him. He'd sat down with the sheriff and Lois after the play. Being the person of integrity that he was, Irwin apologized for hitting him, and told him how important their friendship was to him.

It had eased the pain a little. Lois assured him he'd been a strong contender. But when all was said and done, there was only one heavyweight standing.

Martin sighed. It had been so out of character for him to fall in love in the first place. And now he had good reason to keep it from happening again.

The mayor had insisted they accept the sheriff's invitation for Thanksgiving dinner. He wouldn't take no for an answer and had hung up the phone with, "I'll be there in five minutes."

Fine. But Martin was going to have to be brutally honest with the mayor. It was time somebody gave that man some relaxation techniques, or maybe a Valium. He was beginning to realize the mayor didn't have the capabilities to handle anything out of the ordinary, and in Martin's opinion, the town had suffered for it.

The mayor honked his horn as he pulled into the driveway and screeched to a stop. Martin pulled his scarf around his neck, buttoned his coat, and headed toward the door. The mayor honked again.

"Coming," Martin mumbled. He locked his front door and got into the car. "Good morning, sir."

The mayor growled. "Not so much. The coffeehouse is closed."

"Yes sir. It's Thanksgiving."

"Well it's rude. They get you addicted, then cut you off. Maybe we should drive to the next county, see what's available."

Martin hadn't realized the mayor was such a fan. "Ainsley will have coffee going, I'm sure, sir."

"It's not the same!"

"As what?"

"Look, I know it sounds strange, but if I don't have my double espresso with a shot of Irish Cream, I go insane."

Espresso? *Double espresso?* That's what the mayor had been drinking all these weeks? Martin laughed out loud, and the mayor shot him a look. That was it! No wonder he was shaking like a leaf all the time!

"I don't know what's so special about it, but I can't start my morning without it."

Martin started laughing so hard he couldn't stop. The mayor tried to smile but was left out of what was so humorous. They arrived at the sheriff's house.

"Are you okay?" the mayor asked.

Martin settled down, wiping the tears from his eyes. "Yes sir. I'm fine. It's just that some things aren't what they seem."

They got out of the car and walked inside.

"Martin," the sheriff said, greeting him with a hug. "I'm so glad you came. And you, too, Mayor Wullisworth."

"Thanks for having me," Martin said. "Hello, Lois."

She smiled. "Hi Martin. I'm happy to be spending Thanksgiving with you."

The sheriff said, "Why don't we all gather around the table?"

Everyone took their seats, including Wolfe, Ainsley, the reverend, Oliver, and Melb. Butch walked in.

"You're back already? What they'd say?" the sheriff asked. "He 'fess up yet?"

"Told us everything," Butch said. "He didn't want to spend another night in jail, especially on Thanksgiving. He admitted to breaking into the house."

"I don't understand. What was his motivation for all this?" Ainsley asked.

"Apparently anger," the sheriff replied. "I guess Dustin had outbid him on the Internet and was boasting about it in some chat room for snake lovers. When he let everyone know the snake was loose, Tarffeski decided this was his chance to get back what he thought was rightfully his."

"Is he really from New Zealand?"

"No. Admitted he learned the accent at some Web site called cool foreignaccents.com. He's been trying it on women for years and decided it might be useful for picking up snakes, too."

"Neither successfully," Butch laughed. "By the way, we can all feel safer now. The guy's got a pretty lengthy record and is wanted for holding up a convenience store."

"So what's Dustin going to do with the snake, now that he knows how much it's worth?" Wolfe asked.

"He's not selling it. He says he wouldn't sell them for a million bucks. But the pet store did donate a large tank for them, and the owner is giving Dustin some more accurate feeding tips. Also heard that a few zoos are interested in coming out and taking some pictures of our newest star."

"Dad, that was a brave thing you did. Who knew what could've happened had you not intervened," Ainsley said.

"Well first of all, it was a prop gun, so I knew it wasn't loaded. He didn't know that, but then again, if he'd grabbed my real gun, that wouldn't have been loaded either!"

Everyone laughed, and the sheriff took his seat at the head of the table. Everyone sat down. "Well, it's hard to believe, but a year ago this young man we now know as Ainsley's husband was just getting to know the family at Thanksgiving dinner. So much has changed since then. My only daughter has found true love. Melb and Oliver have found each other as well. Even Thief has managed to settle down. Butch, there's always next Thanksgiving." Everyone laughed.

"I've got my eye on Tammi from the restaurant."

The sheriff looked around the table. "I don't think any of us could've predicted where our lives would be." He grabbed Lois's hand. "Could anyone imagine that I would've found such a unique and lovely woman that I hope to share this house with someday? Especially now that we've cleared things up about the fact that there was no other woman."

The sheriff glanced at Butch, who threw up his hands and grinned.

"What? It took some getting used to. But I know Mom would want you to be happy, Dad. You have my blessing."

"We have many blessings. This family. Our friends. This town. Two new babies on the way. None of us knew what the future held a year ago. In fact, things looked a little grim last Thanksgiving. Wolfe had been kicked out in the snow and nearly died. Thief looked to have been poisoned. But isn't that where our hope is? In the idea that life will get better with God by our side?"

Everyone nodded.

"In the tradition of this holiday, would anyone like to name something they are thankful for?"

The mayor stood. "I would."

"Go ahead."

"We've seen a lot of changes in this town over the years, some subtle, some not so subtle. I have loved this town with all my heart, and given her everything I had. I am thankful for it all. But it's time for me to step down."

Everyone looked at one another. Martin couldn't believe what he was hearing.

"And I am naming Martin as interim mayor, until the election. But I've done some polling, and Martin, you're guaranteed to be voted in. This town loves you. And I can't think of anyone more capable of leading Skary, Indiana, into the next phase of her life."

Martin felt himself choking up. Tears formed in his eyes.

The sheriff said, "Martin, please, stand and say something!"

Everyone around the table urged him, and he slowly stood. The mayor nodded at him the way a father gives a son his blessing.

The mayor said, "You've inherited a town that is divided. It won't be an easy task."

"Yes sir. With division comes a host of problems. This town can become like a two-headed snake, each head wanting to go a separate direction and therefore hardly able to go one right way. A snake like that can't even defend itself against the smallest of predators. But if both heads learn to work together to accomplish a common goal, then the chances of one head swallowing the other are diminished quite drastically."

Maybe that was too graphic an illustration for the dinner table.

"Anyway, the fact of the matter is that what makes a small town isn't the things but the people. Our small-town values can remain no matter what comes our way. But it's up to you all. We must work together to keep Skary, Indiana, a town never to be forgotten!"

Hearty applause followed, and everyone at the table stood and cheered. Martin couldn't hold back a smile. And he knew one thing for certain: he, too, had found the love of his life.

Martin said, "Let's give God thanks for the chance to be part of this delightful journey. And may there be many more journeys to come."

The sheriff held up his glass and said, "To Skary, Indiana. May she always bring us love, peace, and laughter."

SKARY, INDIANA, HAS BECOME a second home to me, and I will be eternally grateful for all of those involved in this wonderfully fun project. What started out as one crazy idea turned into a vision for a series. I never imagined when I first dreamed up the town of Skary that it would be as beloved as it is. I'm thankful first and foremost to all of my readers who allowed their imaginations to be captured by the wacky and lovable citizens of Skary.

The incomparable editorial talents of Dudley Delffs made the books unique and the journey fun. Thank you, Dudley, for all those amazing ideas that translated so well into the story. I'd also like to thank Don Pape for the never-ending encouragement he is so famous for offering. You gave me the courage I needed. Thank you to Mark Ford for the brilliant cover designs that have made these books stand out, and to Laura Wright, an insightfully talented editor who always adds that extra punch to the story. I'd also like to thank everyone at WaterBrook Press for your support and your hard work on behalf of these books.

Thanks to Nessie Ng for your stellar and keen editorial eye. And thanks to my agent, Janet Kobobel Grant. Your support through the writing of this book—and the unseen challenges along the way—went above and beyond the call of duty.

I'd also like to thank Dr. Danny Barnes, for restoring my health and restoring my faith in doctors.

Thanks to my parents, Wayne and Karen, for providing the extra baby-sitting time I needed to complete this book.

Thanks to all my Writing Chambers friends, who continue to be a delight in more ways than I can count. I appreciate all your prayers and your wonderful friendships. Thanks also to my church, WCC, for being such loyal fans and loving friends.

And thank you, Father, for allowing me this great privilege, and for making my journey deeper and broader so that every word I write will continue to point back to You.

ABOUT THE AUTHOR

RENE GUTTERIDGE is the author of seven novels, including *Ghost Writer,* *Troubled Waters,* and the Boo Series. She worked as a church playwright and drama director, writing over five hundred short sketches, before publishing her first novel and deciding to stay home with her first child.

Rene is married to Sean, a musician, and enjoys raising their two children while writing full time. She also enjoys helping new writers and teaching at writers' conferences. She and her family make their home in Oklahoma.

Please visit her Web site at www.renegutteridge.com.

GOD WORKS IN MYSTERIOUS WAYS—
ESPECIALLY IN SKARY

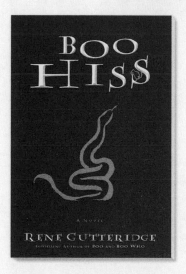

Available in bookstores and from online retailers.